Neil M. Gunn

# Butcher's Broom

*Introduced by Kevin MacNeil*

This edition first published in Great Britain in 2006 by
Polygon, an imprint of Birlinn Ltd

West Newington House
10 Newington Road
Edinburgh
EH9 1QS

www.birlinn.co.uk

ISBN 10: 1 904598 91 9
ISBN 13: 978 1 904598 91 6

The publishers acknowledge subsidy from the

 Scottish
Arts Council

towards the publication of this volume

*British Library Cataloguing-in-Publication Data*
A catalogue record for this book is
available on request from the British Library

Typeset by Palimpsest Book Production Ltd, Grangemouth, Stirlingshire
Printed and bound by Creative Print and Design, Ebbw Vale, Wales

The few traditional poems quoted in these pages may be found, together with their Gaelic originals, in the collection *Carmina Gadelica* (by Alexander Carmichael), to which acknowledgments are made in admiration.

# Introduction

*'It's a desolate thought –*
*to think of all our hearthstones turning cold and the sheep*
*passing over them.'*

A brilliant though flawed talent, Neil Miller Gunn (1891–1973) was one of the principal Scottish literary figures of his generation. He wrote a good many novels, four works of non-fiction and a few rather less successful works of drama and poetry. Gunn, the son of a herring boat captain, was born in the small Highland village of Dunbeath; his work is accordingly suffused with aspects of geographical, cultural and linguistic liminality. Gunn was an important influence on the burgeoning Scottish Renaissance and was in contact with its most notable adherents, including, for example, Hugh MacDiarmid, Naomi Mitchison and Edwin Muir.

I have a remarkable fondness for Neil Gunn. Remarkable because even the most ardent Gunn fan will admit that his writing can be peculiarly two-dimensional. Some of his characters – and, let's be honest, his female characters in particular – can be disarmingly sentimental and unrealistic, 'women' written into corners of pseudo-femininity by a well-meaning but somewhat misguided male.

Furthermore, Gunn, who attempted novels eminently multi-layered with meaning, sometimes ignored to his detriment a key piece of modern literary advice – make sure your symbolic key opens an *actual* door before it opens a symbolic door. And yet, at his best Gunn is something of a literary genius. He is – maybe this is appropriate – a very Scottish, a deeply frustrating genius: hard-working, well-intentioned and successful *to a point*.

I adore Gunn's writing when it achieves its purest pitch of lyrical profundity. For a number of reasons, *Butcher's Broom*, despite its flaws, is not only one of Gunn's best novels, it is far and away one of his most important. In works such as this we can forgive Gunn his imperfections. I intend in this introduction to give a firm but fair, honest therefore personal, appraisal of *Butcher's Broom*, indicating some of its flaws, some of its fine points and some sense as to why it is a book of such great importance.

*Butcher's Broom* was first published in 1934; to place it in a broad literary context, other significant works published that year include Robert Graves' *I, Claudius,* F. Scott Fitzgerald's *Tender is the Night* and Henry Miller's *Tropic of Cancer.* Closer to home, *Butcher's Broom* was always going to be an important novel for Gunn, following on as it did from *Sun Circle,* which was a critical catastrophe. At this stage in his career Gunn was being written off by many as something of a lost cause.

Gunn's ambition was to write a large book with large historical themes: the bitter iniquities of the Highland Clearances and the effect these had on a once proud people's way of life. He found it a difficult book to write – partly because of his own innate humanity. His biographers mention a conversation between writer George Bruce and Gunn, which gives a notion of Gunn's feelings of outrage and shame:

> George Bruce asked Neil once why only *one* novel of the Clearances, and Neil replied, 'Because of the shame of the thing.' 'Why should *you* feel ashamed?' asked Bruce. 'Because our own people did it,' Neil answered.

It is worth remembering that at the time Gunn was writing this novel, there were no fictional precedents. The two other great Scottish novels of the Highland Clearances came later, Fionn MacColla's *And the Cock Crew* in 1945 and Iain Crichton Smith's *Consider the Lilies* in 1968. Though he relied also on his knowledge, through natural osmosis, of local lore, Gunn did a considerable amount of research for *Butcher's Broom.* This was far from easy for him, as he mentioned in a letter to writer Agnes Mure Mackenzie:

> 7 April 1942: I must say that I have found the reading of Scots history at any time difficult. It was either dead uninteresting with no space given at all to real social conditions, the life of the folk, or if really concerned with the truth about Scotland then – it was difficult to read because of the mental complications engendered in the process.

*

*Butcher's Broom* was originally titled *Dark Mairi*; the title was altered due to the original publisher's assertion that *Dark Mairi* was unpronounceable to the average reader(!). One could argue, however, that *Butcher's Broom* is the better title for more substantial reasons, loaded as it is with connotations of violence and sweeping out (one of the most notorious of the perpetrators of war crimes in post-1745 Scotland was the Duke of Cumberland, 'Butcher Cumberland').

Butcher's Broom (*ruscus aculeatus*) is a hardy evergreen plant that may be used medicinally as a diaphoretic and diuretic among other things – knowledge that might well have been part of Dark Mairi's healing art. That the title *Butcher's Broom* is rich in symbolic as well as literal value is a typical Gunn trait. Butcher's Broom is the Sutherland clan badge and as Neil Gunn himself said, 'The awful irony really does stagger me.' The Duke and Duchess of Sutherland, despite being among the largest landholders in the world at the time, were responsible for the Clearances recounted in semi-fictional form in this novel.

*Butcher's Broom* is a polemical, lyrical novel that blends actuality and imagination; it is a historically based fiction that portrays an emotional truth. That emotional truth concerns the community of the Riasgan glen in Sutherland ('. . . the Riasgan with its crofts and hillocks and stream, its mountain ridges and skies, its birch wood, its blueberries, its stones, its trout, its spring poverty, its summer milk, its wild nights, its drink, its dancing . . .') The story concerns the trials the people of the Riasgan face both as individuals and as a group when history conspires against them in a bitterly cruel manner. The novel is split into four sections. In the first part we are introduced to the community and their tough, spirited way of life. They work hard, but they know how to have fun as well. The two central characters in the novel are female – Dark Mairi and Elie. The former is a stoical healer-woman, the latter a beautiful young woman who falls pregnant to a man from the village who goes off to fight in the Napoleonic Wars, unaware that she is pregnant. Elie leaves the village to have her child. In part two, several years later, she returns with her son to a changed village ('Elie's return fitted into the state of mind of the Riasgan with an almost symbolic aptness'). The Riasgan is under threat of being cleared to make way for sheep (sheep being more financially beneficial to the landholders than mere humans). The third section leads up to and finally describes the barbarity of the Clearances and tells of Elie's marriage to the violent brute Rob. Part four finds the people of the Riasgan pushed to the fringes of the land, trying to eke out a living from poor ground and an unfamiliar sea. Although the ending of the novel is not unremittingly bleak, the novel is none the less a tragedy, as befits the subject.

A sad bewilderment prompts me to acknowledge that some of the problems described in *Butcher's Broom* – young people leaving home for economic reasons, religious hypocrisy, a sore lack of political and cultural autonomy – still exist within the Highlands today. *Plus ça change . . .*

The notorious Patrick Sellar, who was partly responsible for those atrocities of 1814, *Bliadhn' an Losgaidh* (The Year of the Burning), is rendered here as *Hell*er (my italics). James Loch and William Young, co-architects of the ruthless scheme, are represented in the novel as Messrs James and Elder.

One tragic aspect of the real-life story is that the only people to benefit from the whole despicable episode were Loch, Young and Sellar, with the latter two becoming two of the richest sheep farmers in the country. (This despite the fact that in 1816 Sellar was indeed tried – and acquitted – on charges including culpable homicide, an extraordinary occurrence in its day.) The Duke and Duchess of Sutherland did not make as much money as they had hoped and – a greater cost, surely – lost forever the trust of 'their' people. Their names are reviled in the Highlands to this day, and Sellar in particular is a byword for opprobrium.

*Butcher's Broom* is a work of great humanity. It exposes terrible injustices with the best of intentions. True, Gunn's anger sometimes spills over into outbursts of didactic speechifying. He does, however, attempt to understand how the situation came about whereby Highland men were away fighting for 'Great' Britain while their very homes were being razed to the ground. The haunting conclusion Gunn comes to is that the allegiance Gaels felt for their chiefs had become an anachronism:

'The chief, the leader, one in blood and tongue and interest with the clansmen, had gone.

'. . . the chief had sold the old order to his avarice and ambition, and was now preparing to sell the children to disinheritance.'

'Their leaders were the enemy.'

As Edwin Muir put it, '[Gunn's] description presumes a definite political point of view, which colours the picture, and with which the reader is indirectly urged to agree; he must take sides.' The novel is biased, yes, but some (myself included) would say it is biased towards basic human justice.

At his eloquent best, Gunn states his case with persuasive power:

Here where they made their own clothing, their own shoes, built their houses, produced their food and drove a few cattle to market to get coin to pay rent, surely the forces that had so shut them in could do without them and forget them. It could hardly be within God's irony that a world which had forgotten their very tongue should be concentrating all its forces of destruction upon them. What could the pride and power of emperors have to do with this little pocket of self-sufficing earth lost in the hills, this retreat, this end of an age, this death of a culture which a millennium before had been no more offensive to the nations of the West than to set Christianity and learning amongst them? When tragedy thus completes itself has it not earned in a people the dignity of saying 'It is finished'?

When Heller and his men hear Tomas MacHamish speaking Gaelic they dismiss it as a 'dialect' and expound a familiarly patronising view: 'We know they are unlearned, and their dialect can have only a very few words, because the things around them are few and they live pretty much like animals.'

One of my favourite aspects of Gunn's writings is his judicious use of Gaelic-influenced English in the cadences and syntactical structure of his prose. This is a laudable feature indeed and one that is rare in serious literature, reserved as it often was – and is – for comedic utterances by stereotyp-ical Highland characters. Though Gunn was not a Gaelic speaker, his English is absolutely shot through with Gaelicisms, and is all the richer because of it.

The Southern view of Highlanders as 'ignorant, shiftless and lazy' represents a bigotry one still, astonishingly, comes across in the twenty-first century – and is, of course, a prejudice as ill-founded nowadays as it always was. Gunn's depiction of the landholders and evictors as being the true barbarians is masterful. Although Gunn's evocation of Highland life is far from idealized, I can't help but think that aspects of it are somewhat romanticized, a notion that goes beyond his near soap-opera-like depiction of certain inter-personal relationships. Gunn can be rather quaint and senti-mental. The extended ceilidh scene, for example, though celebrated by some, seems a little contrived and unconvincing to my Highland ears. Throughout the novel, the prose can sometimes reach a fine and graceful pitch of lyricism and at other times is near mawkish in its sentimentality.

Gunn does however have a brilliant manner of yoking together earthy physicality and very human abstractions:

> To Elie now from this world about her, and particularly from the memoried earth and growing things immediately around her, came a mysterious effluence giving her misery so exquisite an edge that she shivered from the cut of it to a hostile happiness.

He is also exceptional at capturing a person's facial expres-sion, of revealing how a person's character is mediated or hidden by one look or another.

This is at times a shadowy book. When we accompany Heller and Elder as they take a breath of air at night, we are given no description of their actual environs. Although this is odd coming from a novelist whose powers of descrip-tion are such that he can detect colour in voices, ultimately *Butcher's Broom* is a novel of atmospheres, as V. S. Pritchett pointed out in the *Spectator* (though he also confessed to being 'baffled by a book which was so confused in move-ment as a whole and so good in parts').

I always think of this novel's near-hallucinatory quality as being one of its more curious strengths. Gunn is dealing with large human complexities and this is not a book of easy dualities. His voice, sometimes passionate, sometimes compassionate, can also simmer with bitter irony. The notion of the villagers being turfed off their land, as meek as 'lambs of God', is charged with contempt.

Elsewhere, Gunn's ambitious authorial tone is almost Lovecraftian:

> In this darkness of the world identity is lost and time becomes one with the monstrous beginnings of life, which legend recreates in such beings as centaur or water kelpie; or, receding still further, becomes one with the dark spirits, the Nameless Ones, who were before light or creation was. The blood's tale is told in the black night, and the nerves and flesh act the drama backwards.

What greatness, though, when he achieves the true lyricism. Time and again in Gunn's novels the poetic drive speaks of the essence of Highland nature. Such moments – equivalent to Wordsworthian 'spots of time' – developed in Gunn's mind in close relationship with his understanding of Zen, especially the Zen moment of *satori* or sudden epiphanous enlightenment. Though *Butcher's Broom* contains little in the way of such spiritual enlightenment, the lyrical passages are often outstanding:

> The notes of the linnet had now the extra magic of distance, and all at once she was aware of larks overhead, interweaving their songs until the upper air was alive and invisibly patterned with them. The haze on the mountains was like the smoke-bloom on ripe blaeberries. The air was quick with the smell of newly turned earth and manure. All was suggestive of the awakening of life, and the coldness in the sunlit depths of the sky was the coldness of a drinking well.

The text does contain a number of perplexing inconsistencies. On the tricky subject of gender differences – and this novel does seem interested in the balance of tensions between the sexes – Gunn says in part one: '. . . the man in his sphere and the woman in hers were each equally governing and indispensable . . . In life's major dealings, like cattle-droving, marketing, hunting, and war, women would have felt help-less without their men.' And yet when the men are away fighting in the Napoleonic Wars, they do not seem to be 'indispensable' to the village at all.

Gunn, then, has created a hugely ambitious novel, one that is a qualified success. The omniscient narrator's voice attempts rather too wide a spectrum of tones, some of the characters have little psychological depth and, in truth, the novel overall is a little too long. At its best, though – I'm thinking generally of the episodes based on historical events and the nature-inspired epiphanies – the writing is truly great: tight, powerful and moving.

*Butcher's Broom* is an important book because it was published at a time when the elitism of English and Lowland Scots historiography tended to gloss over or ignore alto-gether a shameful period of inhumanity that was akin to what is nowadays called 'ethnic cleansing'. In writing this difficult book, Gunn offered the world a stark insight into mankind's capacity to bring disaster upon itself (and it's worth recalling that it was published the same year Hitler became Germany's Head of State and Chancellor).

Ultimately, Gunn used his literary talents to speak to humankind of historical lessons that ought never to be forgotten and this, I believe, is one of the greatest and most noble achievements a novelist can hope to aim for.

Kevin MacNeil
Villa Concordia, Bamberg
**June 2006**

PART ONE

# ONE

The old woman stood on the Darras, the doorway, between the bright sea and the dark hills; and when at last she turned from the sea and lifted her burden to her back, the door closed behind her. But the vacant glitter remained in her eyes and they held their stare until the valley began to pour slowly into them its dark comfort.

For a long time she was like one who had turned into her own house and found it empty, and walked in a silence that was a hearkening to presences withdrawn beyond the walls and fading away.

Every now and then there was a glint in this vagueness, for she had been born by the sea, and sea-water readily curls over and breaks on the shore of the mind. Looked at from a great distance childhood is little more than the breaking of small bright waves on a beach. And whatever of pain and coldness there may have been, the brightness keeps a certain wild strangeness, a restless fly-away, that the hills do not know and never quite conquer.

The sea had been in a good mood that morning, had had that pleasant scent that is the breath of fine weather. A person could always tell what the weather is to be by smelling the sea. There is the grey dark smell, cold inside the nostrils, ominous; the damp raw smell, husky to the throat, unsettled; the keen dry lifting tang of wind; but when good weather has newly come, how the sea brims and sways and breathes its sweet fragrance on the air! This morning, too, there had been the extra exhilaration of autumn, that indescribable quickening that the skin takes in a shiver.

All of that sea she now carried in her basket as she went back among the companionable hills. For in addition to fish, she had many kinds of weed and shell. The clear pink dulse, gathered not off other sea-plants but off the rocks, was one of her most useful specifics. Eaten raw, it had a cleansing effect; boiled, with a pinch of butter added to the infusion, it acted as a tonic, bracing the flesh, making it supple, and drawing taut the muscles of the stomach. It could be preserved, too, by drying. A man working in a field could put a dry blade or two in his mouth and chew away at them. At first they were tasteless as gristle, but in a very short time they yielded back their juices, which began to run about the gums and fill the whole mouth with a richness that had to be frequently swallowed. When the dried dulse was ground into a powder and taken fasting, it sickened and expelled worms. Other ailments, like the stone and colic, yielded to it.

Linarich, slake, and sea-tangle had also their many uses; though she had not much of each with her now, for slake was mostly needed in the spring, when, after the rigour of winter, the cattle were weak and costive. Linarich, perhaps, was more useful at any time. It helped to soothe and heal the skin after a blister plaster. In the case of sciatica, for example, the ancient custom was to cut spirewort into small pieces, pack them in a limpet shell, and fasten the shell to the thigh-bone in order to raise a big blister, from which the watery matter could be drained away. After the third draining, a linarich plaster dried and healed the wound.

It was in her nature not to return home without such gifts. She had spent two days with a relative by marriage whose husband had been suffering from a mysterious fever and could not sweat. They had sent for her, for Dark Mairi of the Shore.

She had a reputation for healing among the people of that land. She was a small woman, roundly built, deep-chested and straight, yet she did not give an impression of bodily strength so much as of something delicate and hardy that persists evenly. Her skin was pale and little wrinkled; her eyes dark, and of a jewelled smallness. But perhaps the suggestion of persistence, of abidingness, that was the silent note struck by her person, was sustained most distinctly by the cheek-bones that did not obtrude in round knobs but ran straight back towards her ears, each in a visible ridge. These ridges drew the skin taut and gave the frontal expression a curious flattened steadiness. Her hair was black and coarse-grained, with grey strands showing here and there in a good light. It was drawn firmly back from her forehead, tautening the skin at the temples, as the cheek-bones tautened it down the sides of her face. Her head was raised in a watchfulness that was sometimes direct and glimmering and sometimes staring-blind.

This 'blindness' in her expression had often the air of unintelligence, and when she smiled it could be seen as a sort of weakness running thinly all over her face. To move her out of her unthinking self seemed to expose her, to show that apart from what she was unthinkingly she was very little. One might as well have exposed a stone by causing it to smile or a piece of a mountain. Indeed, in her steady unthinking darkness, she might have walked out of a mountain and might walk into it again, leaving no sign.

The sick man had looked at her with expectation. She asked him questions quietly. She smiled her small weak smile. She put her hand on his forehead. Her hand was very cold. Her smile did not touch her eyes at all. She was not concerned. She would soon put him all right. Oh yes. She did not even say what was wrong with him. And the doubt that had clouded the man's eyes faded out, not into eagerness or impatience, but into an almost stupid peace. She prepared her drink and gave it to him. It was hot and harsh to the throat as oily sea-water. 'It's strong,' he said. 'Strong enough,' she answered and packed the extra clothes around him. 'Strong,' he muttered, and his body shuddered as under a convulsion and settled down into the bed, fatally accepting what was coming to it. When it relaxed from its next shudder there was a crawling warmth under the skin. The warmth grew; it became a glowing live heat. Soon his whole body was a white dry furnace. He was being consumed, burnt up. Out of that heat the storm burst. The drops ran into runnels. These runnels tickled his face and his chest, and made his eyes water. 'God, I'm sweating!' he gasped. 'Sweat you,' said she. When she saw his hair steaming, she turned away and began asking his wife the news of the place. The two women sat down and told each other all they knew of everybody, so that their neighbours in their lives and their actions were brought clearly before them. In this way the wife became happy and greatly moved towards Dark Mairi, to whom she unburdened herself, enjoying now what had been her saddest moments. In the morning the man was quite spent, but his eyes and his mind were clear and steady. 'I'm weak as a fly,' he jested. 'You'll be strong as a horse,' she replied. Whereupon the strength of the horse began to trickle into him. 'God's blessing with you,' he said. 'And with yourself,' she answered, looking at him a moment then turning away.

They knew, of course, that she had got her healing knowledge largely from her grandmother, who had been carried away from one of the Islands of the West by the famous smuggler called Black MacIver. Not that they could have called Mairi in her mainland home a foreign or strange woman. She was rather like a little woman from the hills, from any of the small inland glens, and her kind was not uncommen even in townships near the sea. Only Mairi seemed to have in her an older knowledge than was common to the rest of her ancient kind in these places.

As the light mellowed into late afternoon the hills grew darker and the winding valley began to fill itself with an imponderable calm. The frost in the morning had stilled the wind, and it might come again and lay a clear hand on the night. Already the outlines of the hills were sharp and held the eye for unknowing moments.

These outlines and these hills, the winding valley, the many valleys, the breasts of the hills, the little birch woods, the knolls, the humps and hillocks and boulders, the gravel faces, the black bogs, and always for movement the streams winding like snakes in the green or grey-green bottoms. To know one valley amongst these northern uplands was to know all. That was true! as Mairi might say with her thin polite smile. And she might even act as though she believed it. For there are times when all persons are beings moving about in a valley and looking from a little distance as different from one another as does not matter. And no irony is caught in the eye that stares unwinking and, throwing the valley itself out of focus in space, makes it change and curve in the backflow of time.

The backflow of time that is frozen at last in the Ice Age. The ice moves forward and time slowly returns. Vast hollows are gouged out and mountains are planed smooth; seas appear. But the work is rough and the glacier comes again and again. Until the valley is shaped as the eyes of Dark Mairi see it. A smooth shape of slender flanks and fluent spinal ridges, of swelling breasts and wandering arms, brown-skinned except where the region of its fertility lies softly grey-green with grass. Here men and women are at work, concerned forever, too, with fertility in that place and in themselves; turning the earth over and sowing grain seed in it, harvesting, and rearing flocks and herds; making love in youth and story-telling in old age, with a music distilled out of it all as singular and memoried as dark-brown honey: A life shaggy as the legs of an animal, shaggy and tough, with clear eyes above and wary nostrils; and night a small den where the whole body curls in its own thick warmth.

But it is like that perhaps only in thought at a distance; near at hand it is quite suddenly the face of a young woman with its virgin clearness, that brimming clearness forever waiting to be troubled; or children flashing about, or gravely preoccupied, or doing anything but herding the cattle from the strips of grain. The smooth face of a child and the bearded face of a man, with the woman going between them.

They are shut up and shut off in these valleys. God breasts the hill-tops like a giant; but no, immediately the eyes glance at the hill-top, the giant, God, is withdrawn far into the sky where He sits in a stiff chair gloomy with thought. The men with the beards know about God. They have gone into the ravines and the corries, they have climbed the precipices, they have stood on the mountain-tops of God. But only a few of them are true mountaineers, and they are called 'the Men'. All the others forget God for long periods, except now and then when the shadow of Him stills the features, until body and features escape, glad to have been in the shadow – and to have escaped.

As Mairi went on she met no one, for only important business with the outside world would take a man or a woman down that way. There are no roads anywhere, no wheeled vehicles, only paths and shaggy ponies and burdens for the back. What reason then is there for a man to wander into strange places where he has no business? To do so out of idle curiosity would be an odd proceeding difficult to explain. 'I don't know what took me, I just can't explain it; but, anyway, there I was in that place,' a man might begin a queer story.

But when Mairi came below a little cluster of houses, she knew that every pair of eyes there was upon her. A man or a woman might walk down to the path if it could be done naturally, so that Mairi might not feel she was being intercepted. Then that man (or woman) might say in greeting, 'It's the fine day that's in it,' as though he were setting the day in the hollow of the world so that they might with courteous detachment regard it. There was always this detachment, this reserve of the person, removing the world to a slight distance and permitting it to be addressed or discussed in a grave and pleasant voice.

The world was possibly all the better seen for the slight removal. The eyes and the mind fastened upon it, anyway, with curiosity, noting its myriad peculiarities and giving each a name. The old language Mairi used was full of such names, not only for things but for men; particularly, indeed, for men, so that the name evokes each kind of man with an astonishing, almost laughable, magic. Naturally with this go diminutives that are the finger-tips of fun, phrases that snare the heart with a hair. For love-making, it is a subtle tongue.

In truth, it is an immensely old tongue, and a thousand years before Mairi it was richer in its knowledge, wider in its range, and was given to metaphysics and affairs of state. The thousand years have slowly pushed it back, have shut it up in the glens, where it has developed its instinct for human value, and may flash out of the mouth of a tempestuous fighter or grow silent in him who with fixed eyes stares through the material world and sees what takes place outside our notions of time and space.

Yet that may be to give it all a monotone, drawn from the shadows of the afternoon through which Mairi went with the sea in her basket. The round-backed cottages clung to the earth like long animals whose folded heads were always to the mountain. Lying thus to the slopes they were part of the rhythm of the land itself. They grew out of it and merged with it, so that shadow or stillness caught them when it caught the mountain, and the cries of children were no more alien than the sharp cries of moor-birds. In the head of the cottage lived the humans, in the abdomen the beasts, and from the tail-end drained away what the whole ejected. There were little herds of these cottages at long intervals, and every now and then an odd cottage by itself like a wandered beast. Even in a flock of sheep on these hills there is the 'piner'. One may come upon him suddenly round the corner of a birch wood. He stares with a white face and one sees in a moment that he has no concern with eating and has something different in him from all the other sheep. This something is disturbing, for it has been well established that 'second sight' is not peculiar to man. Sheep and cattle and horses have it in one degree or another. Cattle in a byre show great uneasiness when a ghost enters. And there is something sad, too, about a lonely cottage, when one is making for the warmth and laughter of a small herd of them.

Yet there is a quiet luxury in this monotone that Mairi absorbed. She liked the orderliness of the afternoon, and as she went she noted little things with interest. Sometimes she stopped for a moment and conned over what she saw and knew. There was old Farquhar Bannerman with the long grey beard coming from the peat stack. As a leader amongst 'the Men' he prayed with deliberation and power. When he said, 'Lord, look upon us at this Thy footstool,' and paused, the young could have urged him on in order to keep the eyes from looking too long and too closely.

Now Mairi herself could have borne up to a scrutiny of that kind however long it lasted, for she had the wisdom that never looked into God's eyes. She would not even have minded meeting old Bannerman, though news did not matter much to him unless it was news of eternal things, and she wanted to know how folk were, and what women had children, and, in particular, if they had had any tidings of the lads who had left a year ago for America. It was rumoured that one of them, Bannerman's grandson, had gone because he could not stand up to the old man's holiness. Some of the young men in her own place laughed at that and kicked a sod and said that God alone knew.

But their growing feeling of discontent with the minister of the gospel was what deeply preoccupied Bannerman and one or two more of 'the Men'. The minister was concerned, they felt, far more with his bestial than with his human flock. The real field of his endeavour was his glebe, and he was more at home with the factor discussing estate affairs and news of the absentee landlord's doings in the great world than by the humble fireside of one of his following. His treatment of the Word itself was mechanical and peremptory. No seeking after the truth, no wrestling with the Lord, no fervour, no evangel. There wasn't enough hell-fire in it to warm his breath. The people had not wanted him, but the absent landlord had 'placed' him over their heads. How unlike the old days of the 'good Earl'! How the glory of Israel had departed! Not even a strong man like his brother-in-God in the neighbouring charge with his undershot jaw and ready fists, but just a foolish sort of nice man, cunningly aware of his superior tongue that narrowed the rich northern *ia* in the body of a word to the southern *eu*. Nothing much was said openly, but when Bannerman or other elder called at any township, there would be a prayer-meeting of peculiar unction over and above the usual catechetical duties.

Taking to the hillside, Mairi saw the manse and the church with its walled churchyard against the flat alluvial valley-bottom. The whole looked prosperous and superior and well-endowed. The reaping of the oats must just have finished, for a woman was standing with a sickle in her hand while a girl and a youth were stooking the last of the sheaves. Feeling the comfort of the scene steal upon her, Mairi sat down. A lad rushed wildly at some sheep, herding them away from the unfenced harvest fields. Small black cows regarded the action speculatively. A woman and two men walked out from the steading towards the cornfield. Another man followed for a few yards and stopped. It was the minister himself. Outside the pulpit, there was a pleasantness in his manner that was not so much deceitful as evasive. Persons in a high position were often like that.

The lack of the usual gaiety attendant on such a scene

was properly understood by Mairi as respect due to the Church. There was a seemliness in it that established life, an orderliness that Mairi found lasting and good. And the minister would be generous to them with meat and drink. They would appreciate that, and one man there whom Mairi knew, whose pores would grow still more oily with good humour as the supper went on, would defend the minister against no attack. The younger folk would agree, with clipped voices. The end of the night would see good fun beyond the pale blinded light of the minister's window.

The pale blinded light, like the light of evening coming down from the hills, like the light that is the shadow of Jehovah. *That* was the monotone. That was why the land sometimes had a solemn still air, as if it bore the memory of a particularly silent Sabbath evening. Though all Sabbath evenings came up out of the past with this air, and even when the wind was blowing, the rain falling, the tops mist-shrouded, the stillness was in and about these natural manifestations like an ear listening; or if not like an ear, then like a greyness of breath. Whose breath? The body turns away, the eyelids droop against the awful Immanence. At just such a moment a youth may laugh most readily, spluttering through towards daring sayings and subtle lewdnesses. The minister's light, a blinded eye that might open, added an exciting recklessness to the paganism of the barn.

And as with the minister's light upon the barn, so with Jehovah's eye upon the valley. For the folk did not love Jehovah: they feared him. To love would, in its presumption, invite damnation. For the whole sphere of creation was clear and rigid as a crystal ball which an omnipotent Jehovah held on a vast invisible palm. Venerable men like Bannerman knew this, knew there was no room for any but the pure doctrine, knew that mankind must submit in fear and trembling or Jehovah might turn His hand and smash the ball in the End of the World. Beyond that End, Hell ever waited with its tortures for the damned.

Now because the 'fundamentals' of the crystal doctrine were not being rigorously taught by the minister, many of the people were falling away from grace, jesting and telling stories, practising ancient heathen superstitions, laughing, singing songs, and dancing: doing these things that were a challenge in God's face, because of the paganism that was so deep-seated in them. Profoundly did 'the Men' ponder upon this.

But Mairi got up and pursued her way, untouched by doctrinal purity and as unconscious of paganism as she was of the sea in her basket or the glimmer of harvest on her face. Indeed for the moment there was some inscrutable connection between the basket and her face, between her body and the hillside, and when she dipped down out of sight, eyes that had just caught a glimpse of her might well have doubted their vision. But she appeared again going calmly into the hills, to which she would no more have thought of lifting her eyes for aid than they would have thought of refusing to receive her.

When she came to the place where her pathway narrowed to a foot-bridge over the stream, she paused and looked at the mill. From the open door came the click of iron on stone. The grinding wheels were being dressed for the new harvest by Rob the miller, a bachelor of forty. Had there been anyone with him she would have heard his laugh and his challenging jaunty voice. The mill had a reputation as a meeting-place of the wilder spirits of the country-side. Rob's sister, Sarah, who kept house for him, a young sleek woman, was nowhere to be seen. Mairi went down to the stream and took three pebbles from the water immediately under the bridge over which the living and the dead pass, and put the pebbles in her basket. Then she got up and crossed the bridge and set her face to her own little glen.

Though Mairi knew the healing rites and practices, she was not always rigidly governed by them. She should have taken a pebble on each of three consecutive mornings, one for the head, one for the heart, and one for the limbs, made them red hot, and dropped them in water. But Mairi was not going to do that with these pebbles. It was merely comforting to have lifted them, and as she walked along she knew that the pebbles would communicate to the sea in her basket the spirit of her own earth. Thus was the world brought to a healing harmony within her mind. Not that she did this deliberately. It happened to her, as the sun shines upon a harvest, and sun and harvest provide life under Bannerman and God. The pebbles were sun-yellow.

The water under the bridge had had a soft warmth from many slipping ledges and gravelly shallows. This warmth spread all over Mairi and got mixed up with the warmth of home-coming. She was entering her own place and its seclusion gave at any time a snug feeling of comfort. There was nothing here to war against but the treachery of the weather and the leanness of spring and early summer. In the odd years of catastrophe and poverty, when many of the cattle died and the eyes, cleansed of all humours, saw into the human soul with a terrible clarity, charity, sensitive and silent, became a rite.

Through the first shadows of evening Mairi looked on the hump-backed cottages she knew so well. Her own stood on a breast of the steep upslope to the left; it was the highest cottage in the place, not because it was the poorest but because her long dead husband, who had built it himself, had had to find what stance and land he could. In front of the cottage lay the cultivated ground, the potato and cabbage patch, the yellow oats, and the lighter-coloured narrow tongue of bear over towards a stony water channel that was a cataract in the winter but was a small enough trickle now.

Altogether the land in the shallow valley-bottom was not so flat as it was in the main glen; it rolled slightly over humps and hillocks that separated the score of cottages and gave to the whole area a certain variety and expansiveness.

In this first dusk of evening it had the welcome of that which remains forever unchanged. The homes, the knolls, the slow slopes, the grass pastures, the birch wood that began beyond Mairi's house where the hill steepened, the rowan tree with its red berries by each green cabbage patch, all were in the same place, with the same movements and sounds threading them together. Pleasure glimmered on her face like twilight on a loch.

Here where they made their own clothing, their own shoes, built their houses, produced their food and drove a few cattle to market to get coin to pay rent, surely the forces that had so shut them in could do without them and forget them. It could hardly be within God's irony that a world which had forgotten their very tongue should be concentrating all its forces of destruction upon them. What could the pride and power of emperors have to do with this little pocket of self-sufficing earth lost in the hills, this retreat, this end of an age, this death of a culture which a millennium before had been no more offensive to the nations of the West than to set Christianity and learning amongst them? When tragedy thus completes itself has it not earned in a people the dignity of saying 'It is finished'?

Apparently not. There would seem to be a power in nature that once set on harrying is not content to defeat and break, but must with malignant intensity pursue its quarry into a physical death of revolting and bloody cruelty. And to bring this about it uses forces that appear oddly disconnected, set blindly in motion by divergent causes, over great areas of the earth. Napoleon evades the English ships in the Mediterranean and on this October evening has landed in the south of France. He is heading for Paris and the rank of First Consul. The blood of the Revolution has fascinated Europe, revolting its nobility and inspiring its poets. Amid liberty, equality and fraternity Napoleon takes command and plays his game of mythic ambition on Continental squares, removing a piece here, a piece there, to set his own pieces in their place. From the battle of the Pyramids to Austerlitz and Jena. And then across the whole board to the Kremlin of Moscow. Nothing evaded him except that oft-muttered 'England and her gold', which after all had not been a piece so much as the haunting ghost of a piece. Is it contended that Destiny was creating these titanic forces in order to use them to destroy, with a perfection and finality they nowhere else attained, this hamlet in its glen that Mairi stood looking upon in the October dusk? How fantastic a conception! How ironic the universal waste of divine and tragic energy to achieve so trifling an end! Hardly less fantastic to believe that Mairi had in very truth brought to her people the earth and its seven seas in her basket. Yet Moscow rose from its ashes, the battlefields of Europe were tilled, and even liberty, equality and fraternity continued to linger as the waking memory of a Utopian dream. Only this glen here, that was itself and the other glens, suffering fire as did the Kremlin, and destruction as did the battlefield, has remained into time dark and desolate and dead.

# TWO

Mairi was very weary after her long walk, and when she had broken the kindling peat to a flame and set other peats on edge around it, she rested in her straw-bottomed chair for a long time. The fire was set on a flat stone hearth in the middle of the floor and the blue smoke went curling up towards the hole in the roof that was the chimney. The twisted heather-rope that suspended the iron pot-hook from the roof-tree had got coated over with soot and glistened like ebony. Some fowls, nestling over the partition that divided this living-room from the cowhouse, made ruminative sounds, acknowledging their mistress's return. The flame grew strong and began to throw its own shadows.

Presently she would empty her basket and put each thing in its place. How Elie (Eilidh) would like a bit of the salt fish with a new potato! She wondered what was keeping the girl. Lifting her face to the small window in the edge of the thatch, she looked through its open space to the evening sky. The fire danced in tiny spots on her black irises. Yet she did not seem to see the sky so much as listen to it; or listen to nothing, so still did she become for a time. Then a small sighing wind came down the hillside and from her mouth, and vague concern for her cow touched her. She got up, put her basket over by the meal chest, and went out.

Beside the rocky watercourse, she climbed towards a hollow by the crest of the wood. There was one thing about the holding that her husband had understood: the fairly good grazing above the house. Though all hill grazing was common grazing, the upper reach of Mairi's burn was never stocked by anyone else's beasts. In July of their second year, they had sold four head of cattle and the skins of two goats, and had settled down to a long happy life, when her husband's side began to swell from an inflammation of the bowels and he died. Her son was then a year old and she struggled on hardily with the place, for she had the endurance that eats into anything, whether misery or a hillside. Now she had her own five cattle in the herd, her grain and potatoes, and, over all, the providence of her neighbours – the only banking system known to that people, a system that never closed its doors and provided a dividend only for those who had nothing invested.

When her head topped the rim of the hollow, Mairi saw Elie and a young man lying together on the grass. They were talking in a friendly way, smiling, or laughing in a quick note or two, their bodies rolling slightly, their fingers picking small clovers. The black milch cow was eating industriously, but the goat immediately raised her head and bleated, whereupon Elie and the youth sat up; and in a moment Elie was crying, 'Mairi, are you home?' and coming to meet her.

Elie's body was soft as her voice and it approached Mairi with a flowing welcoming warmth deepening in her cheeks to a slight self-consciousness. Her hair was browner than sand and her eyes browner than her hair, a uniform glistening tawny brown, that concentrated and glanced away as her restless body swayed and flowed. A soft kind girl, whose voice hung on her words, 'Mairi, are you home?' with an undernote of wonder and almost shy welcome, while all the time, smiling, she was conscious of Mairi catching her out in something that was half-embarrassing and half a joke. 'I didn't know it was so late. How did you get on?' She was almost putting her hand on Mairi's breast, her eyes lowered. 'Wait and I'll get the ewes.' Her soft throaty laugh swung round with her and she went running up the grass, giving Colin her amused eyes as she passed.

Colin was smiling too, but in a slightly constrained way. He was a youth of middle stature, broad-shouldered and dark, with colour in his cheeks; a frank active lad who now smoothed his smile and said with grave cheerfulness that it was a fine evening that was in it.

'It is that,' answered Mairi, quietly wise also. He politely enquired how she had got on in her journey, and she, thanking him, said that she had got on very well but that she was a bit tired, for it was a long way.

It was a long way indeed. They were talking when Elie returned, with the two sheep on the one tether. Colin explained to Mairi that he had been going up to see the ponies behind the wood and that now he had better go or it would be dark on him. Almost solemnly his well-featured face turned away.

An odd spluttering mirth lay behind Elie's expression, but Mairi never showed humorous subtlety at any time. Her smile was thin, and when she laughed – which was rarely – she showed her gums above small yellowish teeth; it was as if the bones grinned. There was no blood rela- tionship between the two women, as was obvious at a glance and quite apart from their different colouring. Elie's breasts were soft and full; her shoulders tilted upward or drooped, her body had a flowing movement that would come at one with an intimate wheedling voice wanting the fun of breaking away into pieces of teased laughter. But Mairi was tight and upright as a standing stone; she was like an earth outcrop to Elie's brown stream.

As they came down the hillside, Elie drew Mairi's news from her. And Mairi in her clear monotonous rather high- pitched voice related all that had happened, giving the prac- tical details without any reflections, for she was concerned always with happenings and not with thoughts.

'So you went along to see Duncan Mor too? You would go by the sea? You would like that?'

'Yes. It was a nice morning. He was not in his bed. But I asked his wife about him. His bowels had not moved in four days.'

'Hadn't they?' said Elie.

'No,' said Mairi, who made everything so natural that many people might think she had little delicacy, but Elie never thought that. Indeed it was almost an adventure to be with Mairi alone sometimes; like drawing a blind from a secret window.

In her turn, Elie told the little things that had happened since Mairi went away. She was one of a family of five girls, but she lived now almost entirely with Mairi; and this arrangement suited her parents, and suited Mairi, and perhaps suited Elie best of all, because it gave her a lot of freedom and yet hardly prevented her going home when she liked.

It was quite dark at the milking, but when they went into the living-room the peat's pleasant flame threw shadows everywhere.

'Ah, you're there?' said Mairi. The small dark boy came away from the basket. He was like a gnome, his eyebrows slightly tilted. Because he had been stealing from the basket, he was pale and unembarrassed. Mairi knew the sign and questioned him.

'No. I was just—' He began to cough.

'That's the edge of the lie sticking in your throat,' said Mairi.

The coughing brought water from his eyes. He could neither swallow the tiny sharp-edged flake of dulse nor bring it up. Mairi made him take a mouthful of milk to ease the irritation.

'I was just trying a little blade of it,' he said. Elie laughed. Davie coughed again.

'Has he been good?' Mairi asked.

'Oh, only middling,' Elie answered.

'You'd better watch out!' Davie threatened her.

'Watch out for what?'

'Or I'll tell on you,' he muttered.

'What'll you tell?'

'You know what.'

She looked at him rather curiously and, smiling, said in a whisper, 'Tell-pie, tell-pie, sitting on a rock!'

His face grew vindictive. She turned away, smiling still. He hit her across the buttocks. She said, 'Ha! ha!' He hit her again. She caught him and whispered in his ear. He became obstreperous.

'Will you behave yourself!' called his granny.

He punched Elie in the stomach and made out at the door.

'You'll be sorry for that – this night!' called Elie after him. Then she gave her soft chuckling laugh. 'He is excited at your being home again.'

'Maybe yes and maybe no,' said Mairi, intent on her business. 'It's getting very dark. It's a nice bit of salt fish. Have you got the potatoes in the pot? We'll just boil that bit; look.'

'Oh, that's too much,' said Elie.

'Not it,' said Mairi. 'I was thinking of you and how you would like it as a tasty change.'

'My teeth are watering for it,' said Elie, and she drew her breath in through her teeth till the spittle beneath her tongue sizzled.

'And when we have our food, I'll go out and see old Seumas and Christina. Are they any worse?'

They were neither worse nor better. Elie hung the black pot on the hook over the fire and coaxed the flames round its bottom. She bustled about, her skin warm, her hair untidy. There was always indeed this warmth of untidiness about her.

When the potatoes were nearly boiled, they remembered

Davie, and Elie went to the door and called him. He was
nowhere to be found. But she had a suspicion that he was
hiding near at hand, and returned, saying loudly, 'He is
nowhere to be seen, so we'll just take the nice fish and
potatoes without him.'

Presently she lifted the pot off the hook and, passing
through an opening in the partition by the wall, took the
one step down into the byre where she could have strained
the water off the potatoes; instead she carried the pot
outside (the only door of the dwelling opened into the byre)
and, holding the wooden lid against its mouth, tilted it over
until all the greenish water ran out. Her head was up looking
for Davie, when Davie's foot, landing behind, nearly couped
her. He laughed a mocking high-pitched laugh. Her skelp
just missed him, and in the race he was too nimble for her.
He led her round the house, and as he came back on the
pot he stooped and flicked a mealy potato in the air, catching
it and tossing it from hand to hand, as he ran, for it was
too hot to hold.

'That's all you'll get, my lad,' called Elie after him.

'Ha! ha!' and his voice and himself disappeared in the
glimmering night.

But when Mairi and Elie were sitting by the fire on two
stools, with the steaming pot of potatoes between them, a
face peered round the partition. Mairi was talking of the
folk by the sea, and did not appear to hear the scratching
of a finger-nail on wood. But Elie heard it and knew Davie
was watching them, and so she said, 'The shore folk are
lucky having this good fish. It's the best ever I tasted.' She
lifted some flakes off the wooden platter on her knee and
took them into her mouth with a soft lick of the fingers.
The melting succulence of the food in her mouth could just
be heard. 'The little bit of butter makes all the difference,'
she said, and added a piece of potato. The potato was hot
and her mouth held it delicately and blew a fine stream of
steam upon the air. The earthy flavour of the potatoes

pervaded the whole chamber in a warmth that tickled the
nostrils; the fish sent out a salty tang that made water flow
about hungry teeth and mount up on the tongue and slip
down the throat in a gulp. 'The new potatoes are dry as
meal,' declared Elie. 'They are that,' said Mairi, helping
herself to another one from the pot and blowing sharply
upon its laughing face. 'They'll hardly boil, and that's true.'

Her voice was normal, yet full of a quiet thankfulness.
God and the earth had been kind to their labour this season.
Here was the feast of life. The cow beyond the partition
let out a low 'moo-moo'. 'The water will be running from
her mouth,' said Elie, with her low chuckle. Some of the
hens began to croak and fluff their feathers. The old cock
lifted his head and glanced at them with one eye and then
with the other, but had no way of doing anything more
important. He often suffered in his gawky dignity. Elie said
the hens would have a great feed in the morning.

'It's a pity about Davie though. How he would have
enjoyed this!' And she could not help laughing.

'I'm hearing you,' said Mairi firmly. 'Come away in here.'

'Who is it?' asked Elie innocently.

'It's Davie scratching over there. I know his tricks. Come
away in here.'

There was silence. The face was withdrawn. And in
that moment Elie knew that now he would not come in.
He was standing just behind the entrance listening and
growing moody. She could see him and understand him
and immediately grew sorry. For it had all been a sort
of game on her part; and he was often rough to cover
his feelings. But there had also been that little matter of
his taking the dulse and half-denying it. Almost out of
nothing his gnome-like sensitive face had created a situation which irked Elie. She began to hear her heart-beats
as she listened for him. A note of suspense, almost
poignant, invaded the air. She could not stand it another
moment, and laying her fish plate on the earthern floor,

was swiftly through the partition on bare feet. Into the darkness of the byre she whispered quickly, 'There's a ceilidh tonight at Angus's. Come and behave – or granny won't let you go.' Then raising her voice, 'Come on, Davie, or your food will be cold.' As she was returning, a hand struck out from the dark. Deftly she gripped the body and brought it in with her.

His granny paid no attention to him. Elie put some fish on his platter. He sat down by the pot and with some care picked out a potato and slowly peeled it, looking at no one. Elie and Mairi began talking again. He ate his fish at first with a fastidious reluctance, but soon in a gluttonous noisy way that Elie did not like. She became annoyed. His granny told him to be quiet. When Elie did look at him she looked steadily. His whole manner was deliberately exasperating. She wondered how he could so forget and destroy the good time they had had together, for when he was good he was as good as honey and their three days had been a comb of freedom, dripping exciting golden drops. A flush went over her.

'I'm going down to Angus's tonight. I said I'd give them a hand with the waulking,' she observed evenly.

'Are they to be at it then?' asked Mairi. And after a little she remarked to Davie, 'You can stay here by yourself till I come back. I won't be long.'

He made no answer, nor did Elie pay any attention to him. The firelight enriched the skin on their faces and glistened in their eyes. Davie's soiled legs glowed brown beneath his bony knees on which the plate rested. Elie's legs had a reddish tinge in their tan and her ankles were strong and yet delicate. Her broad stained feet had short smooth toes. Davie's face was smudged as by sleep. The fire-tongues played with the gloom around them, and the smoke curled upwards toward the opening in the black roof. In the centre of this gloom was the fire, and sitting round it, their knees drawn together, their heads stooped, were the old woman, like fate, the young woman, like love, and the small boy with the swallow of life in his hand.

Nor did Davie readily let that bird fly away. Sometimes he carried it on his sleeve, often enough it twittered out of his mouth, and when he got a fright it gulped down his throat into the cage of his breast. But it could wing swiftly too. When at last Mairi was ready to go out and turned round to speak to Davie, he had flown. 'He was here this very minute,' said Elie. 'Davie!' cried Mairi. 'He'll be hiding again,' said Elie. 'I'll hide him!' said Mairi. There was complete silence everywhere. But now they both knew that the silence was empty.

Outside there were stars and clouds and somewhere surely a risen moon. 'You'll send him home in an hour,' said Mairi, as they went on their way. Elie said she would if she found him, but her eyes were with the night and the veiled shapes of familiar things; a dark corner was a place out of which a body might come with arms. Often a young fellow would give a girl a great fright like that. Already she began to feel excited, thinking of the ceilidh, and the faces, and the fun there would be. The ceilidh itself was a bright circle out of which secret arms . . . But she did not follow that thought. No one followed that thought for it went into the excitement of the dark, a secret thought half-looked at. She did not look at Colin. She kept him just beyond the rim of her thought – knowing he was there. 'It poisons the blood and takes the pith out of anyone when it's not got rid of,' said Mairi; 'the great thing in health is to keep them open.' 'I'm sure,' said Elie. 'That's what he hasn't done,' said Mairi, 'and he's an old man. The spring will see the end of him.'

'Perhaps no,' said Elie, reluctant that even an old man with poisoned blood should die. There was a tingling keen-ness in the night, sparkling and frosted and crisp, so that one's own arms could grasp in laughing fun – and break away. Her spittle came about Elie's lips. 'Won't you look in for a while yourself? you'd better do that. Do,' she suddenly begged of Mairi; and as Mairi went away on her healing errands, she stood looking after her until the night drew her from sight. Then Elie ran a step or two and pulled up, and went on walking to Angus Sutherland's house.

## THREE

As Elie entered Angus Sutherland's house, life met her in a bright tumbling wave. The women liked her; the children shouted to her in familiar terms; she was a soft kind creature with a singing voice that folk had to guard against. She won her way to a trestle seat by a long narrow board on which six or eight of the women were to waulk or full the cloth. There were old men and young men, women and girls and boys, about a peat fire in the centre of a room as simple as Mairi's but larger. The greatest gaiety pervaded the scene; for folk had not yet settled down, and men exchanging news had now and then to shout above the youthful din.

Several of those present had come down from the summer herdings to tackle the harvest. It was thus one of the most important times of the whole year. Indeed it was the time towards which the year grew and upon which much of another year depended. There was in it, accordingly, before the actual work started, the idea of festival; the feel of the stalks, the rivalry in cutting and binding, the ingathering of sheaves, of bread, of life: with busy hands and stooping bodies, male and female, and glances and smiles and sweat and determination: bread, and seed for the new harvest.

So naturally enough excitement rustled like wind in the ripe barley. There was discussion too. For they were not to start on their own crops tomorrow, but on those of Captain Grant, the tacksman, who was their immediate landlord. His house and his land lay in a bay of the glen beyond the mill, and free labour was given to him as part of their rent. Thus Mairi, in addition to £1 5s. in money, contributed two days' labour in the cornyard and cut twelve stooks. This was a moderate rent in keeping with her indifferent holding, but Angus Sutherland, with his large holding and many head of cattle, had to clear the haylands, shear forty-eight stooks, thresh twelve stooks, give four days' labour in the cornyard, provide one spade and three spreaders of peat, six hens, six dozen of eggs, six bolls of meal, and £4.

This system of land tenure had an ancient source and seemed natural enough to the people. A forebear of the Captain had been given the compact little Riasgan estate by a chief as one man might make a present to another out of recognition of services and blood kinship. No such gift was ever conveyed in writing, for in old Gaelic days a gentleman's word was more held in honour than clerkly scrawling on parchment. The Captain's duty was to supply his chief with men and otherwise to assist him in the maintenance of his position and the rule of his wide province. And though in these last two generations affairs had been changing radically, the people of the Riasgan, because they liked the Captain, still followed the ancient labour custom with natural enough grace. Profoundly within them there might even be a secret pleasure in doing the Captain's work, a satisfaction arising out of the idea of pure service directed towards someone higher than themselves, for the Captain was the blood representative of the chief, and the chief was father to them all.

In a land of tall men, old Angus was small, with a white cropped beard, a quiet humour, and twinkling eyes. He was very knacky with his hands, built cages out of thin birch withies, and bred singing linnets in his barn. He was always willing to try a new thing, and in the spring had bought oats from the coast in the belief that the ground must get tired of the same old seed. And the new seed would have done very well had it not been for the stronger crop of

yellow flowers that grew up with the corn, to the amusement (and perhaps not a little to the satisfaction) of some
of his neighbours. Nor was it of any use for Angus to
suggest now that the flower seeds must have been introduced to the ground after he had sown the oats. The picture
of the old man solemnly flailing sheaves of withered flowers
made good fun. The colour of the bread, it was maintained,
would at least tally with the linnets' wings. It might even
turn the linnets into canaries! Angus had long hankered
after canaries. What about a barnful of them! One young
man there, with a cripple foot, was goaded into impro-
vising:

> 'When Angus Ossian Finn Mac Cumhal
> is turned into a fairy,
> he'll eat a bit of his own yellow bread
> and whistle like a canary.'

Which hit off Angus's knowledge of the ancient poetry and
of the fairies well enough. But Angus answered the poet at
once:

> 'When Murdoch son of Murdoch
> has grown old and hairy,
> alas if he should find
> he never made a tune
> so well as a canary.'

Whereat everyone cheered the old man. In fact this impro-
vising was one of their great amusements, and some nights
at the ceilidh they hit a lucky vein. One or two of the
girls were very good at it. Occasionally a couple of lines
were struck out that instantly delighted and then haunted
the mind. 'That's you on your back, Murdoch!' called
Seonaid, the dark girl, boldly. As enemies, they never
gave quarter.

Murdoch murmured innocently:

> 'If I am on my back
> and Angus is a fairy,
> how kind of you to come
> and offer your canary.'

There was an explosion of laughter, for Murdoch's satire was nearly always two-edged. He had ruddy cheeks, dark eyes, and a quick attractive smile.

With a spot of colour, the girl changed the rhythm:

> 'If you were a whole barnful of canaries,
> if you were a whole green mound of fairies,
> I would sell the lot for Angus's empty cage
> with a crow in it.'

But the great game among the children was riddles, and one boy piped up, 'How could an empty cage have a crow in it?'

'When you are older, Iain my young calf,' said Seonaid, 'you may find that you too may not be in it though you are there.'

'Let me explain it to you, Iain,' said Angus, gripping the boy by the shoulder. 'Some day, like Murdoch there, you may be anxious to draw the attention of a fine girl, like Seonaid, but she, not caring, will look at the place on which you will be standing as though it were empty.'

'I should like to see her try it!' said Iain.

'What would you do to her?'

'I'd hit her one on the nose.'

Murdoch laughed.

'There is meat and drink in its laugh, as the fox said when he ran away with the bagpipes,' misquoted Seonaid.

Then the war of proverbs started. They came hurtling from all corners, sometimes inaptly, but with Murdoch and

Seonaid carrying on the main combat. The company obviously delighted in this, more than in the verse-making, which sometimes had an air of artificiality or strain, except in the case of Murdoch, who nearly always said something that stuck, often with a double meaning, particularly on the subject of women.

When Seonaid had Murdoch floundering for an apt reply, Elie heard Davie's excited voice putting the words in his mouth, 'I am too accustomed to a wood to be frightened of a canary.'

'Is it my friend Davie who's sending fuel to the wood?' cried Angus. But Davie had ducked down out of sight.

'It's invisible you should be, you rascal!' cried Elie.

'I am like MacKay's cat – still in the flesh!' came Davie's voice.

Seonaid smiled, and the boldness of her glance melted into a rare attractiveness. 'The wren may be small, but it will make a noise,' she said.

'Your hour, Davie,' said Murdoch, 'is pursuing you.'

'Now, now,' said Angus, 'Fingal never fought a fight without offering terms.'

'Fingal's door is always free to the needy,' said Murdoch, without glancing at Seonaid, who remarked mildly, 'The heaviest ear of corn bends its head the lowest.'

'That's your head between the door and the doorpost,' laughed one man at Murdoch, whose colour had risen.

'It's never difficult to guess the egg from your cackle,' Murdoch answered him shortly. But the man did not take it amiss for he saw that Murdoch, for all his laughing mouth, was beginning to be nettled. Seonaid seemed to have the power that in the long run cramped his wits. At the least opportunity they got fighting like this. Indeed the very sight of him raised her hackle. And there were times when he could clearly have throttled her.

Anna, the woman of the house and daughter-in-law to old Angus, was tall and broad and comely, with smooth dark hair and pleasant manners. She sat with her hands in her lap, smiling, saying to herself that in a moment she would stop this and call the girls to the waulking of the cloth, and yet delaying because of the gaiety. She liked this sound and fun in her home; she liked old Angus, whom she treated as one of her sons, of whom she had three, the second being Colin, who avoided Elie's eyes as pointedly as Elie avoided his.

Anna now watched the fun climb to the point where Murdoch, desperately pressed, defended himself with the saying, 'The dung-heap is mother to the meal-chest.'

But Seonaid, with a mouth-twist of equal satire, replied, 'It's aye the weed that grows from the dung-heap that lifts its head the highest.'

The creases of Murdoch's smile froze into a horrid grin. 'Seonaid!' murmured Elie, with compassion. That murmur was, unfortunately, heard and Murdoch's expression went dark and impotent. There was silence. Into it piped Davie's voice:

'Going to ruin is silent work!'

Merriment splashed over the company. Old Angus caught the boy from the floor. 'It's Black Donald (the Devil) that's in you this night,' he said. Davie wriggled, his face pale from excitement. Another boy cried, 'I knew that one too!' and trod on a dog that yelped sharply.

Anna got up. 'There would be no work done here this night if we sat listening to you all.'

'You have the warm heart, Seonaid,' said old Angus.

'No wonder, after hunting that cuckoo's nest,' replied Seonaid, upon whom the proverb game had now got a relentless grip.

'Some day you may need a nest of your own.'

'Beware!' came a hollow voice. 'If you take a wife from Hell, she will take you home with her.'

The laugh went full blast against Seonaid. Who had quoted that one? Not little Alan, the mimic? Amid the good humour, Seonaid smiled, flushing, aware of the underlying tribute. Her forearms and hands struck the board. 'Come on,' she said, 'before the witless grow profane. Where's that cloth?'

In addition to Anna, seven young girls seated themselves about the board. Elie, Seonaid, Grissel, a tall good-looking girl, and the mouse, Peigi, on one side; on the other, Flora, slimmer than her sister Elie, Iosbail, the vivid girl with blaeberry eyes, Rachel, the stocky girl who could not let herself go and sometimes looked resentful, and Anna, the woman of the house.

Anna started the song to which hands and arms sent the cloth circling with the sun in a thumping sideways push onwards round the board; then the others took up the chorus. The gay swinging rhythm filled all the room, entering to the heart of each cell in bodies animate or inanimate.

There were necessarily a lot of verses to the song to suit the length of the work, but very soon the verses were departed from and each girl improvised a couple of lines on the gallants present. It was the girls' opportunity and they took it.

Elie, being the first on Anna's left, sang out:

> 'What con*fuses* Murdoch's *mind*
> when he *cannot* find an *answer*?
> Hi-*ho*, for Murdoch's *mind*!'

'By the red hand, you're catching it this night, Murdoch!' roared Alie Munro, a happy, slow-witted man.

But there was something underlying Elie's words that made everyone wait for Seonaid's comment. It came:

> 'I saw *Colin* up the *Burn*;
> He was *herding* Mairi's *ewe*-lamb.
> Hi-*ho*, for Mairi's *lamb*!'

Colin's startled swallow went down noticeably as a cow's cud. He was a gay daring youth, but he now blushed more painfully than a child. Murdoch's eyes mocked him maliciously: You see how she lays you bare? Now you know! When a few more of you get it between wind and water, I'll laugh! But I'll slay that girl Seonaid yet, give me time!

Elie's face was a peat flame.

'Sing up, Elie!' cried Alie Munro.

> 'I saw Alie lead his goat,
> And I saw the goat lead Alie.
> Hi-ho, and make your choice!'

Most of the men came in for it one way or another, and many hidden things and feelings were more than hinted at, and when a hit was made the chorus went with a roar, the cloth getting licked into shape with energy. The minute hairy ends of the yarn knit round one another as the girls' eager fingers knit round the cloth, to the rhythm of the singing, with its bump on the board for the beat of mirth. Shapeless and twisting onward like the mythical serpent, all round the board, sunwise, with music being thumped into it and rare sallies of fun. The girls knew what they were about. The man who wore this would have their spell on him, the spell of his race. And good cloth at that, full of wear!

Two or three more men came in, including Hector, the man of the house, who had been out seeing to a neighbour's horse. He was over middle size, with such fine bone in the nose and eyebrows that his face had an air of distinction though his general expression rather drooped like a weary hawk's. He did not speak very much, and then quietly about anything that mattered. Though often in such talk his eyelids would lift and his eyes smile at some innocent thing near him in such an unexpected way that it was as if one of his father's linnets had come out of its cage. People

relied on him, and when he came to a house to do a neigh-
bourly action, the women of that house offered him their
best hospitality with their most delicate manners.

His entrance now took the personal edge off the fun and
broadened it, so that the younger men in particular experienced a relief, in which they expanded, moving about
with glistening eyes in the crowded space, their faces bright
with conspiracy in the upper gloom where the smoke hung.
The girls at the board knew of their youthful threats and
slapped the cloth with divine derision:

> 'Do you see the itching sparrows
> trying to look like bright canaries!
> Hi-ho! and chirp! chirp! chirp!'

This was a Seonaid stroke and the girls could hardly take
up the chorus for laughing. Repeated 'Chirp! Chirp! Chirp!'
threatened them with the giggles, so Seonaid, taking charge,
averted the feminine weakness by invoking a blessing on
the cloth and on those who would wear it.

So the cloth was waulked and folded and their labour
put aside.

Anna arose, saying nice things to the girls. They could
see she was a trifle excited and mysterious. She took Elie,
Seonaid, and Grissel with her and disappeared from the room.

Hector put the fiddle against Murdoch's hands.

'No! no!' laughed Murdoch, waving it away.

'Come on, Murdoch, lift it!' said several voices.

'No,' said Murdoch. 'Hach, no.' He pushed it aside,
smiling that sensitive but obdurate smile, like light flickering on black water.

'Come on, man!' cried Alie Munro. 'You surely wouldn't
let a girl like that upset you!'

From the black water pleasant venom points flickered.
The others might themselves have been stung, the way they
invisibly recoiled from Alie's bluntness.

'That's what it is, all the same!' cried Alie, nodding and hitting his knee. 'That's it!' He scratched his whiskers noisily, then laughed, turning his face away, knowing that they were against him.

Murdoch knew this too, and it darkened him still more. His smile was now brilliant, his eyes glittering and restless.

Colin drained all stress from his voice and said, 'Come on, Murdoch, give us a tune.' The matter-of-fact friendly tone nearly succeeded. But Murdoch would not play; he could not now; and they knew it.

All in a moment this tension had been created, and one false contact would make the spark flash visibly. Colin did not hit Murdoch familiarly on the back, nor could anyone suggest that Alie was a fool.

'Well, perhaps you'll play later,' said Hector in his quiet way. Murdoch met his eyes and found no stress there. 'All right,' he answered. 'Yes.' His expression was quick and courteous, without exposing anything or receding from anything.

Young Iain, who had been watching this, turned round and, as if something had been released in him, hit Davie a friendly slap. 'Stop it!' said Davie, 'you awkward fool.' 'I'll fool you!' said Iain. Davie, the eel, tried to slip past, but Iain gripped him by the tail. Davie tugged to get free. Iain let go at the right moment and Davie hit full tilt into Alie, who, on the verge of rising, was slewed on to the floor, where he sat for a moment scratching his beard amid the released laughter. And they knew by the way he scratched that, slow-witted or not, he had the common instinct for social balance.

'That's you on your back, Alie!'

'It took a big man to do it,' said Alie.

The women returned, Anna leading them with an armful of newly cut corn. At once the air of festival was created and the boys shouted 'Graddan!'

The girls carried milk-vessels and whisks. All arose and

made way for Anna, who came toward the fire. 'You'll put up a few words,' she said to Angus.

Angus bared his head; the smile on his face faded. He asked God to bless them in these the first fruits of the harvest, and in the harvest itself, in each home and in all homes; and he thanked the bountiful Giver and promised that they would remember His name. In saying these words, Angus to the boys was completely changed. This change made them foretaste their own manhood. They saw the power of reverence and dignity. In the running water there was that rock.

Excitement and anticipation now made everyone restless. They formed a moving ring round Anna and the two girls. A skin was spread on the floor. Anna held a fistful of cornstalks in her left hand and in her right a stick. Seonaid lit a piece of bog fir at the fire and when it was blazing like a torch held it out towards Anna. Anna lit the ears of corn at it. They flared up. At the right moment, she hit the ears with her stick and the kernels fell pattering on the skin. Elie on her knees gathered them into a heap and winnowed them with a little pitching motion through her hands.

Anna's skill was admired. The smell of the roasted oats was sharp in the nostrils and the fire-tongues danced in watching eyes. Anna herself seemed satisfied and proceeded with the work, her expression concentrated and yet calm. She had the unexcited wisdom of the mother. When all the corn had been thus dealt with, she examined the oats carefully. 'We'll put on the pot,' she said. And when an impatient voice cried 'They're right enough' she did not answer, but lifted the big black pot on to the hook over the fire. As the heat got inside the pot she stirred the oats with her stick, and not until she was satisfied that the grain was properly kilned did she lift the pot off the fire. She never liked things half done, whether a funeral or a feast.

Nor did she rush her preparations. When the quern stones

were fixed and Elie was feeding the grain, she set the top
stone turning in order to grind the grain into meal. Out of
the rhythm of the stone rose her voice in the old quern
song:

*Turn the stone sunwise . . .*

The meal from the quern was winnowed clean. It had
a toasted gritty flavour that no other meal achieves. It was
said of one tacksman that he allowed ten cows to starve
while he had stacks of corn in his yard, because he was
reserving the corn for graddaning.

This meal, riddled through the fingers on to a bowl of
roused cream and eaten with a horn spoon, is very palatable. It charges and caresses the mouth, yet one movement
of the jaws is enough to make it disappear as by a divine
illusion, and were it not for the lingering flavour and after-
math in the nostrils, one might well believe in the illusion.
But there the bowl is, and (God between us and mischance!)
another spoonful coming up.

To hold the illusion, therefore, requires care, and even
a thoughtful rumination when the mouth is full. How hard
accordingly it was upon four boys who each had a spoon
but had to sup out of a common bowl! For the agreement
to take spoonful about round the bowl hardly met the
difficulties that arose. To go too slow was not to be waited
on, to go too fast was to spill, while to have an elbow
touched was war. And one of the boys, whose spoon had
a hair lip, protested when he could, until in a moment of
revenge he helped himself out of turn and the bowl was
saved from disaster by a miracle. Seonaid came and acted
as umpire and gave her own spoon to the boy whose spoon
was defective.

She lorded it over the boys like an older boy amongst
them, rapping out her words, threatening or smiting, with
spirit and decision. She had a clear skin over very regular
features with red in the cheeks, and eyes bright on the
surface and quick to turn and flash. In company, the boys

preferred her to any of the other girls. She was slim and could fight; and when she hit them they could run away scoffing, their heads down, and call her names without feeling ashamed or belittled. Amongst themselves they admired her for her witty turns of phrase and put her against Murdoch, though their male instinct was to support Murdoch and say he could lay her out if only he really cared to let himself go.

Her voice gave a cheerful battling air to the soft seduction of the food. Spoons scraped. Tongues licked. Lord, it was good that! It melted like manna! . . . All life was mellow with goodness. There were no bad times, only trials. And maybe there would never be any bad times again. Why should there be? And whether there would be or not, how easy to meet them, after all! The hard times were a testing of the spirit and the memory of them filled talk and made fellowship . . . Lord, the pipes!

The very tuning of the bagpipe coming in from the crisp evening filled the room with excitement. In no time a reel was in full swing in the barn, where a few tallow candles held an unequal fight with the dark. Linking in and out the dark went the dancers, the men going at it with great gusto, the girls laughing when a swift arm-lock sent them spinning. At the beginning some of the older folk looked on from the door, but soon the young began to crowd them out as they gathered from neighbouring crofts, and even from down the glen, for some of the girls who had been in secret league with Anna must have passed the word. The barn was a small place, but it was a clear windless night and over by the black stones, where the women boiled the washing pot, a fire appeared. Seldom had that happened at night, but soon tongues of flame were making shadows dance on the barn wall and on the piper lost in his black art. When the boys first saw him they nudged one another, whispering, 'Look, there he is!' as if they had never seen him playing before! Against the wall, his chest and his pipes

and all the upper part of him seemed to swell and grow
tall in the stillness of concentration. The notes bubbled in
their blood. They were still watching him when couples
took the turf between him and the fire.

It was more magical out here than in the barn, and the
eight dancers were all in a moment a company of origi-
nators. And they knew it; knew they would be imitated;
but for the moment held their distinction with jealous exultation.

The wide earth, the flames of the peat on limbs and
faces, the bodies leaping and spinning in the circles of music,
under a sky with stars paling to the east where a waning
moon was thinking of rising upon her kingdom; here was
more than the joy of the dance, something added to the
mystery of the rhythm, a beat in the blood; freedom from
walls, freedom from rules; escape caught in its own delirious
toils between fire and music. The music put its frenzy in
the boys so that they could not leave the fire alone. Out
of the dark they came running with peats from the nearest
stacks with the guilt of half-theft stinging their mirth. They
would make a fire as big as the world and blind the moon
and stars! Other dancers stole out; at first quietly, as if
intruding on the kingdom of the night, but soon making
the kingdom their own. Then more dancers, until the barn
was deserted.

Between the black piper and the red fire the music
changed to quick time. The women faced each other between
the lines of the men, dancing woman to woman, then,
advancing, linked arms and whirled in a giddy spin, the
men swaying on their feet, watching them, jocular, eyes
glistening and ready. The women broke apart and faced
their men, who danced to them with welcome, who swung
them and left them, to face each other man to man. All
the wild male energy now tore out of them; their deep-
throated cries rose upon the night, pierced the night with
exultation; the dance attained its moment of mad frenzy;

linking arms, they set their strength to the swing. The quiet women who had danced, quietly laughing, watched them, waiting for the sundering of that whirling violence, conscious of the male pride but sure of themselves as of fate.

To one or two of the cottages of the Riasgan the scene presented another face. Old Gilleasbuig, with his bent shoulders and thin white beard with yellow discolourings, long-jawed and narrow-templed, with small wide-open pale eyes, looked down upon the scene with open mouth. The sloping ground set the fire in the bottom of the valley, in the centre of the pit. The dancing figures were like small black devils and the little boys like scuttling imps. The cries were the screeching of demented souls. His wife was behind him in the door and expressed her disapproval in sighing tones. Dancings and carryings-on indoors were bad enough, but this was a defiance of the Almighty Himself. He did not hear her dribble on, and when he said, as one speaking out of sleep, 'That's nothing,' her mouth was stopped, until he added, 'That's nothing to what it will be in Hell itself.' She whinnied, turning from a stirring of the pool of memory, for they had danced in their youth, God save them, and his arms had been strong and his breath hot. He had had a stoop even then, and great strength in his shoulders; a crushing stoop. The music and laughter followed them into the house. He sat staring into the fire; ignored her; got to his knees and prayed. He was dull-witted but he had had passion. And in communion his anger got bathed and caught some of his God's complacency. And so her fear that he might ask where his son was, and particularly his son's wife (for well she knew they would both be at the dance) began to ease. She could see that he was accounting it right-eousness in himself that he had not accused her. Not often did he deny himself in God's work . . .

Seumas MacKay, who was on his deathbed and nearer God than Gilleasbuig, smiled to Dark Mairi of the Shore.

'They're at the dancing,' he said. Then he trembled a little, 'Och-och,' and his hands lifted an inch or two and fell. His hands were emaciated and from the thin wrists to the finger-tips lay straight by his hips. It required an effort to withdraw himself from the upward stare to which he was now committed and the effort gave his smile an extraordinary kindness. The pathos of this did not touch Mairi. She was content that he should stare, because in his staring he was comfortable and committed. She spoke to him in a way that he need not acknowledge. The dancing was at his old friend's, Angus Sutherland's, she told him. Angus and himself had been great companions. It would be to celebrate the beginning of harvest. The minister had his harvest in that day. She took him to the sea and told him of all the people he knew or had heard of. 'Yes,' he whispered now and then, 'yes,' as if to a story of biblical remoteness. When she was going away his eyes turned on her and the smile came, that strange sweet forced smile. He would not last until the spring.

The woman of the house accompanied her a little way. When at last they stood, looking at the fire, a man came upon them. The woman, Morach, gripped Mairi's arm, until she saw it was her own son. 'Is it you, Seumas og?' He did not answer. He rarely spoke. He would sit an evening in a ceilidh-house without opening his mouth, until something came upon him and he would at once get up and go silently out. He had the ghastly power of foreseeing events. As he faded silently from them, Morach said, 'I'll go back.' Her voice, as she thanked Mairi, was like her husband's smile. Mairi stood still a moment, then turned her face to the fire.

When a man and a woman finish a dance within walls they separate. To walk out into the dark of night would be a defiance of reputation. A decent girl would deny the Bible sooner. But where there are no walls, what may one sit on or lean against but the dark of the night? Little laughing groups, squeals from a girl who refuses to show what she has in her hand, abrupt wrestling matches, peat-dust down the neck by the peat-stack, recriminations and the voice that dares, a swift escape round the fire and into the darkness, helpless laughter, a smothering silence.

The little boys become excited. They whisper among themselves. They scout. 'I saw him kissing her!' They become intensely excited. There's something they have never seen and they listen to young Art, who is thirteen and a leader, whispering that he has his eye on Sarah, the miller's sister. There are stories enough about her and the wild happenings at the mill. 'Will the bastard is sniffing after her,' said Art. 'You watch them slide away when the dance starts. Then we'll follow them.'

Murdoch is tuning his fiddle on a mound of turf. He hears Seonaid's voice by the black wall of the peat-stack. It is gay and daring, holding its own, though being interfered with. He hates the voice and its bright challenge. And the voice of the fellow Anndra, interfering with her and trying to be witty, sickens him. 'Lift it, Murdoch!' shouts Anndra. Murdoch smiles to the one or two near him, his eyes black as the bog under wild fire. He makes shy noises in his throat. 'Is it time?' If he threw the fiddle in the fire, he would smile gently like that. 'Uh, do you think?' His voice breaks in a chuckle. 'All right.' He has the magician's finger that always surprises them. He gives the bow its head, and, in his recklessness, strength and clearness combine to astonish himself.

Though fiddle music was Davie's strongest passion, he found himself turning away from Murdoch and following in the tail of Art's little band. His mind floated in a curious clear coldness, but the swallow of life was beating against its ribbed cage in an excitement that was faintly sickening. But he was a man tonight, full of proverbs and wit. Intimations of manhood pulled him away from Murdoch. He followed, hopeful and fearful, as if he were to see the coupling of snakes.

After naming to them the likely spot, Art, knowing the ground, led his following in an outflanking movement. At a certain spot he went to earth, the others wriggling round him. Now they were to crawl – and remember, not a sound! He got up upon hands and knees and so did the others; whereupon they all grew still as stone, for their lifted eyes saw a dark figure standing before them, its wrapped head and shoulders cut off by the far hill crest. It neither spoke nor moved. Art's throat gave way and, backing into his followers, he turned in mad flight, the rest after him, the stragglers screaming and yelling. Davie yelled too, but because he was nimble and there were a few behind him, his head kept clear and wary. Several times he pitched on his nose, but before a hand could stretch over him from the air he was up and off. The fire, the dancers, the music – there they were, and Art had already one or two men round him. Davie thought he heard one man laugh. He swerved away round the corner of the barn and into the house.

Old Angus welcomed him. 'There's the running on you of the dog that chases two deer. You don't tell me you've been at the dancing?' There were a few of the older folk around the fire, with a young one fluttering about for something here and there and others bursting in and out, or resting between dances. There was whisky in the house too, and some mystery and joking accompanied the good liquor. Angus had had one or two drinks with little groups and was full of fellowship. Story-telling had started and Angus now said, 'Because little Davie here likes it better than any of you, I will now give you "The Desire of the Aged Bard".'

There was applause at that. 'By God,' said a man, 'we'll have another drink first on the heads of it.'

'Fingal's door,' said Angus, looking at Davie, 'is always open and the name of his hall is the stranger's home.'

'None ever went sad from Fingal,' murmured Davie.

Angus closed the crook of his arm on him. 'Your kindling will be the great fire one day.'

The drink went round with the usual little speeches of respect and good wishes to the lady of the house and to all in the house and to the house itself. And Angus made Davie sip a drop too. 'Be quiet, Anna,' he said to his daughter-in-law; 'it's at the breeding of men we are now.' When Davie coughed, the men laughed.

Then Angus settled down and gave the argument to his poem. This was done every time, however well the listeners knew it. It was the tuning of the instrument, the tuning of minds to the right reception of the great theme. And occasionally Angus introduced some observation new to his listeners. The look on their faces showed when he did this. And if his observation was at once just and curious, their faces caught the brightness of pleasure.

The Aged Bard, then, lived in days before St Columba came to Iona and came to Inverness; he lived maybe before the Saviour Himself was born. That explains why there are certain things in the poem, and why the Paradise of the Aged Bard is not God's Paradise. He was a heathen. And there were beasts living then which have not been living in Alba since hundreds upon hundreds of years. Where now is the elk that's mentioned in the poem? Yes, and there were wolves and bears and boars and beasts like little lions living then, and stranger beasts too, beasts like hairy men. Yet in spite of all that, and in spite of them being heathens, the people who lived then were wonderful people, like Fingal and Cuchulain (him that was in Skye) and all the heroes, and beautiful women like Deirdre and Maeve and Emir. Now this Aged Bard was not one of the heroes. He was just an old bard who was dying; and he thought to himself as he was dying that there was nothing in all the worlds, here or hereafter, so beautiful to him as his own land . . .

'*O place me by the little streams that flow softly with gentle steps,*
*Under the shade of spreading branches lay my head;*

*And, O thou Sun, be kind to me.*
*Lay softly my side on the grass upon the bank of flowers*
*    and gentle breezes,*
*Let the pale primrose, grateful in hue, and the little*
*    dairy surround my hillock,*
*Greenest when bedewed . . .'*

As Angus went on with that ancient poem, his listeners
came under its enchantment. Angus was a small man, neat
in his hands and clean in his person. His face had a natural
simplicity and kindliness, caught up by a twinkling cunning
of expression in the eyes, that looked for fun round the
corner. Now, however, his expression held a gravity softened by memory, as though the streams and the Sun, the
primrose and the green bank, had been enjoyed by him in
that land that could be seen back in time – as any man
can see his own childhood. It was the land of the Aged
Bard, who was a man like Angus. And this Aged Bard was
not a simple or uninstructed man, but on the contrary was
a man grey with years of experience of life, rich in knowledge, who had faced all things and exhausted all passions,
but who in the end prayed to be placed by the little streams.
All his dealings with gods and men had winnowed to that.
And there came from his words to all their nostrils the
fragrance of the primrose with its grateful hue. And this
fragrance affected them like love. The Aged Bard did not
love them: he loved the primrose. He loved the primrose
and the daisy and the green mound. And O thou Sun, be
kind to me. Their hearts turned in them with love of the
old man who loved the primrose and the streams and prayed
to the Sun by which all things grew. They understood him.
His words ran like a soft fire in their blood. In their bones
they knew him. Their flesh was warm with desire of him.
They would have comforted his head and taken the stones
from under his feet. Their minds ran before them to minister
to him and to listen to his immortal words. They could see

him turn and smile upon them, his face kindly as the face of Angus. And Anna, the mother, would half scold him as she put his head more comfortable on the green mound; and little Kirsteen, who was a whole month younger than Davie, appeared before him like Fand, the Pearl of Beauty, and said that she would take him across the loch to the primroses of Fairyland; and Davie himself was an arrow that flew hither and thither and had magic power to grant all the wishes of the Aged Bard, whose smile would be reward, for Davie liked the streams where the trout were and the stories of the great hunting in the old days . . .

In all this there was both the reverence and the freedom of love. Behind the Aged Bard was the eternal earth and over it the Sun. In instinct and in heart they delighted and worshipped here. What they knew as God and religion interfered with this spontaneous worship and love. The Aged Bard had no Hell. They had no God of Vengeance to fear in those days. But yes now. Therefore when they slipped back with Angus, their hearts opened like flowers and the muscles of their bodies grew fluent with immortal health.

This wisdom of the ancient world, with its kindness and untrammelled feet, was given its shadows and dark mad moments by the music outside and the cries and laughter of the dancers. Lost moments on lonely shores, bird-crying on night moors, spirits in dark woods, swift upflying of the instincts, black passion and glutted mouths; through it all, through all the world beyond the lochs and beyond the mountains and beyond the seas, through the nights of dancing and passion and deeds, had come the Aged Bard – to lay his head by the primroses with longing and desire.

Quietly in out of the night came Seumas og with his face. It was like an owl-cry from a wood; it had hidden knowledge from the well at the world's end; it was cold and sunless and stared. The eyes were a pale greenish-blue; the face thin and bony; the hair dark, but with owl-brown in it in certain lights. He was welcomed in a special way and a seat was given him; he sat down; his shoulders and arms moved in a cold chill; then his expression became fixed on the fire and he paid no attention to anyone, nor did anyone interfere with him. Usually persons with second sight are normal enough in every other way. But Seumas was a strange being, and when the others forgot him, Davie and Kirsteen remained sensitive to his alien presence. He had no favourites; yet he came oftenest to Angus's house, for Angus was fond of him, and when Seumas og had his vision of death, Angus accepted it with the quiet wisdom of a man for whom death is a familiar thought.

Angus was in full spate when Seumas suddenly got up and turned for the door. 'You're not off already?' called Angus, going after him. 'Mind your feet.' Beyond the doorstep, Seumas stood against the night. Nor did Angus put any question to him. As Seumas walked abruptly away, Angus heard him mutter 'Fire! Fire!'

The fire has disturbed him, thought Angus, peering into the night and wondering what vision Seumas could have got. Perhaps a barn on fire, or a house, or perhaps hell. That fire burning in the open pit of the night was enough . . . The figure with dark-wrapped head and shoulders that had scared the boys came towards Angus. His old heart started a little at the quiet apparition; his mouth cried 'Fine night!' The answer revealed Dark Mairi, and he called to those in the house that he was bringing them a great stranger. Anna welcomed her; then they all greeted her.

'Is it here you are, you rascal?' said Dark Mairi to Davie.

But Angus stood up for him and Anna excused him. They were delighted to see Mairi and to get her news. They loved news. And now Mairi had told of her journey three times so that the whole pattern of it was in her mind and what she had to say was of remarkable interest to them all. For Mairi did not embroider anything, but dealt only with facts, and the more she got at the heart of a fact the more marvellous it seemed. She was the teller of mortal things. Angus saw this in her.

Then she related what the people on the coast were saying and what they had heard about the men who had been shipped to America. They could see this was something her mind dwelt on, for her own son had gone there. She had never heard from him in eight years. She told of a letter from London in which it was said that they were getting on well. But some of the people did not believe that letter. 'Uisden, son of Duncan of the hill, who is back from the army with one leg, says that some of the boys were landed in forests and the savages killed most of them. He is a bitter man, though he has a pension, they say, of sixpence a day for life. But I don't know,' concluded Mairi.

How could Uisden know, compared with London, where the truth itself was? And had not the news come specially from the Great Lady (their chief) and her husband, who was an English lord?

But the shadow kept Davie from escaping. His father landing in forests and in snow, being killed by savages . . .

On the way home, he was not rebellious or moody. Once or twice he said to his granny, 'Watch your feet there.' She heard the companionship in his voice, and it comforted her in a strange way.

When they had won to the height of their cottage and paused to look back, they saw the red circle of fire and black figures leaping before it to the cry of the pipes. A strange emotion caught suddenly at Davie: of denial, of wanting to reach out, of tears. Moodily he refused to eat. He curled up in his floor bed. But the feeling had in it also a perilous elation, coming from his knowledge and cunning use of the proverbs that night. The tremor in his breast was like the 'second sight' of greatness. When his granny was asleep he would steal out and take the bread she had offered. She was now at the fire, and as she smoored the kindling in the ashes she invoked a blessing upon the house and all that belonged to the house. It was one of her ancient rhymes and her voice had a nasal reedy sound that he could have mimicked – and frequently did – and would have been half ashamed of before strangers. This little smooring chant had a terrible haunting monotony. He got a vision of his granny as he sometimes got a new vision of an earthy outcrop in the half dark, and watched her dim figure move away from the fireplace into the blackness by the bed. Staring after her, he fell asleep.

And Dark Mairi herself had fallen asleep long before Elie came barefooted across the floor to slide in over her body. But sleep came slowly to Elie.

Her lips were still burning and there was a queer drawn pain in the roots of her breast. Colin and she had avoided each other at the dance, as if they had had to show how ridiculous was the rhyme about Colin meeting Mairi's ewe-lamb up the Burn. The rhyme burned, however, in both their minds. When their arms or hands touched in the dance the effect was so vivid that all other hands and arms might have been made of wood. When the dance was over and they separated, their talk or their laughter was loud as though they were keeping in touch within the dark. Had one of them gone into the night with a partner the other would have known it, would have felt it like a nerve-wound in the middle of a joke. All their play was for each other even when it was invisible – particularly then. Yet neither was sure of the other's awareness.

And the fun increased as the night went on. In the strange haphazard way that memorable nights are made was this night being made. Something extra of freedom, of excitement, gave it the rightness of a magical creation. All felt this in the poise of their bodies; in the flash of their bodies on tiptoe to brimming cups that might spill, might empty, too soon. And when one or two of the older bachelors, on the crest of their liquor, embraced a girl too strongly, or gestured into the embrace a laughing lewd suggestion, tongues could have forked at them and heads swooped like falcons.

The miller began to pursue Elie.

The sky cleared as the moon arose. Girls spoke quickly and sharply in their excitement, as though the kingdom was fully theirs at last and they had to govern it and save its subjects from divine disaster. This rule intoxicated them. The men played their rôles of exaggerated folly in company, or of stealthy sense at a distance. Colin, stung by the miller, swore to himself that he would see Elie home, and from that point onward his cunning became acute. Between the barn and the house he got her at the right moment. Silently she slipped into his conspiracy.

When they were out of earshot he was gay in a burst of pure relief, chuckling at the ease with which they had got away. They were like two playing a game, and they were immensely relieved to find each other frank and open, to be able to speak and laugh. They became extremely friendly and fond of each other. He had her by the arm. He pressed her arm close against his side. They discussed the evening and made fun of certain incidents. They frolicked homeward. Sometimes he pulled her arm in a little race. Her body trembled with laughter. 'O Colin!' said her husky shy throat, and in an access of tenderness she gripped his arm tight. They reached her gable-end where they spoke in whispers. He could not go away. They could not move from each other. What a lovely night it was under the moon! Her voice caught that low note of reluctant shy sadness as it came out of her wonder at the night. Only the flaw of worldly knowledge in her innocence kept her from rising in a wave against him and turning her face from the moon. And this innocence affected him, like the moonlight and the earth and the dying fire. In his enchantment his bodily strength made him tender and delicate towards her.

Now at that time the piper took his own way of dealing

with the night. He had played well and drunk little by little and had come to that state where a man feels it in him to give his best, not only for his own satisfaction, but for the satisfaction of the night and the folk and the stones and the beasts, and as a tribute to his pipes, his own pipes, that only got drunk at rare moments of inspiration. He played therefore the 'big music', and as he played his face went white and cold, and all of him shivered like glass. '*No More*', he played. 'O God!' said the dancers, and the brutality of their bodies gave a colic-twist and passed out of them, 'that's the end!' And some of them felt the music as a piper's revenge, though revenge for what they did not know. But others felt it as the sadness that is beyond joy, the deep sweet sadness for that which will never be caught or will never be born. When a woman has the ache in her breast and a changeling shape glimmers through tears, a man hears the high vanishing echoes of a lost cause.

Colin gave a small nervous laugh and began talking of the piper's odd humours. Elie did not answer. He tried to see her face. Touching her cheek, his fingers got wet. Her glimmering smile came at him on a moon wave; he crushed into it. 'Elie! Elie!' he said. And 'Ah, Colin!' she answered as the wave sank.

When, long afterwards, she left him, the fire had died to a small red eye and all the glen was silent. A wind came down from the hills, a chill night wind from the south. It had come searching along the backbone and between the ribs of ancient Alba, searching up from the plains and the seas that were given over to the game of death and hungry for food.

## FOUR

With its harvest gathered and its meat salted, the Riasgan got through the early winter with a strong pulse. Each season of the year had its occupation and interest, and though none might compare in delight with the long summer evenings and freedom of the shieling life, yet there was a lot to be said for the early winter. Food and fuel were stored in their first plenty; outside labour to a large extent was suspended; stock had been sold for cash and young unhoused beasts strayed over all the holdings at will; nothing could be injured; nothing destroyed; interest in life was contemplative or joyous or malicious; the dark nights called for the ceilidh and fun and songs, for intrigue and love-thoughts, for surprising outbursts of passion or oddities of behaviour, for the visits of 'characters' like the packman with gossip and story and fascinating merchandise in his pack. The packman indeed brought them the latest styles, the best romance, the most scandalous biography, and the catchiest verse of the season. And in the full flow of that, Angus's classics were given a rest. Women carded and spun, the weaver wove, the tailor visited houses and made clothes, youths swung flails and old men winnowed. Even Gilleasbuig grew fluent in his prayers, for God had been mindful of his stock, and he urged God to bring sinners to repentance, to set up His rule on earth, and so put an early and final stop to the Devil and his ways.

With all this there went leisure and a leaning to inclination. The women were the more persistent and fruitful workers, and found the males frequently in their way. Many

of the tasks about a house they would not let a man perform
– even if he had wanted to, which, of course, he did not.
In this matter of work there was so strong a custom that
if a man did a woman's work, where a woman was fit to
do it, the feeling of shamed surprise would be felt stronger
by the woman than by the man. The system worked very
well, for the man in his sphere and the woman in hers were
each equally governing and indispensable. Thus the difference between a man and a woman was emphasised and
each carried clear before the other the characteristics and
mystery of the male and female sex. Men were not knowing
with regard to their women. They left them their realm
and could thus on occasion meet them like strangers and
even make a verse or a song about them. In life's major
dealings, like cattle-droving, marketing, hunting, and war,
women would have felt helpless without their men. Yet
more than their usefulness, men were to them their final
ornament, and their secret pride in them, when worthy,
was complete.

During this early winter season too, what with the new
barley, so readily turned into malt, the menfolk had conspir-
acies of their own. Many of them would be away for days
on end, and old Angus had the reputation of bringing the
liquor from the pot in the distilling bothy sooner and cleaner
than anyone else. His whisky, they said, had a flavour all
its own. So well liked was he by the men that some of the
women thought a man of his years should have more sense,
forgetting that he was only very little over sixty. The men
also went hunting the hill for deer and the river for salmon;
and so ancient had been their gaming rights, that no new
laws or restrictions in favour of landlord or lessee could
ever convict them in their own minds of poaching. And if
poaching it must be called, then so much the greater the
zest in its pursuit.

So that, altogether, this season that followed the ingathering of the grain and potatoes, with its Harvest Homes

and Hallowe'ens culminating in the great New Year festival which continued for the better part of a fortnight, had its own attractions. But once the new year had settled in, a thin quickening, like the movement in a healthy but lean stomach, could be felt in man and beast. The testing time lay immediately ahead, when it was within the providence of Nature to be cruel or kind. It was at this time that the talk got going of conscription for war.

There was a thin covering of snow on the ground when Davie approached the house of Angus Sutherland. Kirsteen cried to him that she was making a great big snow man, but Davie, instead of going to help, stood looking at her out of his dark eyes. Her method of carrying handfuls of snow and patting them into position was adjudged by him to be a real lassie's way of making a snow man. Her living glance caught his disapproval, and, returning a cold dislike, she enquired, 'What are you going to my house for?' 'Not you,' said Davie, and drifted round to the barn where he could hear the clip of the flails. As he hesitated before the door, he heard footsteps, and, turning, saw the young daughter approaching with snow in her right fist and wrath on her face. 'You cheeky thing!' she observed and threw the snow, which, not being properly packed into a ball, broke into ineffective fragments. Davie laughed and went into the barn.

Colin was flailing sheaves of oats which contained a great number of those withered flower stalks over which Angus had been twitted. His body swayed with a powerful rhythm, and so fine was his judgment that the tip of the loose arm of the flail clipped an overhead couple at every swing, for the curving roof was low set to the walls. This clipping sound was the mark of the expert, for it did not seem to interfere with the final thresh of the stick, yet gave the exquisite satisfaction of doing things to a hair's breadth. Davie liked the sound. Colin liked it himself, and when he had threshed the grain – and flower seeds – from the sheaf, his whirling flail contrived to whisk the straw towards his eldest brother, young Angus (Angus og), who gathered and tied it into bundles or windlings.

'How's life, Davie?' called Colin as he laid out another sheaf. Colin's chest looked broad and full of power. Above that chest his features appeared small, but finely made and hardy. Davie liked him at that moment – his compact strength, his clean assurance. Even his cheerfulness had a hard fighting glint. Colin often appeared to have this brisk cheerfulness before his brother, Angus og, who was half a head taller, slow in action like his father, Hector, and had an odd sideways glance from his eyes that appeared to sum a man up craftily when he wasn't looking. Davie respected Angus og, half fearing his reserve. His dark hair had something of brown in it that was absent from Colin's. Colin derived from his grandfather, Angus, as Kirsteen, her fair hair shot with gold, recalled to Anna her own mother. Hector, Angus og, and the youngest son, who was in Morayshire learning to be a mason, were much of a piece physically.

As Colin drew Davie into conversation, he made loud careless jokes that seemed like an instinctive barrier raised against or challenging Angus og. His eyes were clear and bright, his arms and shoulders supple as the flail, his waist drawn to a round pillar above his flexing hips. 'Canary seed!' he scoffed cheerfully. 'What they're going to do with this, Black Donald alone knows!' Happening to turn his head, Davie met the eyes of Angus og.

And when he left the barn, Kirsteen challenged his right of entry to her house. He was having a hard day of it! Nor could he rightly snowball a female on her own doorstep. It must be this talk of the army! She looked sharp and vindictive as a weasel. He actually did not know what to do and was standing with a sheepish expression when Anna appeared at the door and scolded her daughter for lack of manners and hospitality. 'He— he—' began Kirsteen wildly, then, to Davie's amazement, burst into tears.

Anna invited him in and he found his old friend Angus by the fire. 'What havoc is this you're doing amongst the women, Davie?' He was very busy boring small holes with a red-hot wire in a sheepskin spread taut over the frame of a riddle, and Davie knew by his keen interest and extra good humour that he was inventing something. He was asked his opinion of the holes, and if he could guess the riddle. 'They may laugh at you and me, Davie, but we'll show them a trick or two! Put that in the fire again.' When the little black holes were all over the skin and Anna had complained finally about the smell, they got up and went to the barn. Colin welcomed them satirically, but Angus, paying no attention to him, laid the riddle on the floor and with cupped hands lifted the oats and flower seeds into it; then carefully he carried the riddle towards the door, where he began a circular motion that set the seeds sliding over the skin. From underneath came a small rain of the round flower seeds only: the oats remained in the riddle. 'You see how it's done, Davie: the holes are just big enough to let through the seeds but too little to let through the oats. Simple, isn't it?'

Colin was delighted with this; so was Davie; and so was old Angus. The pile of seeds grew. 'Lord, it's great, that!' cried Colin. He laughed, as at some animal performing a ridiculous trick. Even Angus og, leaning on a birch handle, smiled. 'No one understood,' said old Angus, riddling away, 'why I grew these flowers in the corn. But now you know, Davie: I was wanting the seeds for my linnets.' At that Davie himself became noisy with mirth. 'I knew!' he cried challengingly at Colin. Colin, with a quick lurch, couped him in the straw.

It was a moment of divine ease when life bubbles up clear at the source. The joy of creation, first creation, when what is made is not of use so much as of wonder, and attracts ripples of laughter around its sheer surprise. All Angus's inventions gathered something of that about them.

Their usefulness was a divine joke. And to be in the midst of the joke, and welcomed there, was to experience for irresponsible minutes a state of perfect freedom, in which the instinct to play catches its own crystal circles and flings them like lassos to snare and double up.

From the tumbled straw Davie looked up at Angus og, whose smile out of the corners of his eyes had a sly measuring, as of some primordial insight or wisdom; Colin still stood with hands and shoulders arrested in the out-thrust that had couped him; and Angus, like the God of the Jews, moving the round riddle of his creation beneath his beard, separated the weed from the oat.

This vortex of fun in some mysterious way drew others, and presently quite a few men and youths were scattered about the dim light of the barn watching Angus finishing the last of the riddling. They were delighted with Angus's invention, much as they would have been delighted by one of Murdoch's witty sayings. And the old man took their fun with such sly humour that the very sight of the pucker on his face and the wary light in his eyes keyed up their expectations of adventurous sayings. Until one remarked, 'With Angus in the regiment, it would never want!' Immediately the riddling was forgotten and the talk of war on.

Clearly this was become a subject of deep and avid interest, and perhaps for the first time in the history of that place it brought cleavage amongst the men. For a new idea was being introduced into the conception and methods of war. It was not the fundamental issue of war or peace that troubled those in Angus's barn, but the way in which it was now proposed they themselves should be used for war. In days of old men had risen to support their chief whatever the extent or nature of the feud, local, regional, or national. And the fighting was carried on by that impetus in each breast which made the cause its own, so that all men in supporting their chief supported their own leader-

ship and furthered their secret designs of pride or acquis-
itiveness or revenge or justice or courage. The chief stood
to each man for his high secret picture of himself: a long
tradition, courtesy that has the manner of a clever saying,
hospitality that is easy and incurious, freedom of movement that disdains the grinding task, courage, anger that
goes headlong to an end, a love of change above a constancy
that is remorseless: in short, all his history in descent from
the Aged Bard, writ in the one blood and spoken in the
one tongue: and just as a man is delicately familiar with
this secret picture of himself, so is he familiar with his chief;
and when his chief appears in the flesh he goes gladly to
meet him. The land and all it contains is the common
heritage, and as a man would make the moral law out of
this high conception of himself, so is he pleased to leave
justice in the hands of his chief.

But if thus it had been from the times of the Aged Bard,
the century that had just closed had introduced change.
The rising of the '45 had been followed by penal enactments against the clansmen designed to destroy all that was
distinctive in them from the allegiance of their spirit to the
very pattern of their clothes. But desperate as these enactments were – and they were particularly diabolical in the
cunning with which they fouled a man's honour, shamed
him before his ancestors and his children, and so rotted
the root of life in him – he might to a certain extent, by
the intricacy and malice of his mind, have circumvented
them, if only that high picture, mirrored and made tangible
in his chief, had remained clear and unsullied.

But his chief failed him, and in 1747 gave up, for cash,
what rights of dispensing justice he may have possessed.
Some of them got large sums, some got small, but only a
few favourites got as much as they asked, for their demands
were reckoned excessive and greedy. They took, however,
what they got. But they were able to make a better bargain
over the common heritage of the land. Charters could be

granted investing sole ownership not in a clan but in a chief. Wherever it was necessary, the chiefs procured these sheepskins. And even if in recent generations one of them had assigned a tract of land to a cadet of the family (as in the Riasgan case) or other person to whom he had been indebted, such transaction, having been only a gentleman's agreement, and not recorded in writing, was now forgotten by the reigning chief who above all things desired his sheepskin bright and whole and all-inclusive.

Accordingly, by virtue of his sole ownership of the land, the chief came to hold territorial power over his clansmen that was absolute, and their value to him shifted from that of fighting men to rent-paying men. The chief had turned from a great leader into a great landlord, and with the law in all its power behind him, his concern became the acquisition of the greatest possible amount of annual tribute in cash.

For he needed cash. With the Union in 1707 the centre of the affairs of his country had shifted to London, and London stood for a new way of life and a very expensive way, so that he became not only a great landlord, but for the most part an absentee one. The chief, the leader, one in blood and tongue and interest with the clansmen, had gone.

Yet the clansmen still believed in the chief. And even when the penal enactments debased them, they still preserved this belief. Such a faith might well appear stupid beyond pathos, if it be forgotten that they had to believe in him or lose faith in themselves. Just as a man will in moments of misfortune and moral wrong try to remember and idealise some early fine picture of himself, so did the clansmen carry with them a recollection of the golden days of 'the past'. This past, if not in their own actual experience, was summed up in their tales and songs and music, and could be – and was – touched almost every day in age-old ways of work and amusement. There was no getting

away from it, and some of Angus's most stirring and clas-
sical pieces had to do with the thoughts and deeds of 'the
heroes'. Their actual chief could betray them, sell them for
cash, and then sell their land to pay 'debts of honour'
contracted at gaming tables or other places of less mild
amusement, and still, by the subtle alchemy of the believing
mind, retain the outline of one of Angus's heroes of legend;
nay, more, as a courtier of repute and a business man of
sound principle, as one professing ideals of progress and
concern for the material advancement of all humanity, he
could clear his clansmen off the ground their forefathers
had won for him and themselves, burning their houses over
their heads and driving them forth to destitution and exile
and death, and yet retain in him some of the magical
conception of the chief, so deep did their ways of life run
and from so ancient a source.

But if, in front of that change, they felt the impotence
that made them unconsciously idealise the past, yet
consciously they could discern the change readily enough.
And so it was in this business of recruitment for the army
that now disturbed those in old Angus's barn.

For after the '45, the great English statesman Pitt had
known what to do with these troublesome Highlanders: he
had made Imperial soldiers of them, and as such they had
found an outlet for their 'savage instincts' on many a foreign
field. For their valour he praised them highly; their valour
justified his wisdom. But they had enlisted in Fencible
Regiments and had gone into action under their own clan
leaders. Now, however, it was proposed to raise a regiment
of the line, where they were to be professional soldiers
under any officers who might be placed over them. The
old organisation of chief and clansmen as one body in a
common cause was gone. For a long time that organisation had been disintegrating; and though for many a year
to come old conceptions might linger with a sweet bitterness in the blood, yet the day of the men and their natural

leader was dead. Through a long process of personal acquis-
itiveness, intensified and completed in the last half-century,
the chief had sold the old order to his avarice and ambition, and was now preparing to sell the children to disinheritance.

The older men in Angus's barn knew this, if not explic-
itly then in their blood, and they were against the youths
joining up. They mistrusted the appeals of the powerful:
Join for your king and your chief! What was the king to
them but a great menacing power at a distance? And their
chief . . . left them dumb. In the call to arms, too, there
was the definite note of compulsion. Each district was being
carefully listed. Ministers of the gospel, factors, ground
officers were already receiving their orders.

'Why not?' challenged Colin. 'They'll pay us money while
we're in it, and they have promised every fellow land when
he comes back.'

'Who promised that?' asked Angus.

'Haven't you heard? The Great Lady herself spoke it out
of her own mouth. Your chief and your king! . . . *And land.*'
Colin laughed. He looked bright and daring.

'I don't know,' said Angus, and gazed over his shoulder
out of the barn door. Death comes one way or another,
but this business was wrong. In professional soldiering there
was something degrading, with its slavish obedience and
lack of freedom; it denied somehow the individual and religious spirit of man. This call to king and chief did not even
rouse the blood. Angus looked gloomy.

One or two of the youths backed up Colin with a
swagger, as though their elders were trying to prevent their
going on a poaching raid. They were neither solemn about
their chief nor their king. They were going to put some
money in their sporrans – and show the French a thing or
two! Behold Bonaparte standing transfixed before the
charge of the Riasgan Company! Think of Roy the piper
playing *No More* in the vineyards! See Gilleasbuig 'offering

up a word' – like this – to the foreign heathens! They rocked with laughter. Knocking the devil out of them with Angus's riddle! Choking the frogs with Angus's canary seed! Their mirth consumed them.

'You're fine and brave,' said Angus; 'I know that. You're so brave that you wouldn't go against the powers that be. Your chief needs you.'

A bright spot came to Colin's cheek bones. 'Black Donald can take the bitch,' he said gallantly, 'as far as I'm concerned.'

They were all shocked at that, the older men solemnly, the younger with a laugh at the blasphemous irreverence. If he had referred to her husband, the Englishman, it would have been bad enough, but she was of the blood. Colin was merely excited and showing off. The whole atmosphere had the exaggerated air of an unholy Sabbath. There was something somewhere in it that did violence to them. Every time the affair was discussed, this was the result.

The afternoon settled down and filled the corners of the barn with darkness. Outside, the dying light caught the pallor of the snow. Here and there throughout the Riasgan boys' voices were isolated in the thin air. The houses lay to the undulation of the ground like beasts huddling and covered up; and from a short distance Angus's barn was little more than a boulder-hump of the earth itself, with no life about it at all; except that of a little girl who could neither approach it nor leave it alone, and in the disturbed state of her mind kept running hither and thither, adding derisive touches to her snow man.

*

These haphazard meetings and talks grew with the lengthening of the day, until at last men were named and marked down for the army. On a special Sabbath the minister had given a sermon that for point and strength far surpassed any effort of his for years. Their country was threatened.

Their beloved land, if they did not fight for it with the sword of Gideon, would be delivered over to the Papist and the infidel. He extolled their forefathers, he showed how the faith had been kept pure by their earnestness and the freedom to enjoy it by their valour. He had this gift of flowery speech and in the use of it he became moved himself, so that when he ordered them to obey their chief he did it with weight and authority. Their chief was a woman who symbolised the great union of the two countries of England and Scotland in her marriage to an English lord. What she said was true, for had not her husband been our country's ambassador to the court of the French king and had not she been his helpmeet. Who were those before him, who was even he himself, to question their knowledge, their power, their authority? Had these two not power of life – yea, and of death – over us all? Was not this land, this church, homes, harvests, fire – everything, theirs? Yea, everything was theirs. Yet in their kindness they allowed us to cultivate the earth and procure the fruits thereof for our bodily welfare. Not only that, but so generous, so noble, so splendid and magnificent a lady was her lady-ship that she assured all those who would join the regiment that when they came back with their money or their pensions she would see to it that each got land and a home. Think of that pledge, think of it, you second or third or tenth son. He could sooner conceive of the rivers flowing up to the hills and the hills flowing down to the sea than of that pledge not being fulfilled. Your chief needs you to save your land. The great king himself in his majesty demands you. You will be informed of the steps the destined amongst you will presently have to take in this great effort, this holy crusade, to deliver the earth itself from the infamy of our enemies.

In these early spring days the thought of joining the army ran hot in the veins of the young men of the Riasgan. When two or three of them met they laughed and talked. Why not? The glitter in their eyes showed the repressed excitement, and the quick side glance betrayed a novel fear. It was something to play with, to put a quiver in the chest! To leave all this and go away to the wars – I, a plain fellow of this simple little place – to leave this, to leave everybody, good Lord! The thought of the old men and women made them chuckle – and the girls! They became an enigmatic body, drawing glances.

The spring weather was boisterous and outside work delayed; yet here and there a woman could be seen stooping over the crooked spade, as if she were better doing that than doing nothing. The men took little notice of these women. They were more concerned about the cattle that after the long winter had grown thin and, roaming about, could find little in the dun heather or withered grass to sustain them. The beasts inside in their stalls were even thinner, though there were still wisps of bog hay and straw left and an occasional meal-drink. Of the whole year this was the time when the pulse of the earth beat slowest. There were late springs, indeed, when the pulse seemed to stop altogether, and as cold stormy day succeeded cold stormy day, belief in the miracle of re-awakening began to wane in the minds of men. But this spring was not like that, for the cattle sales had been good and the harvest better. Yet this nadir of the year did have its effect on the attitude of all to the army. The old men grew irritable; the young men grew more convinced than ever; the women withdrew themselves into work, out of which they spoke with a curious fatalism or with such personal decision that the men avoided them.

Yet at no time in the year did such a profound kindliness move the heart. Whatever of irritation or silence or moodiness overlay it, it was there and came out most sensibly between man and beast. 'Take that, you poor brute!'

The ceilidhs were often nights of extravagant fun. The

excitement in the breasts of the young men gave the least twist of thought or action a significance and zest. Sometimes an evening would be quite hectic, and girls and fellows would swing to a dance on the crowded floor. On evenings like these the girls became more excited than the youths.

Amongst 'the Men' religious zeal increased. All these wars and rumours of wars were but evidence of the wickedness of the state of the world. The Devil was going about like a roaring lion. But they did not condemn the recruiting for the army. To Caesar the things that were Caesar's. Trials and afflictions were to be borne by the steadfast spirit. The spirit proved itself not in rebellion but in acceptance and grace. God visited His wrath upon them for their iniquities. God would make an instrument of even the Anti-Christ, Bonaparte. And there were sufficient infidels and Papists in the world to make the needs of God manifest and His ways of punishment and justification inscrutable.

The young men began to haunt the house of the old wounded soldier, William MacIan, a gaunt man with a chronic kidney complaint that kept him to his cottage. William was now very God-fearing, but the boys were so eager to learn of life in the army that they drew him out of his reserve into dramatic descriptions of 'actions' in many places abroad.

It was the youth Johnny Gordon who attempted the religious note by shaking his head and saying solemnly, 'Ah, the evil spirit.' But the young fool Fair Alie, looking at him, swole in the face till he went pink and burst. Nor did Johnny's coughing deceive William MacIan. 'We often wonder,' said Johnny, 'what are the temptations of the flesh and the devil we should be warned against.'

William, holding Johnny's eye, told him. They might laugh now, but a time would come when they would 'regret the day'. He had seen what he had seen. What he had seen became too much for him and he named foreign places where soldiers, set upon by harpies and whores, had sunk into the nethermost pits of sin, sin and bestial disease. Like children, they had wanted him to get talking of whores. So he talked to them of whores till they grew awkward and pale and the phrase 'scarlet woman' left no more than a faint unresolved glitter in the eye. So worked up did he become that his internals were disarranged, and when the boys left the house it took them a little time to give free rein to their spirits.

But they give the rein to their spirits, for the call to arms came up through their blood from the generations before in a scarlet bubble of gallantry and mirth.

*

As the cow first blinked in the daylight, the two women, Mairi and Elie, watched the poor brute. The skin round her eyes and on her neck was bare; there were deep hollows below the haunch bones. She picked her way uncertainly, snuffed the ground, jerked her head this way and that, and at last gave a low nasal bellow to the world. There was something wild in her eye, of excitement or fear. Beasts lowed like this when they smelt blood, or were moved to passion in summer pastures. The coming year blinked there before the hearts of the women. Summer and grass and milk and laughter – and for Elie what passion, what promise, what end? Blindly the brute snuffed about, restlessly, her calf moving in her. 'Poor Nance,' came from Elie's smiling lips, as though she had a vision of all the strange sweet sorrow of the world: a profound blind moment of happiness because it had somewhere near its core the understanding of tragedy.

'She'll get little,' said Mairi, 'but the airing will do her good.' Then after watching the brute ease herself, she said, 'I'll get a mash of the broom shoots down yonder or maybe go as far as the shore.'

Elie glanced at the short but firm body, with the black head small and set to the neck with poise. It showed less outward emotion than an animal. Self-contained, it was without the expressiveness of sentiment and almost completely without humour. To something in that deep negativeness, Elie's heart also responded, as it might in other circumstances to a bank or a tree, or to the black heart of the earth.

And though that earth did not visibly move into growth for weeks to come, yet day by day in sheltered spots, by the burn side, in little fertile pockets, Nance and the sheep and the goats found healing mouthfuls of green stuff. The weather was still cold and blustering, but often there were hours of clear fine sun, and in the succession of the days Elie began to find herself up in the hollow behind the edge of the wood.

Now whenever this happened, whenever she passed out of sight of the Riasgan and came into this lonely hollow behind the wintry bare birches, an odd expectancy and excitement beset her. Her face would take on a faint flush and, looking around, she would listen and catch the sound of her heart-beats like the thud of feet in the grass. She had no appointment with Colin here. She could never with certainty know when she would be here herself. Often, indeed, her coming was the result of an unexpressed understanding with Davie, who was the natural herd. 'I'll just take them up myself to see them get a good bite,' she would say unconcernedly to Mairi. And Davie, glad to be relieved of the lonely herding up there, would yet by a certain sly expression convey to her that he was not so easily taken in as his granny; but so elusively – for once at sight of his grimace Elie had changed her mind – that she need not perceive or act upon it. Later, when the coming of Colin was more certain, through an arrangement of signs or appearances, and Davie's knowingness was justified, there grew between him and Elie a sensitive understanding that became less and less shy on Elie's part as the fever of her love fastened on her, until at last there was a deep conspiracy between these two; and not because of the secrecy so much as of a warm compelling urgency on the part of the girl, did Davie now and then have an odd feeling of guilt or lawlessness.

In the Riasgan love-making was not an affair of easy lonely meetings. No girl and boy went walking away into the darkness or, in daylight, into the hollows of the hills together. Even on the way home from a ceilidh for a couple to detach themselves too obviously from a group, held in itself an insensitiveness to good behaviour that brought whatever desire moved them into at least the disrepute of discourtesy. True love-making should be at once more open and more secretive than that. And only in the case of those whose love was at last so strong as to be a fire did headstrong behaviour commend itself to a sly mocking brightness.

Colin soon became very cunning in managing his meetings with Elie. Her home, lying against the hillside, was visible from any part of the Riasgan, and no matter what Colin was doing he had an occasional glance for Mairi's burn, until his heart would give a quick beat. She was there! The bleak hillside became alive with her presence moving upon it in a pattern he understood.

After that first love-making between them on the night of the harvest dance, they had not met for quite a long time, until Elie began to wonder if Colin had regretted his part. This used to occupy her thoughts all day long, and sometimes she would be certain and sometimes uncertain. When they were together in company he gave her no special sign, unless an almost marked avoidance of her could be called one.

There was something more than shyness or perversity in it. Colin with his strong body and open face went naturally to action. Even the satire of his fellows, to which he would have been sensitive, could hardly have overcome a strong impulse in him. Yet he held off – as he fancied he saw the girl herself hold off. And he did not know why he did this. Even at the height of the fun in the ceilidh-house, when he was neither near her nor looking at her, her presence excited not only his mind but every muscle of his body so that he lived at the very heart of the fun he did so much to provoke. Particularly when any talk of the army got going was he most lively, and very early it was recognised that Colin Sutherland, whoever else, would obey the call to arms.

Two or three times during the winter he kissed Elie, but a trifle boisterously and in circumstances where they had quickly to break away, so that Elie had seemed to repulse the action, perhaps for fear of its being seen. The moment was chosen when other and quieter moments might have been.

Something was burning up in them both and he was a little afraid of it; and not until he was committed to the army beyond any chance of backing out, did he suddenly and soberly come within his own mind and, gazing out, see a future that was no longer vague but on the contrary as clearly defined as a hill path that rose up to a skyline – and passed beyond.

This certainty, that perhaps unconsciously he had been waiting on, drove him up through the small birches on the hillside in the early spring and round upon Elie in the hollow. And for the first few meetings that which had kept them apart still contrived to act out of its perverse need: until one afternoon as the daylight passed into the gloaming, he took hold of her and said, 'Ah, Elie, you've got me!' and pressed down his head against her with the strange, almost sad, action of a man who was defeated and acknowledged fate.

This was so remarkable in him that she gave a curious little whining cry and drew him hard against her breasts. They had been sitting on the grass and now as they lay to the ground she nursed him and ran her hand through his hair in a continuous murmuring ecstasy of possession. There was something sad in them both and her eyes indeed grew brilliant though no tears actually welled over.

He could not understand what was happening to him at all. He should kiss her, laugh, make fun. His whole nature was to be quick and if necessary boisterous, whereas he actually felt released and weary. Their mouths met. They clung harder than ever. He was strong. So was she, though her body was soft and full. Then he smiled, a slow glimmer in his dark eyes as of a far reminiscence of fun. This was comfortable, divinely comfortable! O God! and he convulsively gripped her again. They lay together for a long time while the light waned and the chill grew. Not a word did they speak all that time, nor did they know how cold they were until they drew away from their own fire.

'You're shivering,' he said.

'I'm not.'

They were shy a little. 'I'll have to run,' she said.

'Don't go.'

'I must go.'

Their voices were isolated in the stillness of the evening as though all that which had been watching them was now also listening. They themselves became suddenly aware of this and cast their eyes about and listened.

'I'll have to go,' she whispered. 'I must,' she said, and pulled against him. Her brown eyes and warm skin were confused with tenderness. As she kept avoiding his eyes, she laughed. She was all generosity, a shy impulsive generosity. Something excessive about that, caught in her untidy brown hair, a smudge on her jaw, the rumple in her clothes, her open wide kind face, went straight to his heart. He pulled her against him. When she got away again, she put up her hands, the flat of each hand against a cheek, and so cupped his face and drew her fingers lingeringly down, saying, 'Colin.'

'Don't go yet,' he cried, snatching her back. He was all

at once eager and quick. 'Don't go yet, Elie. Look here, what's the good of going?' They were on their feet. 'Don't go,' he said. His face wrinkled up like one worried, not knowing what he wanted. He did not indeed know what he wanted. He was, however, extremely urgent, and there was no trace of smile or fun on his face now.

She must go. Mairi would be wondering, might be coming up . . . But he was not listening to her. There was now something secretive in his urgency, something that was his hidden self. It was pursuing her, following her. They came to the brink of the hollow. No one was coming up. She turned, 'Ah, Colin!' and surged up at him and caught him.

When at last he spoke her name there was in his voice a delicate new tenderness, as if in the wordless moments they had clung together, his spirit had gone on a journey and come back white with love's magic. It was almost quite dark when at last she withdrew her hands and found that old Nance had gone home on her own.

But her hands continued to feel him when he was not there. Her body rustled by him when he was alone. Each was so aware of the other's invisible presence, that when he was, for example, in company he was conscious of ignoring her presence by his shoulder, and yet while ignoring it was so certain it was there that his manner caught an extra mockery or gaiety or fun. And only when discussing the war did this fun catch a slightly hectic note, a something that was a trifle too much or overdone. For Elie this was a period of pure magic bliss. There was a warmth always in her body, a divine well-being, that made work a delicate discipline, a holding of her together, and gave to moments of complete suspension a deep timeless peace.

She awoke from these reveries – when nothing conscious occupied her mind – as one might wake on an immense shore. And yet quietly and secretly, as if she had been trafficking with she did not know what (yet knowing it could be *nothing else*) she would smile and sigh, and staring through the magic moment not even look at the shadow of him in the falling wave.

Her nature was tender and generous to the point of softness, lavish and impulsive; like her body which seemed soft to the point of formlessness. Her voice was husky, and, singing, had a deep artless note that folk found extremely moving. It could now move herself. And one afternoon, crooning over one of the old sad love songs of her race, she suddenly stopped, called the girl of the song by name, and burst into tears, throwing herself at the same time face down on the grass.

Dark Mairi was standing by her when she sat up.

Elie smiled through her embarrassment, wiping dark smears under her eyes. 'It was foolish of me, but I couldn't help it. I felt so sorry for her!'

'Who?'

Elie laughed. 'The girl in the song.' There was something highly diverting in it. Yet through her gaiety she said, 'Poor thing!' and glanced at Mairi sideways as she got to her feet.

'You gave me a fright,' said Mairi. 'I thought something had happened to you.'

'What could have happened?'

'You know best,' said Mairi.

Elie laughed – that easy soft laugh of hers that ever seemed bubbling up as though she had no restraint.

'You take care of yourself,' said Mairi. She had shown no emotion. There was hardly even any double meaning in her voice. Now her face smiled in its thin shallow way. 'You take care,' she repeated.

'Take care of what?'

'I didn't like you weeping like that.'

'Did you have a vision of me?'

'No, then, I didn't.'

But Elie knew it was almost as if Mairi had had the vision of a figure weeping in the future – her figure, Elie's!

Something novel in the idea gave her the shiver of a small thrill. Her face tilted up, eyes bright with mirth, and suddenly she caught Mairi under an arm and pressed it. She overflowed with an affection that included this simple artless tidy stone of a woman, who had no emotions at all. A stone in the hand or a drink of cold water in the mouth. Or a hill or a cow. Or everything from the wind above to the Riasgan stream below. Elie's mind flashed about the fire in her heart. And some of that fire she put about Mairi, and Mairi knew. And a great urge came over Elie to tell Mairi in words, to tell her everything. 'Take care of yourself,' warned Mairi, 'for you have a lot of affection in you,' and she went back to the plot below the house that she was turning over with the foot-plough or *cas-chrom*. Elie went into the kitchen and caught Davie in the act of stealing some bread. He was openly defiant. What he wanted with it was his business, he told her, as he broke the bannock and stowed it out of sight. 'Where are you going?' He turned and put out his tongue at her; then he paused, 'I'll be back in time to take home the beasts – on the edge of the dark.' His eyebrows tilted and his dark eyes caught a knowing gleam. She beckoned him and from the little wall cupboard took down a bowl of butter. 'Give me your bread.' She thumbed some butter over the bread. His eyes gleamed avidly. 'Is it poaching?' she asked. He nodded. Their whispers were warm in their faces. 'Don't be too late,' she said. He slid away. She was a fine one Elie! he thought to himself, all glowing.

Elie was in a glow too as she went down to the plot where Mairi was working. 'I'll take a turn at that now,' she said, and without a word Mairi gave her the foot-spade. Elie was heavier than Mairi and a fine worker. Her breasts shook as she dug in the crooked spade and levered the earth over, humming the song appropriate to the rhythm of this work. Mairi went back upon what she had done, breaking up the clods of ground. She was too finely made

for a heavy earth-worker, but an unanxious persistence gave
her tidier results than those achieved by the biggest-bodied
woman in the district. There was nothing in nature but
gave in to her in time. The two women worked the earth
all through the afternoon. The seed was ready and the time
was near.

From the hill-crests this work could be seen in progress
round all the cottages of the Riasgan; and up beyond the
Riasgan in Tomich where the land was worked in the
ancient run-rig system, and lots had been drawn for the
various plots, the whole community was at work in what
seemed one large field. Along the glens and the straths from
mountain to sea, the soil was being prepared for the seed,
and here and there in suitable places men could be seen
with ponies and a plough. But the *cas-chrom* made the best
job and got the best results. Mairi stood watching Elie for
a little, then lifting her creel went and carried out some
more manure. They worked until the dusk came down and
Mairi said that it was time Davie was bringing home the
beasts. As she went towards the house, Elie called to her
that she would go up to see what was keeping him, and
though her voice sounded normal there was excitement in
her throat.

As she started climbing her heart began beating like a
heavy-winged bird, and if she could not pause and deliberately look down towards the Riasgan, she managed to
look all the same. Many were still working, for though the
air was cold it had been dry for several days and the soil
was in good trim. Someone was still digging below Colin's
house. She went slowly, humming to herself something she
did not hear. It wasn't Colin, she was sure. Not Colin –
where was Colin? Where? The thought of Colin was like
a dark bird up on the crest of the wood. Occasionally a
flush would go over her flesh and make it as weak as water.
She hummed and pulled grasses and tore them with her
milky teeth. She entered the hollow as if her breast was

advancing against a heavy wave. The hollow was empty
and the wave receded leaving her empty as the hollow.

'Where can Nance be?' she muttered to herself, and aloud
called, 'Nance!' Where? She called again – and knew he
was not here by the silence, by the grass, and by the bare
birch trees. She became concerned about the cow and went
here and there, calling, so that her voice could be heard.
But he did not hear her voice. At last she really thought
of the cow and went out over the edge of the hollow and
along the back of the wood. The moor behind rose in waves
with rocky crests, but nowhere in the grassy troughs could
Nance be seen. Perhaps she had gone down into the glen
beyond the wood – and might now be away up at Tomich!
Davie should never have deserted his charge. But he had
done it before, and besides it wasn't the time of year, with
the brute in calf, for her to wander. Her anxiety caught a
petulance. She had forgotten to wash the smears from
beneath her eyes. 'Nance!' She stood in the dusk, alone in
that vast upland world. A sudden sharp feeling of loneliness sent her running back towards the hollow, as if in
some mysterious way the beasts might be there now. And
when she did arrive they were there, right in the centre of
the hollow, eating quietly! The big goat stared at her,
motionless as herself.

Elie came slowly down towards them, stopped and
looked over her shoulder. From the roots of the small birch
trees, Colin's face peered at her. For an instant, Elie held
the look, then moved by an impulse so deep that it lifted
her out of all the self she knew, she went towards the beasts
to drive them home. She went calmly, with no emotion,
like one bewitched by a strange and terrible fate.

She went on alone, nor did she mind that he was not
following. She did not know; she did not care; she did
not . . . he was at her side. 'Elie, it was only a joke! I hid
them – in over.' His laughing voice and his look were
searching and earnest. He caught her arm. She offered no

resistance. She sat down on the grass. The beasts went out over the edge of the hollow. He kissed her. She lay down half-over on her face. She felt tears coming. She was always bubbling. She did not want to cry. She hated – oh, she hated having to cry, because there was nothing to cry for. She so hated having to cry that she burst into tears.

At the sight of her in tears something rose up and choked him. He could cry himself, so he could. 'Don't cry, Elie; for God's sake don't cry, or you'll tear the heart out of me.' He fondled her, lay close to her, but her face she would not show, for she was now very ashamed. And then suddenly in a dry weary petulant voice, he said, 'I know! O curse, I know!' He left her alone. At that queer sound in his voice, all her body became a listening quivering ear. She could not move now; she lay close waiting for the first sharp thrust.

'I'm going,' he said, his voice at once careless and bleak.

But she would not let the meaning come at her, and to keep it away she muttered, 'Where?'

'To the wars.'

She lay still and all the world about her grew quiet and without end. From that quietness her vision came back on her heart in a narrow pain. This squeezing pain stupefied her. To the wars. The wars. Parting. Going away.

She had known of this before, had heard it discussed in the ceilidh-house talks often enough. But the affair had not been irrevocably settled, and she had not somehow thought about it particularly. Why?

The awful revelation came to her now: they had arrived, without knowing it, in love's country. Through all the days of fun and carelessness, when it did not matter what was going to happen next month or next week, she had taken his affections like a girl picking flowers in a wood, suddenly to find herself lost in this wood, which thereupon became strange and terrifying.

The erratic emotions even of this day were now clear,

from the moment when Dark Mairi had found her weeping until, walking down into this hollow, she had seen Colin's face and turned away from it. It had been coming; it had been pursuing her; it had arrived.

She was normally so impulsive, so lavish with her emotions, that the sight of her lying quite still stirred Colin out of his bleak humour. A bitterness got into his throat. 'I gave in my name today. We'll be going soon to join up.' He recited the names of those who were going. But they would come back after joining up and altogether it would be two or three months yet before they marched away behind Roy's pipes! His tone was light, almost airy. He looked at her, stretched out his hand to put it on her shoulder, the tenderness came back in a rush to his throat – but he did not touch her, did not speak.

'What's that?' he asked.

'Why are you going?'

'Why? Oh, our chief and our king need us, you know! Besides, look what we are promised! Not only the money, but a tack of land. Something that a fellow could really marry on. As it is – well—' There was no trace of tenderness in his voice; it had vanished again in the same dryness.

She sat up suddenly and clutched the breast of his jacket. 'Ah, Colin, why are you going?' Her brown eyes brimmed to him. 'Colin?' She tugged his coat. 'Oh, Colin!' Her body had a shuddering spasm and the naked soul rose up into her face in supplication, in offering.

He could not meet it, so deep was the revelation. The quickening immortal look would haunt him until he died. He gazed away, feeling cold and mindless, with a tremor in his body running up to his throat. She hit her forehead against his breast and clung there.

'I must go, Elie. It'll only be a few years; then when I come back, I'll have money and get land, and we'll get married. That's what I've been thinking; that's how I've been working it out.' Actually he had never worked it out like that. Their love had been too young, too fresh, too full of fun, they had been too young themselves, for thoughts of marriage to trouble them. Speaking like this gave him a sense of responsibility, and it was easy enough to believe that what he had said had been always at the back of his mind.

But Elie was not concerned about marriage, nor any bargain about marriage. It was simply that she could not have him *now*. And so she muttered, 'But why do you want to go?'

'I'm telling you.'

'But why – why do you want to go *away*?'

'I don't want,' he said.

'You're going away,' she said, her mouth against his breast. 'You're going away.'

'Don't, Elie. Oh God, don't do that.' He drew her face away. They clung together. He spoke wildly, blaming her for not understanding, for tearing the spirit out of him, while he fondled and crushed and kissed her. They struggled with this blind emotion until its unreasoning strength crushed them both and exhausted them.

Then in the chill darkening air they lay quietly, until at last his mind, grown clear and gentle, began drawing the future again with its money and land and a house of their own. Wasn't it worth going away for that? He would like to have a fine place for her. And then the other fellows were going too – he would feel such a fool if he tried to back out now. And if he did, the factor would certainly have his revenge by refusing him any land anywhere on the whole estate. They had to fight for their land. And at that, clear and chill as the air around them, he got his vision of what underlay all their going. They might talk of chief or king – some of them with a twist of the mouth – and make fun of this or that, but they had to answer their chief as the chief answered his chief, as their ancestors had answered the call of the leader amongst them to conquer and to hold. Underneath it all lay the Riasgan with its crofts and hillocks and stream, its mountain ridges and skies, its birch wood, its blaeberries, its stones, its trout, its spring poverty, its summer milk, its wild nights, its drink, its dancing, Angus's stories of the heroes, its fights – this hollow, this lonely hollow with the thin birch twigs and the withered grass in which Elie and himself lay close catching the honey of that immortal life in the cells of their bodies. Every now and then in the generations it had to be won again and ensured. Not that he reasoned it out thus, but that he had an intimation of himself as the soldier who, with some such faith, goes with a laugh to the wars. They might scoff at the chief as they might scoff at the minister; but in the moment of vision they saw the Riasgan lie under God: the duality that was the ultimate of all earthly vision. And he said to her after a silence, 'Elie, I'd like to go.'

But she could not understand him, and felt that he wanted to go solely for the adventure of going, for the fighting, the camps, the excitements of war. She saw him marching away gaily, laughing, forgetting . . . men's faces, all men; men going away and leaving the women. That terrible unreasoning fighting lust of the men of the world.

Yet a certain shyness, almost wistfulness, in his voice when he had spoken, touched her heart as no reason of his ever could. He would *like* to go. The deep craving in a boy's breast to do what other boys are doing. And beyond all the boys were the dark forces of the world, of chiefs and kings and armies, deploying on foreign or nightmare fields.

She did not speak but he felt the movement of sympathy in her. His spirit rose buoyant in him. She began to take part in his beliefs. She saw the edge of his pride, his vanity, and could not hurt him. Land of their own, money for stock, a good place – something special! Nothing poverty-stricken for them, if he could help it. She knew he would get that. It could not occur to either of them to doubt their chief; to doubt would be to give the meaning of what he was going to do so vast an unreason that it would be like doubting God.

Yet when he made this picture he was losing for her the bright immediacy of their love that would have squeezed out of adversity or poverty an extra sweetness; that desired to squeeze it. Not only her heart but her hands ached for him. Her hands clasped; separated and clutched the grass. She fought down the surge of the appeal in her. And when at last she went away, she was quiet and friendly, with almost a transparent expression on her face, as though her spirit had quickened and purified there, and with only the slightest troubling left in the eyes of pain.

He was so moved that he did not follow her, but sat where he was long after she had gone. When at last he got up and went down through the wood, his mood lightened. Indeed a secret light-heartedness assailed him. He paused now and then and broke twigs with restless fingers while he stared before him, an odd smile on his face. Elie! The whole affair was extraordinary and marvellous. He lay down and came half to grips with it. One could not face it – any more than go home. But when the darkness was on the wood, his body came to rest before the full vision of Elie's love, and such a delicacy and worship invaded him that the offering of himself became light as a leaf on his palm. He went home full of an abounding energy, and when the army talk got going he was first in the foray, as though Elie's tragic plea for him to stay was the only inspiration in his going away to the wars.

Two days after that Elie visited Morach, whose husband, Seumas, had died between Christmas and the New Year. The folk had feared for Morach, who was sensitive as her husband had been; but she had so concentrated on her clairvoyant son and the working of the croft that out of some corner of her maternal being a cunning obtuseness was born. Only occasionally, when she watched her son, did a look of uncanny penetration appear in her eyes.

Seumas og had neither spoken nor looked at Elie since she had entered, but had remained seated and bent towards the fire. Elie began to feel the drooping curve of her body, and all at once it was she who was there by the fire, and a sensation of such grey hopelessness beset her that she broke her body back and glanced about her, struggling to escape. She caught Morach's look and it seemed acute and penetrating. Morach knew what had taken place in her mind, and Elie got up to cover an involuntary shiver. She went out laughing excitedly. A timid near-the-bone kindness looked through the woman's eyes with the brightness of pain. Elie could not find words for the sudden tragic movement of affection in her breast. There was a hand on her shoulder, a pressure of inexpressible intimacy: 'Take care of yourself, lassie.'

Elie went away in a hurry, the smile sticking on her face. The son had *seen*. The mother had known. They had all known, without a word, a gesture. Her steps quickened to a little run to defeat the shudder. That grey hopelessness, everything lost – no, no, it wasn't her body, not yon way by the fire! Oh – no! . . . The exclamation pressed through her lips but was checked by the sight of a number of men beside Angus Sutherland's house. Presently she ran into Seonaid with a couple of wooden buckets.

'Oh, they are the young men,' replied Seonaid, 'who are going to the wars! The Captain himself has come up. Look, that's him coming out from the house. Shaking hands with them. See, they're all shy, by way of it! And that's Colin – bare head and smiling face, the warrior, shaking hands. Though we are poor we are highborn! Aren't they feeling themselves the great ones? And tall Anndra, my love, with his elbows, will you look at him! That's it, Anndra; nod your head, my heart!' She divined so well what the boys were feeling that her astringent humour had an irresistible truth.

For the Captain touched something deep in all the men

and made them slightly excited and gay. One might say what one liked about chiefs and rulers, but when the Captain appeared in the flesh, how instinctively the spirit caught at courtesy and willingness! He was tall, strong-shouldered, finely built, with a full open face smooth and ruddy, dark hair streaked with grey, pleasant easy manners and not the least trace of condescension; on the contrary there was a companionable frankness about him as he shook hands; what he learned about them he learned with interest, and seemed to make a note of it with his blue eyes. There were stories of his strength, his direct ruthlessness, but none of quirkiness or plausible dealings.

When he was politely having his last words with the old men, the young men stood within hearing distance. Old Angus was moved like the rest. Did the Captain think it would be a long engagement? No, a few years should see everything cleaned up. Ireland, or some place like that, possibly. But the War Department seemed to have a high idea of the Highland soldier and of course it might be as well to keep that idea in their heads! The French Revolution? The blue of the Captain's eyes caught a hard gleam and he spoke in short sentences of barbarities. His hatred of the subject stopped him, and his listeners shuddered with disgust and anger.

He was glad they were going. There had been talk of strange officers, but they could take it from him that there would be more Highland officers than Highlanders for them to command.

One or two of the men accompanied him out of the Riasgan. 'I'm going!' said Elie hurriedly to Seonaid. 'Wait!' said Seonaid, who had just filled her buckets at the well near the path down which the Captain was coming. Her being out at all, as well she knew, was a piece of bravado, for all the women were watching secretly what was going on from their own cottages. For Elie there was still time to escape, as her home lay on the opposite slope. But Seonaid held her. Nor could they turn their backs on the approaching men. Those with the Captain understood their discomfort and showed it by their smiling expressions. Seonaid's cheeks caught fire. The Captain looked at the girls, smiled, saluted. His eyes got caught by Seonaid's face for a moment; he hesitated as if about to say something; then bade them good-day, half saluted, and went on. It was all very simply and yet rather elegantly done. Seonaid's heart was thumping in her breast. As she picked up the buckets she felt the tremble in her muscles. Both girls were breathing quickly.

Elie said nothing. Seonaid, anxious that Elie should not detect her excitement, glanced covertly at her and saw an odd look in her eyes, something frightened or petulant behind the embarrassment. Perhaps she was so excited that she was overwrought! She looked closer; there was something intimate or tragic about Elie. Elie felt the look and said, 'Well, I'm off!'

As Seonaid went homeward with the well-water, she was annoyed at herself for having become excited. A girl would do anything rather than meet a man in the Captain's position face to face. She knew that – and rebelled at her common behaviour. As though he had been a divine being in man's image coming down the path! She, who had laughed at the young men for becoming well-mannered and excited, had felt her knees weaken and curtsy of their own accord! Who had taught her to curtsy? No one. And sheer into this little turmoil of vanity came the meaning of Elie's look. *Colin was going to the war.* She set down her buckets. The whole meaning of what was happening came home to her. The boys – her dear enemies – were going away to be soldiers, to fight, to come back years and years after this as pensioners, broken men – or never to come back at all. There was no colour left in her face; no trace of anger or rebellion; only the pale look of realisation.

She turned and gazed at Elie now at the foot of the slope to Dark Mairi's cottage. But Elie was going steadily, without looking back. As she climbed, the loneliness of her figure against the brown slope tightened Seonaid's lips and sent her hands in a quick grip to the buckets.

Mairi asked Elie what all the gathering was about. Elie told her. Mairi was interested and went over each young man's name, deciding he could be spared. Her clear matter-of-fact tones irritated Elie, who had a sudden revulsion against her. A witless woman with no more feeling than a stone. Elie hated her; wanted to flee from her; had an awful divination of her right to the empty core.

'And how is Morach?'

'Same as usual,' answered Elie and walked away. But she had nowhere to walk to. The byre trapped her; the land trapped her; wherever she worked, Mairi would be. She set herself to the hillside, but as she approached the hollow a whistle from the birch wood showed her Davie and his companions at the tree game. She waved to him, but now instead of going into the hollow she climbed over the crest to the left and entered upon the moor. There were ponies and some stirks on the slow downslope to the right. She swerved away from them, now going quickly, and presently came into a lonely place of rocks. In a hole like an animal's den she drew up her knees. 'I'm tired,' she whined. And there she lay with herself, whimpering and licking her sores.

She had slept little in the last night or two and she was now unconsciously soothing herself to forget her trouble in sleep. But this time the loneliness would not work. Every now and then her muscles stiffened in convulsive spasms. But at last a stupor of exhaustion did creep over her, and the earth, damp and cold, pressed against hip and shoulder.

Something of this misery and stupor of the earth was with her when, in the first of the dusk, she crept shivering from that den and went down towards the hollow by the wood. Yet the earth in its stupor had a strange liberating quality; a mindlessness, an end. Black peaty ooze, small hoof-marks, crushed dung, thin heath tough as wire, broken contorted rock, grey lichen everywhere like the frost of death.

When in the hollow Elie met Colin, she rose from the bed of the moor to his warmth. There was nothing querulous left in her. Her love, turned from the doubts of life, rose up complete and unquestioning. At first her ardour frightened him a little, and the crush of her arms choked and hurt his throat, but he felt her escaping from something, full of an insatiable hunger that must bite into him. He remonstrated, half laughing. But her ardour acted on his own strength which rose to meet hers. She held against him till her strength broke. It was the first serpent bite in the innocence of their love.

In this denial of past and future, Elie found freedom, and in its perfect desperation became more variable and attractive than she had ever been. Even her shyness she gave up to him. 'I'll sing you a song.' She sang the song that had made her weep not so many days ago. As she sat beside him, her hands in her lap, her voice had an extraordinary potency, a low rich note deeper than the brown of her hair. Her eyes remembered the song and looked far away at it with an artlessness that was simple in a child-like way, terribly simple, as if her mind had never developed. The tangle of hair, the wide open face, the small fine nose, the warm skin, the neck going smoothly into the full breasts, the soft slumped body, and the eyes staring with a remembering tenderness into some remote innocent age, affected Colin as the mystery of a changeling would. Three notes of her singing voice went straight to any man's heart. Now she sang a song he knew, an ancient song of love forsaken, in the music that was not only music to him but all the impulses and longings of his immemorial race caught for an immortal moment in body and brain. The sheer unconditional nature of this music has nothing to do with thought or intellect but only with absolutes like beauty or terror. They are apprehended in the blood and in the bowels, and the soul gives them light or fragrance, or the blindness of night.

When she was finished her mind was free as a flower. 'The last time I sang that,' she said, 'I cried – and Dark Mairi came on me!' Smiling, she turned to him and saw his face which he made no attempt to hide from her, but held as it was, staring across at the slope opposite them. The teeth were clenched, the eyes welling with tears that, even as she looked, slowly brimmed over. His drawn expression did not alter, and the nostrils continued to flex as they breathed noisily.

'Colin, my dark love!' she said softly. He lay down with her and she had him under her hands.

*

The birch trees put forth their translucent leaves that blew and rustled into the fullness of summer before the lads were mustered to set out for the wars. The eve of their departure saw a great stir in the Riasgan. The old folk had had the certainty of their departure so long with them that they had grown accustomed to it, and many had been the talk and discussion on world affairs. And though men like Angus did not easily give up their mistrust, yet a certain optimism had conquered them, for they now had the news that the barbarous French were out to invade and destroy them, and were therefore a people that must themselves be destroyed. Some of the stories told about the Irish were bad enough, but the stories told about the French had all the marvel of the inhuman, and brought to mind tales of the man-shaped monsters that dwelt in the mountains of their own country in the olden days.

But added to all this was the pleasant talk of material increase. Tomas the Drover from the main glen, was full of growing prices for beasts and produce, and, however fluent and sarcastic his tongue, his probity and acuteness had become almost a proverb. On an evening when Bannerman the Holy had descended upon a dwelling and, after the catechetical questioning, had referred to the awful times we were living in as God's judgment upon us for our sins, Tomas said that to make us richer was an odd way for God to punish us for our sins, a very odd way, and unconcernedly ignored Bannerman's frown and the hushed expectation of the others assembled. To the younger folk the Bible and its stories were made real by the bodily presence of a man like Bannerman, with his long patriarchal beard, his solemn voice, and his intimate knowledge of the Old Testament. Now he slowly stroked his beard and with unwinking eyes full on the Drover asked him if he understood the danger his country was in from the foreign infidel; if he understood how the very gift of their faith was at stake; even if it should come to pass, in God's mercy, that they in this far corner of the world might be spared direct visitation, yet would not the earth be so disarranged that famines and pestilence might spread over its face, now as of old? Who were we that we might hope to escape? Were we not creatures of sin, conceived in sin and born into iniquity? And if God should send the infidel, yea, led by the Anti-Christ himself, who were we that we should say God was not justified, that our deserts did not warrant that monstrous invasion?

The Drover replied that that might well be, but if he wanted to know, in the first place, who we were, he, the Drover, was prepared to tell him.

The Drover's rags were nearly as famous as his probity. He was middle-sized with a stoop that when alone made him commune with himself, but in company gave his talk a forcefulness that caught fire from the glint in his eyes; it was then like a fighting stoop, and indeed he often got to his feet, advanced and retired, tapped his man on the knee or the wrist, and in such ways drove home his arguments – or, for that matter, his stories or his verses; and his Ossianic lore, which was considerable, had received a fervid impulse from the MacPherson controversies. He now started to speak with decorum. 'The Highlanders,' he said, 'are an ancient race. In the beginning of the world they had great heroes like Ossian and Fingal and Cuchulain, fighters whose names are like poems and like thunder. They had splendid and beautiful women to breed that race. All that is known. And there is poetry about it the like of which the people in the wide world had never heard until MacPherson told them one or two little things in his books. But they would not believe MacPherson, saying that he had made it all up himself. Just as if you were to say that the Bible had been made up by the minister because he once wrote it out with his own hand!'

'That's not a seemly way to refer to God's Word,' interposed Bannerman austerely.

'The reference is in good company,' replied the Drover, 'for I'm talking to Highlanders of Highlanders, and if God has not shown favour to Highlanders in the past then they must surely have been all the greater soldiers to have won their victories without Him. For they won great victories, that are like the shouting of armies and the neighing of horses and the rushing of chariots down the centuries of the world. Saxon and Dane and Northman – ah, the heroes, the great heroes of Lochlann, splendid as our own heroes, but of no avail, even they, in the end. The Roman Emperors could not subdue us, and finally had to hide behind great walls and ramparts and fortifications to save themselves from our attacks. That is true, as the dominie down the glen will tell you, and he will tell you too the noble speech that Galgacus the leader of the Highlanders made to his men before they charged the Roman Eagles. He has put Gaelic on the Latin three times for me, and I could hear him a thousand and three times. "When I reflect," said the noble Galgacus, his head up before his vast army of 30,000 men, "when I reflect on the causes of the war, and the circumstances of our position, I feel a strong persuasion that our united efforts on the present day will prove the beginning of universal liberty in Britain. For we are all undebased by slavery. In all the battles which have yet been fought, with various success against the Romans, our countrymen may be deemed to have reposed their final hopes and resources in us: for we, the noblest sons of Britain, and therefore stationed in its last recesses, far from the view of servile shores, have preserved even our eyes unpolluted by the contact of subjection. The extremity of Britain is now disclosed; there is no nation beyond us; nothing but waves and rocks and the still more hostile Romans, whose pride we cannot escape by obsequiousness and submission. These plunderers of the world, stimulated by greed, ambition . . . To ravage, to slaughter, to usurp under false titles they call Empire; and where they make a desert, they call it peace."'

The Drover had got to his feet, and so moved was he by the words of Galgacus that for a moment his stoop straightened. Then he leant forward again and touched Bannerman on the knee. 'That was only the beginning. He reminded his men of their children and relations, those dearest to them in nature, how they would be torn away by the Romans to slave in foreign lands, how their sisters and wives would be the sport of the licentious, how their own bodies would be worn down by stripes and insults. All of it he told them, before he began to move them to victory. He was the great chief! By God, he told them . . .'

'Tomas McHamish,' cried Bannerman, 'do I hear you take the name of the Lord God in vain?'

'He told them,' shouted Tomas, whose excellent memory failed him in his excitement, 'not to give a packman's oath for the Romans!'

'Tomas!' thundered Bannerman.

'Not a – not a damn for the whole lot of them, eagles and legions and all! That was Galgacus, our ancestor.

Galgacus! And his last words: "Here is a general; here an army. Over there is punishment and bastardy and slavery. On this field you'll make your choice. March then to battle," he shouted, "and think of your ancestors and posterity."'

The Drover had been so wrought up that when he sat down he did not appear to listen to Bannerman on the heathen, the vain, and the godless. But presently, as his face stilled, he regarded Bannerman with a steady and vindictive expression.

'I do not think it wrong to invoke the Almighty's name on a great occasion. Furthermore, if we repelled slavery and prostitution by our courage on the field of battle, equally in the Lord's field did we win victories for His message. You can forget Columba, if you like; I don't. You can forget that into a world wrapped in devilry and heathendom, Columba and his missionaries from the little island of the west sent forth the Light, with miracle and martyrdom. And long before Columba, in blessed Ninian's days, and long after him. That's the way Himself has looked on us, as far as I can see, and we have nothing much to be ashamed of. Our history is a proud history, not only in these far-off days, but in the days between and in the days near us. We have never been conquered – never anyway until the '45, and whatever conquering took place then was the conquering of Gael divided against Gael, and the Sasunnoch doing his bloody work on the remnant. We have had our reverses. The world may be leaving us. But our glory is not departed yet. And where the Highlander is true to himself and true to his kinsmen, he conquers still. For what has been happening in the wars of Europe and the wars of America and the wars over all the wide world? The Butcher of Culloden never won a victory – till he won it at Culloden. At Fontenoy – who covered his retreat and saved him from the French but the Highlanders? The very commander himself when it was over pulled off his bonnet and cried, "They have gained as much honour in covering so great a retreat as if they had gained a battle." And as they had been the last in retreat, so had they been the first in the battle. With the Guards they attacked a great redoubt and carried it, with sword, pistol, and dirk. Just as they climbed the rock-faces of the St Lawrence and on the plains of Quebec conquered Canada. Just as they broke the forces of Hyder Ali in India. The 73rd was the only British regiment at Porto Novo and the enemy outnumbered them by twenty to one, but the pipes sounded them to it and where it was thickest and hottest the piper blew loudest and the General shouted to him, "By God, it's silver pipes you'll get for this, my hero!" And silver pipes he did get.' The Drover had risen. Everyone present was now as moved as himself. Seeing this, the Drover concluded proudly, 'And because of all what I have told you, I am not afraid of Frenchmen or Irishmen or invasion or anything else. I have given you my reasons. If you do not think them worthy, you are welcome. To me they are enough.' And he sat down.

The sympathies of the company would have been with the Drover in any case, but particularly the enthusiasm of the younger members. For anything describing a great fight moved them like flame. Bannerman knew this, and feeling the whole as an indirect assault on his authority, remained opposed to concession. The general enthusiasm, from which he could be no more immune than the others of his race, impelled him to a harsh eloquence.

The Lord shall not hold him guiltless who taketh His name in vain. They listened with lowered eyes and solemn faces, but the Drover's fire was hidden in them. And when Bannerman at last got to his knees, and they all got to their knees with him, some of the young men, opening their eyes, tried to get a glimpse of other eyes, and even winked while Bannerman was praying God to look into their hearts at this His footstool. But the older men and the women and the girls remained motionless with devout bowed heads.

When the company got to their feet there was the customary silence which no one liked to break, for it was not seemly to introduce the secular voice too quickly upon communion with the Almighty. Indeed after such prayer, it was usual to feel the presence of the Spirit linger upon the air of the humble dwelling as if the air itself had been moved by a passing wing. There was also the courtesy due to the dwelling, to the father and the mother thereof, and to Bannerman.

Solemnly the Drover thanked his hosts for the happy chance that had allowed him to take part with them. 'Blessings upon your home.'

As the talk became general, though still subdued, he was sure there would be blessings upon their home (for he had not yet scored his second point against Bannerman).

'May it be the Lord's will,' said Bannerman.

'It may also be the will of our enemies in spite of themselves.'

'I do not see,' said Bannerman severely, 'how the Lord's will can also be the will of our enemies.'

'Perhaps not,' said the Drover simply. 'But this war is teaching us many things already. Famine and pestilence come to those working in mines and mills and cities – not to those who are raising the food with their own hands. At the last Falkirk market they were saying that there would be food riots yet in the south. Last year the English harvest was bad. You will get bigger prices this year for your beasts than ever you got. You can take that from me. The Lord works in inscrutable ways,' he concluded humbly.

Bannerman gazed at him. 'May the Lord use him who takes His name in vain for His own purposes.'

'Amen,' said the Drover.

*

Echoes of this catechetical meeting gave extra notes of fun to the eve of the departure of the lads for the wars. Angus's house was the centre of festivities, and old men and women who never came to ceilidhs now visited the house to shake hands with the boys, to offer them greeting and farewell in words of kindness and blessing.

Flushed faces and a swagger carried the young men through the perilous whirlpool. Even the shyest of them spoke loudly, and when Alastair 'the Stallion', a strong-necked, rather dour fellow, threw an arm round old Granny Gilchrist and squeezed her till she squeaked, a wave of wild laughter shook the company. She needed a dram after that. What, not take a dram and drink the lads' healths?

Angus went round the company with 'the mercies' when-ever he saw new faces about – and sometimes just when he saw faces. For he was merry himself, and every little drink the others compelled him to take added to his gaiety. Sure as death, they would have him drunk as a piper!

But the piper was not anything like drunk yet. The summer night was warm, and he blew or sweated one drink away before he took another. The drones were humming like a hive of mad bees, and inside the barn and outside the barn, in the long-drawn dusk of the summer night, they danced with great spirit. The dram went a little to Granny Gilchrist's head, and the slim, bent, but merry soul was caught into a figure and made partner to the Stallion, who braced himself before her, cracked his fingers, flung arms and legs about in grotesque style, then picked her up and whirled her.

Murdoch was there with his fiddle; Murdoch the wit with his dark face that could keep a smile on it like a mask; Murdoch the cripple – unfit for the wars. Mostly he was inside the house taking a drop of drink, but never getting the ease of drink. With two or three men – any men – he would talk and chuckle in a corner.

Seonaid, his enemy, had little time for him this night. Big Anndra was after her, and Angus og, Colin's brother, had a sly watchful eye for her as well. But Angus og wasn't going away and Anndra was – and many another good lad, including three from Tomich. The girls were kind to them, forgave them any extravagance, and often flew the merry flush of tenderness. There wasn't much in all that for Murdoch to look on at!

But when one of Angus's reeds stuck and the shout went up for Murdoch, he had to go out. Seonaid, hunting him, met him at the door, and all in the flush of the moment gave him a strange and intimate smile. 'Murdoch, they're shouting for you.' He neither answered nor moved, but stood looking at her eyes. 'Come on, Murdoch,' and her head beckoned him, the smile gathering an almost tender amusement. It was a moment of distressing awkwardness for him, for her intimate expression had put his body into a trance and he had to grope for his senses and jerk himself into action. Yet it was all so instantaneous that no one could have noticed anything; and he himself had laughed and tuned up and was well into the dance before his wits came back to feel the tremble of the reaction running along his muscles in a jumpy weakness.

But though he refused thought, somewhere thought was at work in him, for a little later, when laughing and talking as he sat on the turf mound, the fiddle on his knees, the vision of her face came vividly into his mind, and more clearly than mortal speech, he heard the words, 'She has pity for you.'

The E string snapped with a sharp crack. 'The damn things are rotten,' he said, with his deep-creased glittering merry smile. His fingers went under the other three strings. He tugged and burst one of them. The bridge collapsed.

'Hold, Murdoch, you're drunk, you devil!' cried Anndra, whose obtuseness was always flattered by Murdoch's company.

Murdoch grinned away good-naturedly. The fingers of his right hand were gripped round the neck of the instrument. The desire to smash the delicate shell was whirling within his head blotting his reason out. Smash it! The whirling frenzy called out for relief from the prison of the instrument, the prison of himself. Smash it! Colin gripped his arm as it was coming down. Murdoch wrestled with him. 'Catch it!' yelled Colin, and Anndra retrieved the still unbroken fiddle.

Murdoch came up from the ground, breathing heavily, easing his neck, and grinning.

'What the devil's got you?' cried Colin, staring into him.

'Uh! What!' said Murdoch, staring through his smile at Colin, then throwing a quick glittering glance here and there. If he had been less moved he could have pretended he was drunk. But now all he could use was his mask, and the reality hiding behind it made those about him instinctively pretend not to see it.

'You're wrong,' said Colin. 'He's not drunk enough! Come on, Murdoch!'

But Colin's hearty tones left Murdoch grinning through them, refusing to budge. 'No,' he said.

'What's the matter?' asked Seonaid, coming up.

'What!' said Murdoch, holding her look with his bright enigmatic eyes. 'Nothing!' The small laugh was in his throat. He turned his head and glanced at Elie. They all felt him holding them at bay. He did not want them. Yet they could not leave him. Nor could he leave them. When Anndra suddenly became boisterously friendly, one or two of them winced. But Seonaid abetted him with a dry voice:

'That's right, Anndra; take this bairn to your breast!'

A blood-dark shadow went over Murdoch's face. Colin, whipped blind by the sight of it, cried, 'Take him to your own dry breast!' Then he turned, 'Come on, Murdoch!'

'No.'

'No, be hanged! Come on,' and gripping Murdoch by the shoulders he heaved him to his feet.

But Seonaid was on him in a flash. 'What do you mean?'

'Mean? Nothing. Come on, Murdoch.'

'You won't insult me like that, Colin Sutherland.'

'I didn't insult you.'

'You did.'

'I didn't. Are you coming, Murdoch? All right, if you're not coming, you can stick.' And Colin walked off.

Seonaid stood looking after him, her eyes blazing.

'Och, he didn't mean – he didn't mean—' muttered Anndra awkwardly.

'Didn't mean what?' flashed Seonaid.

'Didn't mean that you – that your—'

Murdoch laughed. Seonaid turned on him. 'You – behaving like a spoilt child – you and – and – your fiddle!' She was in such a flaming anger that she stuttered. The cheek bones were red as if they had been painted. The term 'dry breast' quivered like an arrow in the quick of her spirit and she could have slapped Colin on the mouth; but that denied, all her venom turned on the old enemy. 'You bairn!' she spat at him.

But though his face darkened, he laughed his familiar mechanical little laugh and shot a glance of subtle bright malice at her. This drew her recklessly, and she was aware even while she was railing at him that she was degener-ating, making a fool of herself, for what was needed was the sting of an improvisation or even of a proverb, not the stuttering spittle of an enraged gossip-woman. His eyes were the eyes of a demon drawing her on, and the more she floundered the more he triumphed.

'Never mind them, Seonaid,' said Elie, gently.

This sympathy stung Seonaid behind the eyes.

'I say—' muttered Anndra.

'You say! What could you ever say? you long beautiful Fingalian hero! standing there like a thaw in a dream! Soldiers! Real cripples would wallop you with their crutches!' Her last sentence eased the sting behind her eyes and she gave Elie a smile, then looked around – and suddenly became ashamed. 'Hasn't Roy got his pipes right yet?' she called with amused defiance. 'What are you staring at, Davie?'

Davie muttered that a cat could stare at a queen. There was a chuckle and Seonaid flushed. At that moment, Roy blew a blast through a naked reed, whose pale inches he then withdrew from his mouth. 'I think I've got her at last,' he said. 'Hurry up, then!' urged Colin, who was bending beside him. 'What's all your hurry?' asked Roy slowly. 'No piper is ever in a hurry. Besides, why complain because your blood is salted?' He fixed the reed in the pipe and blew through it again. 'Man, this is life,' said Roy. 'Many's the day we'll remember this night. By God, you'll dream of it yet.' He looked about him with a humorous smile. 'I'd stuff it in the bag – if I could!'

Colin went boldly to Seonaid. 'Will you dance it with me?'

She drew herself up.

'Seonaid, you know well enough I lost my head.' He caught her by the wrist. 'You know you're a beauty with the tongue of a bard. This is our last night. It may be long enough before you can make a fool of me again.'

'Oh. Who's been teaching you the serpent-tongue?'

'You know that fine, too,' he said.

His fingers crushed the bones of her wrist. But glimpsing the stress of his features, she did not call out.

Rob the miller had Elie as partner in the same set. He was full of gusto and a fair amount of drink. The recent little flare-up had salted life, as the piper said. Rob, though twice her age, was clearly enamoured of Elie, and in his jaunty jocular way did not care who saw it.

With his fiddle under his arm, Murdoch went towards the house, but at the door his eyes glanced hither and thither seeking escape, when old Angus appeared and said in his wondering welcoming voice, 'Lord, Murdoch, is it yourself?' as if he had never seen him before; and he took him into the house.

The dusk deepened its spell on the Riasgan. The thrill in the foreknowledge of the dark touched all the young. The wind had died and the quiet of evening lay along the hills against a blue-green sky whose brightness in fading retained an inner lovely light of unearthly thought.

But the thought coming out from the darkening hillsides and down upon the valley seemed earthly enough, as if indeed the Riasgan were contemplating all her children, whose cries and shouts ran along the sky-gleam in the winding stream, about the hillocks, down the waves of the ground and up them and round the cottages, through the birch wood like fingers through hair, growing smaller, lessening, fading out upon the air beyond the hill-crests, where God's thought in its inner brightness could not hear them – or hear them as a human ear the hive-murmur of wild bees deep in the earth.

Dark-browed, the Riasgan encompassed the hot blood, the old wisdom, the urge through music to the sting of love, the quick foot, the flash, the fire, the withdrawal, the black pain, the red eye, the restless eternal beat, beat, beat of the heart; for already there is the fear that one day, before desire is fulfilled and purpose completed, she will look upon her body and find the warmth gone and the womb barren and desolate.

Dark Mairi, like a thought out of the Riasgan's brow, stood at the end of her cottage, looking across and down at Angus's croft where about the barn and house she could dimly distinguish the movement of human figures. The music and the dance shouts came on the still air clearly, yet with the remote sadness that accompanies the distant sounds of pleasure. A sudden laugh or scream rose solitary as a startled mind before a strange rite. All this was a rite – the sacrifice of the boys led away from the Riasgan, whose features were more to them in the secrecy of sense and lust and beauty than the features of their human mothers.

Mairi's brow was cool as a stone to the night air. The

air stirred about her in a faint sigh as she turned from the Riasgan and entered her cottage. Her little acts were performed with the mindlessness of an immemorial rite. As she smoored the peat in the ashes, her chant of blessing was abstracted into an unhuman monotony. And when the words were finished and her mouth closed, the chant rose up through her head with the released strong-smelling smoke, then slowly died down through her nostrils into the silence and the dark.

Elie and Colin came up the hillside towards the cottage. Though it was midnight, there was about them a ghostly memory of the day, for it was high summer and the northern sky never quite lost the sun's afterglow. Since Elie had sung to him by the birches cold-budded in the spring, the sun had gone to the roots of life and stirred and wakened it to leafage and blossom. And a birch tree, even the small birch trees of the wood, did not come to life with one leaf, or with a few, but with myriads of leaves; and even the stunted and dwarfed trees shook and quivered in a myriad-pointed fire of green.

There was nothing stunted about Elie. However countless the leaves and grasses, however they blew into a flame, that flame was jewel-cold to the countless leaping tongues of Elie's warmth. When she could no longer hold Colin, when she knew that go he would, that go he must by order of forces beyond them, she surrendered her grudge against these forces, surrendered the past and the future, and with that lavish generosity that was natural to her growth, plunged into and breasted the present.

Yet all through their love rites up there in the wood, the certainty of his going, the inevitability of their parting, was an edge cutting the grossness out of emotion, leaving the quickening, the ecstasy, that is so often the premonition of pain or of tragedy.

Occasionally Colin was frightened, and in odd lonely moments would shudder, and grasp, and blot the thing out.

But there was no fear in Elie at all. The days were golden.
The rain was soft. She would open her lips to the rain.
And however cold the wind, her body nestled from her
clothes into it. The bright days had a brightness underneath them that lay on the grass, the heather, the hens
about the door, and on the comb of the laughable gawky
cock. The dull wet days held shadow underneath; and,
drifting along the hill-face, caught in the myrtle, entangled
in the heath, rising out of the grass, were the scents of the
earth, the elusive, wandering, lovely scents that came as it
were privately to one who knew the sunless shadow under
which the body withdrew with its radiant secret delight.
In a hidden nook Elie could bury her face and, laughing,
lick the beads of sweet rain from her lips.

And now of that golden period the last night had come.
Their feet were approaching step by step to a pause, to an
end. The mad loveliness was over; Colin's mind was full
of misgiving, of surging gloom, and in its struggle to get
free it kept his voice going gaily. Wasn't Murdoch an ass?
And Seonaid – wasn't Seonaid an idiot? He, Colin, shouldn't
have said what he had said, maybe, but still, dash it, what
could one do with them? They were always quarrelling.
You would think they were jealous of each other ! Elie
laughed. I wonder, she said. Her voice was quick and
excited. They could feel the constriction of each other's
breast. Their breathing interrupted their words, came in
little gulps from their chests. What do you wonder, what?
I think, she said, there is something between them – and
they don't know it! What's between them? he asked. What
astonishing thing could be between them! What did she
mean? I mean, said Elie, that – that they don't know, but
there is a fire between them – you can see the way they
flare up at the least thing. I know, he said, they do – that's
just it – they are jealous and hate each other. That's what
I say! No, she said, that's not what's beneath it – it's –
something else. Her voice fell away softly, enigmatically,

but also with something tired and terrible in it. He felt this and laughed. Hush, she said, there's the house.

O God, there was the house. They stopped and looked up at its looming shoulder. The constriction was round his chest like a tightening snare. He glanced about him. Look! there was someone over there. A head, he was sure it was a head. Elie thought it might be Davie – it could be no one else. Colin walked over a few paces, whispered into the night, and came back. He must have imagined it! He laughed softly but they went across the hillside a few steps – and stopped again. I'm tired, said Elie suddenly, and sat down. Her legs were shaking; she felt weak. Tortured, he sat down beside her. What is it, Elie? She gripped at his breast, hit her head against it, and burst into tears. He got his arms about her, lay down with her, and the snare-band round his chest burst. Long after that she bade him good-bye. She was calm and quiet and her voice had the low honey sound of the fey woman or the child. Colin. Good-bye, Colin.

And she still stood unmoving when he turned from her abruptly and went stumbling down the hillside like a blinded beast. She heard the surge rising out of him in its blinded rage. Her heart twisted with pity for the love and fate that warred within him and choked him. When the last sound of his feet had passed away, she looked about her at the night with its ghostly light.

She went slowly up to the cottage. But she was weary, ah, she was weary. She lay down, her face against the earth. Echoes of his talk, his eager talk, his home-coming . . . ghost-echoes. Small dry sounds began to wrack her. She had asked nothing, told nothing. She knew too much. She had loved him – to the end. From that end, she would have to – ah, what what what? Her misery rocked her, her mouth tried to escape, she writhed there in her grey sapless misery, one nerve of red fire threading it.

'Elie!' said Davie's broken voice over her. 'Elie, what's wrong?'

She lay still for a little time, then slowly sat up.

'Why aren't you in bed, Davie?'

'Elie, what is it?'

'It's Colin, Davie, who's gone away from me.'

'Ah, Elie, don't cry. Never you mind him, Elie. Don't you mind him.'

'I'm not crying, Davie.'

'Come on to your bed, then. Come on in, Elie.'

She sat still, gazing into the night. He pleaded with her again. His voice grew gruff.

She turned her face to him, spoke his name so tenderly that it fell like a leaf into the abyss of her woe. The sound of it frightened him and he clutched her roughly at the neck.

'All right, Davie,' she said, 'I'm coming.' And they went into the house.

\*

With Roy at their head, the lads went marching away from Angus's barn, a handsome set of fellows, swinging down the path, across the stream, and up over the shoulder of the hill on the short-cut to the sea and the south. Little boys followed them, racing through the heather, tumbling, keeping step, staring at the tall warriors, their excitement bursting into shouts and cheers.

At the end of each cottage figures were grouped, many of them aged and bent, some of them carried out to see the last of the men who were going from the Riasgan to the wars; from the little district of the Riasgan that was as intimate to them as their own bodies.

Those who were not so old said, 'Well, there they are off, anyway!' Occasionally a man joked. 'Roy is keeping the bag tight, though the hill will test him!' They swayed restlessly. In some faces was a vague emotion of yearning or envy. Lashes flicked over bright eyes. Already the figures of the marching men were growing smaller, and the big pipe was gathering into its lively march the sound of *going away, going away*, the terrible burden of every march to those who hear its heart-beat growing fainter and fainter.

Now they were taking the hillside. Roy was keeping at it! He wouldn't give in now, not Roy! The watching men became interested in whether Roy would play his lads right out over the top, and on their faces there was a fixed smile. Many of the women were crying, and the smaller children looked shamefaced and awkward. Anna, Colin's mother, had her lips pressed tight and tears now and then rolled down her cheeks. The yearning in her eyes was in the eyes of all the mothers. The music that was going away threw back upon them long thin fingers that went in behind their hearts, in behind the milk roots and fibres, and struggled to tear them out. Many of the women had their arms crossed over their breasts. Their bodies would now and then twist slightly from side to side, and small sounds would pierce their closed mouths.

Many times in the long past of the Riasgan had the mothers watched their sons go, single sons and married sons, out over that crest of the hill at the summons of the fiery cross. On this morning all their history stood tranced.

Yet there was a difference in the spirit of the trance. In past times the women would not have ignored the children about their knees. They would have snatched them to their breasts, for who knew what would come back over the hill-crest, hunting and hunted? No danger threatened like that now. By their men in the past the Riasgan and its homes had been made secure for all time. These were their sons, answering still the call of their chief, not for the forays of the glens, but for campaigns and battles on foreign fields, so that not only their homes but their country might have peace with honour.

Their bodies rose against the skyline. They were on top! Roy had done it! The music ceased.

Arms waved against the sky and a cheer came down upon the homes. The cheer was returned from every throat in the Riasgan. Roy started up his pipes again, and, waving still, the figures passed down the horizon and left it blank.

Beyond that homely horizon, lo! the far bright sea and the infinitely remote horizons of the world. Down all the ways in that northern land are similar little bands passing, leaving behind sudden blankness and shadow.

Marching away to what new lands and strange adventures, glittering seas, and fears so nameless that the chest swells with the surge of the piping and a reckless gaiety mounts to the head. For the fears are in some high fatal way part of the nostalgia of leaving, and the spirit must keep the body going with the colour and flash of a banner moving to the heart of the hostile forces of the world.

For far and wide over the earth these hostile forces are moving and counter-moving in a game so inscrutable that surely Destiny herself could hardly work out its meaning, or even dimly discern its end. These men marching down the glens will take part in it in places as widely apart as the streets of Dublin and the mountains of South Africa. The man walking by Colin Sutherland's side and staring at the band of bright light that lay along the utmost rim of the sea, with a set enchanted smile on his face, was already saluting his death in the surf of Lospard Bay, and Colin's own expression would not be less intense when, the desperate charge over that won the crests of the Blue Mountain, he would lie under strange stars thinking of that death and its link with the soil his feet so lightly trod now. As though destined to outflank the earth itself rather than move to the game's centre on the plains of Europe, these lads had their eyes fatally drawn by the sea. Anndra, tall and angular and red, walking in front of Colin, a queer sad surging in his breast, not because he was leaving Seonaid but, profoundly now, because he knew Seonaid was never for him, would meet his death in the insensate carnage before New Orleans when their regiment, under criminally stupid command, lost more men in a few hours than in the whole course of the Indian Mutiny, surely the bloodiest move in that intricate art of the meaningless that Destiny contrived to play with them.

The sea, that was to bear them to the ends of the earth, that glittered there before them this summer's morning, was the second of Destiny's arms. Napoleon had known its power – and was to know it better still before it finally bore him to his last rest on a rock lost in its wastes. But now he is in Paris, received in triumph after two months of conquest, with Italy, Switzerland and Germany under his hand, and Austria preparing for disaster at Hohenlinden. Thus freed from Continental wars, he would be able to direct his whole strength against England, get the ports of Europe closed against her, starve her out, invade and smash her, as the Normans had done long ago, this England with her usurpation of the lordship of the sea. Crushed by taxation, starved for food, bread riots amongst her ever-increasing hordes of industrial workers, wheat soaring to its 120 shillings a quarter, were not her people clamouring for peace? In May her King had been shot at in a theatre. Saved hitherto by her seas and her endless capacity for raising gold to bribe others, England's hour of doom was at last about to strike.

To keep going, England needed food, food from within her own borders, and her borders now included the glens, for after the '45, what with penal enactments and other fruitful works, Pitt the elder was able to declare of the barbarous Highlands, 'I sought for merit wherever it could be found. It is my boast that I was the first minister who looked for, and found it, in the mountains of the north. I called it forth and drew into your service a hardy and intrepid race of men; men who, when left by your jealousy, became a prey to the artifices of your enemies, and had gone nigh to overturn the State, in the war before last (the '45). These men in the last war were brought to combat on your side; they served with fidelity, as they fought with valour, and conquered for you in every quarter of the world.'

And now Pitt the younger was draining this remote part of his kingdom once again, draining it of the surplus commodity of men. Was there no other commodity left of which it could be drained?

Food? Pitt would not let His Majesty's Government interfere with the free interplay of the laws of commerce as shown in their 'immutable laws' by that logical Scotsman, Adam Smith. Supply and demand would regulate prices, not Acts of Parliament – scarcity, bread riots, starvation – but man must not interfere with the upward march in price. All man could do was profit by it – where he could. But not in the Highlands, surely not in these ancient glens, where food was often scarce enough, where poverty in an odd spring stalked lean-bellied as ever it did in the industrial lands.

But if food was under the divine law of price, it was under the secular law of human ownership. And the man who owned the land owned the food before it was produced.

In these 'mountains of the north' the chief owned the land.

But what food could be produced from these mountains?

Flesh, and before the flesh, wool. Food and clothing.

But could they be produced in vast quantities?

Not while they remain inhabited as they are.

How then? What inhabitants can you put in their place?

Already, farther south, other inhabitants, four-footed, non-human.

The beat in the heart of a march can sometimes have a more searching poignancy than the beat in the heart of a lament. Quick, living, moving, it has not the final calm that sits at the heart of sorrow. It goes on, on, and it draws after it the phantoms of those left behind . . . phantoms coming down the glens, the terrible army of phantoms driven down the glens, down the same paths that these lads go marching with such brave show to fix and hold in the ends of the earth the outposts of the British Empire.

## FIVE

When, a little later in the year, the lads were followed by a small group of girls, there was no brave show of bagpipes to set them off on their march to the south. The girls, of course, were only going to try to earn some cash for themselves and their folk at harvesting possibly as far away as the Lowlands. There was, however, much amusement and chaffing over the event, for the girls were by no means forced to go. The Riasgan was a tidy community, with wide hill grazing, pasture and cultivated land by the river, and winter shelter in the birch wood that with its small trees lay to the hillside like a green or brown blanket. There were many worse-off places than the Riasgan. Indeed in a way its comparative comfort was what gave the girls the spirit to try to fend for themselves. Other districts did it. Many went from the main glen. Why shouldn't they from the Riasgan? Thus the girls spoke, pointing out furthermore that it hadn't been a good year for the crops. 'Suppose,' said Seonaid, who was the ring-leader of the four, 'that blight sets in and then a very hard winter, like some hard winters of the past, and the cattle die in the spring, and we have no money to buy meal. Suppose—' 'Suppose,' interrupted old Angus, 'that you find the lads that are left pretty dull?' 'Suppose I do,' answered Seonaid, throwing a cool look around, 'would you blame me?' 'If you go,' he answered, smiling, 'it will be withered grass in a ditch for my old hair and I'm saying nothing of anybody else's.' 'You stick to your canna locks,' said Seonaid, 'and leave the other fleeces to their own sheep.' 'Where's your tongue, Murdoch?' asked Angus. 'Is she going to conquer us while she's here in the flesh – and trouble us in the spirit when she's gone?' 'I can think of nothing,' said Murdoch, 'but the old saying – The nature of a hen, of a sow, and of a woman: to take their own way.' They all saw Seonaid drawing up and held their laughter till she spoke.

They were at it again! And Seonaid now could readily become personal and even bitter in her retorts, while Murdoch would flush a bit but gleam as if, though beaten, he were almost having the better of it.

'I knew I was missing someone,' said old Angus. 'Where's Elie?' 'Oh, Elie,' replied Seonaid carelessly, 'she said she mightn't be down, she has so much to do before leaving.' One or two smiled, for Colin was gone. 'Ay,' retorted Seonaid drily, and was turning the talk when Anna, looking at her, asked, 'Isn't she coming down at all?' Seonaid met the look. 'She'll surely be coming down to say goodbye,' she answered. There was colour in her cheeks and a touch of reckless good-humour in her manners. The few lads who were in were wary of her. She had the air of wanting to slash them if they spoke. She was restless and dangerous and very good-looking. The freshness of the shielings was about most of them, but its bright wind was in Seonaid's eyes. The four girls had come down from the summer grazings accompanied by a small band. Tomorrow they were going to make a night of it. Meanwhile Elie was the wise one, to be getting things ready . . .

Though it didn't take a great deal of time getting the few things together that Elie would carry in a bundle over her shoulder. Yet she made much of it and worked away after the daylight had faded, stitching a garment that Mairi had shaped, for Elie was a good but not a very neat worker. As Mairi stuck a new fir candle in the wall, she said, 'You're looking tired a bit, lassie. Are you vexed now you're going?'

With her eyes on her work, Elie laughed. 'Oh no,' she answered.

'There's no need to go,' said Mairi. 'You know that.'

'Yes,' answered Elie. 'We'll be all right. It'll be something for us. I think that'll do fine now,' she added, and rolled the garment up.

'Yes,' said Mairi, 'we'll do the rest with the daylight when we'll see better.'

But she could not sit by the fire with Mairi. She was restless and got up and went out. Mairi then blew out the fir candle and went to the door. It was quite dark outside. She listened for a long time. The wind blew in fitful rustling eddies. Mairi did not like wind eddies that stirred up earth dust or moved over the heather tops with spirit-feet. When an eddy like that met you on a path you stood still and let the spirit pass. She went to the end of the house and looked over at the Riasgan, then, baffled, turned her face to the dark hillside. The wet season had kept water in the burn which now came down in its monotonous plunging song. Through the sound of the burn she heard, up on her right, the surge of the wind in the birch leaves. Caught in the centre of these sounds was a small cry that was not a real cry so much as the crying heart of the sounds themselves. Mairi did not like it. It was the voice out of the eddy, the voice left behind. She went back to the door where she stood again for a long time, then went in to the peat fire and sat down beside it, bent forward a little and very still.

She was in bed when Elie came back.

'Where have you been?' she asked.

'I just took a run over,' said Elie.

Mairi did not ask her to what house she had run over, because she knew that Elie had been to no house. Elie was a poor hand at telling a lie.

'Did you see Davie?' Mairi asked.

'He'll be over at old Angus's, as usual,' replied Elie.

Again there was a long silence.

'He gets too much of his own way, and stays out too late for one so young,' spoke Mairi. 'No good will come of it.'

'Will I go away for him?'

'No. I wonder he's not frightened in the dark by himself.'

'He runs the whole way home,' said Elie.

'What are you doing now?' asked Mairi, after a long time.

'I'm lying down in Davie's place,' answered Elie. 'I'm not sleepy yet.'

The silence inside the house grew so heavy that no natural voice could rise above it.

When Mairi sighed the sound was solemn as the misery that is squeezed out of religion.

'I cannot get my sleep,' she said, querulously.

Elie could not help her, could not by a chuckle and a few words ease the uncertain burden on her mind. She could not . . . Her teeth bit into her lips, her throat and her face swelled up, but she choked back the dreadful spasm, and then tried to let her breath escape quietly. Mairi heard the suspense and the quivering.

'What's wrong with you?' she asked, and when she got no answer, stirred to her elbow.

'It's nothing,' said Elie, 'just this going away. I'm foolish.'

Mairi heard her face being buried.

The sounds of the night came about the house. 'It's time that rascal was home,' said Mairi. Elie was a soft girl, too good-natured and soft, and warming. Perhaps it was no more than that she was going away. Perhaps not. But she remembered again the queer way Elie had looked into the mouth of the night, earlier, before turning away round the house.

The burden of the silence pressed down on Mairi who was so used to a state of mindlessness that she fell into a drowsy coma. Perhaps she had actually fallen asleep before Davie came in, but if so, all in a moment she was wide-awake and gave Davie her tongue. 'Unless you mend your ways this is no home for you. Mind you that. You should feel shame of yourself, a young thing like you thinking you

can go on the houses like a grown man. What you need is
a thrashing, a sound thrashing, and it's a thrashing you'll
get.'

Davie chuckled under his breath to Elie over whom he
had tripped and fallen.

'I'm hearing you!' called Mairi. 'And I've a good mind
to get up this minute and slap the side of your head.'

'Be quiet,' whispered Elie into Davie's ear.

'You're tickling me,' whispered Davie. Elie held him.
'Hush.' She began to laugh softly. Davie, half-smothered,
tickled her under the arms. Elie's laugh quickened to a
scream. Davie slid from her like an eel.

Elie could not keep back her laughter. Davie was on the
floor, frightened and wary. Dark Mairi wanted to know if
it wasn't late enough for all this carry-on. They could hear
Elie stuffing her mouth. Then through the smothering came
a loud hiccough.

'Ha! ha!' issued from Davie abruptly. Then he edged
towards the door as Mairi came from her bed.

'What on earth's taken you, lassie?'

Elie hiccoughed, convulsed with laughter. Mairi moved
through the darkness towards her, for the fire was smoored,
and there was no light anywhere. Davie listened to the
women. At last Mairi drew the ashes from the peat and
blowing the kindling to a blaze lit the fir candle. When she
had got a drink ready she made Elie turn over. Davie saw
Elie's face; it was swollen as if from some dreadful fever
or pain. The laughter now had died down but the hiccough
remained. She drank like a child, gulpingly. Mairi set the
shallow wooden bowl on the ground, and placed one hand
against the back of Elie's head and the other against her
brows. 'It's all right,' said Mairi, in her monotonous voice.
'It's all right.' The monotony caught its own rhythm, became
an old child lullaby humming in Mairi's nostrils. The queer
thin sound of it brought a tingling sensation of mad laughter
to Davie, who didn't, however, even smile.

Elie fell forward and gripped Mairi round the hips. Davie saw the desperate clinging of the fingers. Mairi's right hand passed slowly over Elie's head, while the nostrils continued their witch-chant. It was like being at the end of the world, with everything stricken into an eternal peace, including Elie's hiccough.

'Come to your bed,' said Mairi, lifting Elie gently to her feet. Davie watched them go over to their bed in the corner, as if he were prying on some secret procession of women, and it was not until he had smoored all light and slid into his own bed that the tingling in his chest passed away and he regained his own secrecy and the laughing free feel of his boy's body.

In the morning the noise of the two women getting up wakened him. But he was still sleepy, and not until he heard Mairi say in a curious voice, 'What's wrong?' did he open his eyes. He caught a glimpse of Elie rushing through the doorway and of Mairi standing looking after her with queer puckered mouth and face. She looked silly, as if someone had hit her in the wind and she did not know how to draw her breath.

When at last Mairi went towards the door, Davie slipped into his clothes and stepped warily after her. She was standing just outside, gaping and listening, her mouth wide open in that inane way. Then Davie saw her eyes glisten, and, rounding the door post, he beheld Elie coming towards them, her face the colour of meal.

Davie's own mouth fell open. The hens brushed against his legs as they rushed out, noisy and hungry. The cock kept his head so high that he tripped over himself. The cow lowed in the byre. The tethered goat maa'd and then stood stock still with a face grey as Elie's. Suddenly Elie herself stood still, swayed, then fell to the ground, where she doubled up and retched.

Mairi did not go towards her, did not move at all, but stood looking at the writhing girl as at some final act of revelation. Davie glanced at her face, then slowly, awkwardly, edged away from them both.

When the spasm was spent, Elie lay quiet, knowing that all was now exposed, but hardly caring, so utterly exhausted did she feel. When she got to her feet her face had a thin unnatural flush. She looked about her wretchedly in the bright morning light. She took a step towards the house, then hesitated, and turned her face away.

Mairi went over to her. 'Come away in, Elie,' she said quietly.

But Elie did not look at her, did not move.

'Come.'

'No,' said Elie. Her voice was weary and stubborn. Her whole body was stubborn and wretched. The garish morning light mocked her wretchedness. The hens came about her legs. The world was vast and bright, eager and bright, with no black pit anywhere.

From the hollow of the watercourse, Davie peered over at the strange play of the two women. They were in a world apart from him, apart from all men. The difference between them and him was more than the difference between their bodies (which was marvellous enough): they had their secrets, their griefs, their queer hidden ways, from which he was shut out – into freedom. A shiver of male satisfaction went over him and stuck on his face in a thin smile. Mairi now had Elie by the shoulder and was half-dragging her to the house, as if otherwise she might run away, as the goat did sometimes, maaing and bleating and taking to the hills. Davie felt something move in his throat. Elie's head was down. But once she stopped stubbornly and threw it up and Davie heard a thin stifled cry. Then, her head down again, she went before Mairi's hand into the house.

Davie looked into the small swirling pool before him, his mouth pursed up and making the frightened smile crinkle round his eyes. Digging stones out of the bank, he hurled them into the pool. He was very hungry but his gorge felt sickish a bit too. Action left him, and he grew still as a stone, staring into the pool, black hair falling straight over an eggshell brow, dark eyebrows uptilting over hazel eyes, nostrils that moved, and a closed sensitive mouth. The arch of the eyebrows occasionally gave him a puckish slanting look, but now his might have been the spirit-face of the burn itself. Sometimes action came to him out of stillness and lack of thought, as it did to his grandmother, Dark Mairi; and all in a moment he was up over the bank and going warily towards the house. As he went in at the door, he half-expected to hear Elie crying, but he heard not a sound. He tiptoed towards the partition, intensely curious. To learn what they were saying to each other, to catch the woman secret between them, drew him with a sharp sense of guilt. But so long as they did not know it would be all right and he would take his knowledge with him to the hillside and look at it. He became aware of Mairi and started guiltily. She did not say anything, but stood looking at him, as his body twisted with affectation of innocence, then she went over to the cow and milked her.

'You'll put her up the hill,' she said quietly. 'I'll give you some milk.' He drank the milk like a calf and went away after the cow.

At first he lay about, and would wake from half-formed thoughts to glance around him. Restlessness got the better of him, however, and he told the cow she would have to stop there, or he would give her what for! Backing away with a fierce face, he at last, when she was quietly eating, slipped into the wood, and in the upper end of it, where three rowan trees grew, he broke a slender forked branch, and with the aid of some sharp stones by the side of the stream, rough-shaped what might have been the handle of a catapult, had such a weapon been known to him. An hour after that, Kirsteen surprised him in the barn cleaning the three ends of his stock with the reaping hook.

'I'll tell,' she said.

He looked over his shoulder at her and said nothing.

'I'll tell,' she said excitedly. 'I'll tell Angus og.'

Old Angus darkened the door. Swiftly Davie thrust the stick out of sight, and then slowly, without looking at his old friend, went and hung up the hook.

'What are you doing, little Davie?'

'He was cutting a stick with the hook and blunting it,' cried Kirsteen.

'I was not!' said Davie.

'The stick is up under his clothes,' cried Kirsteen.

'You weren't hurting the hook at all, were you, Davie?' Old Angus lifted down the sickle. It was a very valuable possession and to blunt it would be an awful sin, not only against value, but against the art of the cutting edge. The old man and the boy were in complete understanding over this, and Davie waited in bitter anxiety while Angus thumbed the edge. How different this from the woman trouble up at the house, where he had looked on as at a strange happening that could never really affect him! Angus hung up the hook. 'What were you wanting with it?'

Davie looked on the ground and did not speak. Kirsteen watched him, fascinated, her voice mumbling on the edge of further accusation. 'Won't you tell me?' asked Angus. Davie's body twisted away from Angus's hand. His betrayal of Angus's friendship cut him with the round terrible cut of the reaping hook. 'Won't you show me the stick?'

Davie kept his head down.

'All right,' said Angus, and walked slowly away.

Davie left the barn, Kirsteen following him. He swung round on her with a look of such intense hate that it brought her up like a hand.

'You're a cheeky thing,' she mumbled.

He went on.

'Cheeky thing!' she cried.

Picking up a stone he pivoted and let fly. It hit her in the body and knocked her down. Her screams caught at

his flying heels like the red beast of sin. Down by the bank
of the burn he got into a hole and hid. He heard voices
coming out of the ruined world. Two or three of his companions found him. 'You threw a stone at a girl,' jeered Iain,
their leader. Three more boys came running up.

'Shut up!' said Davie.

'Say that again!'

'Shut up!'

Out of his stagger from Iain's wallop Davie came in a
white madness. Iain grounded him twice. It made no difference. Davie came tearing at him and in blind fashion
smashed his nose, so that it suddenly began pumping blood.
The fight was immediately stopped. While Davie stood
panting he saw little Rob Sutherland lifting the forked stick
from the ground. In a moment he was upon him and tore
it from him. The other boys saw the stick, and even Iain
himself tilted his head forward from the cold stone that
was held to the back of his neck to stop the bleeding. Davie
stood proud and trembling. 'Keep him, till I get hold of
him!' shouted Iain. Davie's steps quickened, then broke into
a run, the boys following and shouting. Stones splashed in
the water as he leapt the boulders. Soon he had outdis-
tanced them and was lost in the birches.

From his hiding place near the top of the wood, he
looked down on the Riasgan. Every house he knew, though
with less intimacy the further it lay from Angus's house,
and one or two outlying ones were familiar to him by a
sense of smell. Gilleasbuig's house, for example, smelt like
a chest with the mournful breath of prayers shut in it. In
a house like that he was always very polite and stood until
he could get away. As he watched, a woman would come
out at a door, do something, and go in again. Several girls
were laughing at the end of Seonaid's house. A man was
coming slowly down the path from Tomich. Figures moved
here and there over the land. Young folk ran, in a hurry.
Many had come down from the summer grazings. There

would be great fun in Angus's house that night with dancing outside, and stories inside, and proverbs. From all of which, he was shut out forever. He remembered the glow that had come over him when he had given the saying, 'Going to ruin is silent work.' How everyone had laughed! The memory of it wrought silent ruin in him now. Perhaps Kirsteen would be in bed and her body grow up all deformed. He could never go near that house now. What trouble had one like Elie compared with this awful and eternal exclusion from the life of one's kind? His eye was caught by the movements of the boys at the river. Iain was now nodding his head slowly up and down and then standing still to see if any blood came. The stoppage must have been complete for a council of war was held and a combing of the wood clearly decided upon. A certain rabbit-hunting collie was added to the band, and the attack advanced in wide formation.

Davie might elude them in the wood, but he might not. Anyway, he did not want to try. For solitariness was in his heart and he desired to go away into solitary places and be lost where no one would ever find him. Then they would see that a little hurt to the pruning hook – or even to Kirsteen – was a small thing compared with the sad mysterious disappearance of his whole body.

It was probably the influence of the forked stick that ultimately brought him in sight of Tomich and gave his feet courage against the barking dogs. Though Tomich was little more than two miles from the Riasgan, it was to Davie a strange place near the end of the world. In the Riasgan the houses were scattered about the land each at a little distance from the other; but here in Tomich they all lay huddled together as if they were frightened. Every person he could see was standing looking at him, as at a being from another world. They worked their land in common, drawing lots for their various portions, and did many other queer old-fashioned things that often came into the ceilidh-house stories. Anything incredible or fantastic was always placed in Tomich. It became the home of the laughable and grotesque for the young practical jokers of the Riasgan. But old Angus said that in his time the Riasgan ran things in exactly the same way, and that that way was as old as the beginning of time.

One or two boys of about his own age were now circling round him at a little distance, but a young man came to him and called him by his name. He was very kind to Davie, and when he saw that Davie was shy and appeared to have no particular business he whistled one of the many boys who came up and was presented as Eoin. Davie was now very embarrassed and wished he had never come. But the freckled fair-haired Eoin gazed at him with bright curious eyes and Davie did not fear him. When the young man turned away they had not a word for each other. Davie pulled out the rowan stick, saying, 'I was wanting to see the changeling.' Eoin instantly coveted the stick and Davie gave it to him. The boys came up and met the stranger from the world outside, and the little band moved away with him in their centre, until Eoin called a halt and, when he saw a man leave a certain house, advanced towards and into that house, announcing politely to the back-bent woman who gazed at them, 'This is Davie of Dark Mairi of the Riasgan and he wants to see the changeling.'

Some of the woman's teeth were missing and her eye-teeth were long, her skin was yellowish, and her hair was drawn back from her forehead in an untidy way that left wisps sticking out here and there. There was an aged sadness on her face, though she was no more than forty. When she had gazed at Davie in a rather startled vacant way for some moments, she smiled and said, 'Oh yes.' Plainly his grand-mother was widely known.

The cradle was a narrow rounded wicker basket and in it lay a being that horrified Davie. A very old man had shrunk and shrunk until he had become the size of a child.

A little withered old man, wrinkled and impotent, and dreadful to look at. The lips were blue, the eyes lidded and half-closed, the forehead deeply scored.

'That's him,' said the woman sadly. 'That's what they left in the place of my own boy.'

That the fairies had stolen the woman's child and left this wretched wight of their own in his place had for a whole week been the talk of the Riasgan; and whatever anyone may have said, no one really doubted the truth of the story.

As the woman turned away, Eoin, who was on his knees at the foot of the basket, jerked the forked stick from under his clothes and poked the soles of the changeling's feet with the two short ends. At once it let out a high old man's moan. The woman turned back but Eoin had the stick hidden. It was clearly an excellent stick for that had been about the best moan that Eoin had ever got. The next time it was not quite so good. The third time he gave the soles a decided jab, and the strange wrinkled thing began to whimper. The sound made Davie shiver, and the woman was now in such a strange mood herself that when she bared her breast and stooped for the child, the boys filed out, and, when they got clear of the houses, began to run. By closing their mouths and pushing a thin cry up into their nostrils they tried to imitate the changeling's moan. This game they played for quite a time, with bursts of laughter, running round in circles, their heads in the air. Then they played other games. Davie had potatoes and milk in Eoin's home, and it was not until the sun was sinking that he started for the Riasgan.

It had been a great day. He had been made to feel like an important ambassador to a small court. When he was alone this feeling buoyed him up; but when he got his first glimpse of the Riasgan, it turned into the old remote hostility. Immediately he left the path and bore away sharply to his right so that he could get in behind the birch wood and drive home the cow. The sudden thought of the cow made him run.

He would not have found her had not a glimpse of his hurrying figure made her, now thinking of home, low from a moor hollow far in towards the rising ground. He knew when he came upon her that she would never have left the sweet grass about the wood and crossed that peaty waste unless she had been driven. Iain and the others would have done that! The dusk was now falling quickly and he herded the brute to a run. When finally he got her into the hollow, Elie was there. All day he had forgotten Elie and his granny. Elie was quiet, and he began to explain hurriedly that when he wasn't looking the old brute had gone out over the top.

'Take her home,' said Elie.

'Aren't you coming yourself?'

'I'll be down in a little,' she answered.

A small clutch caught his breath, half in wonder, half in fear, and he turned away at once. Before going out of sight, he stole a look back. She was walking slowly up to the crest of the wood.

When Dark Mairi had challenged him about his day's doings and why he had not come home for food, and got no answer, she set about milking the cow in a preoccupied way.

'Have you been running the cow that she's got no milk?'

'No.'

'Where's her milk gone to then?' Her voice was sharp yet weary, as if this new misfortune might have been expected. She gave him oaten bread spread with new cheese, and a bowl of yesterday's milk. 'Did you see Elie?' Yes, he had seen her up on the edge of the wood. In the firelit gloom, his granny's face was wearied with vacant thought. In a little time she got up from her seat by the fire and went out.

He listened, then went to the meal chest and noiselessly lifted the lid. His nostrils had told him his granny had been baking. Now he saw the round oaten bannocks, standing on edge, and hesitated, for they were obviously meant for Elie's pack. The meal had been bought from the miller, for their own had been finished a few weeks before. He dare not take a bannock, so he stuffed his mouth with the meal, and when his jaws wearied and his gums got dry, he gulped a mouthful of the new warm milk, and started on the meal again. When he judged he had taken enough, he closed the chest, wiped his mouth, and went to the outside door, where the dark hillside faced him.

He was normally frightened of the dark, but by tightening himself all up, he could walk past the fearful spots and take to his heels. He had suffered agonies of fear between Angus's house and his own after listening to ghost stories, but he had never given in like some of the other boys, for Angus had always called him his little hero. Many grown men would be frightened to go the distance he went, Angus had said. And it only required the women to ask, 'Are you sure you're not frightened, Davie?' for him to face anything.

Now, however, as he looked up that dark hillside with the peculiar intensity that darkness always inspires, he thought he heard the thin cry of a child. It was at once a cry at the very heart of the night and yet a wandering cry, and his skin went cold all over. In some way he felt that Elie and Dark Mairi were near this cry and that their woman secrecy had something to do with it. Then even as he stood, taut and trembling, there came before his vision the awful face of the changeling with its blue lips and lidded eyes and wrinkled forehead. He slipped going in at the door and cried out sharply as he fell, but in no time was beyond the partition and crouching by the fire, staring at the entrance through which the thing would follow him. Something flickered there and he screamed. The scream banished the flickering thing, and he crouched back.

*

It was a cold winter evening when three of the four girls who had gone south for the harvesting came back upon the brow of the hill and looked down on the Riasgan. The sight of the familiar land brought warmth about their hearts. Each house was in the same old place, recognised with a short eager ridiculous laugh. It all looked like a nest, with a soft brown blanket coming up to the chin.

The girls had rehearsed over and over on the long day-marches from the Lowlands what they would say about their experiences and about Elie, and so when they came to a certain point in the descent, Seonaid bade them good-night and went along to the home of Dark Mairi.

Davie coming out at the door started back before her. 'Hallo, Davie!' she said, and her bright eyes challenged him. 'You're growing a big fellow!' He flushed and looked away. 'Is your granny in?'

'Yes, she's in.' And he drew back quickly. It was the same Seonaid, only stronger in some way, and quieter. It was not until she had left him that, with a sudden tightening in his breast, he recognised why she was quieter.

Dark Mairi looked up from the fire as Seonaid came in and greeted her, and not for a few moments did she get to her feet and take Seonaid's hand. 'It's all right, Mairi,' said Seonaid, and they sat down. 'I'm very tired. We walked a long way today. And I haven't been home yet. I'm not going to stay long with you, but I had to come to see you first and tell you that everything will be all right. No, I won't eat a thing, so you needn't get up.'

Seonaid spoke in a sensible voice but with a tired inflection in it. She was never soft like Elie at any time and now it was as if long days of wind and hardship had blown emotion out of her. Moreover, all that could be thought had been thought. She told Mairi a little about their journey and their experiences. They had been lucky enough to get work at once. Indeed they had very nearly been late, for the harvest down there was earlier than in the Riasgan.

The farmer had been honest enough but a driver. At night they were glad to crawl into the straw and lie down. Mairi listened to her. Seonaid fell on silence for a little, then went on in the same voice, 'We left Elie all right. She is not coming home because she got a job as a dairymaid. She'll stay on there for a year and make a little money. She said she would be able to make sure there would be work for us when we go down next year. That's why she's staying.'

Mairi knew this was the story the girls had made up. She could not speak.

'So I thought I would tell you first. We'll tell her mother tonight.' Seonaid smiled. 'Elie was so good at her work, so cheerful, they liked her so well, that they asked her to stay.'

Mairi looked at her with her dark misery-vacant face.

'When she called the cattle in the Gaelic they would come running. The people there laughed at that, for they had no Gaelic. And when she sung her little milking songs to them in the byre, the cattle let down their milk, so that the extra milk would pay her wages before she was done. So they were saying anyway. One night, at the harvest home, they asked us to sing. It was a terrible night of fun and dancing. The three of us wouldn't sing but we pushed Elie on. So – she sang. And she sang – you know the milking song that goes like this ... well, that one. And she bent down and did this, as if she were putting the pail between her knees, and then worked her hands up and down and sang. They were greatly taken with that. So she had to try it on the cows. And that was the beginning of it. She gave them more songs. And we gave them a waulking song, too, and I made up one or two verses – and the girls couldn't sing for laughing, because of the things I said about some of the people there, but they couldn't understand a word, so it was all right. Elie became a great favourite – so they prevailed on her to stay. That's why she hasn't come home.'

Seonaid, smiling, looked into Mairi's face. It was so still

that it seemed stupid and unable to understand anything. Yet all that she had said she could see falling upon it, like dew upon a stone, faintly darkening it with thought. She was beginning to believe! Her dry misery was taking the dew! Seonaid's smile twisted aside, but so faintly that even Davie, watching her face through a tiny interstice in the lattice work of the partition, wondered if his eyes had been deceived by a sinister flicker of the flame.

'I'll be going away down then, Mairi. Elie just told me to tell you she was fine.'

Mairi did not move. Seonaid looked at her again, and, though held by her vacant misery, grew also suddenly tired of it. In the last fortnight they had tramped over two hundred miles. It had been a long way home. She was weary, and now got up and moved away.

'Goodnight, Mairi. There's nothing more you would like to know?'

The old woman arose, the thin shallow smile on her face.

'There's nothing to know.' She came towards Seonaid. 'It was kind of you to come to me first.'

'Oh no,' said Seonaid, feeling she now wanted to be away at once. But Mairi was only accompanying her to the door.

'Goodnight,' Seonaid called, turning to look at the still figure. 'I'll come up soon again,' she had to cry. There was no answer.

A sharp spasm of misery and spite caught Seonaid as, in the gathering dark, she stumbled down the path from the cottage on her bare feet. It had taken them nearly a fortnight to come home, tramping day after day until they could have dropped; sleeping anywhere; driving sleet in their faces; then inches of snow coming over the Grampian mountains. 'There's nothing to know.' God, how true! she thought, her weary body full of a man's bitterness. The endless barren leagues of the Grampian mountains. Weary and barren as that, and dead as the ooze in the bogs and the frost in the passes. Burst chilblains, red hacks, and Anna, the youngest, sitting down and crying.

'There's nothing to know.' True enough for you, Dark Mairi, with your thin smile like wind on the grey loch of death! Your empty stupid earthy face! No questions, no tears, no gossip-gossip-gossip. 'Nothing to know.' How true that, dear Lord! *Nothing*!

It had been bitter enough – leaving Elie. They had gone because of Elie, had gone as her secret escort. Half their wages they had handed to her – and left her. No bagpipes blowing; no young men away to the wars in their case! Over two hundred miles on their bare stumps for a few shillings – to hide Elie – and leave her to her fate; then over two hundred miles back. The only red gleam of satisfaction in it all was the man she, Seonaid, had smashed in the face and then, when he had momentarily mastered her, bitten to the taste of blood. He had yelled, that brute!

Man, the brute. What was there to tell about him? or about woman's suffering?

Mairi was right. Dark Mairi of the Shore had plumbed it all. In some straw barn, Elie would have her travail. Beyond that red terrifying fact, what was to know? And the days after – the days and leagues – barren as the Grampian mountains – that Elie, cast out, would have to wander and tramp.

Who wanted a woman with a child? Not the brisk Colin going off to the wars of his chief. Not Gilleasbuig with prayers as long as the wrath of God. Not Bannerman with his, What's man's chief end? Seonaid knew what man's chief end was all right!

And now all she had to do was to tell these pretty stories about the singing! Nice little business for the ceilidh-house, that! And everyone would be delighted and think, Wasn't Elie the wonderful one, getting on so well! Perhaps she would be marrying a wealthy man down there yet!

Perhaps. Who knows!

That drained the last of her spite and in the lull of her mind she saw Mairi's face and caught some of its mindless calm. At that moment she could have sat with Mairi saying nothing for a year. Elie had told how kind Mairi had been to her, not with kindness but with an acceptance awful in its steady-faced look. She had told Elie everything that would happen to her body and what cares she should take and what she should do. All Mairi's morals and religion about the thing was a sigh which spent itself before she spoke. Thereafter everything was straightforward yet somehow heavy too, freighted with the darkness of the doom of the body. Dark Mairi was like a bit of the earth that was given hands and eyes; that took from the earth and the edges of the sea healing weeds and herbs; Dark Mairi of the Shore.

No one thought of her as a witch, yet there was an odd half-hinted, half-jocular conception of her as a being that went in and out of the earth, as a dark sea-beast can go out and in the caves of the ocean. Her shadow was sometimes seen when she wasn't there herself; and often her still face frightened boys in the wood.

Elie's story of her last night in the Riasgan had been a story like that. She had been up on the edge of the wood where Colin and she had so often made love. The bushes, the scents, the memories, the silence, were all around her, and then in the heart of them, as in the heart of a circle, her mind cried, 'No more.' Her mind cried it before she could stop it. *No more.* Ah, it wasn't within her own mind only; it was a great cry that rose and shattered the Riasgan. Elie could not explain the utter certainty which came upon her then that Colin and herself were separated for ever. She fell down and cried into the earth, beating back the certainty. She could not live without Colin. She would die. She clawed into the earth. 'I'll die. I'll kill myself. Listen to me.' Then as if the earth were indeed listening, it put a hand on her shoulder. In the dark, when she had scrambled to her feet, she saw the quiet figure of the earth; it was the figure of Dark Mairi. Up there on the edge of the wood, Mairi had sat with Elie's head against her breast, rocking her and crooning to her as to a child, crooning out over the Riasgan the pain and the tragedy of women, over the wide earth – from which on its winds came the stench of men's wars and the sounds of their machines grinding out starvation and disease and death for the poor.

When she won free of the hillside, Seonaid turned and looked up at the crest of the wood against the cold wintry sky. The thought of the warmth and generosity of Elie's love up there chilled her to a sudden shiver, and her last weeping in Mairi's arms became something dark and mythic, as if Mairi and Elie were figures in an old and terrible legend boding forth destiny for this place and for them all. Mairi the black earth mother that bore and nourished them, with love under her crooning mouth. Listening, Seonaid heard the wind that Gaelic legend feared and she from her travels had come to hate, hunting the wintry birch with its bared fangs and whining nostrils.

# PART TWO

In the little village of Golspie, the Drover, with some new white whisky inside him, was animated by the spirit of Galgacus, whose speech according to Tacitus he now had complete. Golspie, with its new inn going up and its proximity to the seat of majesty, was used these days to the sight of strange faces, and it was not a difficult matter for the Drover to gather an audience at any wayside. In fact, his bright eyes scanned faces with a certain piercing acuteness, for how could one otherwise be sure of his man? Not that the Drover would have cared who carried tales to the factor, so long as he had the satisfaction of knowing the bastard and letting him know that he knew him. There were not many such; hardly one at all, to tell the truth, yet eyes must hunt for that one as for the Devil.

For clearly enough the Devil had visited this county like a roaring lion seeking whom he might devour, and he was devouring them by the hundred. 'By the hundred!' cried the Drover. But that was nothing. He would yet devour them by the thousand. By the thousand! No, by the tens of thousands. He would not be satisfied until he had devoured every mother's son of them – and then devoured the mother herself!

'Now what form did the Devil take?' demanded the Drover, swaying a trifle on his feet, head stooping forward, eyes glinting with their suppressed joke. 'You think it was a lion. But a lion would need to have a belly as big as Ben Laoghal to hold that cargo. No, not a lion: a lion would be as useless as a capercailzie cock. It's the Beast,' said the Drover. 'The Beast of whom your minister has thundered to you out of the Revelations of St John. *I saw a beast rise up out of the sea, having seven heads and ten horns, and upon his horns ten crowns, and upon his heads the name of blasphemy. And the beast which I saw was like unto a leopard, and his feet were as of a bear and his mouth as the mouth of a lion: and the dragon gave him his power, and his seat, and great authority . . . And the people worshipped the dragon which gave power unto the beast; and they worshipped the beast, saying, Who is like unto the beast? Who is able to make war with him? And there was given unto him a mouth speaking great things and blasphemies and power was given unto him.* That's the Beast!' cried the Drover. 'But no one in the history of the world has ever known his name, and no one has ever read the meaning of his heads and horns except myself. Myself, Tomas son of Hamish, son of Tomas of St Donan's chair, shall reveal unto you what the learned and the sages have never discovered. Are you listening? Are you prepared?' The Drover looked from face to face, each expectant, smiling slightly, and more than slightly awed, then leaned still further forward and in a harsh whisper said, 'The name of the Beast is – Sheep.'

For a little time all were held by him as if he had indeed by some infernal or magical spell named the unnameable, and it was only when he overbalanced and snapped the link that the meaning entered them. By that time the Drover was drowning in his mirth.

'Sheep! . . .'

'A cheviot ewe!' he cried.

His high voice cracked, while his knees gave under him and brought him near the ground.

With a scared humour in their eyes, some of the listeners began to laugh at the Drover, whose head was now waggling in helpless profundity. The Beast and the Drover's drunkenness might have overcome them, did not the Drover's eyes keep glinting at them like the eyes of a weasel out of a ruined dyke. This burning life in the ragged figure held them at bay and dared and mocked them, yet included himself amongst them as one acknowledging the Beast, indeed as that one who had the originality and vision to perceive the Beast. His discovery, his joke – his infernal revelation!

Down the glen from where the inn was being built a woman and a small boy appeared at a little distance. With the shyness of a stranger, the woman hesitated when she saw the men, and, calling the boy, took his hand. By her clothes she was manifestly not a woman from these parts, and in her whole gait and appearance there was the manner of the vagrant, if not of the beggar. But through the change in the system of land tenancy, which had been taking place spasmodically further south, and by which large areas were being cleared of their human inhabitants to make way for sheep, the hapless vagrant was becoming a common enough sight in those places where still the ancient system prevailed. And this woman's apparent shyness was enough to stamp her as the decent timid dispossessed human being. The very clutch of her child's hand had an air of distress in it and, from the look she threw over shoulder, she would clearly rather have retired, had that been possible. But some greater difficulty must have threatened from behind, for she came on slowly. Before she had quite reached the group, three gentlemen appeared on the road behind her; and when the group saw them they did not even glance at the woman, but whispered amongst themselves, swiftly looking this way and that as if they wished to escape. Two of the men did in fact at once slip away. But the others, of less decision, were pinned by the Drover against their instinct. For the three who drew near were none other than the factor of the estate and the two gentlemen who had arrived by the packet vessel less than a week ago from Burghead, and who had been going over the country since their arrival carefully studying the land and all that it contained.

The Drover, like many of his race, was a man of cunning mind, and his native independence, finding it could clothe itself in a parable, gave an extra zest to his utterance. For he had disclosed to them so far only the meaning of the Beast itself. Now they knew who the Beast was. That was something that had never been known before. Why? Because there was no Beast in the whole history of the world that was devouring like this Beast. But that was only the Beast. Who were the seven heads and the ten horns on the Beast? '*Behold*,' said the Drover, '*three of them approach now!*'

He did not abate his sway nor in any way lower his voice, and seemed unaware of those who were now almost at his back. To them it might well appear that this strange figure had not heard their approach, and so the voice that could speak so loudly in their presence might not be conscious of its incivility. But on the other hand the natives at whom he spoke were manifestly so uncomfortable that he could hardly be otherwise than knowingly unaware. The factor's face showed its annoyance, but the two who were with him half-smiled in a measuring amusement at the sight of this queer half-drunken figure spouting a lingo of which they knew nothing.

Only when the factor stopped and looked at the men, who slouched their bodies awkwardly, did the Drover turn round and exhibit his surprise – and Gaelic welcome. 'How do you do, Mr Falcon?'

'You're drunk!' said Mr Falcon briefly, and clearly making a note of the fact.

At that moment the little boy, who had slipped his mother's grasp, appeared before one of the factor's two guests and begged, 'Gi'e me a haepenny.'

This gentleman was so taken aback at his own Scots tongue in a land of Gaelic and, whatever else might be said about it, of complete absence of the beggar, that the importunacy of the pale half-starved face made his brows involuntarily frown about grey hard eyes. The mother's voice was now heard calling the boy in harsh low tones of distress. Her language was Gaelic, so the boy had two tongues – unless he had merely got up a few begging phrases in English for such an occasion as this. It was a problem, and the grey intelligent eyes of Mr Heller were fond of problems.

'Run away!' ordered the factor angrily, as he turned from the weasel light in the Drover's eye and resumed his walk. The mother, who had come wretchedly back, snatched the boy by the arm and was hurrying off when Mr Heller enquired of the factor if this curious type was common, as he had not come across anything like it so far.

'Here!' called Mr Falcon. 'Stop!' And finally the woman, with lowered head, waited.

'Who are you?' asked Mr Falcon.

She lifted her face in a pleading look, then glanced away, scared and mute. The hair that escaped from the plaid drawn tightly over her head was brown as tow, and her eyes were the colour of half-melted demerara sugar. The cheeks had fallen in below high cheek bones in a gauntness of poverty that made it difficult to judge her age, though if the face had been filled out it might conceivably have been smooth enough and still in its twenties. There was in fact a softness about the whole face that gave its predominant hunted expression an extra misery. Altogether there was something too untidy and wretched about her, to draw sympathy. Her legs and feet were bare and red and frost-hacked; and the soiled plaid ill-concealed the rags beneath.

'Can't you speak? Where do you come from?'

'The Riasgan,' she said in a low voice.

'The Riasgan! And do they teach the children English in the Riasgan?'

She was dumb.

'Where have you come from?'

'The south.'

'From the south. And where are you going?'

'The Riasgan.'

'Do you belong to the Riasgan?'

'Yes.'

'What's your name? . . . Come on, answer me; what's your name?'

'Elie.'

'Elie what?' The factor was growing impatient. These dumb dour people always angered him. 'Answer me; are you married? . . . So you're not married.'

'Yes.' The low harsh defensive sound told its obvious story to the ears of the three men. But the factor went on remorselessly, 'Did you say yes? Where is your husband?'

'In the wars.'

'Oh, he is in the wars! I see. Did he belong to the Riasgan too?'

'Yes.'

'And you were married there?'

She was dumb, but when pressed again muttered, 'Yes.'

'Who married you? . . . So you don't remember who married you?'

The brown of her eyes began to dissolve.

'Look here, my woman,' said the factor, 'you go away south again where you come from. We have plenty of your kind here. There's no room for you at the inn up there! Nor at the Riasgan nor anywhere else on this land. Do you understand? You go to the south again. Do you hear me? Well, march off! Do you hear? Off! And never let me see your face again or—'

It might have been thought that a woman who, whatever else she had done, had clearly fended for herself and her offspring along the tortuous ways of poverty, and the more bitter ways of the outcast, would have become inured sufficiently to her position to stand against factor Falcon's strictures. But apparently not, for suddenly her whole miserable frame began to heave with sobs, that, as they mastered her, gathered a dreadful gulping noise.

As the three gentlemen turned away from this offensive sight they heard the Drover's voice rising to a frenzy. And, in fact, the Drover was now so moved by his own oratory, by the whisky he had drunk, and by the sight of the woman breaking away in tears from the three heads of the Beast, that he mixed his own revelation with that of Galgacus and St John.

'These are the heads of the Beast whose arrogance we cannot escape by obsequiousness and submission. These plunderers of the world, of our wives and sisters, moved by greed and ambition, with blasphemy set on the horn in their foreheads. They ravage and slaughter and usurp under false titles; and where they make a desert they call it peace.'

'Who is that fellow?' asked Mr Heller of the factor. At that point the Drover gave a final shout and started stumbling after the weeping woman and child. Mr Falcon threw a look over his shoulder and then stood still, clearly half of a mind to go back and interfere more definitely. For though he deservedly had the reputation of being a highly respectable and even just man, with almost finical neatness in his person and habits, he was completely overbearing in his demand for unquestioning submission to authority. And if authority meant *his* authority, yet, to do him justice, it also carried a conception of the immutable in it like the authority of God.

'He's a drover,' said Mr Falcon, moving on again, 'and he's drunk. But I shall find means of closing *his* gab.'

'What was he gabbing about?' asked his second guest, Mr Elder. 'I mean was he really making something in the nature of a speech, or was all that just gibberish?'

'I know very little of their dialect,' said Mr Falcon. 'But I do know that they are utterly ignorant, lazy, and filthy.'

'I mean,' said Mr Elder, rather interested in the point, 'was he really making sense when he spoke? We know they are unlearned, and their dialect can have only a very few words, because the things around them are few and they live pretty much like animals. But what could he have found to say intelligibly at such length?'

'They can say enough,' remarked Mr Falcon briefly, 'and what they can't say they drone and sing!'

He was annoyed at what had happened, for his guests had found everywhere complete civility. In fact the people had shown themselves so courteous and shy that, when they could manage it unobtrusively, they would go out of their way to avoid meeting himself and his gentlemen guests; which was delicate and proper of them.

'I had the feeling,' said Mr Heller, smiling, but getting at the real point, 'that he was rather trying to have one at us!'

'He wouldn't dare!' said Mr Falcon.

'Why is he sore? Has he been ejected?'

'No. He belongs to the main glen. His turn will come. But though you saw him drunk today, he is not often drunk – and never on business. He has the reputation of being a very honest man, as a matter of fact. But he droves the black cattle – and the days of the black cattle are numbered. He knows that. Besides, he is what you would call a bit of a character, and as he does business with the tacksmen, they sometimes make a lot of him. Oh, I know him all right. He's reputed to be a favourite of Captain Grant of the Riasgan. It was only drink, I assure you.'

'And of course, in a way, these tacksmen – like Captain Grant – are naturally enough, no doubt,' said Mr Elder, 'against this change of tenancy.'

'No doubt,' said Mr Falcon succinctly.

'So that – I see; your drover has probably been imbibing more than whisky!' Mr Elder was interested in the complete thought process.

'That woman,' said Mr Heller, turning the conversation, for clearly Mr Falcon was not yet sufficiently restored to pursue estate intricacies, 'that woman – all a heap of lies she told you?'

'Obviously – as I brought out,' said Mr Falcon. 'As a Riasgan woman, where did she get English? The fact is, the thing will have to be put a stop to. Whatever the ignorant may say about the change of tenancy we are trying to introduce – not that anything has been said except by those who don't know a damn thing about the circumstances and – and—'

'If I may interrupt you, Mr Falcon,' said Mr Elder soothingly, 'those people who were cleared by you off the Larg sheep farm – well, naturally they have a sense of grievance. Anybody who loses anything has a sense of grievance. I mean, that will pass. It's only temporary and, in a way, natural enough. After all, you have been very kind to them. There was no obligation upon the estate to do anything for them. The land is absolutely his lordship's, to do with as he likes. In Perthshire they were cleared off – and could go to the devil for all that Atholl cared. Atholl was within his rights. But here you have provided them with some new ground. And as that is to be your policy throughout, well, I mean, you won't get rid of temporary grumbling, for humanity has little gratitude, but at least you can congratulate yourselves on his lordship's unexampled charity.'

'That's true,' nodded Mr Falcon eagerly to Mr Elder's smile. 'That's the whole thing. And when that charity is not understood – well, you can understand how it annoys me.' He smiled himself.

'That woman—' began Mr Heller.

'Yes, as I was going to say,' and now Mr Falcon's voice was pleasantly excited, 'that must really be put a stop to. You mentioned Perthshire. There is also Ross-shire and Inverness-shire. The whole fact of the matter is that people who have been driven out of these counties would come in here; a few have come in and squatted, without a word! It's a fact. The thing is absurd. I – really – when you hear people talk—'

In this pleasant manner, and in complete accord, the

drover and the vagrant woman having suitably acted the part of stimulating their conversation, the three gentlemen continued on their way. And when, later that evening, Mr Falcon had gone to attend to some personal matter and to bring back some charts and figures, Mr Heller turned to Mr Elder, with the whole 'change of tenancy' policy of the estates as a query in his shrewd and now subtly calculating face.

'I don't know,' murmured Mr Elder, and he tilted his head back, considered the ceiling, and stuck out slightly his lower lip. When he looked at Mr Heller there flowed between the men a faint intangible excitement. 'It's big.'

'I know,' said Mr Heller. 'How big?'

Mr Elder's fingers investigated the bone of his knee. 'Well,' he hummed a note or two, 'are you going to take the farm?'

'Possibly,' answered Mr Heller. They were both silent. Mr Elder waited.

'You know,' said Mr Heller, 'that's not – the real issue.'

Mr Elder waited in a silence brittle as glass. Mr Heller broke it.

'The real issue is – are we going to take the whole thing?' His grey eyes were bright as steel. 'It's as big as that.' His hand closed on the table between them.

Mr Elder's eyes sought the roof. 'I know,' he said. 'But how?'

Mr Heller got up. The shrewdest thought to him meant action and came back in action on his body. He shoved his chair aside with his knee.

'Let us look into the whole damned issue,' he said, outrightly, his breath coming in a surge, 'for this is big, or I'm mighty mistaken. If it's big, then – are we to be in on it? And we've got to be in right away – or others will come and take what we hadn't the guts to take. This isn't the sort of thing that we have to suggest, or arrange, or work up. *It's the policy of the estate.* It's what *they're* going to do – though all that it means may have to be made plain to them. We've only got to walk in.'

'Uhm,' said Mr Elder abstractedly.

'Take that single Larg sheep-walk. Good God, the thing stretches from nearly one end of the county to the other. One hundred thousand acres! And it isn't as if we didn't know how the cheviot is going to do. Reed has shown in the north that the cheviot thrives as nothing else does. Remember that shepherd this morning who came and spoke to Falcon? You saw me having a talk with him afterwards. He's a Northumbrian; one of Atkinson and Marshall's men. Born a shepherd. Knows the Cheviots like the back of his hand. Doesn't like being up here much, but says the feeding is in it all right. I asked him what that meant exactly. And he confirmed the rotation of the alpines. When the snow melts, the cotton grass is found to have been growing rapidly; excellent and healthy food right up to the beginning of May, when it goes to seed. But right on its heels comes the deer hair and covers the whole place. Burning is needed for that, of course. All that rank heather will have to be burnt right out. Well, this deer hair and the bents keep them going until the end of July, when the cotton grass again springs up and, with the pry moss, comes into flower for the second time in September. After that the heather and more heating plants provide abundance until the winter.'

'And the winter?' asked Mr Elder.

Mr Heller stood quite still for a moment. Then he said, 'In these areas in the glens where at present the crofting townships are, there would be first-class wintering.'

'You mean—?'

'I mean,' said Mr Heller, 'that the whole of the interior of the county from one end to the other will have to be gutted out – man, woman and child.'

'To provide wintering for the sheep.'

'Yes.'

'I see,' said Mr Elder. 'It might take a little time.'

'Not so long,' said Mr Heller. 'Where tacks fall in – they won't be renewed. Within a few years, we could make a clean sweep.'

'As a legal man, you are satisfied of that?'

'Absolutely. When Falcon and I were going into the Culbaile farm he wants me to take, I made sure of that – not only for Culbaile but for all over.'

'It's pretty big,' said Mr Elder.

'Not too big – for a man like you,' said Mr Heller.

Mr Elder now looked at him. The stillness drew taut as a wire between them. 'How do you mean?' asked Mr Elder quietly.

'You are the one man in the north whose improvements on your own ground and knowledge of affairs and markets – the one man in the north fitted to carry out his lordship's improvements on his northern estates.'

To the last words Mr Heller gave the intonation of a man making a statement to some high authority not present – but understood. The half-ironic intention was perfectly appreciated.

'And you?' asked Mr Elder.

'Your under-factor, perhaps, and law agent – my time mostly being given to the practical work of farming – on rather an immense scale.'

'And the cash?'

'You wouldn't need cash. It's only I who should need cash from the estate – for its improvement.'

Mr Elder was silent for a thoughtful moment. 'And how do you know the estate is prepared to advance cash?'

'We may see – when Falcon comes back.' Then he added, 'Uh, about Falcon, he would have to be . . . what do you think of him?'

'Of Falcon?' Mr Elder smiled.

'There he is,' said Mr Heller, and as he smiled back the tension he had been under eased most pleasantly. They were actually relieved when Mr Falcon came in, and turned to meet him agreeably.

Mr Falcon had charts with him and soon the three men were bending over these charts spread open on the table. But when questioning Mr Falcon, his two guests were indirectly speaking to each other. For example, Mr Heller said, 'Now let me see if I've got this clear. Take this glen Strathuile as an instance. It stretches from the sea – here – right up and up to the Heights – and then—'

'Yes,' Mr Falcon took him up; 'then it goes down – excellent sheep ground all that – right into the sea – there on the north. Apart from some small bits – thereabouts – all this hasn't yet been touched.'

'It's an immense stretch of country.'

'It is,' agreed Mr Falcon.

'How many families would you say are living there?'

'I couldn't tell you offhand precisely at the moment. Perhaps two thousand or more.'

'As many as that?' said Mr Elder. 'Hm. It would be rather a job removing all these, wouldn't it?'

'Well, of course, we haven't got that length yet!'

'No, but . . . uh . . . would you be prepared?' asked Mr Elder mildly, as he examined the map.

'We are prepared for anything – if we get the offers. That's what it amounts to,' said Mr Falcon.

'It is really all a business matter. I quite agree,' nodded Mr Elder. 'By the way, is that really true about the Ross-shire men who had some old grazing – on whose estate again? They paid £15 a year for it, but a sheep farmer from the south offered and got it at £350 a year – half the value of the whole estate?'

'Quite true,' said Mr Falcon. 'But we need hardly hope to get an increase quite so satisfactory, though of course we are naturally not making the change for the worse!'

They laughed at Mr Falcon's joke, and then Mr Heller said, 'Here, Elder, I think that's hardly fair of you, reminding

Mr Falcon of such terrible extortion at the very moment he is fixing up a price for me for Culbaile!'

'Ah, but,' declared Mr Falcon, twinkling, 'the price is already fixed.'

'Oh, is it?' said Mr Heller, smiling a trifle self-consciously.

There was a moment's pause, but the business was rather large for Mr Falcon to come out with it in any light manner.

'We recognise, Mr Falcon, that all this,' and Mr Elder drew the backs of his fingers over the charts, 'is really a tremendous affair. In a sense, we can see it has a very direct bearing on Mr Heller's decision. This farm of Culbaile is quite a tidy proposition in itself. It raises the question of removing existing tenants and expending pretty hefty sums of money on improvements. Assuming all that is done, it then raises the question of a continuing market – and continuing peaceful conditions among the community. I think you will admit there is the element of a gamble in it to a considerable extent. Let me put one aspect of it this way: you are prepared to go ahead with your designs. You get the offers – satisfactory offers, let us say; you accept them and clear the ground. Well, two thousand families from that main glen – have you any reason to suppose that they will not offer physical resistance, and by means of public outcry and what not bring at least some of your plans into danger? Please do not imagine,' he added somewhat hurriedly, 'that I am deliberately suggesting obstacles. It's merely that we should like to have your ideas.'

For Mr Falcon's eyes had glistened at mention of resistance. In fact anything suggesting lack of respect for, and lack of instant obedience to, authority never failed to empurple his fresh ruddy cheeks.

'My ideas are quite simple. By the law of the land a man may do what he likes with his own. In this case, however, he is not only doing what the law will protect and assist him in doing: he is also benefiting the land. I think we have gone into all that,' said Mr Falcon with some restraint.

'I know, I know,' replied Mr Elder. 'I thoroughly agree. But there was some trouble – some bloodshed even – in Ross. I was merely wondering how they'll take it here?'

'They'll have to take it,' said Mr Falcon. 'I know them. They'll pretend this and that. But they're ignorant, shiftless, and lazy. They'll grumble, but they'll go. There's only one bad nest of them and they're up on the Heights – MacHamishes, a sept of the Gunns, thoroughly godless dangerous ruffians. There are some Gunns, too, but they'll be evicted first of all, because they know enough to organise the Strath – and they would. All that lot live by breaking the law. It's worth a man's life to try to serve a summons there. In fact one man who did try was never heard of again. But they'll go – in a body.'

'Where?' asked Mr Elder.

'They'll ship abroad – to the devil, and good riddance.' Mr Elder laughed.

'However,' said Mr Falcon, 'that's all right. All over they're a timid half-starved lot. You needn't worry about that. And the Church will help the law in the matter.'

'The Church? Do you mean the ministers of these people?'

'I do,' said Mr Falcon. 'Every one of them will threaten their people with the fires of hell, if they don't go peaceably.'

'Really? All of them?' Mr Elder sat back.

'Yes. There is one weakling, named Sage, I hear, who may lament with them – but he doesn't count. And, anyway,' said Mr Falcon, 'it is intolerable that we should even have to contemplate trouble from them. Are we not bettering the estate, are we not civilising the people, rousing them out of their sloth, aren't we going to make this instead of a peat bog a great productive area for feeding England with wool and mutton? Isn't his lordship putting his own money against the Government's to construct roads and bridges? And on top of all that aren't we giving them plots by the sea and – and encouraging them to fish? Do you expect us to wipe their – their noses?'

His guests laughed. Mr Falcon was a respectable God-fearing man, neat in his person and habits, but the rumours of what the people who had been turned off the Larg sheep-walk were saying about the sasunnoch sheep-farmers and their sasunnoch shepherds had for many months annoyed him acutely. There had, too, been one or two small 'incidents'.

With their laughter, his two guests seemed to wave the matter aside as being in truth unnecessary to discuss further. What really had to be discussed were the Culbaile terms, and on these Mr Heller was sure that Mr Falcon was not going to – well – rob him!

There was quite a little good-natured rallying before Mr Falcon finally said, 'Three hundred Scots acres at twenty-five shillings an acre. The mountain pasture behind. And an advance of £1500 at $6\frac{1}{2}$% – to assist in the improvement.'

Later that night, Mr Heller and Mr Elder, well warmed with the whisky that had sealed the Culbaile bargain, were taking a last breath of air to ease their long restraint.

'God,' said Mr Heller, 'I'm in it now! The whole thing is shaping like fate!'

'It's big,' said Mr Elder. 'Corn and sheep – with Europe in its present state – the industrial areas growing – Bonaparte doing his best to shut us off – there will be a demand for this territory right enough!'

'I'll have a shot at the corn, if that's what you mean,' said Heller. 'I'll guarantee you that. But the big thing here is sheep. I know it.' His native accent came strongly through. 'Old Falcon is an important man of business – with the brains of a confidential clerk!' He chuckled. 'He talks about the natives, like a Napoleon Bonaparte!'

'Don't let us miscall our friend Bonaparte,' said Mr Elder. 'By the way, do you know that Falcon exacts a tithe on the fish landed in the village – one fish out of every ten for his own use.'

'No!'

'He does. The emperor levies his taxes.'

'Good God! I've heard a lot about the great Gaelic people and the Gaelic heroes and heaven knows what. When you think of them in these bloody filthy little cabins – with Falcon their almighty! They're sheep!'

'Not yet,' said Mr Elder.

\*

It had been a hard winter with plenty of high wind and the roof of Dark Mairi's cottage had suffered, particularly over the byre gable. The young man, sitting on a stone seat that leaned against that gable, was busy twisting a heather rope. He had started by taking one long heather stem, doubling it, and weaving into and from each end stems which he picked up one by one from the pile on the ground beside him. The twisted double strand of the rope thus made was extremely strong, yet not half so thick as his wrist, which was slender enough. His fingers too were slender but deft and persuasive. He whistled a low liquid little tune, drawing out a note now and then to help his fingers or to suspend the work altogether while his eyes estimated the rope's length. At one of these pauses his glance was caught by two figures on the skyline. It was a clear chill May evening and against the darkening hillside the sky was a bright frosty green. The diminutive figures were outlined extraordinarily distinctly, and he thought of them at once as a mother and child; for even at that distance the woman's shoulders seemed rounded and drawn by her plaid and the child beside her stood arrested in her thought.

They stood so long that he became quite silent and still watching them. Obviously they were strangers. There was even something sad and outcast about them, as about all figures wandering on the edge of light. And cold. Vagrants. He gave an involuntary shiver. It was cold. His face was pale and thin, with dark eyes, and black slightly uptilting eyebrows. An attractive unusual face, with some of the detachment of the moor adder about it.

At last the figures came over the horizon and he lost them. It was growing dusk and the hillside heath was still a dead dark brown. Lifting his head after a little while, however, he discerned them coming across the hill-breast towards the cottage. A faint ironic expression flickered in his eyes. If they thought there was anything to be got here, they were hopeful! They kept coming, and presently the woman's features could be distinguished. He got to his feet, even as she stopped and looked at him, and with an odd catch at the heart went round the gable corner and in at the door. Dark Mairi was twisting wool by the fire-light.

'Granny, there's a woman and a small boy out there.'

A curious hushed note in his voice arrested her. She looked up at him and her mouth fell slightly open.

'Who are they?'

'I don't know.'

In the quietness the room waited for the footsteps that presently came in at the door and along to the partition like footsteps in the half dread of a dream. On the threshold the woman stood quite still and looked across the fire at Dark Mairi.

There was silence for a long time, then Dark Mairi said, 'Is it you, Elie?'

'Yes,' answered the woman.

When Dark Mairi had stared at her yet a little while, she got up and went towards her. The little boy clung to his mother's skirt. Dark Mairi looked at him and looked up into Elie's face. She caught Elie's hands. 'Come and sit down, my sweetheart; you're cold, cold.'

Elie's face became gaunt, and when she sat down she lowered her head.

'Every night I have thought of you,' said Mairi; 'and when I smoored the fire I put up a word for you in my own mind. Warm yourself at the fire, my little calf.' She banked the peat in closely; flames leapt up, and she added new fuel to the outside of the fire ring. 'Warm you yourself, my love. That's you!' said Dark Mairi, her thin monotonous voice going husky with welcome that had in it a haunted undernote, as if they were going through a memory of what had happened long ago.

Elie's head drooped a little lower. From the cold circles of the world she had wandered by many a blind path, drawn back to this fire at the centre, at the heart. Its warmth went all around and over her, closing her in, like soft wings shutting her away from life, suffocating her. She felt Mairi's hand on her head, and her body began to shake and tremble as in a shivering fit.

'Poor lassie, you're cold,' said Mairi.

With a choking cry, Elie threw her face upon Mairi's lap. Mairi's hard firm body, sitting upright, began to sway. The little boy stood gazing at her, fascinated. Then as the old woman's speaking voice began to pass into a rhythmic chant, something seemed to pierce him from sources beyond the experience of his little life and in a passion of crying he tumbled to the floor and clutched at his mother. Davie, who had been standing in the shadows with his pale watching face, made quietly for the door, crossing the line of vision of the old woman, whose staring eyes were blind.

Outside he listened, his expression held in a queer silent half-laugh. Then he looked about him and began to breathe. He slipped away very quietly and by the time he was going down the hillside, the smile came twisting drily now and then about his mouth. Sometimes he paused as if he were listening; then he would snick a grey grass and his lips would curl from the sharp teeth that chewed it.

For all the wariness with which he outflanked old Angus's barn, Kirsteen, hurrying round its corner, ran bodily into him. She drew back in a flurry. 'What a fright you gave me!' She threw back her fair hair, some of which had entered his mouth. Her colour mounted. He looked awkward and guilty, as if she had found him out in something secretive. All in a moment, their bodies caught an extraordinary awkwardness in which there was a strange naked shame. The colour ebbed from her face and her features twisted in a frightened way that exposed them and stripped them bare. The smile on his pale face disfigured it, left it thin and hungry and weak. 'Oh,' she said, 'I—' She glanced on each side of him, 'Oh,' and went blindly back the way she had come.

They had been friendly hitherto, with perhaps an extra teasing interest now and then. Nothing horrid like this had ever happened before – and it had happened all in a moment without any reason in the world.

He drew back, leaned against the wall, the odd characteristic smile arrested on his face. His heart was beating painfully, as it can beat in a body exquisitely underfed. But if the encounter made his blood labour, he did not think much about it, and in a few moments he was peering round the corner of the barn. The sight of Angus og at the house door made him withdraw his head quickly and he stood as it were on tiptoe hearkening for the footsteps to approach, when he would immediately hurry away. They did not approach. Presently one or two men and two or three girls drifted into the house. He heard the laughter in their greeting voices. It was getting dark. He looked around at the world bleak and cold in darkling mound and black shadow. Old Mairi's upright body and staring eyes above the two figures on the floor came before him, her weaving hand and high thin voice. There was nothing in the house but a few handfuls of meal. He lost himself for a time gazing away in front of him, and his face grew ghost-white with the cold. Old Angus's voice at his elbow made him jump.

'What are you doing here, Davie boy?' The voice was gentle and kind, the eyes peering at the lad.

'Nothing,' said Davie. The beat in his throat choked him.

'Won't you come into the house?'

Davie was looking away into the night. Angus's fingers went round his elbow and held their grip, but he did not speak again.

'Elie came home tonight,' said Davie.

'Elie!' repeated the old man.

'Yes.'

'What is it, Davie? What's wrong?'

'Nothing,' said Davie. 'She has a little boy with her. It's her own.'

'Has she? God's blessing on her! She was a sweet girl, Elie. Don't you worry about that, Davie. The women all knew long ago, anyway. I'll tell Anna when I get her alone this night. She'll fix up every thing. She's wise, Anna. You and I will say nothing. Won't you come in, man, for a little?'

'No, thanks,' said Davie.

Angus peered at him. 'What is it, Davie?' he whispered.

The boy's face was turned from him and the body was stiff and lean as a post. Listening acutely, Angus thought he heard the sound of swallowing, and in a moment he felt that tears were creeping down the drawn cheeks. He gave the boy time, and presently Davie said abruptly, 'We have nothing in the house.'

The grey void of the world pressed upon Angus and smothered his speech. Poor lad! God between him and the torn pride that had to admit so terrible a thing.

'How could you have anything?' he answered at last. 'It's the great wonder you have managed to keep things going at all. In the winter before last when your four beasts perished, wasn't it hard enough on you without the frost getting at your potatoes after that cloud burst that nearly swept you away with it? And then the old cow dying this spring – though she was old enough and had stood by you well. Families get hit like that now and then, and often it takes them years to recover. Indeed I've been meaning many a time to speak to you directly about it, for I knew fine that no drover had taken a beast of yours last July and you had the rent to pay. But when I did hint at anything, you always put me off. But, Davie boy, I'm glad you have spoken to me now – and you can trust me to let it go no further.'

'I could have sold a young beast – we had enough to pay the rent – but—'

'But you had to work your stock up again. Of course. God bless me, what else! Come on into the barn with me, Davie. It's the time of year when it's lean enough for most of us, but I smelt the summer this morning and I've been turning the potatoes in the dark corner of the barn so that the sprouts won't be growing on them.'

On his knees, old Angus kept whispering to Davie while he stuffed a small straw bag with potatoes. There were two young calves in the byre. 'You wait here, Davie, and I'll see if I can get a drop of milk somehow for the child. I know where there is a bottle.' He stopped. 'Have you salt?'

'Yes,' said Davie.

It was not very long before Angus returned with a bottle of milk and some butter wrapped in a cheese-cloth. 'I was in luck's way,' he said. 'Here you are, boy. Smuggle the bottle back tomorrow and we'll have a talk together.'

'Thanks.'

'Off you go now!'

Davie stood quite still for a moment, then, without looking at his old friend or saying a word, walked away. Angus watched him fade into the dark and turned towards the house. Kirsteen was alone by the gable wall. He asked her what she thought she was doing there. She was his great human ally, particularly in the matter of the linnets. She was a linnet herself.

She did not speak for a little, then in a curious strained voice she asked, 'Are they hungry?'

'Hush!' he said. 'Didn't I tell you not to say anything about the milk?'

She was silent.

'Come on in.'

'I'll be in in a minute,' she answered in the same voice, and turned away towards the back of the house.

*

When Davie entered the outer door, the young cow lowed in a manner that pulled him up abruptly, and of their own accord his nostrils began sniffing. All in a moment he felt certain that his granny had bled the beast, for in times of want, when nothing was left but a small hoard of meal, a palatable and nourishing change of diet could be given by mixing the meal and some fresh blood into cakes and frying them. A pang of disappointment shot through the boy, and for a moment, curiously revulsed, he wondered whether he should walk in with his store of food or not. Only once had his granny bled a beast to his knowledge, and the occasion would sometimes rise in his mind with a strange mixed effect of religion and horror. He had sat waiting for his granny, listening to every sound the cow made, hungry-sick with excitement, until his granny had at last come in with the new blood in the bowl.

He went on, however, almost at once, and as he entered he saw Elie get up from the fire, but he did not look at her until he had laid his goods on top of the meal-chest in the dim corner by the foot of his granny's bed, then he turned round and Elie said to him shyly, in the soft brown voice he had never forgotten, 'Davie, what a size you have grown!'

He shook hands, smiling and looking down and to the side. The smell of singed oatmeal was in the air. All at once he liked Elie, but could not look at her.

'What have you there?' asked his granny.

'A few things,' he answered, with an indifferent voice but a pleasant manner.

'What things?' She got up and came towards him.

'A little milk for the boy, a few potatoes, and a bit of butter.'

His granny stared at him. 'Where did you get them?'

'Never you mind!' Smiling, he moved towards the fire. The little boy was watching him with profound attention. He bent down, stopped himself from asking the name, and picking up the thin figure lifted him in the air. The solemnity on the young face never altered. When Davie began to tickle him as he set him on his feet again, the boy drew back.

'Don't be frightened of Davie, Colin; he only wants to play with you,' said Elie.

The name Colin flashed through Davie's thought and sent a momentary heat pricking at his face. He stooped again, but neither the boy nor himself made more of it at the moment. Dark Mairi had in any case now investigated Davie's gifts. 'Have you had nothing to eat?' she asked him.

'Uh – no,' he answered, carelessly.

She turned away, close-mouthed, and put on the iron pot.

Everything that came from old Angus's place was good. 'There's both bounty and quality in his store,' was one saying, and 'He never put a poor mouth on it,' was another. His potatoes certainly did justice to Angus's reputation. Their old tough skins burst with goodness, and the mealy bits and balls slowly melted the butter to running gold. And as the potato melted the butter, so the tongue melted the potato. It was better than fairy food because it was hot and cheerful and the nostrils got all prickled with the flavour in the rising steam. There was one thing about Dark Mairi: she was not mean. She could scrape and save and gather a bit here, a bit there, with a neater economy than the niggardly; but when the time demanded it, she would give away her store with a blessing, and on the morrow set to the gathering again. Had she been expecting guests, there would certainly have been food awaiting them, though it had been no more than nettle broth. Surprised in her moment of destitution, she had drawn blood from her cow and fired cakes for the mother and child who had travelled on bare feet all that day and eaten nothing. The beast would recover rapidly for the grass was springing in sheltered spots here and there up the burn and into the hollow. The economy of life she held balanced in an unconscious wisdom. And that wisdom now produced a large pot of potatoes. For at such a moment it was not waste to eat much. On the contrary, it induced cheerfulness and belief and hope, the conquerors of tomorrow. Davie ate potato after potato. Dark Mairi picked out good ones for him. She also picked out good ones for Elie. 'They're all the same!' she said. For Colin she put a little milk in a bowl. He gulped it down at a draught. 'That's you!' said Dark Mairi; though well Elie knew he should have taken the milk in little sips while eating his potatoes. When the potatoes were all eaten, Mairi poured out some more milk and they each had a good mouthful. The milk of the small cattle was very rich and left a fine silken taste. Mairi's own old lean stomach was so taken aback by the comforting meal that it made her belch abruptly. Davie's eyes met Elie's and, smiling, he got up.

When he was gone out, Elie asked about him, and Mairi, as she scraped every skin and speck of potato into a little heap, was complimentary. 'I don't know where he got the food tonight, but maybe it was from old Angus. I never expected it, for he would cut his tongue out rather than beg anything. Though he's very good at bringing things home. He had half a deer in the winter time and I salted it. He had a good few rabbits too, and more than one salmon. But I cannot close an eye when I know he's off like that, for if he was caught it would be the end of him – and indeed of me too. All the rivers are being watched, and you can hardly stir out of the place but there's an eye on you. This life is no longer what it was in the old days. It is not.'

'Had you a bad season, the year before last? I was often thinking about you. It was a harvest year of famine all over.'

'It was bad enough. We lost four of our best beasts. We haven't got over it yet. I have only three hens left. There had never been the like of it for twenty-five years. And then somehow there was this talk of clearing people off the land, and that did not help any. Poverty can be borne well enough when it comes in nature, but – I don't know – when the spirit is troubled in itself with fears it takes the heart out of the body. Indeed I sometimes think it takes it out of the land too. I have seen the earth glad to take the seed, and I have seen it with the sour look that draws in the seed to rot it.'

The two women would talk now the whole night. There was in truth a terrible hunger of talk upon them. The little boy with his round tight belly fell into a deep sleep, but Elie merely smiled down at him and went on talking. The fire was warm, their bodies were comfortable as much from the food as from their spent emotions. Indeed Elie felt bathed and a little remote and exalted. Her voice often caught the old accent with its reflective honey-sweetness, and the girl of nineteen softened the features of the woman of twenty-seven. Mairi, who did not look a day older to Elie's eyes, sat with upright body and hands upon her knees, staring through the fire at Elie's pictures, making little nasal sounds now and then and sometimes, under the stress of Elie's struggles, swaying a little and shaking her head.

For Elie had had many strange and terrible adventures. The farming life had been hard enough to begin with, especially for her. These people in the south thought very little of the Highlanders. They called them a wild hungry thievish lot. 'They looked on us as savages,' said Elie. 'When they heard us talking, they laughed and cried ach-och-ach-och and cleared their throats and spat. The little boys shouted, "Kilty-kilty-cauldbum!" They thought we were trollops – and worse. But we did not understand their talk. Seonaid was good too! Oh, she was good! She fairly put them in their place! What's happened to her, Mairi?'

'She married Murdoch, the fiddler. They have got a tidy little place and he's got a loom and does an extra bit of weaving.'

'Oh, I'm glad!' said Elie, and her eyes sparkled. 'I got terribly fond of Seonaid. She has the courage of two men. Is there any family?'

'One,' said Mairi, 'and one coming.'

'Proud Seonaid! Tell me—'

'Tell me yourself first,' said Mairi.

'Seonaid was sorry leaving me. Indeed she was for staying, and you have no idea how I had to fight with her to get her to go away. But in the end she went and the others with her, but not before they made me take half their money. I think my heart would have broken in me that night when I was alone in the hay-loft, if it hadn't been for the thought of what lay before me. And as the days went on that made me cunning, and the great fear was the hiding of my money. Then something began to happen. I was working for little more than my food, for the farmer's wife was terribly mean. When anyone is mean here it is a joke amongst us; and when it's really necessary the mean one will give with the rest though it's tearing the heart out of him. But this woman's meanness was so terrible that you thought of her heart not as one stone but as two stones grinding on each other. It was awful. Well, her husband was a silent red-faced man, kind enough, but sly and a hard driver maybe because of his wife. She was hard in the face and her eye was like whinstone, and she smiled on Sundays to people dressed like herself. He was good enough to me and would some-times stand in the byre and point to things, saying *coo, milk, coggie* and so on in the English. He always laughed softly when I said the words after him. I'm sorry for him. Then I began to feel always that he was about. If I was singing very quietly to the cows to let down their milk, I would feel him listening or watching me. I began to get afraid of him. It went on like that. Twice he tried to catch me. Then one night in the loft he came in. By that time I had a stick always by me. It was dark. I got up and fell. He kicked over me. He got me. I cried out loud. I had lost the stick. He was on top of me. Then her voice cried behind us in the dark. It was so terrible that he began to choke me with his hands. He didn't know what he was doing. I lost my senses. I remember hearing her voice far away, "*Come oot o' that!*" Then I came to myself, and if I didn't know all her words, I knew what they meant. She hardly gave me time to gather my things, before she turned me out in the middle of the winter's night. And in the middle of that night I started my wanderings.'

Elie could not get employment anywhere at that time of the year. There was terrible misery and destitution in the villages and little towns where people worked all day long like slaves. She was afraid of them, afraid of their faces, and, besides, her condition was now becoming such that she could not hide it. So she kept to the lonely country places, buying what she needed in a frugal way and sleeping where she could. Once or twice she was challenged for being a vagrant, but she always got over that by saying that she was just passing through the parish on her way home, which was in the far north. It was not an easy time, and often and often she lay and wept and wished that she was dead. Days and days she never spoke to a soul – and even if she did see anyone coming, she would hide. This loneliness grew on her and she became frightened of it and of herself. Her mind too would keep dwelling on the past. 'Sometimes I would cry "Mairi! Mairi!" and I would get all knotted up in a convulsion and I would roll there and cry out loud loud, for I knew no one would hear me. I think maybe I was going out of my mind. And then I met the tinker woman.

'She came out of Appin, this woman. She was a Stewart, with hair like my own, and she had the Gaelic – different from mine but we could understand each other well enough. There was a few of them and at first I was terrified. But she befriended me and I think the only thing I was able to hide from her that first night was the money that I had folded up in a band and tied round my skin.'

She was silent and Mairi said, 'She would help you, for she would be skilly and would have delivered many a woman.'

'Yes,' said Elie, in a low voice. 'It was dark, and when Colin came she asked me if I wanted him to live or not.'

'Did she? It was hard on you, that.'

'Oh, it was,' said Elie; then she breathed heavily through her nostrils and composed herself. Mairi waited for her.

'When I said yes,' said Elie, 'she told me to think of what it would mean to me. Myself and the child would be taken up as vagrants and sold into bondage. If I stole anything, even a turnip out of a field, I would be put in prison or transported to the plantations beyond the seas. And the boy himself would be working twelve hours a day before he was six years old and would be slaving like that for ever. And oh, those terrible faces of the colliers – the brute faces – that used to frighten me when I was wandering – they came to me then. And I saw little Colin with a mouth like a snout – it was pretty hard on me.'

'It was indeed,' said Mairi. 'Are the colliers like that then?'

'They had been slaves – tied to the mines from their birth. They could not leave. No one else could employ them. There was one village of them – oh, Mairi, I will never forget their faces. Great big mouths, thick lips – open like that. They ran after me in my sleep like swine. Terrible. Terrible. A law had been passed the year before freeing them from their actual slavery. But they were there still. What were they to do? And in other work it was as bad. They were sending children, years younger than Colin here, to work from four in the morning till nine or ten at night in new factories or mills: droves of them, and them crying like the lambs on the hills here when you take the ewes from them. In one place I knew they buried them all together in a field.'

'That could not be true.'

'Yes, it's true,' said Elie.

Mairi looked at her. 'Not the boy there?'

'For over two years,' said Elie.

'Mother of Christ,' intoned Mairi, smooring life's fire in the ash.

Elie bent her head and uncurled the child's fingers.

Mairi, having looked at the fingers, began to sway.

'The most terrible crime of all,' said Elie, 'is theft. A woman was transported to slavery beyond the seas for seven years for stealing a cotton gown.'

'Seven years!'

'A woman and her child were put in prison for sixty days for taking a little meal.'

Mairi looked at Elie's drawn mouth. 'You – Elie?'

Elie nodded.

'My heart's love! my grief!'

'You make me softer, Mairi, than I have been for many a year. Many's the time I dreamed of this. The memory of poverty here – it's difficult to tell you – it seemed like something that brought out all the kindness and sweetness in the heart. Through it we saw each other to the bone. If we had been quarrelling, it drew us together. And the boy who gave – and the woman who took – like Davie coming in there with these gifts for Colin and myself. The memory of that would tear at the heart. And these hard times of ours were far and seldom among the good times.'

'Why did you not come back sooner?'

'I don't know that I would ever have come back, if it hadn't been for the boy. You can understand what it will be for me in this place now, Mairi. It's over for me, but if you will keep me here, I will work hard for you.'

'Don't speak like that, Elie.' But Mairi saw the gaunt disillusion behind Elie's face, even if that face might still come all over soft and break weakly in tears. For Mairi knew that no circumstance, however it may affect action or response, ever alters the essential nature of a human being.

'Anyway, it would have been difficult for me to come back,' said Elie, 'for we were always in one difficulty or another, except for one year. I had happy moments too. I will never forget the morning I left the tinker wife and had my young bairn all to myself. I was just beside myself with happiness. I cannot tell you how foolish I was and the things I did. He was as good as gold too and crowed and played with me. I think I was happy too, for a queer reason, and that was that I felt I should have given the tinker woman a little bit of money – and I hadn't. But I hadn't because I was hoarding it up for the little one. Somehow even that made me happy. For I had a plan. My plan was this. I would find a country woman who would take the child while I got work on a farm. I was prepared at first to work for nothing; but my money I would give to the country woman. Many and many a poor respectable woman would be glad of the chance of a few shillings. My story would be that I was married, but after my husband had gone to the wars I was cleared off the croft. That has happened in many a place anyway,' said Elie.

'And will happen in many more,' said Mairi, 'so you were right enough.'

The women were silent for a little.

'If Colin – had known – he would—'

'He would indeed,' said Mairi, 'and that's certain.'

'Mairi – you are not against me for it?'

Mairi looked at Elie's averted face, as if the idea that she might be in a position to judge life were strange.

'No,' she answered.

Elie's eyes filled. 'I knew that,' she said. 'You would do the same for any animal. I love you for that.'

'Tell me,' said Mairi, 'what happened after you left the tinker woman.'

'Yes. Well, there I was. It was a sharp but sunny early spring day. I gave him a drink in the corner of a little wood and sang to him and he went to sleep. Then I wrapped him up and put him on the ground and opened my clothes and took off the band with my money which was tied round my middle here. I opened it out, and do you know what was in the place of my money? . . . little flat round pebbles.'

Mairi looked at her stupidly. She didn't understand what Elie meant at all.

'The money had been stolen,' explained Elie. 'It had been taken out of the band, and the stones put in its place, so that I would think I still had it.'

Mairi's mouth remained open, and indeed for years afterwards this simple theft obsessed her mind. Presently she got it clear that Elie had not a farthing left and she began questioning her about whether she had ever taken the band off her waist, who had been near her, could she remember if she had done this or that, might it have been one of the boys in the tinker camp for surely it could not have been the woman. The mysterious vanishing of the money seemed to grip her more than the position in which the lack of the money left Elie. Nor was she in the mood to listen to any more for a time, but sat with loaded mind marvelling over what she had heard.

Elie too grew silent, for the tale of her wanderings would fill many a long night and the prospect at that moment held a strange warm comfort for her. She had not come home so much as come back into a place of old security and detachment, like her den up in the rocks. The stream of life would flow past her, while she sat like a traveller telling her story. And Mairi was the great one to tell it to, because she did not judge, but was herself of those who are judged.

When Davie came back he found them still talking, and Elie looked at him with friendly brown eyes that both knew and wondered where he had been; bright dumb eyes, craving and quiescent. He glanced away, smiling, the frosty night pale on his face.

Mairi compelled Elie and the little boy to take her bed. They needed one great sleep, she said. Tomorrow Davie would make a place for Colin beside himself. They wrangled over this until Elie gave way.

Lying in her bed, Elie listened to the burn as it came tumbling down through the frosty night from the crest of the silent wood.

*

Elie's return fitted into the state of mind of the Riasgan with an almost symbolic aptness. Stories of the way folk were being cleared off the land to make room for sheep provided most of the talk these days. Nor was it vague talk as of something happening far away: it was happening just over the hills, and now and then a crofter who had been evicted would be personally known to a man here, or down in the main glen, who spoke at length, recalling the virtues of the dispossessed, as if something had happened to him fatal as death. Tomas the Drover could entertain folk for whole nights on the subject, leaving behind him an impression of profound uneasiness.

In this way the ancient peace of the Riasgan suffered invisible disintegration; at times it became vague and formless, spread open, waiting for the stone to fall and crush it; at other times it curled its fear back into a bud that youth carried with a laugh; for there remained the feeling that what had happened to places over the hill could not happen to the Riasgan even if they were all on the same estate. Her ladyship, the chief, could not clear the whole of her lands. She could hardly sweep clean a county! And already there had been such an outcry against the iniquity of what had been done, that those who still held possession could feel safe. Their best plan was to hole up and say nothing.

And the ministers of the gospel all over were preaching obedience to the law of the land, and many of the finer natures amongst the congregations, bred in the fear of God, were sensitive to the cardinal stricture: God was visiting His wrath upon the people for their sins. The ways of God are not only inscrutable: they are always just. It was inconceivable that the ways of God could be other than just. And it wasn't as if He did not know. He saw everything, even to the fall of the sparrow.

Unto Caesar the things that are Caesar's. Unto the chief, her land, and all that pertained thereto. The law ordained it; the forces of the law would maintain it. Those who rebelled would be outcast from His Church. Thus did the ministers, who held their charges from the chief, support against the people the policy of the 'change of tenancy'. And indeed they did so with much harsher and directer injunction than was contained in any heavenly argument; for with factors, ground officers, and other servants of the estate they threatened and bullied in other than God's name.

There were rebels, however, to these churchmen; men of narrow piety who derived from the Covenanters who had been hunted for their faith. When the Reformation had been accomplished, the chiefs and barons had laid hold of all the Church lands they could get, thus proving by their acts that their interest in reforming the Church had been temporal rather than spiritual. The first minister of Durness had been a man of such Christian zeal that he had, for his people's education, turned into Gaelic verse great portions of the Scriptures, so that his people could in truth have the Scriptures at heart. He also composed hymns of creation, the fall, redemption, and other of the mysteries. But that happy state of affairs was not allowed to continue long and in the north, as in the south, the Presbyterian ministers were hunted.

But their strait piety was remembered by such men as Bannerman and Gilleasbuig, who strongly objected to the 'place men' that an absentee landlord now set over them. But even these new reformers, though against their ministers and against the 'change of tenancy', yet adjured the people, even more sternly than did the ministers themselves, to offer no resistance but to bow their heads and look into their hearts, for manifestly in this matter the Lord had a controversy with the land for the people's wickedness and in His providence, and even in His mercy, he had sent this scourge to bring them to repentance. It was the spirit that, a generation later, brought about the Disruption of the Church.

The Riasgan, then, into which Elie returned, had, in the years of her absence, become vaguely aware of the disintegrating forces at work in that northern land. For the religious factor, so powerful in keeping the people unrebellious and dumb, was brought into play primarily by secular issues, amongst which the most powerful was the fear of being evicted. And eviction was a terrible thing, for it meant the tearing up of life by the roots and the throwing of it on a sea-beach or on a foreign strand where everything that made life comely and happy and to be desired would forever be denied; where life itself, through exposure and lack of physical sustenance, would become wretched beyond reason and starve and die.

The news of Elie's return with her bastard son went over the Riasgan like the lick of a flame. The following day Rob heard of it in the mill and an aspirant to holiness mentioned the matter to the venerable Bannerman.

If the minister was too busy to do his duty, 'the Men' themselves would call the girl before them in a searching assize. For did she not come back amongst them as the living witness of that general sinfulness which the Lord was to punish by using the chief and her factors as His instruments?

But rarely does a whole community become truly religious in this way. Often the more extreme the leaders, the more of secret and profane rebellion runs through the animal spirit of youth. The thought of Elie before the elders became to boisterous young men a secret joke, which warmed them curiously and lewdly.

Of all this Elie had a vague uneasiness. She did not mind Davie not looking at her directly, not overcoming an odd shyness. She understood what it meant to his mind. She knew that his thought would flash or brood over the times when, as a little boy, he had seen Colin and herself together. The living secret was now before him. She would live that down in him. But Mairi's mind and sayings reflected the spirit of the place itself.

Elie had been through too hard a school to be afraid of anything except what might happen to her son. She could become dour and refuse to answer – beyond saying yes to any question about his baptism. She would lie. Hell had never got a strong grip on her imagination.

Upon the edge of the wood, with the young cow foraging in the hollow, Elie sat with her thought. 'The Men' would probably terrify her into telling everything, including not merely matters relating to birth and baptism but what had preceded birth. Fornication was the word. And with whom, and when, and where. Every question, pertinent or impertinent, would be asked. 'And you continued in this state of sin with him whom you call Colin Sutherland? . . .'

And Colin would not be there. If he was dead it would be like dragging his corpse through a dirty pool. His people too would suffer by reflection. Anna, his mother, what was she thinking? Dear Anna. Whom could she blame but Elie? Hardly her own boy, fighting in foreign lands. Was it not sad that the very sacrifice she had made of her son should be dirtied in this way? And Elie's own mother, ashamed in her heart; and her sisters and father, ashamed before the people of this place – to which Elie had come back. How they must secretly wish that she had stayed away! For with both Colin and herself absent the affair took on a different air, one of distant tragedy, for which no one at home could be held responsible. But with the girl here, pushing the unbaptized child in their faces . . .

And it wasn't as if Elie had merely come to understand this for the first time. What she was experiencing now was but setting the seal of certainty, of doom, on thoughts old as her misery.

Yet in face of all this, a strange thing was happening to Elie there on the crest of the wood, where the birch buds were bursting upon the faint dusk of her first day in fairy flakes of green snow. The scent of the earth lay close to grass and heath like a breath not yet breathed. Upthrust wrists and fingers of small trees held wintry memories in a ruddy gleam. Beyond the Riasgan the air became visible against mountain-side and skyline in chill blue. Down below by knoll and hollow and stream lay the homes of her world, with roofs curved tight and inimical against her.

If all the past had come to her, here in the central place of her heart's growth, as something dead as a corpse, and the future as a dread array of forces, against which, with dull instinct, she would plod and war, then the strife would have been so wretched that even tragedy's self would grow weary and die and any record of the issue had hardly been worth the making.

To Elie now from this world about her, and particularly from the memoried earth and growing things immediately around her, came a mysterious effluence giving her misery so exquisite an edge that she shivered from the cut of it to a hostile happiness. This hostility to the forces withdrew her from them, and in her loneliness she dared outward upon the air and did not care. It was something more than the defiant pleasure of the outcast, for at its core was this positiveness of the earth, and the memory of love defeated, denied, but sweet-scented as the earth. She wept and pressed her face against the earth, and dug her fingers into it, and called upon it, or called upon her lover – she hardly knew which.

Her son, Colin, put his hand on her shoulder and, as she sat up, stood back with a half-scared understanding in his face. Something in the square set of his bones beneath his underfed skin recalled the bodily build of his father. He was not quick enough to avoid her lunge, but he soon struggled from her embrace and stood free again. In his hand he had a switch which he had broken from a birch in the wood. There was a gravity in his expression that recognised and feared her emotion. 'Drive home the cow,' he muttered.

She appealed to him to come to her.

'Come home,' he said, turning away from her towards the cow.

*

When Elie came down from that mount of her lonely vision, she found need for all her courage. There were now four mouths to feed, and though old Angus contrived to make Davie carry away at night further supplies of food, manifestly so large a household could not continue to exist upon charity. Old Mairi was contemplating a trip to the coast to see if she could raise, against payment after the July stock sales, a supply of salted or dried fish. As the grass came on, milk would be plentiful everywhere. Meantime they needed meal.

On a day when they had risen from such a frugal repast that their quietness was the colour of their grey faces, Elie said that she was going for a walk into the Riasgan. Mairi looked at her, for no one had yet visited Elie, and Elie had not visited even her mother.

Elie did not go into the Riasgan; instead, she turned down the stream towards the mill. Davie had said that Rob had no more meal to sell, but Elie remembered Rob and how he had had a daring and slightly terrifying liking for her. Rob had always been the sort of man that made a woman conscious of her flesh. His glistening eyes said, 'I know what you're for, my beauty!' yet not ungallantly, for there was a wild generosity in him.

But all that was in the past and Rob, who must now be about fifty, would be kind, for at least there had never been anything hypocritical or sanctimonious about him.

He was sitting whittling a piece of wood and whistling to himself, when the shadow in the doorway made him look up.

'Lord God, is it yourself, Elie?' He was not so much older as tougher, and his eyes pierced in a more personal and searching way than she had remembered. With the rush of open-hearted welcome to his face, he in no time had her by the hand. 'Is it you, Elie, yourself? Lord, I'm glad to see you. The same Elie too, blushing there like nineteen!' He laughed. 'I am delighted to see you. God bless me!' He embraced her.

When she had got free of him, every cell of her smiling face was flushed with blood.

His whole spirit rose to a jaunty boisterous height.

'Lord, Elie, you're sweeter than ever. And many's the sleepless night you gave me!'

She tried to stop his nonsense, but he would have none of her sense. 'Ach, never mind that; tell me your news. Sit down there.'

He sat down beside her, swore it was like old times, and put an arm round her, tickling her in the ribs. 'Cheer up, Elie!'

She had not met this sort of generous personal warmth since she had first left the Riasgan. Her whole starved body tingled with the too sudden flow of hot blood. Her joints eased and melted. She thrust his hand away but he gripped her fingers; then suddenly let her go and chuckled. 'Elie, you're soft as you used to be, and you used to be a little soft red devil. You took the heart out of me then and threw it away. So you did.'

His hilarity was infectious, his hands hard and strong. 'I'll have my own out of you for that! Ach, never mind me, Elie; it's only that I'm so glad to see you.' He kept on talking, meeting her every expression, courteous, obstreperous, full of fun.

'Rob, you're mad!'

'Mad, am I? Tell me, how long is it since you've felt so mad yourself? Do you think I don't know what you've come through?'

She was all flushed and soft and looked down at her hands.

He ran his eyes over her.

'I've come down to see if you could give us some meal. We have – very little,' she stammered.

His eyes lifted from her body, a hot glint in them.

'I have little enough left, but I think I could manage half a bag for you.'

'Oh, Rob! When we sell the beasts in July, we'll be able to pay you.'

He laughed.

She looked at him.

The light in his eyes made them glitter. 'You'd pay me, would you?' he teased her. There was a beat in his throat, a slight quiver in his hand. He gulped his breath and laughed, 'Come on and let's see what is in the girnel!'

She got up, but as though her legs had suddenly turned to lead, she could not move. He bore up against her shoulder. In the narrow passageway between the wheels and the wall he caught her abruptly and brought her to the floor. His breath was thick and hot with passion. 'Elie, Elie; God, Elie!' His hands, tough as iron, went over her. She struggled, but the brute beast in him could tear locked joints apart.

She began to sob, but the sobs quickened him. She heaved over, sobbing wildly and crying out. He spluttered and cursed her. But her sobs beat him. Mad with rage, he scrambled to the front door to shut it. His sister Sarah was there with her lank hair and sneering face.

'Get out!' he shouted, shoving the door shut, 'you sneaking bitch!'

Elie came stumbling towards the door.

He stopped her. 'What are you shouting about? Have I done anything to you?' Her dishevelled appearance inflamed him. His hanging hands knotted.

She looked up at him and with the pitifulness of a child said, 'No, Rob.'

He stared at her. His body went slack.

'Let me go,' she muttered.

'God, Elie, I . . . dammit, I . . .'

Tears now came streaming down her face.

'I – I did not mean anything. Sure as heaven, I did not.' His words jerked rapidly in a queer echo of his previous hilarity. 'I – I—' He took a turn away from her, came back, roughly put his arm round her shoulders, embraced her abruptly and stood away.

'Let me go, Rob.' There was no resentment in her voice. Her eyes shone through a dumb profound misery.

She was not blaming Rob; she was blaming no one. This was her fate.

He could not let her go like that. 'Dammit, Elie, you can't go like that. This is bloody silly. Honest to God.' He stamped, writhed his hands and arms.

'I'm not blaming you.'

'Oh, Christ, shut up!' he cried.

She laid hold of the door. He caught her roughly by the shoulder. In the swing round she looked at him with dumb fatal understanding.

At that he threw his hands up, cried out, and strode back into the mill, kicking things viciously and blaspheming.

Round the door of the house a few paces away, Sarah's face was peeping, and when Elie appeared the face cautiously drew the body after it. She was about the same age as Elie, smaller in height, with lank hair over a pale face smooth except for furrows in the forehead and between the eyes that gave the eyes themselves a knowing look, emphasised into nastiness when the upper lip lifted from the gum.

A sleek cautious nastiness, that could be astonishingly foul-mouthed after a fashion unknown to the other women of that place. The young men had their own stories about her, and any drunken braggart boasted her as fair game. The mill itself, as an out-of-the-way meeting place of ranting spirits, had known many a wild night, and Sarah's tongue may have gathered much of its armoury in sheer self-defence. Besides, for a younger man it was such an unholy thing to hear a woman swear that the thrill urged him to temptation.

Her knowingness now by being politely veiled was complete. 'Isn't he a coarse bastard?' she whispered, smiling and greeting Elie. 'How are you?'

'Fine,' said Elie, embarrassed as she had not been before Rob.

'Your hair is all down. Put it up before anyone sees you.' She took a pace towards Elie to help, for were they not both women in, as far as women were concerned, life's only conspiracy? But Elie involuntarily recoiled.

Sarah's lip lifted.

'I'll put it up in a minute,' muttered Elie quickly.

'It may keep you from giving yourself away.'

Elie was sorry she had repulsed Sarah, but somehow she could not make up for it. She only wanted to get away.

'I'll be going,' she mumbled. Her queer embarrassed smile of goodbye kept Sarah's mouth shut.

As she went slowly up the glen, she felt weary and a little dispirited. She had become used to an attack like Rob's, but that it should have happened here brought all the south into her own homeland. She could never get away from her past, but she had hoped that, whatever new trials the north would bring her, at least she would be able to leave the south behind.

The two enemies that had stalked her in the south had been hunger and lust. Perhaps she was not very good at dissembling, but she had finally come to expect that folk would not believe she was married. And the mere thought of an unmarried woman with a bairn made men's eyes foxy. Where one man had succeeded, another could.

Continually she had had to be on her guard against that. Always the furtive half-smiling look. And even in youths in their teens, awkward, almost miserable in their embarrassment, she had seen it. Davie at first could hardly look at her at all. His instinct told him how other men would look at her.

Somehow she had not expected this in the Riasgan, possibly because to her the Riasgan stood for her youth, which had known nothing of it.

Yet she was hardly disappointed. Or was it that she was beyond disappointment? She scarcely knew. For she had no conscious moral sense of the kind that gives rise to anger or righteousness. She knew that to let a man have his way with her was wrong, but the wrongness was vague as misery. Far keener than any such knowledge was the instinct that kept her from being devoured by beasts. Once she threw her body open, it would be devoured under her passive mind, and the cord that bound her to her son would be broken, and she would sink and the ends of the world fall in upon her.

Thus detached, her vision of herself was curiously

profound. It was so profound that at extreme moments her own unimportance almost made it disinterested. That was why she could look at Rob and in her eyes show him the dumb revelation of understanding and misery that in all ages has made man beat his forehead and cry on God – or blaspheme.

Murdoch called that night. 'Since word of your home-coming, our place has not been fit to live in!' He shook Elie's hand as if she had only been gone a month or two. It was the same subtle face, with the smile darkening it; friendly and full of welcome.

'What's wrong now?' asked Mairi.

'It's that Seonaid. Every time she miscalled Elie for not coming to see her she snapped my head off. There's no peace yonder.'

Elie found her voice. 'Why – why didn't she come—?'

Murdoch gave his quick ripple of laughter and his face went very dark. 'If I hadn't come tonight, she threatened she would come herself.'

'Is her time as near as that?' asked Mairi.

Murdoch laughed again.

'Oh, Murdoch, I'd like to go,' said Elie in a gulp.

'Well, why not come just now? We'll go together. You'd be doing me a good turn.'

'Will I go, Mairi?'

'Off you go!'

Elie was bewildered for a little. She didn't know whether to step backward or forward or how to get ready. They ignored her, for Mairi had a lot of questions to ask Murdoch, and by the time she got half-a-dozen answers she had the human pattern of the Riasgan fairly clear.

'I'm ready,' said Elie, and stood waiting in a heart-beating excitement.

'I'll be over to see her the day after tomorrow,' promised Mairi.

'I won't be long,' said Elie.

'I'll see to him,' Mairi answered her.

'I'm forgetting,' said Murdoch; and taking a whistle out of his pocket, he went over to Colin. 'This is a little present to you. It blows like this . . . I made it out of a tree. Try to blow it yourself.'

Colin did not even look at the offered whistle, his eyes were so gravely bright on Murdoch's face. Murdoch blew the whistle again, and by moving one of his fingers gave it a bubbly sound.

He put the whistle in Colin's hand and guided the hand. 'Blow! No, don't make a sound; blow – like this.'

Colin blew. The whistle whistled.

'That's you, you rogue,' said Murdoch.

Elie turned her face away and went out before Murdoch. When he spoke she did not answer. As they were rounding the gable of the house, she started.

'Did you see anything?' he asked.

'Yes – someone – round the house.'

'It'll be Davie. Davie!' he called.

There was no answer.

'Fancies!' he rallied her. 'Give me your arm – it's dark.'

'No – I—'

'Ach away, Elie! You were equal to me at any time! And you owe me a lot. For if ever anyone was to blame for me having to marry Seonaid it was yourself.' His laugh was infectious. He squeezed her arm.

Elie had to use all her restraint to keep her from starting away from him. 'I—'

'Hadn't you? Hadn't you great arguments with Seonaid when you were both in the Lowlands together and would be teasing each other?'

'I never teased Seonaid.'

'Didn't you? That's not the tale I heard. She said you proved to her that she was in love with me and I was in love with her, and it used to make her that mad she couldn't help thinking about it. She's mad yet.'

Elie laughed, remembering the arguments. She remembered also that it was the last argument Colin and herself had on the very spot they were now crossing over. Then, too, she had imagined she had seen someone in the dark. In a magic way the past came up to the present and life wavered like a candle flame in the hollow between them.

Seonaid's excitement was extreme. She squeezed Elie's hands and scolded her. 'Remember, I'll never forgive you! You should have come to me first. I expected no less. I wept – I, who have never wept in my life. You may think I'm pretending. But I'm not. I'm very angry. I can't tell you how angry I was at the slight you put upon me.'

'Didn't I warn you?' said Murdoch to Elie.

'Can you expect me to forgive you ever – seeing *that* in my house?' and Seonaid indicated her husband. 'My nature would need to be made of honey and running over.'

'Sweet as is the honey, who would lick it off the briar? – Ah, here's Davie. Come in, Davie boy. I've got the better of her in the proverbs, but God knows what'll happen to me in another minute.'

Seonaid told them to run away and play themselves at weaving the Captain's kilt. Her face was fuller than it used to be. Colour burned tonight in her cheeks and a feverish light in her eyes. The comeliness of the woman had caressed the lean places of youth. She would yet be a big, perhaps heavy, mother of sons, who would remember her for ample warmth and security, inspiration and grit. Now she could not get enough of Elie, and she stopped her remonstrances only when she saw their effect, for Elie took them as such sweet compliments that her lips began to tremble.

Seonaid caught her by the knees and whispered fiercely, 'Don't, Elie, or I'll burst out crying like a fool.'

In another minute they were both rocking with laughter. They were like lovers who saw all their past as an endless series of humorous pictures.

'You'll hurt yourself,' called Murdoch to his wife.

'*Mind the coo!*' she echoed, and rocked.

Neither Murdoch nor Davie had a word of any tongue but Gaelic and the short Scots sentences that Elie produced for Seonaid's benefit had no meaning for them.

'*Ah, ye stot!*' gurgled Seonaid.

She sobered as if she had been struck and went deathly pale.

'Didn't I tell you, dammit!' cried Murdoch, crippling across to her. 'What's the sense in carrying on like yon?'

'I would rather she was born with laughter in her mouth than curses,' said Seonaid, mocking him out of her pain. But Elie had now got her arm round her shoulder and was compelling her to her back on the bed.

While the women were whispering by the bed, Murdoch was restless and smiling with temper. Davie got ready to go but Murdoch told him not to be an ass. Davie had never seen his friend so erratic. Clearly Murdoch could have hit Elie. When she came up, he smiled to her deceitfully. Elie said things were all right but she would go home and see Mairi, and Mairi might take a walk over tonight yet.

'Elie, that would be kind of you! Could she come early?' he wondered, all at once eager as a boy.

Elie smiled. 'Yes, Murdoch.'

'Elie,' cried Seonaid, 'how lovely it was to see you! Do you mind the time—'

'Be quiet, woman!' shouted Murdoch.

'Do you hear *that stot!*' she cried, and began to laugh. 'Oh! . . . Go away!'

When they had gone, Murdoch crippled in black temper to his wife and said, reasonably, 'What's the sense in behaving like that? God damn it all, have you no more sense than a hen? What—' and stopped, for his voice was rising.

'Murdoch,' she said, regarding him reflectively, 'after all these years I am still not sure.'

'What about?'

'Whether I care for you or not. Strange, isn't it?'

Murdoch groaned.

'I have a grudge against you,' she said, 'for never having met anyone I liked better. I think I'll never get over it.'

'You'll get over it in a day or two,' he said, 'if only you could stop being a fool.'

'Ah, Murdoch,' she sighed, 'you know the things to say. I was always frightened of your tongue, though I never let on. The thorn on your briar is frozen honey.'

'Now look here, Seonaid,' argued Murdoch, calmly desperate, 'let us be sensible and stop quarrelling for once. All you have got to do is to take things easy and not excite yourself. Why, in heaven's name, run any risk? You know how I got my foot. It's just sheer silliness to – to run a risk. I mean, here you are, in grand trim, all you have to do – it's so simple – is just to be reasonable and not excite yourself and – and take things easy.' He turned to her, but before her smile his further words dribbled out and his face darkened.

'You mean, it's so easy to take things easy,' she helped him.

'You make me mad as the devil,' he said, and turned away.

'I think it's the bad light,' she suggested gently, 'that's hurting your eyes.'

He walked towards the loom.

'Murdoch,' she called him.

He sulked.

'Murdoch!' she yelled.

At the high sound he came in a rush, beside himself with fury. 'Murdoch,' she murmured, 'bend down.'

'I will not!' And when he bent down he muttered, 'Why do you always tear the heart out of me?'

'To warm my own with it for a little,' she answered.

*

On the way home, Davie made an excuse about having to see someone, and, adding brightly, 'I'll be home soon,' walked away from Elie.

'Don't be too late,' she called after him, and because her voice was gay, he answered back. She heard the bright note ring its delicate understanding between them, a happy withdrawing eddy in the dark.

She could not believe she was so happy. Murdoch had been mad – out of sheer wild concern for Seonaid trapped in her pain! She laughed to herself and her feet quickened. When she was a girl and laughter came on her like this, she used to run! She had thought when Murdoch had taken her arm coming down here – he had been gay in the sort of forced way she knew so well and dreaded – that he was to have behaved to her . . . no, she had hardly thought this, she had merely had the sickening sensation of it go to her knees for a moment. And it had all been because he was upset about Seonaid! He was literally mad about her! What quarrels they must have! Elie laughed softly. Murdoch in some way had freed her, and Seonaid had taken her back into the old circle of fun. Of course, Seonaid was really enjoying her tantrums, renewing herself. Lovely Seonaid, who was strong as a horse and could drop her child by the roadside any day!

The figure moved by the side of the house again, and Elie's heart stood still. At last it came towards her. It was Rob the miller. All the happiness drained out of Elie and she felt tired.

'Is it yourself, Elie?' His voice was low and merry. 'Hang me if I could get peace till I came back and told you what a fool I was. Do you forgive me at all?'

'Yes, Rob.'

'Oh, God, Elie, look here; don't speak like that. You make me feel as if you carried the sins of all the men in the world on your back and put me sitting on top!'

She was silent.

'Let us sit down and have a talk. Let us go down a little way first out of the ear of the house.'

'No, I must go in. I've got to go in.'

'So you don't forgive me, then?'

'Yes, I do.'

'You sound dour. You won't let it down on me.'

'I do.'

'I see you don't,' he said. 'Well, I can't help it. To hell with it anyway, I can't do more.'

She was silent. When her head turned towards the house, he caught her arm and said with wheedling friendliness, 'Elie, ach Elie, dash it all, be kind to me, or I'll go about rampaging and blasting, as if hell's fire was on my heart. You know that fine. You know I would kill anyone who blew a hair of your head out of place.' His grasp tightened. 'Tell me, anyway, you know that.'

'Rob, when you're in that mood, you would kill anyone for very little.'

He laughed, delighted at any lightening of her mood. 'Elie, you're full of fun. A word from you and I'll be over the moon. Look here now. Let us sit down. Why won't you sit down? I know you think I'm a bad lot. Look here, Elie. I'll have no rest, no peace.' He caught both her arms. 'No rest, no peace – Elie, give me a kiss. That – that will put it right. Then – I'll know.'

He was encircling her. She protested weakly. He embraced her, murmuring in her hair, pressing his mouth against her head, hurting her. 'Oh God, Elie,' he groaned. She hung for a little, drained. When she struggled free, he was in a passion lest she would not now forgive him for this new offence.

'Rob, why do you behave to me like that?'

'There you go again! That voice. I'll be bad as ever.'

She backed slowly away from him.

He went after her, caught her hand. 'Elie, say you forgive me. Just *say* it.'

'I forgive you.'

He stood for a moment upright and perfectly still. When he spoke his voice had a curious deliberation. 'If I didn't care for you so much, I think I'd strangle you. Goodnight, Elie. I don't know yet whether I'll get my peace again or not.' Then he walked away from her.

Inside Mairi was waiting with her question, 'Did you see Rob the miller?'

'Yes.'

'I'm glad of that, for you would be able to thank him.'

Elie went forward, saw the half-bag of meal. 'Did he bring that?'

'Didn't he tell you?'

'No.'

'That's like him,' said Mairi. 'He kept us in fun tonight. He said you had arranged with him to pay it later.' Mairi was blessed when she had stores, and she got Elie to help her to empty the bag into the chest.

\*

Before the harvest was ready, the Captain came up to the Riasgan on an afternoon and met a little group of men at Angus's croft. All the Riasgan knew he was coming, and every pair of eyes that two feet could carry watched him from one place or another.

He had a pleasant duty to perform, and that he should have elected to carry it out himself added to its value in the bright reserved eyes that greeted him above the strong handclasp.

'The money has been sent to me to distribute, and I was glad to have the chance to come and meet you myself, for in these days who knows how much longer our meetings may continue? However, I am glad to tell you that your lads in the army have never forgotten you. They have as little use for writing as I have myself and they arranged that so much should be taken out of their pay to make you a present. Now there are ten of them and the money can be divided into ten parts. If they had all been spared there would have been twelve. But two could not contribute because they were killed, the brave fellows. I have also to say that each one of them has behaved with bravery and courage, and the Riasgan will never be shamed by any of her sons who left her. My own son is now with them. I share in this honour with you and am happy with you. Here is the money.'

No one made a move.

'I'd better share it out. I've given my receipt for it. What have you to say, Angus?'

'I will only speak,' said Angus, 'because I feel that my son's wife would sooner take my advice than my son's.' This sally made everyone's eyes bright as children's. The Captain gave his short throaty laugh. 'We like that you came up yourself, Captain, and feel honoured by it. We knew the boys would do well. They could not help that. We cannot forget the two who were killed. If they had been living, their share would have been here too. Myself, I don't know, but I have the feeling that the boys who sent this would not like the other two to be forgotten.'

'I think that too,' said Neil Mackay, a thin thoughtful man. 'I think so.'

Others nodded and repeated Neil.

The Captain looked at them. 'You mean, I'll divide it into twelve parts?'

Yes, that was apparently what they meant. Oh, yes.

The Captain shook each one of them by the hand again. He was moved. They were all moved.

'Truly, they could not help it,' he said, as he shared out the money. The task accomplished he looked as if he might say something more, but apparently found it difficult to be personal again. They all understood this.

'How are things looking generally, Captain?' asked Angus, easing the moment.

'Damn bad,' said the Captain.

They waited.

'Indirectly, I have been approached, I may say. You needn't trouble talking about it, but I would see them shot sooner than turn this into a sheep-walk. Unfortunately, the thing is not in my hands. My right is no longer acknowledged. All I can say is that I myself will never consent to see any one of you evicted. Before they evict you – they'll first have to evict me.'

His face had gone the purple of a doubtful heart. This colour was still in his face as he approached home. His yellow-haired wife looked at him with a half-smiling, half-humorous expression. 'Were they pleased?'

'They were pleased enough.'

'Anything go wrong?'

His eyebrows had a way of bunching and ridging that gave the eyes a strained look as if he were suffering from a dark headache.

'She's a bitch,' he said.

She laughed a note or two. 'Was it her ladyship again?'

'They insisted on dividing the money so that the mothers of the two dead boys got an equal share.'

'Oh, did they?' She regarded his restlessness. 'They would do that to keep bad luck away from the living boys.'

He stopped and gloomed on her. 'They never thought of it.'

She smiled. Though pleasant and never obtrusive, she was a woman of clear mind and strong character.

'What do you mean?' he asked.

'Oh, it's nothing. They did not think only of themselves – and of the other two families – they also thought of the boys in the wars. At least they felt all that. They – have that sort of mind.'

'You like them for that?'

'Yes – I'm rather proud of them for it.'

He did not quite get it yet, but the half-laughing pride

in his wife's voice, with its soft undernote of embarrassment, appeased him in some way – as it nearly always did –
for he knew that her mind was clever and acute and he
accepted it, like any other natural gift about him. He would
rather that she were like that than he himself. It left the
force of manhood to its own straightforward road.

'They asked me if anything was happening. I told them
I had been approached indirectly. But I said I'd be cleared
– rather than clear them.'

'Uhm, I'm glad.'

'I – I – damn them!' he exploded.

'The bitch,' she said pleasantly. 'I rather agree.'

'If Falcon comes and has a talk with me himself, by God
I'll tell him too!'

'He won't come. He'll send a note – asking you to call
on him.'

'What! That jack-in-a-box! That – that—!' He was like
a towering black cloud ready to burst.

'We needn't get excited about it,' she said, rising. 'After
all, he knows you *can't* take it on. Out of courtesy, he may
ask you to call to discuss it.'

'Courtesy, by heaven! Ha-ha! . . . *Can't*, you say?'

'Well, we can't, you know. They would want six times the
rent we pay. You'd have to stock the whole place with sheep.
People would have to be driven away. What do you know
about sheep – or want to know?' She stood looking through
the window, then turned on his restless mutterings and oaths.
'It's no use, Donald. Here is a landlord who can get six rents
for one. Nothing stands before that. It is the new measure in
the new age. The old age is doomed. It's done.'

'Done, bedamned! Who is she to dispossess me? Didn't
her forefather give mine this land, not on a rotten sheepskin but *on his word*? Haven't we fought for the family in
the past – increased it – increased its land and held it? Not
with sheepskins! God, no! And aren't you of the true family
blood?'

'A man's word doesn't count now unless—'

'Unless it's been spewed on sheepskin by a little clerk in a factor's office! Don't tell me! The vermin!'

She gave her small chuckling laugh, but her eyes had a curious brightness as of restraint or pain.

'She's a bitch, that's what she is!'

'I know,' she answered. 'There are times when I hate her. But it's little use, perhaps, blaming her. She never thought of it – or started it. Her husband – he's bent on something he calls agricultural improvements. That's the excuse, anyway. He has been doing it on his English estate. He has—'

'Well, why in hell's name doesn't he stick to his English estate? Who wants the bloody sasunnoch here?' He walked up and down in the silence. 'Besides, you know that if *you* were in her shoes, *you* wouldn't let it happen. Well, why does she? And she's of our blood.'

'She was brought up in the Lowlands and in England. She lives in England. They were at the court of France. She – she hasn't it in her.'

'True for you! She hasn't!' The rake of his laugh sounded worse than any oath.

She became restless and at last said with a throaty excitement, 'I sometimes wonder if we have done our duty.'

He stopped, blank. 'What's that?'

Her smile distorted her face a little. 'They say, you know, that we – that we live on these crofters and – and use them like slaves for harvest work and so on.' And because she had said such a terrible thing, she looked at him squarely.

'What?' His face had gone almost black.

But she could not call it off now. 'In the factor's office. It's one of their excuses. I overheard Tomas the Drover repeat it to them outside there. We pay over as rent the money we get from the crofters. Therefore we sit rent-free on the best of the ground and get the crofters to do all our work for us. We are little better than useless slave-drivers.

From the factor's office. I thought you might as well know. It's been on my mind.'

She thought he was going to have a heart-attack. His eyes seemed glazed with pain, but out of the netted eyebrows they kept searching for understanding. He was inarticulate. She murmured to him.

Huskily at last, almost quietly, he asked, 'Do you think that?'

And suddenly it was as though her naked soul were confronted.

She looked away. 'No,' she said. 'All the same,' came her voice in a burst as she walked to the window, 'I wish we could pay them for their work.'

'What?'

She stood silent.

'Good God!' he cried. 'What next!' He strode from the room.

She listened intently. The distorted look on her face lost its semblance of a smile. Tears stood in her eyes. She loved her husband and the tenants on their small estate. She saw that her husband was exactly like one of them, more obtuse than many, stronger willed than most, but deep in his instincts just the same. She loved them, not on the surface, actively, but in the marrow of the bone. Their ways were her ways, their people her people. Doomed – helpless as children. Betrayed. She gazed at a branch of a shrub, bearing rigid sharp-spined green leaves, in a brown jar on the window-ledge. The badge of the family blood! she thought. But the family blood had dishonoured it; therefore she herself had dishonoured it. Only the dispossessed of the clan might ever after wear this shrub with honour.

'Muiril,' said her husband, coming stamping back, 'I can't take that from you. I won't take it from anyone. You're wrong!' His voice was rising. He had instinctively gone beneath her 'No' – to the silence which she now observed, standing there with her back to him.

He was angered and tortured. At this moment of all moments to say such a blasting thing! 'Damn them, the swine!' he shouted. 'Have we not had our men in the past? Have we not won this – more surely than she ever won hers? Is not this the old clan way? Can the clan do without leaders? Are you taking their side, or what?'

When he saw the back of her hand brush her cheek, he grew blacker still.

She turned round. There was no trace of a smile about her face now. The window light glistened in the coils of her yellow hair.

'The clan has no leaders now. The chief has betrayed them. Many placed like you will take the chief's bribe and betray them also. And you cannot help them.'

'Yes, yes,' he cried impatiently, 'but you talked of us making them slaves. The labour is part of their rent. It was all labour once—'

'I didn't,' she said, distress gripping her voice. 'That's what they said. It hurt me.'

'Why? How could it hurt you – if you didn't believe it?'

'Why should we give them even that excuse?'

'Agricultural improvement!' he shouted. 'You're late! The clean bloody sweep is on!'

She turned to face him again. 'You're right, Donald,' she said. 'I was merely being sentimental.'

The look in her eyes beat him.

Slowly she withdrew the piece of shrub from the jar and gazed at it.

'In the Latin this box-holly is called Ruscus Aculeatus.' She turned her face to him. 'Do you know what it's called in English?'

He stared at her. 'No.'

'Butcher's broom,' she said. From the moment's obliterating irony she turned away, and with a quiet gesture threw the shrub in the fire.

*

But there was no talk of defeat or betrayal in the Riasgan that night. Old Angus's home was crowded. Davie was there and his contemporaries became, like himself, young men. Kirsteen and two or three of her age were carding the new wool. Anna was twisting yarn, a goodness about her that made thought mellow, dissolved care, and disposed the mind towards argument or fun; disposed the eyes, anyway, towards old Angus, who made the appearance of the gift of money amongst them as wonderful as any story of Cuchulain or Ossian.

It was indeed an extraordinary thing that money should just drop on them in this way. Like raining cattle from heaven! They made jokes about it, and contemplated the thought of Gilleasbuig going out in the morning and finding five goats before his door. What a length of prayer he would make next time – on the off-chance that it went by length! But Anna told them to leave Gilleasbuig alone, for too many of them needed a good long prayer as it was!

'Wasn't that a wonderful thing too about our boys in South Africa?' said Angus. 'The Captain has had it from his son. You see, when a soldier has to be flogged, all the other soldiers have to watch the flogging as a warning to them. Terrible floggings and torture some of them get, seemingly. All the regiments have to parade out and watch the flogging – except the Sutherland Highlanders. They are excused because, as the Captain put it, "because their conduct is so honourable". Now isn't that wonderful?'

All agreed it was about as wonderful as the money.

'I was against them going,' said Angus, 'and I'm against it yet; but now that they did go, do you know, when the Captain said that, it put a shiver down me.'

They all grew fond of Angus at that moment, and the young men became secret soldiers in their own minds. It was great to be not only brave and courageous but also honourable, so that your conduct was observed and spoken of behind your back. It was splendid, that! A fellow could go walking into the thick of it . . . And on top of all, to send money home. The full hand. Just to give it away, like that. The generous gesture appealed to them most, for it was easy enough to be brave and honourable; anyone could be that. But the sending of the money home, knowing how the old folk would meet and talk, that was an exquisite delight, full of secret fun and laughter. The tramp of their heroes' feet came from the plains of the world upon the secret reaches of their hearts. One stocky lad – a younger brother of the dead Stallion – with dour-looking flushed face, was merely embarrassed before his own secret generosity. For indeed if anyone should thank him to his face, he would not know what in the world to do.

'But,' said Angus, 'what should make us perhaps more pleased than anything else is that in all the killing and cursing you do have in the army, the Sutherland Highlanders kept the old faith, as the minister said on Sunday, "pure and undefiled". I'll admit I was moved when I heard that they wanted their own church. Usually someone just reads a prayer to the men on parade. But the men from our glens made themselves into a congregation, and appointed elders, and got a minister, and paid him out of their own pockets. Away yonder on the burning plains of South Africa!'

'Ay, it makes you think,' suggested Norman Sutherland, a quiet man with a sharp-pointed nose.

For a little there was silence, as if someone had said a prayer. They all now came under the influence of the religious feeling. *The Lord has a controversy with the land for the people's wickedness.* The land had been spared to them. The Captain was on their side. But were they worthy? In view of what their sons were doing in heathen lands, were those gathered round this fire worthy?

The generous hearts were affected most. The older men spoke simply. There was no elder in the company, for 'the Men' were going against ceilidhs or any secular gatherings that ministered to the sin of amusement in these latter days of the Lord's wrath.

Thus in a few minutes from expectant fun and merriment the spirit of the ceilidh was caught in the fine rush of religious duty and wonder. For a little while the eternal rightness of religious experience was perceived with intense clarity. The light on the mountaintop beyond the valleys of the world.

But they did not like to gaze openly, to speak freely. The young were embarrassed and remained quite still until their eyes, lifting, caught other eyes. One or two got up. Someone said, 'Go on, Davie.'

'Ay, give us a tune,' said Angus. 'Let us lift up our hearts and rejoice.'

Davie broke into a reel. The whole company got caught up. Bright faces challenged and laughed. Davie was playing with such fire that his face went pale and his hair shook over his brows. The girls looked at one another, smiling slyly. Some of them went out. One, passing Davie, tugged his jacket.

In half-an-hour a dance was in full swing in the clear night; an hour, and some whisky was presented to Angus. They must celebrate the occasion; drink to the lads who were away. What would they like better? Isn't it themselves would be at the heart of it? Remember the fire outside yon night? the mad devils!

A fire! Who said a fire? Were the new ones less mad? In a way, they were more, for to the sheer exuberance of the older day they added something hectic, the thin note of an escape, escape from what was stealing upon them, threatening them, between the land and God.

Without facing her directly, Davie watched Kirsteen, who danced like a witch. She was thin and lissom and quick as flame. There had come between them, since the night she had run into him at the corner of the barn, a certain self-consciousness that she could not defeat, or that he could not let her defeat. There was something miserable in it, wretched, as though in that shameful moment he had stood exposed to the core. Whenever he thought of it his flesh writhed. Yet it was nothing that could be expressed or even rightly understood. The intimacy in it had been so dreadful that she had run away.

As he used to watch Murdoch, his tutor, so now little boys watched him, and gathered about him when the dance was over. Suddenly Murdoch himself was amongst them, swearing the music had played the devil with a sett on the loom. He was heartier than he used to be, not given so much to enigmatic humours. He went into the house to pay his respects, saying he would be back in a minute. They had to haul him out in the end, when he played like a hero.

Davie danced, but not with Kirsteen. Presently the humour for dancing went out of him, and drawing his old enemy Iain and two others aside, he proposed a poaching foray. Iain at first couldn't be bothered, for he had been having a rare whirl with the girls and was attracted by Kirsteen, but the idea of going away from all this, certain of being missed and spoken about – especially after all they had heard about the heroes in the wars – became too much for him and after the next dance the four slid away. 'They'll wonder where on earth we've gone!' chuckled Iain. Davie looked about him and silently laughed at the hills. The long sinuous rise and dip of the skyline ran through him. There was nothing he loved better than this.

Later, when Anna had answered the last goodnight, she sat down by her fire, heavy with thought. 'Hector,' she said, 'I'm troubled about this money.'

When his steady eyes saw what was in her thought, he looked into the fire.

At last she said, 'If Colin knew everything, would he want us to keep it all?'

Her husband made no answer.

Angus og came in and glanced at them from under his

brows. If he was no one's favourite yet no one had anything against him. A quiet persistent worker, he got things done without apparent effort, and the older folk held him up as an example of industry to the impatient young.

'Have you nothing to say?' Anna asked her husband.

'I don't mind what you do,' he answered quietly.

'That doesn't help me much.'

Old Angus came in, whistling under his breath, his eyes twinkling. The little drink had put him in good fettle. 'Where's Kirsteen?'

'We're talking about the money,' she said to him. 'How would Colin, if he knew what was being said, want the money divided?'

He regarded them with a growing air of surprise. 'God bless me,' he exclaimed, 'I never thought of it!' He became excited. 'Anna, truly, I never thought of it! Amn't I the selfish one?'

She did not raise her eyes from the fire. Old Angus saw the misery in the restraint of her face, and his look grew bright as a bird's.

'You never think of money,' said Anna levelly.

'That's true,' said Angus. 'Don't you be at me, Anna. You're troubled because you know Colin would like you to give the money. And yet if you give it, it will be recognising everything. And how do you know for certain? How indeed? That's true.'

'What am I to do?' asked Anna. 'How *can* I?'

'Do you believe Colin is the one?' asked her husband quietly.

'How do I know? I don't know. It's hard.'

'Do you think Elie would tell a lie?' asked Angus of the fire.

'How can I say?' replied Anna, as if they were baiting her. 'It's easy for you to talk. But – he's my son, and – I hate that anything should be against him. How do we know? It's pretty hard on me.'

From the gloom of the innermost corner, Angus og's face turned over his shoulder and looked across the room at Kirsteen, who was by the door-post. She met the look and ignored it with a drained expression that centred again on the three by the fire.

'Well, Anna,' said Angus, 'as you know, I was fond of the boy. That they were together a lot, we know. I believe Elie. I have, to tell the truth, never doubted it. I may as well say that and be done with it. It would be easy enough to blame the girl and dislike her; but if it hadn't been that Colin had to go away to the wars, we mightn't have had this to think of. Strange times give rise to strange doings. Human is our nature. There may be strange doings yet in this land before we go to our graves. All I know is that without the kind heart life wouldn't be worth living. I have now lived the three score and ten years of the Psalmist, and that's all I have learned. I would rather make a mistake that way than the other. That's all the wisdom that's in me, Anna.'

'What should I do?' muttered Anna.

'When a man gets old,' said Angus, 'he gets miserly. The nearer he comes to the grave, the more he grips what he has. I know that on myself. But I wouldn't like to die like that. If I were you, Anna, I should give the whole of it to her.'

Now plainly Anna herself had never thought of such generosity. Hector looked at his father and shifted on his seat. The thought was so big that it unsettled them.

'Anyway,' said Angus, perceiving this, 'give her something. Go up yourself and see her, Anna. Give her something.'

'You could, perhaps, give her half of it,' said Hector reasonably. 'And if we said nothing about it, no one would be any the wiser.'

But Anna made no move for a long time, then she said with an odd conviction in her voice, 'If I give any, I'll give all.' When she looked up, something like an air of renunciation changed her misery into a strange smile. Uncomfortable, they turned away from her and got up, recognising the movement of the feminine mind in a way they could not follow.

As old Angus went through the dark corner of the outer door, young arms were thrown round his neck. But when Kirsteen came into the room and Angus og happened to look at her, she thrust her tongue at him, clear to the root.

Anna paid no attention to her. Indeed far into the night her thoughts kept her restless. Once she woke from a dream of a procession of feet walking over her grave, to hear two feet in the night outside; stealthy feet, that had gone before she could be quite sure she had heard them; then silence in which the dead feet passed endlessly and without sound.

The four boys who had gone poaching had parted a few minutes before, and as Iain and Art were padding past Angus's house, Davie was climbing the slope to his own home. When a voice spoke to him from the dark gable, he staggered and his forehead went bone cold. By the time he had realised it was Elie, he had all he could do to make his legs carry him to the stone seat.

His silence and the way he slumped down made her whisper urgently.

'Leave me,' he said. 'I'm tired.'

She felt his surge of anger and was so vexed with herself she did not know what to do. 'I'm sorry, Davie.'

'Ach, I'm tired,' he said.

'I was wondering where you were so long and if you had got any food. I could not sleep tonight with things going on. Did you get any food?'

'No.'

'That's why you're weak. Come on in. I have something for you.'

'Let me rest, Elie. I'm tired. We were away poaching. I

have got half a salmon here.' He unrolled it from his clothes. 'They came on us. One of them smashed my shoulder. But we got off. When I heard your voice just now I thought—' He gave a soft laugh and lay over on her in a dead weight. 'Wait a little, Elie.' Then he began to breathe heavily like one who had fallen asleep.

She put her arms round him, holding him from slipping to the ground and whispering compassionately over his head. The dancing, the fire – Mairi had said there hadn't been a fire since she had gone away – had stirred feelings she had believed herself incapable of knowing again. Not that she wanted to be amidst the fun herself; hardly even that she felt an outcast. It was something ghostly in her listening to a legendary echo. Now and then her blood had whimpered, 'I'm not old. I'm not old.' She was not old; she was not a ghost; life was not a legend. And the echo: old, a ghost, a legend.

She clasped Davie firmly, defeating the echo with urgency and warmth, whispering his name, commiserating, protecting him, soothing, caressing him.

He stirred; his head pressed between her breasts; he burrowed into her like an animal seeking shelter; then lay still again, breathing heavily.

'Poor Davie,' she whispered. 'You've had a hard time with us all. Dear Davie. But never mind. Never you mind.'

She felt his face against her again; the warmth from his mouth. He muttered, 'Elie, I'm tired,' and put his arms round her waist.

She felt the tension and tremor of his arms; the life stirring and rising in him; and the little phrases faded from her lips. Then very gently she said, 'Let us go in, Davie.'

'No, don't go yet, Elie.' He clung to her fiercely, burying his head between her breasts; then loosened his arms and let his head fall down.

She pushed his hair back from his forehead. 'Poor boy,' she murmured, 'you're hungry.'

'I'm not hungry now,' he answered. 'I feel I could lie here forever.'

'Let us go in. Mairi will be wondering where on earth I've gone.'

'Wait for a little while yet. What were you doing out here?'

'I was restless,' she said. 'I was thinking of the past – the dancing and the fire.'

He became very still. Then he sat up. She watched him staring before him.

'Come, Davie.'

He paid no attention to her. Unsteadily he got to his feet. 'All right, let us go,' he said indifferently.

She picked up the half fish by the tail and whispered what a lovely bit of fish it was.

At the door he stood, reluctance upon him, torn from her by that past, jealously hating it.

She caught his arm and in a quickened friendly voice drew him in.

'What time of night is this to be coming home?' scolded Mairi from her bed.

'Be quiet, Granny, and him with a half salmon,' said Elie in the darkness.

\*

Anna reckoned she got some of her own back when the daylight had the men moving about. Angus og had said nothing last night and, of course, said nothing now, but Anna did not altogether miss a mysterious byplay that often went on between him and Kirsteen. Kirsteen meantime was triumphant and Angus og mocking sly. They had had a few words amongst the cattle. Well did Anna know that her son would consider the giving away of the money as folly, yet would maintain towards the action a certain critical detachment. He never became involved as chief actor in any emotional scene. But his glance went slyly over the whole scene now, enjoying it.

Not that Anna considered her children in this matter; indeed the only thing that disturbed her in their conduct was Kirsteen's unspoken alliance. She would rather that Kirsteen had been against her. Her obvious sympathy with Elie did not bode well in a girl whose emotions were so easily stirred.

However, the conduct of Hector and old Angus was what really interested her. Hector never had very much to say, but somehow one got used to that and liked it, for his quietness at difficult times gave strength and assurance. When a crofter and his wife were waiting for Hector to visit their sick cow, the very sight of him in the distance made them regard the beast confidently, realising that the trouble was not so great perhaps as they had thought. But this morning Hector's assurance was ragged, and even old Angus was unusually silent. No reference was made to last night's talk, and when, as they were finishing breakfast, Anna said, 'Well, I'll go up to Dark Mairi's this afternoon,' neither Hector nor Angus made any comment.

Anna's face retained its composure. The tone of her voice implied she was doing what she was told. Angus og smiled into the bottom of his porridge bowl, as he scraped it carefully. Kirsteen hated that smile and her face drew cold and firm. 'Ay, ay,' said old Angus vaguely as he got up and went out to the barn.

In their wicker cage the linnets were hopping and whistling excitedly. As old Angus was feeding them, Kirsteen came in. He paid no attention to her. She had plenty to do and his restlessness soon got the better of her. 'What's wrong with you this morning?'

He turned and looked at her, his face wrinkling up. 'What's that?'

'Oh, you know fine,' she said petulantly, and left the barn.

Anna waited for the first of the darkness to screen her visit. There was a perverse satisfaction in her thought that the men were now not so certain about parting with the money. It was easy for old Angus last night when his heart had been warmed with the liquor. In that mood he would have given the world to any stranger. At any time he would give of his worldly goods to a needful person. But money – this money, that had been such a beautiful gift, wonderful as a poem – *money*.

Little boys were playing at soldiers along the river bank, charging and shouting in the gloom.

Money and war.

She listened to them. 'I stabbed you first!' 'You did not!' 'I did!' 'You didn't! I did that, and that cut your throat!' There was a dispute and voices appealed to 'the rules'.

Bravery and courage, conduct that was honourable, and the sending home of money. Money. Gold.

The outside world seemed very near Anna as she climbed the hillside. The outside world was indeed sweeping up to the ramparts of her world. War, money, sheep. War on the far beaches of the world where her son Colin was shouting and slipping in the red scum; money that brought the tide up over the plains and sent it swirling about towns and villages, up, up, into the glens, sucking the people to the sea, leaving the grey sheep like woodlice about the desolate hearth-stones. Night, like the dark spirit of that rising power, leaned over the hill-crest and with his long curious spear stirred the children by the stream, Hector and Angus at home, those everywhere who desired money and had got none, the young men who were secretly envious, the holy who prayed exceedingly, the unholy who cursed jauntily. Would the waters ever withdraw, the spear fade against the stars, and immemorial peace settle again?

Elie was milking when Anna's body stood black in the grey of the door. Elie's voice in the low milking song had an extraordinary potency and for a moment Anna neither moved nor spoke, for the voice seemed disembodied. She listened to the silence, the hurried scared feet, the frightened intense whisper, 'There's someone at the door!'

It was the moment for an unearthly visitor! At the partition Anna asked if she might come in, and entered.

By Elie's face, she was still a ghost. But Mairi got up and welcomed her friend with happiness.

Anna had great courtesy and ease of manners, for she was a comely woman and the rhythm of speech was natural to her tongue. She turned to Elie, while Mairi brought flames from the peat, and greeted her and shook hands. 'Is this the little lad? Won't you shake hands?'

'Shake hands, Colin,' said Mairi.

But Colin was shy and backed away round his mother into the gloom, Anna's eyes following him. Mairi made Anna sit down. Elie remained unmoving, her face with a scared hypnotised look; then she broke her feet out and made for the door.

'Don't go away,' called Anna. 'I should like to speak to you and I can't wait very long. Won't you come and sit down?'

Elie went slowly and sat down.

Anna and Mairi discussed their mutual affairs and the affairs of the Riasgan until they naturally came to the money.

'They tell me,' said Anna to Elie, 'that the father of your boy is my son Colin.'

Elie was silent.

'Is that so?' asked Anna.

'Yes,' said Elie, her head down.

Anna turned her eyes on the fire.

'It was hard enough on us all,' said Mairi.

'Yes,' said Anna. 'It was hard.'

In the silence Elie's breathing could be heard; it was deep and irregular.

'Does Colin know?' asked Anna.

Elie did not answer and Mairi said, 'No, he does not know. She did not tell him.'

'Why?'

'How could she tell him, and him away?'

'Did you not know, before he went?'

'If she knew, she did not tell him,' said Mairi.

'Did you know, Elie?' asked Anna.

'I knew,' said Elie.

'And you did not tell him?'

'No.'

'Why did you not tell him?'

Elie was silent and quite still but for her heaving breast.

'If he knew that he had any obligation to you,' said Anna, 'he might want to do something about it. You see, he has sent some money home. We don't know what he would want to do, but we would like to do right.'

'I don't want anything,' said Elie. The tempest in her breast lifted her to her feet. 'I don't want anything from him or anyone,' she cried, and broke away from them and went out of the house.

Mairi called her back. 'She won't come. She won't come now,' said Mairi sadly. Then she went on and told of all the terrible times that Elie had been through during her years in the south, giving in detail the story of the tinker wife who had stolen her money.

'I cannot yet understand how she did it. Do you think she would do it?' asked Mairi with fresh wonder and concern.

'She might,' said Anna.

'She went away into the world in the morning, and in a little wood she gave him the breast and put him to sleep, but when she took off the linen belt that was round her middle next the skin, and rolled the folds out of it, lo in the place of the money there were little flat stones! My grief,' said Mairi, 'I'll never understand it. I try to think of the woman doing it at this time or that time, but I cannot see her. It gets the better of me.'

'Money has a strange influence on people,' said Anna.

'I'm sorry Elie did not stay, but you and I can settle it between us. I took the money with me.' She unwrapped four sovereigns and showed them to Mairi.

'It's a lot of money,' said Mairi, fascinated by the round yellow pieces on Anna's palm. The firelight danced on them. Anna took her hand and tipped them into it. 'No! no!' muttered Mairi, nearly letting them fall, and then there they were, bright and magical, on her own seamed palm, heavy and real. 'They are pretty to look at,' she said with her thin smile, and made to give them back.

But Anna's hand was withdrawn. 'I would rather that Elie had taken them herself. But she has her feelings, I suppose.' Anna spoke now with a certain sad pleasant solemnity. 'If the boy is Colin's son, this, we felt, is what we should do. We do not know Colin's feelings, but he had always been a good son to me and never did he do anything that anyone had to be ashamed of – until this happened. He might have liked me doing this. We don't know. But we thought he might.'

Mairi's hand continued to expose the coins. Her mouth fallen open in a weak stupid dismay, she was staring at Anna.

'You can give them to her,' said Anna. 'When she gets calmer, she'll understand.' Her tone was now more detached than ever; almost weary.

Mairi's arm and body gave a series of little forward jerks. Gently Anna thrust her hand back. 'She may need them. We can do without them. It's all right, Mairi.' She gave a deep sighing breath and smiled. 'I'll have to be going now. It's not long I can leave that house of mine.'

In her stupid bewilderment, Mairi looked pitiful. Then suddenly her voice whined on its highest note, 'No, no! Take them back! Take them!'

'No, Mairi. I have decided.' The renunciation had been made already.

'Ah, you cannot do that,' said Mairi, her voice dropping mournfully. 'You cannot.'

'Why?'

Their eyes met. 'You cannot deny your son like that,' said Mairi. Then her head drooped and her body began to sway in the rhythm that used to make Davie feel he could laugh or scream at her. 'No, no, you cannot,' she muttered mournfully.

Anna's eyes fell to the fire. They began to glisten. Her fine air of superiority and renunciation faded from her body so that it slumped a little. The tears welled over and ran down her cheeks. She was very still and silent now.

'It's hard on women,' said Mairi. 'It's always hard, however you look at it. Ay, it's hard.'

Then Anna broke down and sobbed. She was weary from the strain of it all – the long absence of her son, his danger, the dishonour of the bastard, the wrongness that could never now be mended. The brightness in her son was dead. Yet her flesh clove to him, for she had loved him specially.

Mairi comforted her, and because it was not so much divination of Anna's feelings that moved her as the impulse of her own deep instincts, she expressed something which was outside Anna and against which Anna could lean. For as things were, Anna had still part of her son, 'and may you have that part forever. You will therefore take two of them' – and Mairi pushed two sovereigns into Anna's hand – 'and I will keep the other two for her and for the boy, who, whether it was right under God's law or not, has some of your own blood in him, Anna. I will do for him what I can as long as I am spared. And you can try not to blame too much the girl Elie, for she is a good kind girl who has come through most of the sorrows in the world and I cannot help having great affection for her. Your son, too, was a happy brave lad, who would say a bright courteous word to me many a time, and oh, they were young, young and fond. Who are we to judge them? It may be a terrible thing to say, but I cannot find judgment in my heart, and if that's wrong and full of sin, maybe in the Last Day Himself will not punish me too hard for it, for He will see that it's only poor Dark Mairi of the Shore and that she knew no better.'

Anna was strangely moved by this speech of Mairi's, for Mairi spoke with a deep simplicity. The Christian religion to her was very difficult, being charged with words and commandments and prophesyings of evil to come and punishments. It was beyond her brain to encompass 'the arguments' or even any small part of them clearly. But she had the feeling that God (or, more likely, Someone under God), seeing that she was a stupid old woman who did not mean to do wrong, might, in a moment of errant kindness, wave His hand and admit her far back amongst the throng, where she would be unnoticed and could go on doing what she could.

And perhaps here at last in this profound sense of unimportance, of namelessness, lay the quality that drew Elie and Mairi together. Its natural manifestation was an expression of kindness, of giving, and it could work towards this with the selfless ardour that is seen in birds when they are feeding their young; it desired brightness and pleasant talk and fun, as trees aspire to the sun and the rustle of leaves in a summer wind; all primitive peoples know it, if they are not cursed unduly by their own witch-doctors or the witch-doctors of 'civilised nations'; and the utmost wisdom achieved by man has made a symbol of it in the breaking of bread.

Anna made no protest when Mairi arose to offer hospitality. And Mairi felt at that moment that God was indeed good to her to have left one oaten cake in her meal chest. It was the last and it might so easily have been eaten. She spread butter upon it and a thick layer of milk cheese, and brought some milk in a bowl. She broke the cake and they ate it together. 'It will help you on the way down,' said Mairi.

When parting, at the corner of the house, Mairi pressed her guest strongly to come back soon again to see her.

Anna returned the invitation, and then, after an involuntary pause, added, 'And tell Elie to come to see us too.'

For a moment 'the arguments' swirled serpent-arms around them in the night.

'Watch your feet in the darkness,' replied Mairi. 'And may God bless you.'

Anna still held the sovereigns tight in her hand. She had not liked either to expose them again or put them away. As she went down the hill she felt them burn in her palm, and paused to wrap them in their piece of linen and push them deep into the pit of her skirt pocket.

*

The Captain tried to hide his satisfaction, but Muiril could see that he was pleased. The harvest work was going on well, the folk labouring happily and with a will. She had never, she felt, known them so cheerful, nor observed such friendly rivalry in the fields. On her part, she had seen to the preparation of unusual food and had let it be known that if any of them wished to organise a dance or harvest-home or anything of that sort, it might be done on a free and even lavish scale. She had been a trifle secretive about all this and had said nothing directly to her husband.

'Everything going all right?' she asked.

'Why wouldn't it?' He lifted his eyebrows.

She laughed. 'You want to prove to me that I was wrong! I know you.'

'I'm glad you're so pleased with yourself.'

'Be nice. Tell me.'

'Well, I won't,' he said gruffly.

'You needn't mind me,' she retorted.

His brows darkened. She could so easily enravel him. She waited for him to burst out; which he did. 'I asked old Angus about what you said about money. I asked him. I had to ask him three times. He thought I was mad. Dammit, I was mad myself that I had opened my mouth.'

'I bet you swore at me.'

'Well, who wouldn't? making a soft fool of me! It will go all over the place. What will they think?'

He was now genuinely angry, yet he had meant to tell her with an air of offhand triumph.

'I'm sorry, Donald.'

'You often annoy me. You say things that pierce a man and drive him on. You do.' He turned away muttering, and as if looking for something.

'You're a tyrant and a bully,' she observed cheerfully. 'Can you tell me who the brown woman is with nothing on her hair?'

'Neither a married woman nor a virgin.'

She looked at him swiftly.

'Who is she?'

He paused. 'She has had a bastard to Colin the son of Hector the son of Angus who thought I was mad.'

'Oh – so that's the girl.'

He grunted. 'Would you like me to take her in and introduce her?'

'I would – but she might not like it,' she answered thoughtfully.

He glared at her. 'Sometimes I think you go clean mad!'

'Two of us mad in that case!'

At the end of the day she met Elie. 'Oh, old Mairi is not down today, I hear, and you are taking her place?'

'Yes, m'am.'

'I hope she is quite well?'

'Yes, she is well, but I thought if I took her place—'

'I didn't mean that!' Muiril flushed slightly as she smiled. 'Give her my greetings.'

'Yes, m'am.'

Muiril wanted to say something to the girl but couldn't, and in a moment they both became awkward. Then Muiril flashed a smile right into the brown eyes and said in a friendly voice, 'Goodnight, Elie,' and turned away.

Pleasure tingled into Elie's heart. This had been her first real outing amongst the people, and nowhere had she encountered anything to remind her of her position. There were, of course, the tongues, ever ready for a suggestive healthy jibe, that curbed themselves consciously within her hearing; the few who went out of their way to be too nice to her; and the young girls who exhibited a certain excitement in her company; but beyond these natural manifestations, there was little to destroy the picture of the old days. The months at home and her natural modesty had brought her own people to accept her at last.

That night as she approached Mairi's house and her little son came running to meet her, a warmth of happiness suffused her tiredness. She would be a woman whom the people of that place in their inmost feelings would forever set apart from themselves, but they would not do this obviously or unkindly. With their pleasant tolerance she would be content, for it was only natural that they could no more forget what she had done than she could forget it herself.

This lull of happiness continued through the harvest work at home. The crop was not heavy but the harvest weather was golden. Elie and Mairi worked all day long, Davie helping them, and little Colin, who was growing into an active lad, busy as he could be wherever Davie was. He would have followed Davie all day long like a little dog, and the old cunning frightened look was seen on his features only when Davie, unable to take him with him, ordered him home.

Davie was a little erratic in his temper those days and inclined to go a lot by himself. Sometimes Elie felt vaguely disturbed, for his avoidance of her now and then was noticeable, and occasionally she caught a pinched evasive

smile on his face that she did not like. There had always
been a lonely sensitiveness about him that had appealed
to her. Once or twice when she had seen that queer
pinched look, a strong desire had come upon her to put
her arms round him and comfort him. A similar impulse
she felt at times for her own son, but in Davie's case it
was deeper and warmer, as though to meet the greater
need. And she would probably have given in to it, had
it not been for her vague fear of what might follow. She
could not forget that moment by the end of the house
when his arms had clasped and quivered, while his face
went burrowing between her breasts. It had been a blind
craving for her body that had dismayed and frightened
her. Its unexpectedness had kept her awake half the night,
with tortured moments when she was certain she carried
a curse.

But, as she saw later, at those moments she had really
been thinking of herself. She knew that Davie was not
consciously and secretly lusting after her. It was something
far more intricate than that. Her mental difficulties she
resolved, not by any process of close reasoning, but, as it
were, by dramatising their moments of significance in
pictures. She did this involuntarily. Almost against her will,
she saw Davie accepting her kind impulse, clinging to her,
squeezing her, kissing her blindly – followed by revulsions
of shame, hiding his face, saying he was sorry. The picture
faded out, through repetition of itself, to what miserable
hopeless end?

And at such a point her heart would overcome her with
grief and sorrow for him. Poor boy, she understood him
so well! And to understand all is, in certain natures, not
only to forgive all, but to give all.

However, she could hold all that poised in her experience and knowledge, and if necessary she could speak to
him and explain.

Yet on the evening when Mairi's harvest was secured

and Elie and Davie and little Colin stood at the corner
of the house looking over the Riasgan and the late workers
in the small irregular fields, Elie had an experience which
shook her belief in her own powers. They had been
congratulating themselves on being the first in, and Davie
was full of banter about buying a fiddle which a certain
fiddler in the main glen was willing to sell for a few
shillings. He would teach Colin too. Colin had some grand
tunes already! He was greatly moved the other night when
old Roy (father of the Roy who had piped the boys to
the wars) played *The Lament for the Children*. 'Weren't
you? Go on, show us how it went!' Colin was shy, but
Davie pleaded and threatened – and prompted – till at
last the small figure began to pace slowly, chanting the
theme in a boyish voice. 'He's got it!' cried Davie,
delighted. 'Now tell us why the tune was composed. Go
on, now!'

'This great Lament was composed by Patrick Mór
MacCrimmon of the Island of Skye. The MacCrimmons
were the greatest pipers in the world, excepting only the
MacKays of our own county, though the MacArthurs
were good pipers too.' Colin went on to relate how the
blind piper, Iain Mackay, picked out the MacCrimmon
in a piping contest, giving his reasons why he would
have known his playing from that of a thousand others.
'They were the two greatest pipers in the world of that
time, of the time before it, and of the time after; and
there will never be their like again until the end of the
world . . .'

'Now Patrick Mór MacCrimmon had seven—' prompted
Davie.

'Now Patrick Mór MacCrimmon had seven sons,' said
Colin, and proceeded with the tragic tale of how all seven
sons died in the one year. 'Sometimes we think that we know
of grief, that we have fathomed the well of sorrow, but it's
only when we hear *The Lament for the Children*—'

'Who's that?' interrupted Davie sharply.

As the figure breasted the rising ground, Elie knew it was Rob the miller. She did not answer.

'It's that Rob the miller!' snapped Davie. 'What's he wanting here?' His hostility was instant.

'Don't go, Davie,' said Elie quietly.

'He doesn't want to see me.' His sniff was a sneer. But he did not look at Elie.

'Please, Davie, wait with me.'

Rob called to them cheerfully from a distance and greeted them as he came up. 'I thought you'd have been away at the graddaning with the girls, Davie. You didn't know he had a girl, Elie, did you? What?'

'No,' said Elie.

'He's a sly one! The pick of the flock at that!'

'Oh, shut your mouth!' said Davie, and he turned on his heel abruptly and walked away.

'What on earth's wrong with him tonight?' asked Rob genuinely.

'He's sensitive,' said Elie.

'Sensitive!' scoffed Rob. 'If I was his age and had a girl like Kirsteen Sutherland looking after me, I wouldn't be sensitive. I'd be proud. Sensitive!' He laughed, greeted Colin, and asked after Mairi. There was life in him, and readiness. Inside, he got all Mairi's news about her crop. Mairi liked him, liked his cheerfulness and stories about folk. 'He's a wild man maybe, but there's good in him,' was her judgment.

Later, when Elie escorted him to the end of the house, he asked her to come down the hill with him a bit. She pleaded tiredness, and immediately the silence between them became charged.

'So you won't come,' he stated.

'I'm tired, Rob. I am really.'

'So you won't come. Very well. I knew I was making a fool of myself. It'll be the last time, so help me God.' He gazed at her in the half-dark, and she felt that, in his violence, he might readily and suddenly lay hands on her. He had not come easily. His pride was torn again.

Weakly and against her inclination, she said, 'We like you to come. Mairi enjoys your visits.'

'Mairi, yes!' He laughed 'Don't make a bigger fool of me than the fool I am!' Then suddenly and directly he asked, 'Do *you* want me to come?'

The question was final. She knew it. It stretched time thin as a thread that a syllable would snap.

'Yes,' came from her mouth.

He brought his eyes close to her. 'Christ!' he muttered before her expression, and swung round from her down the hill.

Elie went up to the edge of the wood. In her despondent weariness, her mind became fatally clear. Rob's mention of Kirsteen Sutherland had let in sudden light on Davie's perverse behaviour. If it did not explain everything, it explained a lot. Something must have gone against him; the poverty and the begging might have hurt his pride and led to some action that he was ashamed of. For he had his secret pride, like Rob, like everyone, the dark rat that went gnawing at the breasts of their men folk. And Davie was sensitive beyond the ordinary.

Mairi's house – four of them in it. Two too many – with a young man growing up like that. It wasn't giving Davie a chance. What could he do but go wrong?

Rob was tortured not so much because she would not give herself to him as because he could not ask her to marry him. He could not tear the black rat from his heart. To marry a woman with a bastard! It was too easy to see him toss up his hands and shout, 'O God, that's too much! Anything but that! A girl with another man's child! Taking the leavings! Christ!'

And he would be tortured now because she had said yes – looking as she had felt. Elie gazed around at the slim birches half-denuded of their brown leaves. This was the scene of all that early life which now struck her as unreal as a fairy tale. Colin was nine years older, a hardened soldier, with what new ties? And it would be twelve years more, it was said, before any of them need be expected back. For the great ogre Bonaparte was out to conquer the world and they would have to go on fighting him until he was killed or they were. Colin might never come back. Anyway, it was so far ahead that they would be old, and perhaps it would not matter then. Besides, all the talk about giving land to the soldiers had been a lie. It was all a lie, everything. She saw the parishes over the hill that had that year been cleared of their folk; the miserable herding of them on seashores and barren moors, their desperate and destitute cries.

If little Colin and herself took the road, where would they go? Who could help them? And even in the Lowlands, had she not seen the parishes cleared of the cottars to make room for big farms: a whole village turned into a single steading?

There was no place for the poor anywhere.

And if the decent poor were in this way accursed, who was she? . . .

In the brown of the deep dusk, the Riasgan was a quiet land, very desirable to her eyes.

She sat so still that the cold ran over her skin and she suddenly shivered, desiring to turn away, to turn away blindly.

There were footsteps on the grass. At two or three paces Davie stood looking at her.

All strength and virtue went out of her body. No last protest, no word at all, was left in her melting flesh. She was delivered to whatever might come upon her.

But Davie could neither move nor speak, and so she was given time to struggle out of her weakness; at first with the dreadful ineffectiveness of the flesh in a nightmare, and then, when she was conquering, with weariness and almost with regret for she did not know what. As she got to her feet the blood surged behind her eyes and made her dizzy.

'Are you coming home, Davie?' The blood mist cleared.

He did not answer, but as she walked away he said in a queer strained voice, 'Don't go.'

'It's late,' she answered; 'come away.'

She went down the hill alone, her legs trembling and tired. She was very weary and leaned against the wall by the partition, listening to Mairi and her son Colin. Mairi was making him say his prayers. She had a great number of ancient rhymes and verses, many of them not known to the folk of the Riasgan; but little Colin, who was developing an abnormal curiosity in these things, as if he had wandered by incredible chance into a magical lost land, would draw upon her when they were alone with persistence and the solemn voice of an equal.

He liked his prayer:

*'God and Christ and Spirit Holy,*
*And the Cross of the nine white angels,*
*Be protecting me as Three and as One,*
*From the top tablets of my face to the soles of my feet.*
*Thou King of the Sun and of Glory,*
*O Jesus, Son of the Virgin fragrant,*
*Keep Thou us from the glen of tears,*
*And from the house of grief and gloom,*
*Keep us from the glen of tears,*
*From the house of grief and gloom.'*

'Now go to your sleep, for it's tired you are after the hard day.'

'Granny, I am not sleepy now. What's the one about the stars? "The Rune of the Muthairn." Say it, Granny. Ach, do.'

Mairi recited:

> '*O King of the moon,*
> *O King of the sun,*
> *O King of the planets,*
> *O King of the stars,*
> *O King of the globe,*
> *O King of the sky,*
> *Lovely Thy countenance,*
> *O beauteous Beam.*'

> '*Two loops of silk*
> *Down by my limbs,*
> *Smooth-skinned;*
> *Yellow jewels*
> *And a handful*
> *Out of every stock of them.*'

'Granny—'

'Now will you go to your sleep?'

'I wish, Granny, you would say the one about—'

'I will not then. Have I got a minute to spare to myself? Is not the wool to do, and have I anything ready for your mother and Davie? Do you think I can listen to you all night?'

'Granny, do you remember, when we started the reaping? I heard you say a Blessing. It was something about On Tuesday of the feast at the rise of the sun and the back of the ear of corn to the east.'

'You hear too much, you rascal. But I'll say it to you another time if you go to your sleep at once.'

'Granny?'

'Well, what's it now?'

'Ask God to shield the house.'

She could not refuse that:

*'God shield the house, the fire, the kine,*
*Everyone who dwells herein tonight,*
*Shield myself and my beloved group,*
*Preserve us from handling and from harm,*
*Preserve us from foes this night,*
*For the sake of the Son of the Mary Mother,*
*In this place, and in every place wherein they dwell*
*tonight,*
*On this night and on every night,*
*This night and every night.'*

Mairi intoned this in her high voice, with its echo of religious mournfulness, but her voice dropped on the last line into silence that carried behind it the white wake of wonder.

The silence lasted a long time.

'Granny?'

'Aren't you off yet?'

'Did you ever hear *The Lament for the Children?*'

'Maybe I did.'

'Do you think it's a great tune, Granny?'

'Maybe it is then.'

'It's the greatest Lament in all the broad world. It was made by Patrick Mór MacCrimmon of the Island of Skye, when his seven sons died in the time of sorrow. I'll tell you the story if you like, Granny. Would you like to hear it?'

'I would.'

Colin told her the story.

'Ah, my grief,' said Dark Mairi, 'that was hard on him. And the fine lads to die like that. Sad, sad it was. Who told you of it?'

'Old Roy the piper. I often have a news with him.'

'Do you now?'

'Yes, and listen, Granny, to what more he said. He said that not only seven sons but seventy times seventy times seven sons, ay and more, and old men and women, and little boys and girls besides, would yet be turned out and driven from their homes down into the sea. "I'll play you the Lament for them now," he said, and he played *The Lament for the Children*. Do you think it will come true, Granny?'

'How can I say, little Colin? Who can say?'

'Granny . . .'

# PART THREE

## ONE

Mr Heller was walking through St James's Park in London, accompanied by a man who was speaking earnestly and to whom he was listening intently. The goal of his long journey was almost in sight and within himself he felt the fine excitement or assurance that knowledge gives. All he desired at the moment was an understanding, for tactical purposes, of the mind of the exalted peer upon whom they were about to call. This was being conveyed to him by a tongue more fluent than his own, controlled by a brain hardly less acute.

'As commissioner of his English estates, you can imagine I have got to know him pretty well – I mean, not merely his personal foibles, but the whole drive of his mind. And he is set on this agricultural improvement policy. It's not entirely a money transaction – though he is wide awake, of course, to the fact that even if he has to forego immediate returns in many cases, ultimately he will benefit enormously. Naturally there's that in it. Take your own case. He has advanced you a pretty large sum of money and cleared off the cottars from your ground who were paying a small rent. But you are going to pay in the first place twenty-five shillings an acre, in the second place 6½% on the money advanced – and that's very good *certain* interest for a man with capital to invest – and in the third place the land is already, through your work, raised tremendously in productivity and value. I am talking plainly.'

'I appreciate that,' said Mr Heller. 'You want me to understand that he has a clear grip of the business side and to speak accordingly.'

'Precisely. But, remember, never assume before him that this is a mere merchant's way of making money. He is concerned, you must understand, about developing his estates so that they may be an example of advanced agriculture to the country. Of course, he stands to increase his heritage, but that's a duty he owes to his great family. Besides, if his schemes did not make money they would be no good.'

'I have you,' said Mr Heller, 'I think, exactly.'

'In a word, he will back you to the end – if he feels he can justify his policy along these large lines. You need not be afraid that any little local criticisms will affect him. On the contrary, they will stiffen him. That has happened already on the Shropshire estate, as I have explained to you.'

Mr Heller nodded. 'What he saw of the French Revolution would not dispose him towards local criticism of that kind, if I understand you!'

'True,' said Mr James. An ironic smile flickered over his face and, like a sound Edinburgh Whig, he enjoyed the moment. 'Of course, what we have got to remember is that we are discussing not only a great statesman, a great peer, a wealthy landowner of vast estates, a man who was our ambassador at the court of France before the brute-mob took charge, but a man who knows about botany, chemistry, and Latin, who talks French as well as you or I talk English, and who is a great patron of the arts.'

But Mr Heller glanced at Mr James and smiled also. 'What a handful of half-starved savages in the lost glens of the north may say is nowhere. Yet that is our business, and when talking to us he will make it his.'

'I have an idea, Mr Heller, that we shall get on very well together,' said Mr James pleasantly. 'You be guided by me. He suffers a lot from inflammation of the eyes. He was never very strong and never a blood like the other young gentlemen of his class. But he knows when you are talking sense. Be brief and definite.'

'And what is her ladyship like?'

'She has the customary sentimental weakness for her own people; the romantic attitude towards her Highlanders. You know the sort of thing. But she once gave clothes to a queen and her children when the mob had imprisoned them. She knows where lack of respect for authority lands a people. That's all right! And now here we are.'

As he entered that very magnificent house, Mr Heller got a quite curious shock at the sight of doorkeepers in full Highland costume. His eyes widened and stared for only a moment, yet the vision persisted with an indefinable and not unpleasant irony, and accompanied him past the liveried servants with their powdered hair, remained impalpably with him as his eyes flashed over the grand staircase and hall, the pillar-supported gallery, the statuary and gilded balustrades, and somehow came to a strange still life in the sombre oils of the paintings.

Mr James, whose manner had undergone a delicate change, paused, disregarding the lackeys, and indicated to Mr Heller whatever was considered of striking interest with an easy gesture and the casual tone of voice of the governing classes. 'These all along there are paintings of the Spanish school. Some Masters amongst them. And these here—'

'Who did that?' asked Mr Heller.

Mr James smiled. 'A Flemish artist, I believe. Does it appeal to your Covenanting blood?'

It was a scene in which only two faces were clearly lit up by a candle and the effect was rather striking. The contrast between the faces was still more arresting. One was calm, resolute, with final knowledge of approaching doom: the other was eager, disturbed, and questioning. Mr Heller stooped to the words on the frame:

> *He was wounded for our transgressions,*
> *He was bruised for our iniquities,*
> *The chastisement of our peace was upon him,*
> *And with his stripes we are healed.*

'Christ being examined before Caiaphas,' said Mr James. 'It's the sort of picture that attracts. Not really a great work, though fairly good or it wouldn't be here. Perhaps later on, if you would care to have a look around? His lordship allows artists in here to make sketches.'

'Does he?' said Mr Heller, astonished.

'Oh yes,' said Mr James, amused in a slightly aloof but not unpleasant way, and Mr Heller felt receding from that smile the greatness of his lordship that included French courts, English politics, statuesque Highlanders in full regalia as a more uncommon possession than Nubian slaves, Spanish pictures, Caiaphas and Christ. If Mr James had designed the moment to redress any balance of undue intimacy in their previous talks, he could not have succeeded more perfectly.

The total effect indeed was strong enough to endow the weak-eyed face with the large Jewish nose, to which Mr Heller was duly presented, with a certain ease of nobility and quiet-smiling power that Mr Heller might altogether have missed in a crowd.

'So you have been travelling and studying?' said his lordship.

'Yes, my lord.'

'Pray sit down. And what do you make of it? You went over the Cheviots, I believe, into Northumberland?'

Mr Heller did not know quite where to begin. His lordship waited with his reserved smile. Mr Heller decided to be definite and businesslike.

'I studied sheep-farming there. I wanted to see how they worked the flocks. Our people in the north know nothing about flocks. The system followed by the Border store-farmers is very exact. They divide their flocks into hirsels; for instance, the ewes are a flock by themselves. When the lambs are three months old they are taken from their mothers and put into a separate herding. When they are twelve months old, at which time they give their first fleece, the males are generally separated from the females; the females are returned to the ewe hirsels and give their first lamb at two years old, and the males are sent to wether ground, from which, after a year and a half, they are sent to the feeders. The ewes are sent to the feeders after giving three lambs.'

'Very interesting. Do Atkinson and Marshall follow that practice on their venture in our lands in the north?'

'No, not exactly. Instead of returning their gimmers – that is, the yearling ewes – to the ewe hirsel they send them for about eighteen months to land called yell gimmer land. By the time they are returned to the ewe hirsel and have their first lamb they are three years old. It means the wethers don't go to the knife until from four to five years and the ewes at five to six. The character of this Highland-bred cheviot mutton is going high in the feeding countries.'

'I'm glad to learn that. Now let me ask you a direct question. Are you satisfied that sheep-farming in the north will be successful? Are all the conditions there to make it successful?'

'I am absolutely satisfied, my lord.'

'I see. I am rather interested in botany. How about the grazing there, compared with the Borders?'

Mr Heller explained the providential succession of grasses or alpine plants in the north, adding that there were only two rather critical times, the first in April between the fading of the cotton grass and the springing of the deer hair, and the second in August between the fading of the deer hair and the coming of the harvest moss. His lordship was very interested in this, and Mr Heller ventured upon botanical facts that had already come under his particular observation. The subject was thereupon pursued into the arrangement of a sheep-farm, including the number and disposition of shepherds and the best kind of sheep for the ground. On all these matters Mr Heller was ready with facts and speculative wisdom. The cheviot he declared to

be the true moss and mountain sheep. 'The merinos, for
example, range all in one lot, but the cheviots spread over
the ground in twos and threes. The same quantity of ground
in the north will keep three hundred cheviots for one
hundred merinos, with one half the care and one third the
winter risk. Within the last fifty years, too, the cheviot has
been very much improved in his quarters and in the staple
of his fleece by crosses with sheep recommended long ago,
as you will know, my lord, by Mr Bakewell.'

'True. Have you, ah, ever computed what we might raise
in the north in the way of these cheviot sheep? I should
not be surprised to learn that you are as well versed in the
politics of Europe as in the hirsels of Northumbria!'

Mr Heller took it upon himself to smile also. 'No, my
lord. I have in my own way tried to find out as much as
I could—'

'I mean, you know,' interrupted his lordship, 'that the
condition of Europe is critical. That is, our condition. It
might become pretty nearly fatal, if we don't learn to feed
ourselves. If it hadn't been, even as it is, that we kept
command of the sea – you follow me? And the danger is
only now working to its climax.'

'I hope I understand, my lord.'

'I think you do,' said his lordship, peering at Mr Heller
thoughtfully. 'Now about the number of sheep?'

'If we are given a free hand to carry out your improvements, my lord, I have estimated, on a basis that I can
make clear to your lordship, that within a very few years
– five or six – one hundred thousand fleeces and twenty
thousand ewes and wethers for carcases would be sent from
your northern estate.'

'Really? As many as that?'

'Yes, my lord. Taking as a basis—'

'I am satisfied, Mr Heller. And I should like to compli-
ment you now on your grasp of the situation. It is always
a pleasure for me to meet a man who knows the facts, has

come to the proper conclusions, and can act. I am glad to think that we have secured your services in this important work. You will be of great assistance to Mr Elder, and so long as you drive ahead on the agreed lines, you may rest assured of our backing.'

'Thank you, my lord.' He hesitated. 'Your lordship may trust me to do my best. If anything is ever said to the contrary, all I ask is the special favour of being allowed a personal explanation.'

'Well, I hope we are civilised enough for that! Eh, Mr James?'

'My lord,' said Mr James, 'Mr Heller, I think, is trying to say delicately that he has to meet a certain opposition, that—'

'Naturally. We have received letters direct, as you know. My wife is in truth at the moment very disturbed – however, tell me, Mr Heller, what do you think of those people, generally, who may consider themselves unfortunately treated?'

Mr Heller hesitated. 'I am reluctant to offer a personal opinion, my lord.'

'Oh, come away! You won't tell us anything but the truth and, I suppose, we must be prepared to meet that at all times!'

At last, though still with a proper air of reluctance, Mr Heller said, 'When I first came to your lordship's northern estate, I was under the influence of Sir John Sinclair's book and much else that had been written and spoken on the ancient habits and manners of what are called the Children of the Gael and the cruel inroads that were being made on them by certain landlords. Before I had been two years in the country my opinion completely changed. By that time I had investigated conditions for myself. If I am to speak the truth I should like to speak it plainly. The truth is, my lord, that the people of the glens live in sloth, poverty, and filth; the men won't work; the women slave.

I saw starved cattle and scabbed ponies and sheep staggering all over the place, picking up half an existence, and
in bad weather dying in hundreds like flies. Their miserable little patches of grain get mildewed every other year.
It's not a place for cattle. You'll find them dying wholesale while the cotton grass is withering untouched, for the
cattle don't crop it. I do not wish to appear prejudiced,
my lord, but the sooner they are cleared out the better for
themselves and for those who have the right use of their
country at heart.'

'Hm, pretty definite.' He pulled a bell cord.

As the servant withdrew, his lordship covered his eyes
with his cool fingers and remained quite still and abstracted,
the beaked nose curving out from beneath the hand over
a firm mouth drawn inward a trifle at the corners in a
manner faintly saturnine.

Mr Heller glanced at Mr James, who nodded just percep-
tibly and with veiled satisfaction. The door was opened
and a lady of from forty-five to fifty entered. As Mr Heller
arose he had the impression of the whole room centring
upon that approaching face. For here at last was the Great
Lady herself, the chieftainess of the blood, the goddess of
her people. She walked unhurried, her expression steady
and calm, but when Mr Heller was presented, she smiled
with a sudden graciousness; and in a moment he saw interest
glisten in her eyes.

Her husband explained briefly the circumstances of Mr
Heller's visit. 'With Mr Elder, he has the destiny of your
Highland subjects in his hands.'

'I hope you will deal with them faithfully, Mr Heller.'

When he hoped that he would do his best in what might
be very difficult circumstances, she was really listening to
his Scots accent and regarding the hard bone in his cheek
and jaw, the grey eyes, the set of his mouth. The accent
was familiar and the type, for she had been brought up in
the Lowlands of Scotland by her grandmother, a scheming

worldly woman. As servants they were faithful to the last. But they could be harder than the bone in their faces.

When the talk had gone on for a little time and she had asked various personal questions about the north, the real reason for her presence was introduced, for she had known quite well of Mr Heller's projected visit, and had indeed been awaiting her husband's call.

'We have perfect confidence in our agents and hope to be guided by them,' she now said. 'I have come to recognise that it is impossible to carry through improvements without disappointing or even hurting someone in some manner. Naturally enough many who are disappointed express their disappointment directly – often very directly, I'm afraid. I—' she hesitated, then continued – 'I have a great affection for my northern home and people and should like to do what is right. I should dislike anything to be said implying that I . . . I should dislike it.' Her expression troubled.

'I think,' said her husband, 'you should tell them of Captain Grant's letter to you. We must, as you say, be guided by those to whom we have entrusted our affairs.' He turned to Mr Heller. 'Do you know Captain Grant of Riasgan – is it?'

'Yes, my lord.'

'What sort of man – of tenant – is he?'

Mr Heller's expression suitably conveyed how embarrassing the question was. Not to be too blunt about it, he began, 'The position of gentlemen like Captain Grant is peculiar. There are many of them in the north. They have a certain amount of land. The best part they keep to themselves; the inferior part they sublet to natives who crowd in dirty little cabins and contrive to sell a few half-starved cattle in order to pay rent to such as Captain Grant. The result is that Captain Grant sits rent free. Not only that; all the tenants have to give him a certain amount of forced labour. In this way his harvest is gathered and secured free of cost. And he is almost good to his tenants compared with most of them, who sublet at a figure that no tenant could pay, unless he procured the money in some illicit way – such as smuggling.'

'That's not really true?' came her ladyship's voice.

'I can put it on paper, with name and place, if your ladyship so desires.'

She gave a wry smile, as if she were always somehow being caught out when it came to her Highland subjects.

'I do not know,' proceeded Mr Heller, whose legal mind required a conclusion, 'what Captain Grant may have said to your ladyship, but I think it is not difficult to understand why he should be against any change of tenancy. Otherwise I should prefer to say nothing against him, nor retail what rumour carries regarding his sentiments towards your ladyship.'

'Oh?' she interposed sharply. 'What precisely do you mean?'

Mr James tried to catch the eye of Mr Heller, who, however, had been roused a little and now firmly said, 'It would not appear that he is friendly disposed towards your ladyship. That is all.'

'Caught out again,' murmured her husband, caressing his eyes.

She regarded Mr Heller very directly, and clearly would have liked to make him confess to precise details or words, but she succeeded in repressing the desire and shrugged slightly. 'It would appear that I can get little credit in my ancestry! I suppose you, too, have found my clansmen savage, dirty, and illiterate.'

Mr Heller was silent.

'You would rather not venture an opinion?' Her irony was delicate but direct.

'They live,' replied Mr Heller discreetly, 'in unfortunate circumstances.'

'I see.' She smiled in a certain way.

'It is really simple enough,' interposed her husband, 'if we look at it in the right way. You have seen yourself the beneficial results of our improvement policy in Shropshire. The tenants were displeased. They no doubt said things behind our backs; possibly even: *sacré aristos!* But if we had left the place as it was, I would have been called the worst landlord in England. It really was a mediaeval mess, undrained, wasteful. I either had to clean the place up, put it on a business footing, make it progressive and profitable – or let the old wretched conditions prevail. I think that is clear.'

'I know,' said her ladyship. 'I quite agree. And—' she continued with a certain inflection after a pause – 'I recognise your parallel.'

He smiled. 'I know it's annoying to get letters and to run the risk of being called a tyrant, who has lost all feeling for one's own people and has denied the great ways of one's ancestors. Well, we have seen things that happened across the Channel, where landlords carried on the ways of their ancestors with real thoroughness. Assuming for a moment that they had bent their energies – and money – on improving their estates?'

'Oh, I know. I'm not arguing against improvements. That's not what's troubling me.'

'Let us be clear on this,' continued his lordship, with a note of decision. 'The landlord must retain his power – or abdicate. I propose not to abdicate. Very well. I am going to improve. Now on your estates you know the conditions. Apart from whether the people are ignorant and slothful and bestial in their habitations, we do know that they live in poverty, and some of them have got charity from you. As tenants they are of little use to you financially, and none at all to the country. Well, here's a scheme that is going to use the land in the only way it profitably can be used. You will benefit largely, but not more than the country, for the estate will now export huge quantities of wool and mutton.

Ultimately what benefits the country as a whole benefits the people as a whole. Thus England will benefit. Against a conception as big as that, no personal criticism can ever prevail. That is why I consider we must go ahead with improvements to the logical limit. Again, consider it this way. As a nation we are more and more becoming industrial. Industrial workers need food and clothing. If there is no food there will be food riots. We have had them already. We shall have more of them, because we cannot yet feed ourselves. Our enemies, recognising this, have done their utmost to shut the world's ports against us. They would starve us into submission. But before we would ever be starved into submission, what would happen? Our ever-growing industrial population, demanding the bread of life, would rise in blind rebellion and the whole order of our society would be submerged. We hardly need to be reminded of the way it was submerged in France. Do I make myself clear?'

'Too clear,' said his wife, with an involuntary shudder.

'It really comes to this,' concluded his lordship, 'that what benefits the landlord benefits the nation. The greater his rent from the land, the greater the output from the land, for no man can pay a high rent who is not himself receiving a high return for his labours. Consistent with that fundamental fact, every good landlord will act as humanely as possible. I admit that what has been said by some of your Gaelic enthusiasts has sometimes irritated me. A landlord must have absolute power over tenancy arrangements on his own land. If you cannot, within the law, do what you like with your own, the whole basis of our state is dissolved. I simply will brook no interference, in the slightest degree, with my absolute ownership of my own lands.'

The last few words had gathered such an edged conviction that for a moment no one cared to speak. Mr Heller, in truth, had no desire to speak. The ease with which his lordship had spoken, the effortless manner in which he had touched upon the vital factors not merely in the disposition of his own lands, but in the whole fabric of the state, gave to Mr Heller the conception of largeness which had already, in the minor matter of Caiaphas and Christ, come impalpably upon him; but when his lordship in that final moment had flashed his steel, Mr Heller was definitely thrilled. There was nothing that he himself desired more than possession and power. Its expression in another he secretly worshipped. This man stood for England's power. His power was England's power, because he governed her. It was going to take a mighty revolution to upset that! Never in his whole life had Mr Heller been so moved, so sure of himself and of the fundamentals of life.

When he spoke, this was heard in his voice.

'I am indebted to your lordship for your noble words. May I remind your lordship and your ladyship that your improvements in the north have been – and will be – carried out as humanely as possible. With that absolute power to dismiss your tenants completely, you yet have provided them with land by the seashore. The food resources of the sea have never yet been properly touched by your people. They will be, to the great benefit of the country. This is the greatest movement towards progress that has yet been contemplated in the far north.'

'You are a strong advocate, Mr Heller,' observed his lordship. 'Let me thank you. At the same time, when we get this change of tenancy into operation and complete our other schemes, particularly the construction of roads and bridges, I think, by the time we have finished, that the romantic Highlands will be a different land.'

'I am certain of it, my lord.'

'Very good.' The smile on his lordship's face gathered about his mouth and was sucked in at the corners in a saturnine manner. Even in the weak eyes there was, for a moment, a pleasant ironic concentration. The cause may have been no more than Mr Heller's accent and a definite appreciation of Mr Heller's strong convictions; added, possibly, to the fact that his lordship himself had apparently been rather convincingly fluent.

If Mr Heller saw the smile, he perceived it as evidence of that aristocratic largeness which, by virtue of its being unfathomable, must remain enigmatic. Its very restraint and aloofness stood for power.

Certainly, anyway, as he passed out, he did not see Christ's face in the candlelight, nor did any flicker of interest rise in him over the Spanish paintings, nor did the powdered male servants in any way distract his pleasurable feelings. Once again, however, his eyes steadied on the doorkeepers in full Highland costume; then his mouth closed as he took the air, and a smile more forceful and ironic than his lordship's played over his face and glistened in his eyes. For his lordship, it seemed to Mr Heller, had certainly solved the problem of airing Highland dress and Highland pride – in their proper place.

Between Mr Heller and Mr James many mutual compliments passed as they walked over towards Buckingham House; and Mr Heller's estimate of his lordship's powers and attainments might well have made that nobleman's ears as red as his eyelids. After viewing Buckingham House they set out for St Stephen's, for Mr Heller was anxious to be introduced to the Mother of Parliaments. Buckingham House and St Stephen's between them represented the greatest organised Power the world had ever seen. He was walking, as it were, between the double heart-beat. Greater than Greece, greater than Rome, greater than Spain. It was difficult to realise, so quiet and pleasant and normal everything was, so simple – so sure of itself, like his lordship's expression.

Throughout the interview Mr James had himself borne a reflex of this expression, and as he now directed the conversation towards political affairs Mr Heller became aware of a far-seeing ability in the man, and suddenly he felt that he himself had spoken too much and too openly. The momentary resentment, however, was quickly controlled, for he had the wit to see that his resentment was against his own crudeness and lack of finesse. Conscious of being more cunning than these men, more forceful, he yet lacked their easy smooth manner, the pleasantness that was the glove to power.

Mr James was explaining the weakness and inadequacy of the Addington administration. 'Actually what we must never forget,' he said, 'is that our country is finally governed by a handful of the great English county families. Important public figures rise and fall, but *they* remain. It is at one of their houses that every new move of importance is initi-ated. It was at his lordship's that the conception of a ministry of all the talents was mooted and realised. He himself intro-duced a motion, "On the defence of the country," in the House of Lords. The Government fell. But Pitt, by excluding Fox from the new administration, disappointed everyone. Grenville broke away. It is impossible always to control these personal feuds and feelings,' explained Mr James. 'His lordship stuck to Grenville. Grenville succeeded Pitt and His Majesty conferred upon his lordship the highly exclu-sive distinction of the Order of the Garter. I am aware you know all about that – but at a distance you don't get the same personal understanding, if I may say so.'

'I can see that,' said Mr Heller.

'This business of political power,' continued Mr James, 'is very interesting – and can be very valuable – I mean, not merely in the large political affairs of our country, but in the much humbler affairs which you and I administer. His lordship talked of making roads and bridges. For our schemes to be successful, the country in the north must be opened up, as you so well know. Accordingly the Government were made interested in the backward condi-tion of these areas. Roads and bridges must be constructed. If the Government pay half the cost, will his lordship pay

the other half – so far as his lands are concerned? His lordship agrees. And now the construction is *en train*. The
Government pays half. You see – uh – what I mean?'

'I do,' said Mr Heller.

'Now there is one thing arising out of all this that I must
impress upon you and Mr Elder, and that is her ladyship's
attitude. You have already, no doubt, come to your own
conclusions about that. But we must not lose sight of the
fact that her ladyship, who quite agrees to the change of
tenancy, will yet be very sensitive about any public criticism coming back upon *her*. You understand what that
means – precisely?'

'Precisely,' said Mr Heller.

'Good,' said Mr James. After allowing that important if
delicate matter to sink in, he proceeded, 'Here, again, political power would help us. Nothing ever goes wrong in the
House of Lords. The public discussion ground is the House
of Commons, where *questions* can be asked. It would be
extremely valuable if we had someone there to guard our
interests and actions – and, if necessary, explain their greatness.'

His companion glanced at him.

'May I say to you confidentially, Mr Heller, that it has
been suggested that I should stand for the Northern Burghs.'

Mr Heller drew up. The thrill he got now was stronger
than any he had received in the course of the interview.
The skin along the bones of his face whitened. Even the
crudeness was burned up in the fire of admiration that
exclaimed, 'My God!'

\*

To the introduction of any great change in the social and
economic life of a people there is technically no obstacle
other than what may be found in the law of the land. In
the bold and extensive venture upon which Mr Heller and
his coadjutors were embarked, the only real difficulty lay

in the existence of certain tacks or leases of farms or small estates held by individuals. Until the expiration of these tacks, it might not be possible to clear the ground of its human stock, unless the tacksman was willing to dispose of his unexpired term for some compensating benefit, such as remission of past debts or an advantageous offer of land elsewhere. This, however, was a minor difficulty, inasmuch as the vast bulk of the land was held in direct yearly tenancy or by tacks due to expire at early dates. It thus became possible and business-like to parcel out the vast territory into large farms and sheep-walks, and to offer them by advertisement to suitable tenants.

Accordingly, for the first time in the history of that land, it became a common sight to see strangers traversing the mountains and moors, examining valleys, and otherwise inspecting closely the geographical, botanical, bestial and human features in their potential money-making aspects.

To the people of the glens these strangers were very literally visitors from another world, and the mere sight of them on a skyline raised emotions of wonder and fear and even of terror. For they were endowed, not altogether wrongly perhaps, with the godlike powers that dispose of human destiny with a nod and a rustle of parchment.

While the old prayed God secretly that the stranger might find their place poor and undesirable, the young turned gloomy and rebellious, or laughed openly at uncommon oaths. The process of disintegration was slow but remorseless. In a little time the old would be praying not merely that the stranger would pass them by, but that their evicted brother would pass them by, for to give hospitality to the homeless became, in the eyes of the factors, so heinous an offence that it was visited by summary expulsion from house and land, thus adding the homeless to the homeless, and setting as leader over that ever-growing company the spectre of death.

For the cleavage between the desires of the people and

the desires of the landlord was fundamental and could never be bridged. On the people's part there was love of the land, love of its visible features as something near and natural to them as their own limbs; they grew out of it as a birch tree grows out of it, and could be removed only by a tearing up of roots. The sun, the wind, the shapes of things, the smells, the sound of their own voices, the singing, the laughter, the sorrow, the lore, the passion – all that centuries upon centuries had fashioned in man's or God's image moved behind their eyes and lay on their hearts and in their palms. It was no phantasy that gathered the Riasgan in Mairi's brow or set Mairi wandering for the roots and lichens of colour in the brow of the Riasgan. Deeper than desire, more selfless than love, silent as the cry of the unborn. Sunlight, mist and night; or gladness, tears and death; to that land and its children.

Opposed to this on the part of the landlord and his factors was the conception of material gain arranged in a pattern called Progress. That this progress has proved illusory merely destroys the name they gave to their excuse, and strips their lust for possession to its naked strength.

Now when any man opposes the fundamental principle of life in another, he must, by the irksome consciousness or subconsciousness of what he is doing, become antagonistic and violent, and will hunt about in the other's life for what he can despise and hate. What with ignorance, poverty and pride, Mr Heller found plenty to despise. But now that rancour was being raised against the stranger, that the blackened sea-coasts, where the disinherited subsisted on food that their four-footed brethren rejected, were lifting audible rumblings of complaint, he became very wroth and cast about for some large dramatic stroke that would have the double effect of strangling the life principle altogether and showing the action as one of regrettable compulsion under the law of the land.

But while Mr Heller – and his name may be taken to

represent (or shield) superiors and underlings – was driving on his clear-sighted course, the great bulk of his victims were dumb in the grip of their Church, their chief, and his law. The old might pray, the young curse, but when a stranger was seen on the valley crest or boldly walking up the river path, the many retired to the shelter of their homes as birds to cover beneath the hovering hawk.

Such a stranger was seen on the day that Elie was married to Rob the miller. There were two pipers at the head of the procession from the Riasgan to the miller's house, long-bearded Roy and a black giant from the Heights, one of the wild McHamishs. The instinct to look back in farewell on some place dear and familiar made Elie turn her face towards Dark Mairi's cottage. Dark Mairi was there by the gable, the kind soul, humped a little as though she were muttering one of her invocations. In a moment the old woman could bring a poignancy to life sharp as a knife thrust; the blind thrust that draws a cry of protest, of sorrow, of hate against life the fool whose stupidity is a black maze. Elie's eyes flashed to the brow of the wood . . . and there, springing out of it, was a man's body, small at the distance and dark and extraordinarily still. Those behind saw the awful quickening on her face and heard the small sharp cry she gave as she stumbled. Turning, they too observed the figure on the edge of the wood, but not knowing Elie's association with that particular spot they cried urgently, 'Look, there's one of them!' and all along the line the rhythm of the marching feet was broken. Exclamations were heard, defiant, full of boastful laughter, for clearly at that distance the figure had a strange power over them. They were afraid, and hated themselves for being afraid, of this sinister portent of disaster. Cheers broke out sporadically. They shouted jokes in unnecessarily loud voices. The girls giggled and screeched, or told off some of the more playful gallants in ringing tones. Anticipation of the marriage-festivities got a reckless hold, and when the mill hove in sight the unexpectedly large group that was awaiting them responded with hurrahs and the waving of arms and bonnets. 'By God, it's going to be a great wedding!' shouted a young man barely out of his teens, who thereupon, on the grass in front of the mill, danced a few steps to imaginary swords. There was at once something amusing, good-natured and debased in his exaggerated drunken manner, for he was not a child of the Riasgan and had come to take part in festivities that by the known nature of the contracting parties must step over the normal restraints of a decent wedding into the irresponsibilities of debauch.

There was, in truth, this unlicensed air about Elie's marriage for most minds, consciously or not. As the party approached the mill, the false gaiety roused by the stranger ran into a deeper channel. Delight in its eagerness could afford to fumble with restraint and crush it good-naturedly. There was almost no hurry. The festivities would last for days. And when minds backthrust at the stranger, it was in a sort of smothering triumph.

For at odd moments the stranger did rise up in their minds, like a devil-shepherd driving them on. To what? The marriage of Rob the ranter to Elie the mother of a bastard!

The newly-built half of the mill, with its fine stone walls and unusual use of timber, was somehow the very keynote of the hidden joke. For the mill had got burned down on the night when Rob had laid open Johnny Slaumach's head for agreeing with him that Elie was a bitch.

*

It had been a wild night, the last of a long stormy period in Rob's career, when even to his most intimate friends he had seemed heading straight for some inscrutable hell of his own, whose secret fire was already consuming him.

The black giant, McHamish, had been one of five

gathered by Rob's grinding-stones to savour a particularly strong whisky – trestarig or thrice-distilled – conveyed from the Heights by the giant himself, who was fond of Rob and his quick-tempered, erratic, generous ways. 'Take that home with you,' Rob would say, and in the early hours, still only three-parts drunk, McHamish would stumble away almost unconscious of the bag of meal on his back. An exchange of gifts between men who would have scorned to bargain, yet knowing the gifts were in it.

On this particular night, whether through the quick violence of the liquor or the invisible presence of Rob's demon or as a result of Tomas the Drover's visit to the Riasgan, Elie's name was mentioned. Whereat Rob flamed up. 'What!' he cried. 'That bitch!'

'Ach, away, Rob!' replied Murray, a Riasgan man, good-naturedly. 'She's not a bitch.'

'Ho!' said Rob, swinging on him. 'How do you know about her? I say she's a bitch and a whore!' The last words rose to a roar.

'Well, and I say she's not,' replied Murray, equably. 'She made a slip; but, damn me, she's a nice kind girl.'

'I say she's a whore!' yelled Rob with unnatural violence.

'She was covered,' said Murray. 'But she doesn't peddle it about. And if it hadn't been for the bloody wars—'

But the very words used by Murray so acted upon Rob that McHamish had at once to interfere.

'No fighting amongst friends, boys. That's our law. Keep the fighting for the factors.'

'Take your hands off me!' shouted Rob. 'Curse you; don't handle me!' And he tore his shoulder from McHamish's grip.

Whereupon Johnny Slaumach sidled up to Rob and in his pacifying pawing way said, 'Never mind them, Rob. You and I know she is a bitch.'

For a moment the sly silly grin hung on his face, then Rob's fist smashed into it with such astonishing force that

Johnny heeled over backwards, came his full length on the flat millstone, and lay still. The sound of the blow, followed by the head-thud on the stone, induced a profound quiet.

'Lord Almighty, Rob,' whispered McHamish, 'what the devil did you do that for?' They were all gazing at him, for the violence with which he had hit Johnny was something entirely different from the hostility with which he had opposed Murray, the difference between human quarrelsomeness and the lash of a demon.

'To hell with him!' cried Rob – 'and you, the whole rotten herd of you!' His eyes blazed in the flickering tongues of light from the burning wall-faggots and cruisie lights; for Rob always started – and generally ended – his male gatherings in the mill itself rather than in the living-end of the dwelling with its peat fire. It gave him privacy; it was his own place; and dealings in whisky or unlicensed talk were unhampered by that domesticated form of the female presence which Rob declared had never had anything upon him but a cramping effect.

McHamish now turned from him towards the figure on the millstone. Rob went swiftly past into the obscurity behind. There was a rumbling of mechanism, a gurgling and splashing of water, and the millstone began to revolve. 'Here, hold on!' shouted McHamish, going round with the stone. As the speed increased he yelled imperiously. He could still have slid off and dragged Johnny with him, but in his increasing anger he concentrated on dominating Rob, who now stood on the edge of the light again, his eyes lit up infernally. As the speed grew he began to laugh. 'Hold on, McHamish!' he roared. 'That's you, my hero!' God, what fun! Look at them! . . . And they were now revolving so fast that McHamish had all he could do to hold himself and the inert body of Johnny Slaumach to the wheel. If they were whirled off and hit the wall they would smash their heads in. Once McHamish's heel touched ground and the foot was jerked in the air. 'You for a dancer!' shouted Rob, and doubled up.

But by this time Murray was upon him, his mild face dangerous. Rob cursed him and grappled and they rolled in the passage-way. Over their bodies the Drover climbed. He had been shouting steadily for the last minute, and still addressed herds of fools as he stumbled in the dark, groping for any handle that would twist or bend. He was stepping into certain death in the yawning water-hole, when his outflung hands caught on something that gave – and held. He swung his feet back and leaned, sick and gasping, against the wall. The water-wheel slowly ceased to revolve. Tomas sank to the ground, muttering that they could find him, if they liked, the cattle. He vomited, and succumbing to an exquisite drowsiness, went to sleep.

Murray had retained the sanity not to struggle with Rob for struggling's sake, and when McHamish's wild yell tore through the building, he disengaged himself, giving Rob a heavy blow in the face as he did so.

Murray found that the wheel had won its contest, but had had the grace to fling McHamish and Johnny against a heap of bags, where they both lay, Johnny inertly and McHamish twisting and grovelling in an extravagantly drunken manner. Having finished its job, the granite wheel came to a standstill.

To Murray's anxious questions, McHamish gave no answer. In a slow deliberate effort he got on hands and knees, but stuck there, head lolling and waggling like a sick beast's.

'Wrestling with the Lord, McHamish?' cried Rob, while in the same instant he dealt Murray a blow in the spine that snicked his head and sent him sprawling.

McHamish slowly raised his head and looked at Rob. There was murder in the look, not furious or vicious, but cold and concentrated. Rob could see him draw upon that concentration, forcing its governing strength to his legs. He

got one foot on the ground and levered up his trunk with
his hands.

'That's you!' Rob encouraged him. 'Now for the other
leg!'

With a superb effort McHamish got to his feet, held
swayingly for a moment, then spun, with the motion of
the wheel, collapsed full length and started retching.

Rob laughed loudly. This was the best sport he had ever
had! The whole field flattened out! Murray was embracing
Johnny Slaumach! Lying with his ear upon his breast as if
he loved him! Where was Tom the Drover? Where? Rob
looked swiftly about him, stared at the black passage-way.
'Tom!' he yelled.

'He's dead,' came Murray's voice.

'What?' shouted Rob, wheeling upon Murray's pale face
and steady glittering eyes, and watching him in a curious
fascinated way as he slowly got to his feet.

Rob looked down at Johnny Slaumach's body. 'Serve
him damn well right!' he said. Then he shouted on Tom
again and, snatching the butt of a faggot, made for the
passage to the water-wheel. When he saw no upstanding
body between him and the hole, his heart constricted and
he exclaimed sharply. Staggering quickly forward, he tripped
over Tom and the faggot described a fiery arc into the
watery darkness. He fondled and shook the body urgently,
muttering to it not to be a fool and, in God's name, to
speak to him.

The body grunted. 'That's you, my hero!' cried Rob
gratefully. 'Up with you, my darling! I thought you had
stuck the wheel!' In his arms he bore Tom triumphantly
into the light and set him down gently.

But Tom was not now going to wake easily just to please
Rob. 'Leave me,' he said, in an irritated yet sepulchral voice,
while his beard drooped on his chest and his eyes remained
closed. The mouth fell open and the sound of his breath
was half a snore.

Rob laughed, and pulled Tom's beard. As he straightened up he said to Murray, 'God, he gave me a fright!'

Murray kept looking at him with a queer infernal smile, then went and bent over McHamish.

'Give me a minute yet,' muttered McHamish, who was now lying perfectly still on his face. Murray got up and went to the door. Rob heard him speaking to someone. Sarah's voice answered. Murray gave her a sharp half-whispered order, then he came in and shut the door carefully. Catching Tom by the shoulder, he shook him roughly. 'Get up!' Nor would he leave him until Tom was on his feet, blinking from Murray to Rob in a startled way. When Murray had brought McHamish to a sitting position, he said in a voice which they all heard very distinctly, 'I think Johnny Slaumach is dead.'

There was silence for a little while, during which all their personal angers fell from them. McHamish, without saying a word, staggered across to Johnny. The Drover was quickly on his knees beside the inert figure, about whose nostrils and mouth the blood was already congealing. Murray brought light and stooped over them.

Standing erect in the middle of the floor, Rob looked on as if what they were doing had neither interest nor meaning for him. There was a faintly embarrassed or self-conscious smile on his features, but when he jerked his head up, as if he were listening to something very remote in the night, the smile was seen as a furrowed tormented anguish, drawing red threads upon the strained eyeballs. In a moment it was clear that he had forgotten them, and the Drover's voice, swearing softly and urgently that he believed the heart was still going, disturbed him only as voices might out beyond the walls. He looked at the probing hands, watched them lift the body and carry it past him towards the door and the warmth of the kitchen fire in the dwelling-house, saw that they completely ignored him, did not even glance at him.

Which was right and fitting. In the silence of the empty mill he remained quite still, the creases of his ghastly smile deepening, the head tilting again, listening to the thudding feet dying away, then listening to the world beyond, to the slope of a hillside with a figure on it, a face turned, looking down at him.

Ah, that look! that face! His body broke away – to pull itself up rigidly – to break away – what had he been saying? What had he called her? But the real violence had gone out of him. He was entangled, he was snared. Her white look pressed back his face, coiled its awful humility about his feet.

In one of those spasmodic jerkings of the body by which he normally blotted out thought, he saw the two-gallon wooden vessel of the thrice-distilled whisky, and in the same instant, picking it up, flung it with all his strength against the lighted wall, so that when the whole wall shot up in an explosive blaze, the fire ran along the arch of spilt whisky into his body and face. Blinded and scorched, he swayed backwards, his hands crushing chest and face and eyes. By the time he found he could still see, the small battens of bog pine that lay against the roof couples were on fire.

'The whole place is up in a blaze,' he said in his normal voice, and carefully rubbed his eyes again. 'The whole bloody place will be burnt to the ground!' It was an unusual happening, almost humorous.

The thought of those next door, of the meal in his girnel, of certain personal possessions, attacked his mind in the rear and twitchings went over his flesh, but he held his ground. It was fairly getting a hold now! One or two battens fell to the floor, flaming furiously. He watched their writhings. Another lot! Phew, it was getting hot! Murray burst in at the door, staggered back, remained looking at Rob for a stark moment, then let rip an oath and disappeared.

Rob went out after him, but stopped before his own house, overcome by a paralysing reluctance to enter. When the others came out carrying Johnny, however, he forced himself into movement. Yet it was cunning useless movement. The others ignored him as if he were tainted or mad or a child.

It was his sister Sarah who brought him back into his natural violence. Her screeching and yelling had been distasteful enough, but when suddenly she stood before him and in her frenzied voice told him what he was, her hands clenched, her clay face working in an ugly way beneath disordered hair, he conceived for her a hatred so intense that it locked the muscles that ached to smash her.

Not until she flung from him was he released, and then, in a voice rising to a scream, he yelled, 'Get out of my sight! Get out of my sight before I murder you!' He made after her, but a fist felled him. When he got up, McHamish was waiting for him, his black face lit up by the burning house.

'So it's you, McHamish!' said Rob, eyes gleaming in the triumphant expression that had watched him on the wheel.

The Drover went in against McHamish's breast, but with a flick of his hand McHamish sent him rolling on the ground. As Murray came out of the door under a chest, the roof of the mill collapsed and the roaring upthrust of flame and flying timbers staggered him to a headlong few steps, McHamish saving him from being crushed under his burden. When these two men straightened up, Rob was gone.

'We can do no more,' said Murray. 'The beasts are clear. It's got to burn out.' He was panting heavily.

They retired to where Johnny Slaumach was recovering his senses rapidly before the spectacle of the fire. There was a bloody hollow in his head but he seemed sane enough in his questions. Speculation on the origin of the fire drew from Murray, 'It was whisky. The place reeked. He must have heaved the cask against the wall. The bloody fellow is mad.' And then he added sharply, and for no apparent reason, for McHamish was perfectly silent and still, 'Look here, McHamish, it's no good feeling like that. Leave him! Damn him, leave him!'

'But,' stammered Johnny Slaumach, 'why – why did he—'

'Oh, shut up!' said Murray.

'Murray,' said McHamish quietly.

'It's all right, McHamish. You needn't use that tone on me.'

'Quite right,' said the Drover. 'Rob's the kindest fellow – by God, I tell you—'

Even as McHamish silenced him, Murray was on his feet. 'Come over here with me, McHamish.' McHamish followed him.

'I don't know what's taken Rob, but I'll tell you what I think. He cursed that girl Elie of Dark Mairi's. But I know he has been after her. She has a bastard. You see what I mean? The thing is tormenting him like hell; that's what it looks like to me.'

McHamish was silent. Then with soft astonishment he murmured an oath and sank into a thoughtfulness from which Murray had to rouse him physically.

When they returned to the other two they found Sarah there, glancing about her in a frightened or threatening manner. But now there was no sign of Rob; and when the fire had burned down she went away in the company of Tomas and Johnny Slaumach to her sister's home in the main glen, Murray advising her to stay there for good.

Her forceful words made Murray remark soberly to McHamish as they stood alone, 'God knows who's to blame for that.' Then he added abruptly, 'You'd better come home with me. We'll make up the accident that put the place on fire.'

But McHamish now did not like leaving Rob and insisted

on walking all about the premises. At last they went away together.

*

When, a few days later, Elie saw Rob the miller coming up the hillside, she knew, by a slowness in his walk, in all his bodily movements, a head-hanging deliberation completely uncharacteristic of him, that at last he carried her fate upon him.

By a curious sympathy for him at that moment, she did not retreat into the house. As her strength ebbed, she thought of the ceilidh-house saying, 'My hour is pursuing me.' A vague smile flickered over her features and drained them too.

He greeted her quietly, pleasantly, with a quick look at her and a long look away, during which he asked her if she would come down the hill a bit with him as he had something to say to her. She went at once.

When they came into a little hollow out of sight of the houses, he sat down and she sat down beside him.

'It's a long story,' he began, staring before him. Then, somehow, he was silent, as though all the words within him had withered like grass. From a flushing in her breast, a sickness rose into her throat. A strong desire came upon her to lie back. 'Will you marry me, Elie?'

'Yes,' she whispered.

He turned and looked at her. She was smiling.

'O Christ!' he groaned before that look, and buried his head in his hands, pressing the palms against his ears.

All she had to do now was to put her hand on his head. He would then bury his head in her lap or crush her nearly to death. But she couldn't lift her hand. She stared at the sandy hair that showed grey about the neck.

'I know,' came her voice, 'what you have been thinking.'

'What have I been thinking?' His head lifted sharply; his eyes challenged her.

'I know,' she murmured, looking away from him.

'What?'

She looked at him. 'It was hard for you to ask a girl like me.'

'O God, shut your mouth!' he cried. The swift convulsion passed from him and he spoke quietly, through a bitter smile. 'I knew it was no use. Yet, to tell the truth, I came with a different feeling in my mind from any other time. I wanted to do it. I had made up my mind. When I burned the mill, I thought I had burnt all the damn nonsense out of my mind. I let it roar. I got rid of Sarah. I was free. But it's no use. I see that. No use at all.' He plucked a grass and began chewing it, a greenish froth forming at the corners of his mouth. 'Ah, well, Elie, it doesn't matter. I'm sorry that I troubled you. I am. You have always been – before you went away – you were just a young girl and I a man about forty. I used to think of you then too. I used to think of you till I'd be burning, sure as death. But I could see – ah, well, it doesn't matter now. And I'd have been all right, if you hadn't given me yon look. It's not that you had been through sorrows and hard times. That's nothing very much. But instead of making you hard and coarse, it made you look like the mother of sorrows herself. Damn you,' he said, beginning to get worked up, 'you had no right to look at me like yon. You had no right to understand, to feel for me, to forgive me – no right, for if I'd got half a chance I'd have had my way with you whether you liked it or not.' He stopped and looked at her, with a bark of laughter. 'And I suppose you'd have forgiven me even that!'

'Why should you let it bother you,' she said. 'I'm only an outcast.'

She spoke simply, almost unthinkingly, and was amazed to see the extraordinary change that came over Rob's face.

'By God, Elie, that's what you are!' he said, gazing at her with wonder. 'You're an outcast!' His face lit up. His eyes opened wide and, shining, centred upon her with no faintest shadow in their depths. He was completely transformed, and began to chuckle. The note of the man, too, was not now possessive, but kindly and combative, as if he were in that moment of revelation not her lover but her ally. So all the world was against her, was it? Ha! ha! . . .

The conflict emerged from the tortuous centres of his mind and became visible upon the plane of the earth. He could take part in that! He could slaughter a few!

Had she refused him, he would never have rebuilt the mill; he would have gone away to the ends of the earth . . .

Trembling, she waited until he would look at her again.

*

She told Mairi of it that night, after little Colin was asleep and before Davie, whose hours were growing ever more erratic, might come in.

They were sitting by the fire and Mairi said in a sensible voice that she was glad to hear the news. 'He has got a nice place yonder, and I've heard them say he's got a bit of money laid by. I was hoping it would come to this. What do you think yourself?'

'I don't know,' said Elie quietly.

'Never you fear,' said Mairi. 'You'll come to like it fine. He needs a good wife; and, whatever else, you'll be a good wife to him.'

'I'll do my best.'

'That's you.' Mairi nodded. 'He's sometimes wild and uncertain, they're saying, but there's kindness in him, and I would sooner have him than many. When did he say he was wanting you?'

'When the mill is built again and everything is tidy. He says he will make a great place of it now.'

'That's like him.' The thin smile disfigured her face. 'That will put my mind at peace about you.'

Dark Mairi could show none of that impulsive warmth

or intimate understanding which such an occasion might seem to warrant. But Elie did not expect it of her, and so Mairi's matter-of-fact attitude helped her to a calm, almost detached, perception of herself and her position. She was grateful to Mairi for this, and only some wayward submerged mood, washing softly, threatened now and then to spout up.

When Mairi got down to the business of fitting out the girl for her wedding, she became full of knowledge and resource. More and more Elie grew interested. Mairi told stories of marriage-customs in the Islands of the West in olden times and was reminded of the famous tale of the woman whose portion fate and the brutality of man had made tragic.

She told the tale as she might tell little Colin a rhyme. The strangers who arrived in ships, the fighting, the death of the husband, the cunning deceit of the woman to save her child, and the wild sorrowful end.

No over-sensitive sympathy in Mairi made her realise during the story's course that it might be unsuitable for the moment. She told it unfalteringly, thinking not at all of Elie, who was lifted by that far vision of life and love and death to a plane whereon her own story drew strength from these fateful sources. This old tale of Mairi's exposed Elie's story and purified it.

Yet there was no intention on Mairi's part to perform so high a service; as there was no consciousness on Elie's part of being instructed. And by some still more profound alchemy, the very tragedy which ended Mairi's story gave to the possibility of tragedy in Elie's story the last strength of all.

And if, so expressed, their natural communion may seem to draw on deeps far beyond their simple powers to trouble, yet in reality it need not be so, for through countless generations the ultimates have been caught by these women in legend and poem and music known to them as intimately as their breath.

A quietness came about them and about their talk. And though sometimes Mairi sighed, at the end of the long exhalation she would exclaim mildly and smile, as though what had been dealt with had been dealt with finally and the matter was removed from their hands.

In Elie, too, this manner could be seen, so that in some curious fashion they were like two figures giving judgment amongst men, while leaving the unravelling of the final mystery of human conduct to unearthly powers. Their namelessness, like their hour, had pursued them and caught them up. Man was the child over which their eyes brooded. They could be all things to him and nothing. Life must go on.

When Elie had gone into bed, she watched Mairi prepare to cover the red embers with the grey ash. Tonight, as if still deeply preoccupied, she went about her task slowly and carefully. The embers she spread into a circle, then divided the circle into three parts with three peats that met in a red centre. This she did in the name of the Three of Light. Over the red she spread the ash; and in the spectral glimmer, Elie saw her extend her arms and intone softly:

> 'The Sacred Three
> To save,
> To shield,
> To surround
> The hearth,
> The house,
> The household,
> This eve,
> This night,
> Oh! this eve,
> This night,
> And every night,
> Each single night.
> Amen.'

At that moment Elie's heart was uplifted into the mystery of God's twilight, wherein ineffable calm and longing commingle, swirling faintly in ring upon ring outward to eternity.

But when Mairi came to bed, her complete resignation penetrated her voice in a slightly exhausted, almost petulant, way, so that when she said, 'Well, we'll go to sleep,' it was as though she said, 'That's all we can do: we're only mortal.'

In no time she was sound asleep and Elie was listening to the wheezing of her breath in her nostrils and open mouth.

It was not a pleasant sound – to arrive so quickly too! Mairi's body had never had much warmth. To come against her was to come against the bones of her knees or her elbows.

Elie suddenly felt desperately lonely, and her mood ran along the deep-worn groove in her mind that led to the crest of the wood. There was only one answer that she had prepared for Rob. But Rob had not put the question that day – though well she knew he would put it yet – and many like it in the unreasoning tormented moments that were as bound to happen to him as fire to smothered peat. She repeated her answer now, 'Colin is dead.'

On the crest of the wood, as often happened, his dark body rose up.

*

And now on her marriage morning, while the others were using the vision of the stranger on the crest of the wood as a lash to their gaiety, Elie had had her own dark vision. She had conquered it quickly enough, as she always did, but it had startled her, and something of omen or fate about it remained to give her laugh a curious catch and lift.

The wedding feast was rich beyond measure. All the neighbours had seen to that, with gifts of fowl and meat greater than custom required, as though in some such way a generous hand might smooth out what was unfortunate in the circumstances of the occasion.

The eating and drinking were generous as the laughter and noise – perhaps, again, over-generous by just that amount that a sensitive spirit might catch now and then in the compliments of some of the men. Their eyes were bright, and in roundabout subtle ways they made it clear that everything was splendid and the future assured. Therefore – here's to you! And once again! The happiest wedding I have ever been at!

A genuine happiness and brotherliness did begin to pervade them all. It was, astonishingly, a splendid wedding! Elie's unassuming ways, her shy smiling responses, and something in her eyes like light in the bottom of a well, drew the women unfailingly. The twenty years' difference in the ages of Rob and Elie had a rightness that somehow would not have been there had Rob been a young man of Elie's years. Altogether it was an occasion for merriment, for irresponsible pleasure. And talk – they could not stop talking, and scoring off one another and laughing. The Drover made a memorable speech, into which he worked all sorts of half-veiled allusions. Nor did he forget the Beast. His most brilliant invention was the Wedding of the Sheep, wherein he indicated, without directly naming, the tup, the ewe, and the principal wethers. And he had all sorts of vivid connecting phrases, such as, 'Now when the lord tup himself looked round upon that glen from which everything on two legs had been removed except the hoodie crows . . .'

The guests revelled in this sort of invention, for it was born naturally out of their love of the ancient tales of their race, of proverbs, of impromptu satirical verses, of song-choruses, of witty sayings and divinations. They relished the finer turns with a far keener appreciation than they relished differences in food or drink or shelter. They laughed excessively and noisily. They banged the board. 'Stop him!' They swayed, and leaned against one another. They were proud of the Drover, while they wondered if somebody couldn't choke him.

All difficulties or awkwardnesses were broken down. Their natural selves emerged untrammelled and heightened. There were no barriers here, nor consciousness of barrier. Each being was a distinct – even an extreme – individualist, as diverse in physical and mental characteristic as the Drover and McHamish, or Rob and Davie, yet all combining in a communism or community of interest, not merely complete in its material aspect, but sustained by a singular spiritual force.

It was an interesting gathering, and eyes looking on each other could see the something extra of self-consciousness in the hectic gaiety that was like the first faint touch of dissolution. And when, the feast over, a knot of men on the grass before the mill spied the dark stranger now on the hill-crest above, the sudden discoloration of their faces exposed the underlying fear and hate.

'Let us stone the bastard!' muttered the Drover.

The drones of McHamish's pipes clicked together again as he lowered them and laughed good-naturedly. 'When I was coming down yesterday at the Cnoc, one of them – he turned out to be Read, manager of the sheep-farm – was looking down like that. Some of the boys said, "Let us give him a fright!" So they spread out. Young Rory said he got him in the back of the neck with a turf. There was then, for a little, a tearing fight between his dogs and some of ours. But the boys did not let themselves be properly seen. They laughed afterwards and said it beat poaching. But the old folk were angry, for never before, they said, had any stranger been treated inhospitably.'

McHamish's quiet manner was full of pleasant satire, but the Drover said abruptly, 'He wasn't a stranger: he was a spy, a damn thief!' His eyes were burning beneath their bushy coverings. The success of his speech put him on the crest of action. He extended a hand. 'Is there no one here with the spirit of the Cnoc boys?' His body, inclined to stoop forward from the hips as if always on the verge of intimate or dramatic speech, straightened itself and his beard shot up as his hand swung round and pointed at the body of the stranger.

At the mill, the valley narrowed, so that the stranger was nearer than he had been on the brow of Mairi's wood. For a few moments no one moved or spoke, then, of all voices, Davie's rose through an odd laugh, 'Come on!' and he beckoned with his hand.

Some of the older men peremptorily called, 'Don't be mad!'

But already half-a-dozen youths were on the run.

Amid the commotion Elie suddenly appeared, crying, 'Stop them!' with a vehemence totally unlike her, almost hysterical. 'Where's Rob?' She found him. 'Oh, Rob, stop them! stop them!' She caught at his jacket. Her appeal, her instinctive turning to him for help, left him dead-still, gazing into her face. He muttered something about its being nothing. He could not take his eyes off her.

'Rob! It's our wedding day!'

At that he came awake. 'What!' He looked after the running figures. Then he broke into action, his eyes blazing with light. 'I'll stop the Earl of Hell,' he cried. Others followed him, including all the small boys and a number of dogs.

Soon the first runners, headed by Davie, were at the foot of the steep rise. Rob's voice was heard bawling at them to stop. The dogs and the little boys yelped. The watching women were crowding about Elie, full of concern and elderly lamentation, Seonaid alone amongst them regarding the race with a certain satisfaction. When the youths were half-way up the incline, Elie screamed to the stranger to go away, as if the man could hear. Seonaid gripped her by the shoulder. 'What do you care?' she asked, almost roughly.

Elie paid no heed. 'He's gone!' she cried, with relief.

The stranger had disappeared. Rob's voice, too, was beginning to have its effect. But Davie and three others topped the hill. They paused for a little, then Davie went on alone. Uncertainly, the other three went after him. Rob kept up his pursuit, and on the crest of the hill let out an angry bellow and also disappeared. Soon quite a company were on the skyline. After a few minutes there was some obscure commotion amongst them, then they all began to troop back. The little boys arrived first, saying the stranger had taken to his heels with Davie after him. Some said that Davie had felled him, but others that he had missed him; they were unanimous, however, in agreeing that Rob had threatened to smash Davie's face and had to be restrained from fulfilling his threat – while quite a few had to restrain Davie.

They all called the stranger a sasunnoch who was looking for a sheep-farm.

One or two of the wiser heads prophesied that evil would come out of the incident, for they suspected that the factors would be glad of any excuse to condemn the local people and justify their own ends. In this they were proved singularly correct.

Meantime Rob had arrived before Elie and was telling her that everything was all right. 'It was that fool of a fellow, Davie,' he said. 'I told him I'd knock his head off.' He spoke blusteringly, for already he was uncomfortable over the way he had turned on Davie. But, to his great relief, Elie smiled bright-eyed, apparently unconcerned.

Rob immediately became charged with the utmost good humour. He dispensed hospitality with two hands and a forceful manner, and rallied McHamish on not having enough wind left to fill his rotten old sheep-skin.

The Drover, cackling, backed him up. 'This may be the last wedding the Riasgan will ever see.'

'If it's the last, it'll be remembered!' swore Rob.

This incident over the stranger proved the sort of diversion that was needed to lift them entirely into that unreasoning uncurbed state beyond the generous. Yet that which was over measure was subject to a mad rhythm of its own. And even if one or two of them had fought – which they did before that protracted wedding was over – the wild emotions and counter-emotions would have been caught in the one swinging circle.

This was seen that evening when, between two of the dances, Elie was called upon for a song. There had been a quickness of gaiety and response in Elie's behaviour ever since the flight towards the dark stranger, giving her an unusual attractiveness, a certain erratic manner, that had the air of a wild shyness. It suited her and the occasion, and accorded more and more with the ever-rising spirits of her guests. When men looked at her, their eyes brightened and held. The women understood.

She did not make any pretence of not wanting to sing, but there and then, without moving from where she stood, prepared herself. In a moment the whole place was silent. They could see her searching her mind for a suitable song, yet for some reason no one prompted her to a favourite air. All at once she started on what had come into her head.

From her first note she had her guests under her dominion. Out over them her voice came like an invisible hand. The notes of the old love song were slow and full, brown as wild honey, a globule of honey between the eyes and the moon, between the spirit and the dream.

For there was honey in the song and despair. Once in the middle of it she had fallen down and wept for the girl of whom she sang. And once she had sung it with her mind clear as the evening light over that beautiful tragic world which Colin, beside her, bore on his back.

Now she made her audience carry the burden, while she

herself rose up and with an artlessness more terrible than swords desolated the field of their emotions.

She knew now the song she sang. Remembering it, she sang it to herself. She circumscribed the song and held it and conquered it. For she was not Elie nor any known person. She was nameless, and what was happening to her was no more than what might happen to her hair from the wind, or to her eyes from falling stars, or to her ears from distant music. When she had had for her answer, 'Colin is dead,' she had really meant, 'The past is dead.'

Yet nothing was dead, and she herself was alive, recording life in death, this strange pattern of emotion and action, existing no one knew why, catching the body and soul into its whirl, throwing them aside, for no reason that anyone could think of – perhaps for no reason at all.

Here was the girl in the song comforting this unreason with humanity's final logic, tragedy. Elie knew all about that girl and gave her the dignity due so ultimate a rôle. Her voice could not be shamed by any sound between earth and heaven. And no personal stress or sentiment flawed its nameless power.

Yet it went deeper than that. For she sang in a tongue and a rhythm that were not merely countless centuries old, but had been born out of the earth on which they starved and feasted and against which their feet pressed now, so that all the millions of influences and refinements that had shaped themselves to make the incommunicable understood were from the very first note altogether at her service. Indeed they were at her service before she started to sing, and the first note had come out over them like a hand, whose passing fingers stirred their hair to its roots.

Kirsteen sat with a face as white as death. Angus og's fixed unconscious smile gave his expression a foxy cunning, emphasised by the glitter in his eyes beneath the heavy eyebrows. Davie's teeth were gnawing at a corner of the upper lip in a way that twisted his mouth, while his eyes remained uncomfortably conscious, occasionally glancing at Elie but refusing to be held. The black uptilt of the eyebrows against the pallor of the skin gave his face a curious distinction, as though, not quite of these people, he might very well be the reincarnation of some high-placed ancestor out of a stone cist or a long barrow. Three elderly women, whose hearts had been warmed by a drop of whisky, were uncaring of their tears. McHamish the piper was full of tenderness as a young girl. The Drover's features were consumed by an inner fire. One or two mouths had fallen slightly open. Anna and Hector were not there, but old Angus was, with his grey beard like a nest to his bird-twinkling eyes. Elie's mother and three of her sisters, rest-less at the beginning of the song, had grown quite still. There was a troubling look on the mother's face, as if some inner conflict were with difficulty being resolved. Elie said to her, 'Here is destiny'; and presently the mother sat with her hands in her lap and her head bowed. But Seonaid's face was open, and in its strong affection full of a firm dark beauty: only in the eyes did a glitter of emotion pene-trate through Elie and her song to the secret life they had shared. Young men and women, boys and girls, standing in groups, leaning against the walls, dark faces dark-eyed, an occasional fair face blue-eyed, all centring on Elie, whose autumn-brown hair had come untidy in answer to the warmth and fullness of her body, singing this love song of tragedy out of the heart of their race, out of her own heart – as they knew with that terrible cunning of intimacy that was born with them. Rob had forgotten them all. He was staring at his wife with the strange fascinated incredulity that has the extreme brightness of discovery and assurance at its core.

Presently the older folk began to talk of going home. 'It's time for all decent married people to be in bed.' Excitement got its extreme edge. The bride and bridegroom very nearly evaded the young company – but not quite.

There were screams and laughter and advice and a dark rabble from barn to kitchen. Some of the women should have put the bride to bed. But – well – it was Elie – she did not need advice! In any case, Rob wasn't having any of that damn nonsense. And when at last, panting, he got his shoulder against the inside of the door, he crushed it shut and barred it. He remained for a moment, his shoulder to the wood, hearing, however, not so much the shouts and laughter outside as the silence behind him in which Elie stood unmoving.

'By God, he's got her now!' said a man's voice in the group beyond the door. While they were conspiring what joke they might play, Davie slid away from them and in the blind instinct of his going collided with some girls.

It was star-dark and Kirsteen's low voice said intensely, 'Don't let them do anything.'

He had known her body even as he had bumped it. 'They won't,' he said, 'or McHamish will murder them.'

The three girls and Davie hung silent, throat-choked and tremulous, half-hearing the voices, the odd burst of thick laughter, aware of the two behind the closed door, sensitive to all the under-currents of thought, of suggestion, for this particular marriage warmed and loosened certain instincts to a deep natural mirth.

A solemn voice said, 'Rob's millstones will grind out many a harvest yet.' Davie found himself going towards the barn with the girls. There were squeals of laughter out of odd corners. Excitement ran like a fire, licking here and there into sound, into a crush of action. Yet, like fire, the action was not inward and concealed, but outward and swift-footed. There was time neither for the slow sentiment of love-making nor the deliberation of lust. Deliberate or calculated pursuit would have shocked the wildest. Love is a fire – even a destroying fire – or it raises the gorge.

Old Roy's fingers were clean as ever on the holes of the chanter, for he drank, in the way he had taught his son, little by little into that cold sobriety that may have an imaginary analogy in frozen fire. A bearded father to that excited happy throng of dancing youth, he ignored them, staring far over their heads as he played, so that one look at him, catching something of the wild antique in his whiskers, gave a curious enravelment of mirth to the swing and the laughter.

Kirsteen, gazing at the dance, felt Davie slip away from behind her. At once she turned her head. He was making for the glen and in a few moments disappeared in the night – not to return, as she knew more certainly than though he had sworn it. Yet all the young folk – and some old folk too – would sleep about barn and mill – anywhere – when tiredness overtook them, and pursue the festivities on the morrow. Most marriages lasted the better part of a week. Rob's was not likely to err on the ungenerous side.

The smile had gone from Kirsteen's face as she gazed at the dancers again. Her lips were compressed, her features sharp in a pale anger. Her companions had noticed nothing. 'Look out!' said one of them. Kirsteen was whirled into a dance. She was extremely light on her feet and soon her gaiety and quick-witted fun, flashing hither and thither, ordering, condemning, provoking, became the night's centre. Many a youth got a vision of girlhood that troubled his peace for long enough.

She troubled Davie too, going up the glen, but not happily. A strange kink had developed in his nature over the last year or so that he could not explain. Secretiveness had come upon him like a disease. His mind now worked inwardly upon itself with extreme sensitiveness. This bred a desire for loneliness, and in this loneliness he sometimes daydreamed the most extraordinary images. Of many of them he was ashamed, but not of all. Out of this came a subtle lack of assurance in the outward worldly affairs of men, and particularly in personal relations, perfectly masked by a more subtle pride.

He knew quite well that Kirsteen was not indifferent to him. But he would not help to bring matters between them even to a reasonable friendship. Had he been sure that she loved him, he would yet have hung back – perhaps more certainly then – to get the deeper savour out of it.

Yet in images he could secretly meet her. And tonight if she came up the glen, flying after him, her face pale and drawn in that vivid way that was like white fire, together they might fight and struggle and pierce the hills and pass beyond the hills like falling stars – and in a moment not really have risen at all, but – her voice, her fingers, his buried face.

He looked back to see if she was coming, half under the delusion that her hurrying face and hair would be visible in each feature, lit like one of those balls of fire or death-portents.

There was a small wind in the dark glen that went searching out all the humps and hillocks, scurrying about his feet, invisibly passing on. This wind gave a humped life to all inanimate things, as if they had drawn their shoulders taut against it and bowed or buried their heads. In the absence of wind they were still and menacing. But in a gale they wrapped themselves around and swift feet could pass them rapidly before they had noticed; though, again, within the gale, any one of the monsters, released, might come roaring in a lust more terrible than at any other time. Certain beings did ride the dark wind, but overhead, and only by a chance might they come low enough . . .

In this darkness of the world identity is lost and time becomes one with the monstrous beginnings of life, which legend recreates in such beings as centaur or water kelpie; or, receding still further, becomes one with the dark spirits, the Nameless Ones, who were before light or creation was. The blood's tale is told in the black night, and the nerves and flesh act the drama backwards.

Everyone in the Riasgan had this fear of the night in

one degree or another, and a wraith-story could set lonely apprehension quivering intolerably, so that the clutch, the cry, and the entombment in the black maw could be experienced by the imagination in the one instant.

Yet men bore against this by a deliberate obtuseness that, while believing, was prepared to combat fatally. It was some such spirit that had delivered time from its black womb.

Davie had by internal burrowings so far riddled his objective identity that now he was in the mood to meet the monstrous and fight it with strange bitter weapons out of his eyes and will. Indeed he would have welcomed any monstrous fight, however crushing and smothering the final negation.

Yet this very preparedness and defiance, with its secret pride, wrought him up into such a state of apprehension as he had never previously experienced; and for a considerable part of the way he walked like one disembodied, or with no more embodiment than a cold skin and pads for feet.

While all the time he was not so much subject to the mythic night as to another conflict, in a black inner consciousness, over what was taking place in the millhouse he had left behind him.

As he climbed the familiar slope to Dark Mairi's cottage he suddenly found himself slack and tired, with all tension gone. 'Lord, I'm tired!' he muttered, with a sort of disillusioned spite. His mouth was so dry he had nothing to spit. He lay down and feeling rolled from his brain in an emptying wave that the ground slowly drank. When he sat up he was shivering, with the lees of his tired mood in him.

He passed the cottage and climbed steadily up the hill, without knowing what he was doing or where he was going, without thinking at all. On the crest he stood erect and looked around upon his world, with its mountain waves and hidden glens, its immense dome of sky, cloud-wracked and star-strewn.

His walking hither had been a walking away from his own place and his own people. It suddenly came to him: his fate was to go beyond these hills, to emigrate. It had been working up to that ever since Colin and the boys had gone to the wars. The thousand meanings and acts, the loneliness, the pride, the house, Elie ... Elie ... and that terrible moment today when Rob and himself had glared at each other with murder in their eyes. All the strands of dissolution coming together. They would be herded and dispersed; he was merely herded away from them a little before his time, as if to symbolise the total process. He had seen it in their eyes today, in the fun that was overdone, in the marriage ...

He sat down, doubled up, with his forehead on his knees, so that he no longer looked like an emigrant, but rather like one of his remote ancestors whose only record are the occasional bones doubled up in a stone cist.

When he entered the darkness of his home Mairi's voice met him, asking how the marriage had gone. She was not only awake but eager, and this eagerness released something in him like a hot flood, destroying all his spectral fancies and finding brutal outlet in the words, 'By God, he's got her now!'

'Why don't you speak?' she asked, frightened by the rumbling sounds in his throat. 'What's wrong?'

'Nothing,' he answered in a clear voice. 'Everything went all right.'

'Davie! You're keeping something from me!'

So she had been afraid of something going wrong!

'What was I going to keep from you? I'm tired,' he said.

'Make a light.' She was wanting all the gossip, to be told all the details! Her voice was thin and whining in its eager scurry. He heard her body rustle in the bed.

'I don't want a light. I'm tired.' He should be kinder to her, but he couldn't help it.

She mumbled and then sighed. The peculiar drawn-out

sound of her sigh maddened him, as did the sound of some of her more mournful invocations. It stripped the nerves bare and exposed not only them but something that should forever remain hidden and forgotten, something of the past, misery-ridden, haunted, or God knew what. He lay down beside little Colin, clothed as he was, and pressed his brows against the bolster. She sighed again, but now with that sort of mindless detachment that was like the sighing of all the winds of the world.

A sudden compassion for Elie shook him profoundly.

They had handed her over.

He crushed his face into the bolster, through the ghost of her body.

## TWO

The pursuit of the stranger, who had not been hurt or even touched in any way, was just the sort of excuse that Mr Heller and his group needed to bring to a conclusive issue the now widespread misrepresentation of their humane efforts to institute schemes of progress. For two very important points could be made clear to all the world: first, that the natives with whom he had to deal were still the turbulent savages of Highland feud and rapine, of whom hundreds (as Mr James, M.P. for the Northern Burghs, stated in public a little later) had not heard the name of Jesus; and, second, that by thus exposing them and thereupon using the legal and military forces of the land to overawe and crush them he might once for all settle their grumbling and growling and proceed in peace to the completion of his great work.

For really it was exasperating enough to hear on every hand the protests of these poverty-ridden illiterates, in themselves and their ways of life hardly advanced beyond the 'lean kyloes' and 'scabby sheep' they herded, without having the same article adorned with rhetoric by 'Gaelic enthusiasts' who had never done a decent day's work in their lives – apart from soldiering, of course, when, all dressed up, they could strut and salute and exhibit themselves to the top of their bent.

Children of the Gael! The glens, the bens, and the heroes! With Bonaparte carrying in his pocket the Ossianic exploits of their forebears!

If these people who raved all that sort of romantic twaddle could only see the reality! They would then understand the greatness of the schemes for improving the estate and introducing civilisation into the Highlands; essentially a work of sanitation!

Old Falcon had warned him in the beginning that they would not work. They were above being hired out to work; as gentlemen of leisure they were too proud to become anything so low as day-labourers. And it was true! Once, it was said, a Highlander did start working on the new road, but after a little time got tired of it and went away home!

At the very moment when Bonaparte is sweeping across Europe to subdue the remote Russias, and have all the world under his thumb! Probably Ossian is biting him! And what is he, when all is said, but another strutting upstart? Thrown up by the grumblings of the gutter-rats who started the French Revolution.

Yet how articulate these Highland gutter-rats with their claim that the land is theirs! Her ladyship has no *right* to turn them out! They are the heirs of the heroes, every man a landlord in his own right!

But though Mr Heller occasionally indulged himself with such exclamations, he knew how necessary it was to meet cunning with decisive action.

*

When the word went through glens still uncleared that the factors desired to consult with the people about the vexed position of affairs and accordingly requested their attendance at the castle on a given day, a first flush of hope went over the face of fear. At last they were to be listened to! Some of the bolder spirits aired the opinion that what had been wrong all along was the way they had taken things lying down. They had let themselves be treated like sheep: one lot of sheep driven out and another lot driven in! If they had put up a fight they would have been respected. That's what some of the Ross-shire people did and they

were still on their crofts. But no, the people here were so
law-abiding, so holy, so influenced by their ministers who
had promised them hell-fire if they didn't go quietly that
they had trooped away from everything they possessed like
sheep. From their ancestral homes, humble no doubt but
their own and built by their own hands, they had allowed
a lot of money-grabbing tyrants to drive them forth to the
disease and destitution of the seashore, without hitting back
with anything stronger than a lamentation.

But see what happened immediately one of the sheepmen
got a fright! They were all invited to a conference!

These scoffing spirits may not have been many in number,
but they unquestionably had an effect on the men who now
came in driblets, forming into tributaries, and ultimately
into a single stream flowing down the coast upon the castle.
Many of them would be two full days on their bare feet
before the objective was reached; but any flicker of hope
to relieve impending doom would more than make up for
physical effort a thousand times more exhausting. Nor did
the head-shakings of the greybeards, who said they feared
the factors when they offered gifts and who accordingly
professed to see in this very conference some inscrutable
signal of disaster, make much impression on the pervading
optimism. Greetings were flung to newcomers; stories and
jokes and speculation flew from mouths like ribbons from
the drone-pipes; meal was mixed with water and at one
glorious spot the contents of a straw bee-skep was added
to a drop of illicit liquor, a food that in many produced a
pagan godlike laughter that the misery of those who had
already been evicted along that fertile coastal strip and the
sight of ruined townships hardly failed to extinguish. Yet
when at last they saw the castle-keep in the distance, and
between it and them the great new fields, drained and stone-
dyked, the inner fear found again its own subdued pulse.
For these fields were more terrible in their aspect even than
the castle. One square alone would hold the arable land

of a large township. It was as if a little boy, brought up by a lochan, were suddenly set on the shore of a sea. Even Davie, well to the front amongst the leaders, had a feeling of shrinking before these immense smooth fields, where a man and two horses looked like slow toy-figures turning over a thin black ribbon of earth, with gulls and rooks thrown about him in the wind. Simpler minds gazed and marvelled; but Davie's antagonism grew taut as his fear. There was their real enemy, moving upon them slowly and inexorably as the plough drawn by heavy horses, guided by the English tongue. There was the dark writing on their land.

When, therefore, a man leapt out before them and quickly and excitedly told a story of deception, they listened in complete silence. Police and officials were at the castle and several of the men were to be arrested in connection with an attempt upon the life of Read, the sheep-manager. If they could all be incriminated, the conference would be completely successful!

'Attempted murder.' It sounded an ugly phrase. But uglier was the man's question, 'You see what they're getting at?'

They all saw it. It was a bitter moment. The scoffing spirits became blasphemous. What's that he's saying now? The castle guns are charged with powder and shot? No! Not that! What? By God!

They marched on, and when they came abreast of the castle, down from them on their left among the new plantations, they held steadily upon their course and did not pull up until they reached the new inn in the glen.

But if they would not go to justice, justice would go to them, and in quite imposing array – policemen, factors, magistrates, on foot and in saddle, headed by the sheriff of the whole country. Mr Elder and Mr Heller had staged their affair effectively.

What was the sheriff saying now? Why the devil doesn't he speak in Gaelic? Can't you speak in Gaelic? We don't

know what you're saying. What's that? Davie of the
Riasgan, Nial McHamish of the Heights, and who? and
who? What? Hsh! here's the Gaelic on it.

When at last they understood that certain of the company
were about to be taken into custody for an attempt on the
life of the sheep-manager, they roared their protests,
declaring that the whole thing was a lie, that there had
been no attempt on Read's life, that the men were innocent, and that no power on earth would make them give
the men up. All they wanted was to be allowed to remain
on their lands and pay their rents and obey the law. A
dozen voices asked the sheriff to listen to them. They only
wanted justice and fair dealing. They had never done
anything wrong. In the heat of their protests, carried away
by the injustice that had been done to some of their people
and would soon be done to them all unless the sheriff in
his nobility would listen to them and come to their aid,
they pressed towards him, a surging eager mass, protesting,
clamant, anxious.

The sheriff, holding his ground, began to read from a
paper. What was that? What was he saying now? We don't
understand!

The sheriff was reading the Riot Act.

This Act, passed in 1715, being originally prompted by
fears of Jacobite risings, might be said to have a particular
relevance to the Highland scene. It gives power to magistrates to apprehend as felons persons who, to the number
of twelve or more assembled, refuse to disperse within an
hour of the reading of the proclamation. But the Act also
indemnifies any who assist the magistrate in carrying out
the law; which in effect means that the magistrate has power
to call in the military to disperse a mob.

Here, then, was the very mob, loud-mouthed enough
over its wrongs; but the military were fifty miles away in
that Fort, named after His reigning Majesty's august grandfather, which was the farthest north of three on the line by

the Great Glen from the North Sea to the Atlantic, erected to overawe and keep in subjection the turbulent children of the Gael.

Arrest, felons, attempted murderers – the Drover was driven into a previous incarnation and as Galgacus spoke through Agricola, Tacitus, and the dominie in the main glen. But many swore quite shortly. Dismay was in every face. All were in that wild-eyed state of not believing what was happening to them, of hardly believing in themselves, so that they cried out or swung an arm or pushed or stared or hated or swore. It passed belief! It was a damned shame!

An ugly-looking, incomprehensible-muttering mob. Mr Elder and Mr Heller got to saddle and rode hot foot for the castle, where they in truth trimmed the guns and put the whole place in a state of siege, while an urgent message was despatched to the Fort to send the military, complete with artillery, by forced marches. Murder had been attempted. The country was up!

The mob turned away from that place muttering louder than ever. They had been tricked into a false position, cheated of their legitimate hopes, made to appear rebellious and criminal. There were loud voices amongst them – braggart voices – declaiming they had stuck to their own, but it was the last loudness of rage and dismay. Behind it lay the sickness of defeat and hopelessness. The chief, his factors, the sheriff, the police, the military – all the forces of law and order and ownership were marshalled against them, not only bent on crushing the life out of them, but on making the act appear necessary.

On their homeward journey they did not go near the castle, and very soon their energy died down and in straggling line they trooped silently, contemplating their homes with despair. A man here and there might still threaten rebellion; but that was just talk. They were finished.

Not a touch of that legendary herosim of their ancestors to make them concentrate on the castle and so strengthen Mr Heller's hands. No last kick left in them. As the night came down Mr Heller looked towards the hills into which they had faded like so many wraiths.

*

The pursuit of wraiths by a regiment complete with artillery and cartloads of ammunition may well have seemed fantastic even to Mr Heller, yet under express order the soldiers came by forced marches, night and day, the distance of fifty miles.

An important engagement to suppress rebellion, to vindicate the law, and to ensure the peace of His Majesty's realm.

It proved an interesting reflection that the soldiers from these glens who some dozen years before had marched away to the wars had seen their first service in Ireland, where a rebellion against His Majesty's kingdom was being ruthlessly stamped out. And now here was a regiment of Irish being marched into the Northern Highlands to even the balance of immortal justice. So naturally these Irish were more eager for the fray than Mr Heller or any of his prompters, for they came muttering of their own defeats and wrongs, of Tarrahill and Ballynamuck.

The bloody Highlanders!

The bloody Irish!

Each oath in the Gaelic tongue, while the officers rapped out their governing commands in English.

There was something in this impartial holding of the scales of justice that appealed to Mr Heller so profoundly that his smile lingered before it died out in an appreciation unusually fine. For it recalled St James's Park, Buckingham House, St Stephen's, the faint smile at the corners of his lordship's mouth, the power that was Roman in its certainty and perfectly mannered. Mr James had said that a few county families ruled England. As much could be deduced from the present happening, for it was based on a knowledge of statecraft so assured that it was instinctive, and discernible in its wisdom now to Mr Heller because, in the press of circumstance, he had become one of its instruments and had even been permitted to touch at a given point the rim of its circle.

Mr Heller had no love of the Irish, the dirty low Irish, who tried to hit England when she was in difficulties with other nations. And though he had no first-hand knowledge of the Irish, he was certain he knew what they were like: they were like the mob he had had to deal with here. In fact they were first cousins, same stock, jabbering the same Gaelic gutturals; though perhaps the Irish were a trifle more treacherous, more brutal – or at least they had more guts for a dirty fight.

In the past both these sections of the children of the Gael had threatened the safety of the realm with Jacobite risings and Irish rebellions. How wise, therefore, the state-craft that should generate hate between them and send them to destroy each other, never for any mere vindictive or brutal reason of course, but entirely in the interests of lasting and civilised peace.

How deep instinctive wisdom lay in his lordship's breeding and in the breeding of those others who, with him, carried on wars simultaneously in Europe, Africa and America! And even while carrying on such wars, while ruling an Empire and shaping a world, they found time not merely for the practice of the arts and graces, for deco-rating their halls with legend and colour, Caiaphas and Christ, but for ensuring that an officer, speaking the fine clipped English that Mr Heller so much admired, should say to Mr Heller, 'God knows what might happen if my men got out of hand!'

And Mr Heller could see that the man, who was an officer and a gentleman, was really concerned.

How the sense of responsibility and justice percolated through from the highest to the lowest! If it were the right thing for his men to get 'out of hand' and teach a salutary and bloody lesson, then – well, a man does his duty; but if any affair of that kind should cause a public outcry, it would never do, really.

'I don't think you need worry,' said Mr Heller.

'Oh?'

'I mean,' said Mr Heller, removing his eyes, which for a moment had caught a curious gleam, 'that the local disaffected will give your men a wide berth. They have not that sort of courage.'

And, in truth, no resistance of any kind was offered. Even the few who were apprehended were released on a precognition being taken. Deeply disappointed at this tame ending to what they had hoped might have in some measure balanced the killing of Tarrahill and Ballynamuck, the Irish were marched back the fifty long miles to their barracks.

Despite the tempting speculation as to what might have followed had the Irish got 'out of hand', Mr Heller had reason to congratulate himself and his colleagues on the complete success of their strong measures. If the Irish were disappointed, the local people were more crushed than by any bloody defeat. Mr Heller was content to leave them to the tender mercies of his friends, the ministers of the gospel, whose God had increased in wrath and Hell in torture, while he got down to his charts and papers.

New farm steadings, new and better manses and glebes (for which there were special little evictions), new roads linking up the new policy, for which the new poll-tax on every male of eighteen and upwards would be useful. They had not wanted the roads, apparently, and they hated the poll-tax, but if they didn't pay they would be re-evicted; and as there was no place to which they could be re-evicted except into the sea or into eternity, Mr Heller felt he had rather the better of the position. Mr Elder had been talking about an estate law forbidding the evicted to marry – and clearly something like that would have to be done to stop them from breeding like rabbits and becoming a nuisance.

Something like that was done, and enforced under pains and penalties of being banished the country, with odd results in prostitution that were as new to the people as the new diseases that attacked them, such as typhus, bloody flux, consumption, bowel complaints, eruptions, piles, and maladies peculiar to females, thus making of new dwellings 'family hospitals and lazar-houses'.

Yet no great schemes concerned with progress and improvement and backed by the wisdom of inherited statesmanship but will draw its own meed of help from outside sources. A Lowland earl came personally into the country and, by fair promises and alluring encouragements, induced a number of the already distressed outcasts to enter into an arrangement with him to emigrate to his estates on the Red River, North America. A whole shipload of them consented and set out on that arduous passage – to find themselves, as it happened, alas, deserted by his lordship to an inclement wilderness which he had no doubt sincerely hoped they would make to blossom like the rose. The savages of that new country, however, did not give them much chance, for they plundered them on their arrival and finally massacred them, except for the few who escaped across trackless wilds.

But Mr Heller had made more certain of his savages than that. All the riots and disturbances, desperate enough as has been indicated, were treated by him with masterly decision and display of force. They were at last behind him. Peace was in front. Into that peace he now prepared to move, excited a little, it is true, by the prospect of taking over one of the largest divisions of the country and cleansing it for his own private use and profit as an up-to-date progressive sheep-walk.

\*

Out of these carefully arranged excursions and alarms, one personal incident had a direct bearing on the Riasgan.

Davie, who had fled to the hills when the soldiery appeared, made up his mind to join the band of emigrants for the Red River. This decision he kept from all his friends until the very morning of his departure, when, as he tied his personal belongings into a bundle, he at last explained to his granny what he was about to do.

Her legs gave way and she sat down and gaped at him. When at last she breathed his name, he paid no attention to her.

'Davie!'

Her appeal pierced him to impatience.

'There's nothing here,' he said levelly. 'I'm going.'

He stood up and turned his face towards the small square of window, his bundle hanging from his right hand.

'O Davie, my heart, you're not going?'

Perhaps for the first time he felt the awful power in the sad cry of her voice. 'First my son, your father, went; and now you go; and I am left desolate.'

And even now it was not that she alone was desolate; the whole world was desolate; desolation of desolation.

'Well, I'm off.' He turned to throw her a look of farewell. She had risen. Instantly from her face he walked away. For a little there was unnatural silence, then she was following him, crying like a demented animal, the fool! They would see her from houses in the Riasgan. 'Go back!' he cried angrily, then held on his way. From the crest of the hill he looked down, but could see no sign of her about the house. Out from the house in the heather a dark bundle stirred and got to its feet. Forgetting to take farewell of the Riasgan, Davie went over the crest.

A bitter pallor on his face, his eyes dry and staring, he stumbled down the footpath to some stunted birches that lined a narrow watercourse. The impetus of his leap across the rocky channel bore him almost against the body of the girl Kirsteen Sutherland, who in her brown-crotal tweed, not unlike the brown of the birches, was standing with a small straw bag in one hand and some lichen in the other.

As far as Kirsteen was concerned, this was not altogether an accidental meeting. Someone had said that Davie had 'a good mind to go', but as Davie himself had said nothing the matter had been forgotten – by all, that is, except Kirsteen. From this hint and her own powers of divination, for she knew more about Davie and his secret life than that youth dreamed of, she was now gathering lichen in this comparatively remote place.

Yet the very combination of all her fears and divinings coming down the slope in such bodily reality had had a strange tremorous effect upon her, and now she stood quite rigid and pale.

It was a rigidity that looked extremely sensitive and brittle – and indeed as he stared at her, her lips gave a tiny twitch. The ribbon that tied back her light-coloured hair seemed to lift her face, increasing its drawn expression and somehow its independence, so that she could fly remote from him even while she stood there sick with suspense.

Into this meeting, before they could drag a word of conventional greeting, there entered some of that secret shame which had so mysteriously attacked them one evening round the corner of Angus's barn. It came from some terrible vision of the eyes, an involuntary pitiless stripping and laying bare, hateful and shameful. There was little love or lust in it. It was a bone and blood intimacy, ultimate and aged, without beauty or other excuse.

He found he could utter only a gulped word at a time; and his smile felt stiff and foolish. Well, he was off! He looked at her; and then without stirring, without even an involuntary muscle-twitch, she offered herself to him. This look in her eyes clothed all the shame in shimmering beauty. Silently she said, 'Davie.' Yet more than ever was she wrapped round within herself, so that the very poise of her young slim body was too exquisite to be endured.

As he stumbled away from her, muttering an incoherent half-laughing farewell, she remained quite still. She had meant to talk, in some way to express her fiery spirit, to lash him with it if need be: she actually had not said a word.

The half-laughter stuck to Davie's face, and ke kept muttering through it like a fool. His flesh was all jumpy and exceedingly cold, as if he had been drinking strong whisky too quickly. In this state of mind he passed out of sight of that little valley and presently felt curiously freed, and looked around him, a thin bleak smile giving his pale features, with the dark up-tilted eyebrows, a secretive unhuman look. Quite suddenly he was on his face tearing at the heather with his teeth, and crying, 'O Christ! O Christ!' This expression was Rob's, and when he had heard Rob use it his skin had always shivered, for if God would not hold him guiltless who took His name in vain, how much deeper the guilt of him who took Christ's name in vain!

When that insane spasm had passed, his face, earth-streaked, looked less human than ever. There was, indeed, a secret element of the earth spirit about it, a wary challenging expression against the very vacancy of space, as though it were invisibly peopled. He drew himself back against it; then in a profound hatred of humankind, stepped from the path and made inland for the hills.

He passed the night under a heather ledge, curled up like an animal, sleepless at first from the cold that gave his vision an extreme clarity but towards morning drugged into a mindless misery. In the hang-over of this misery he finally came in sight of the emigrant ship.

Apparently his place had been filled, but he did not exert himself in any way. Almost without any feeling at all, he watched the scenes of farewell. Men shouting, women wringing their hands, children crying or screaming, the brave air of the men going away, the flying laugh, the grim mouth, the silent men, the lonely girls with the faces smeared and swollen from weeping, and – the eyes, the eyes of them all, looking through this play set on the sundering sea-beach. It was a tragedy catching up the whole of life in an hour's farewell. For these men who were going away would never return. A last gesture, a final salute, before turning to the unknown, wherein Death beckoned with his dark kinless hand.

The shadow of that hand is already in the loss of that which is loved. It is in each heart; it stands behind the eyes that gaze back on the hills of youth, the mother-breasts of the hills, with the running streams; it is beyond the sea's rim, beckoning, so that the horizon, its last curtain, may be drawn and the play forever ended.

Lamentation and woe. Davie heard the Gaelic chorus and, when the beaches were empty, he turned towards home.

A division began to trouble his feeling as he went. On the one side, why should he be ashamed to go back and meet the looks of those who would courteously congratulate him on not having gone, after the experience of such a departure as he had seen; and on the other, why had he not gone with that deathly band, to whom, in some mystical way, he felt himself pledged and bound?

There was shame in it however he looked at it. And this shame got linked up with all their land, with the bitter shame of the clearances, with a recognition of some inner futility and weakness in their character, a fatal central dividing within them, paralysing all power of decisive action. Children of the Gael! Children of the tempest! Children!

And all they felt urged to do at such a moment was to raise a lamentation. A Lament for the Children!

Dark Mairi, his grandmother, and her invocations! 'Davie!' And Kirsteen with her eyes inviting him, 'Davie!' The eyes – O God, the seeing eyes!

They were all eyes and nerves.

Flashing intuitions of this affected him with a sense of pain, as if raw flesh or nerves were exposed.

But he was wrong about the two women. Mairi had not moved from her home and no one had visited her. To little Colin all she would say was, 'Davie has gone away.' And the news in her mouth was so terrifying that he did not speak of it outside. Naturally enough, perhaps, Kirsteen made no mention of her meeting with Davie. It was not, in fact, until several weeks had passed that the Riasgan got to know of Davie's expedition and his failure to find a berth. They traced his secretive peculiarities to many sources, but principally to Dark Mairi's blood. Davie himself treated the matter then with an easy indifferent manner.

'What possessed you?' asked Murdoch.

'God knows!' laughed Davie.

Seonaid caught his eyes.

'Going to ruin is silent work,' she said, and held his eyes until he flushed deeply.

## THREE

In the appropriate seasons of the year Dark Mairi went gathering lichens and roots and plants, from which she extracted dyes of many colours. In this matter, as in the concoction of healing draughts and plasters, she had a methodical skill. What she had learned had become part of her and was expressed in the unmeasured yet flawless manner of a normal function. She never became excited or feared that a result would go wrong. Murdoch depended on her entirely now for his tartan dyes; and any problem in colour he ever set her, she solved in due season.

At these times, when she went quietly through the birch wood, head and shoulders bent, rooting amongst the tufts, or was seen far up the hill-slopes on rock-ridges, there went with her a loneliness that to young watching eyes shut her off from her kind, and at moments, indeed, of her sudden noiseless appearance, endowed her with the uncanny quality of coming out of, and disappearing into, the earth at will.

But Mairi knew the earth at once in a more magical and practical way than that. She saw bright crimson in white lichen and bright red in the rue root; violet in the bitter vetch, dark orange in the bramble, and purple in the sundew; yellow lay hid in the bracken root and bright yellow in the bog myrtle; scarlet dripped from the tormentil and clots of black from the dock root; 'human flesh' lay sheathed in the suave willow bark. But the lichens that spread over stone and rock provided her with her greatest treasures in scarlets and browns and in reds more vivid than blood.

Sometimes, as she threaded this bright world which the human eye obscures to grey or brown or the pallor of roots, she would have moments of communion with certain persons and now and then her lips would mutter a few words, by which incantation she brought them into her presence or herself went and visited them in their homes. Where all is magic, only the utterly practical person like Mairi can use it, troubled neither by the self-consciousness of the sceptic nor the idealism of the poet.

'I must tell that to Elie,' she might say when some thought had come upon her mind as a plant or root upon her eye. And then in a little time she would be deep in private communion with Elie the miller's wife. For in the past two years of married life Elie had had a difficult time.

At first Rob had been kind to her – indeed his attentions had been so lavish as to be publicly embarrassing. He did hundreds of little things for her and kissed and petted her at any hour of the day, fulfilling the saying that there is no fool like an old fool. And the quietness with which she accepted these attentions did not displease him in the least. On the contrary, it emphasised for him the soft resigned ways of what he imagined was the true woman. Besides, he had more than enough energy for them both. Elie was wise too and let herself fall away into complete self-abnegation. When at odd times she protested, flushed and shy-looking, he adored her.

Then she brought her trouble to Mairi. Rob was beginning to look at her and wonder.

The two women knew what was wrong with Rob. It was not, perhaps, so much that he wanted a child as that he was secretly gnawing over the thought: here was a girl who had had a child to one man, but not to another. Why?

The question would become an increasing torture to Rob, for there was the possibility, from the public point of view, of a reflection upon Rob's manhood. And this, as Rob well knew, was exactly the reflection that would be slyly made. But Rob might overcome the public attitude, if only he was certain in his own mind . . . It was the doubt that gnawed.

And it would increase, driving him to all sorts of excesses, wherein his certainty in himself would flame out in accusation of the woman, necessarily brutal and terrible. In this he would not be able to help himself and moments of repentance would grow fewer and fewer, until the black devil had him completely in his toils.

The women could foresee that ultimate end and they discussed the subject with unashamed and complete freedom. Elie had no partialities or woman's fancies or any egotistic nonsense of that sort. Her difficulty, as she suspected and told Mairi, was probably caused by her experiences in the south, where she had absorbed so deep a disgust against evil male faces pursuing her for the one object that somehow or other the whole thing had got an evil taste and the utmost she could do was to let her mind fall away and meet it quiescently. She was vexed about this but she could not help it. 'And then Rob himself – if you saw his face – no matter how I have prepared myself, I – I fall away again.'

Mairi understood all that, said that Elie was doing very well, that she was a brave girl, and that everything would come right. Then she drew on her knowledge and exemplified it by stories of other women who had known Elie's trouble. She even went back into legend, until Elie saw herself as one of innumerable women whose suffering and endurance were like little black knots holding the web of history together.

In the gloom of her kitchen Mairi gave Elie a herb drink, over which she had repeated a certain charm. The extreme intimacy in this proceeding brought upon Elie a certain bashfulness, and after the drink she experienced some of the warm blushful feelings of a girl of seventeen.

When she returned home that evening, however, she found Rob had male friends in the mill. None of them came near her, and at an early hour in the morning Rob, in the flame of drink, entered upon her and let loose most of the evil in his mind, whipping himself with his unclean tongue into a madness that ravished itself and her in physical brutality.

On the morning of that dreadful night she was aware of a strange lonely influx of strength. Rob, scowling, neither ate nor looked at her.

In the evening he spoke for the first time, growling, 'What's that?'

'A drink Mairi gave me.'

'What for?'

She turned her face to him for a moment, then looked away.

In that quiet glance he stood revealed before himself to the last shred of his desire. Throwing up his arms he cried, 'O Christ!' and the fingers clenched as if a nail had entered the palm. He went quickly from the house and did not return until an early hour of the morning.

She watched him come quietly in and sit by the fire, where he remained hunched up and still.

She thought of speaking but could not. Neither could she move nor otherwise show that she was aware of him. Even a sigh in that eternity of stillness would startle him. His brooding figure had upon it the naked-handed crimes of the world.

Then an old weakness attacked her, though she thought she had conquered it, not having given way to it since her marriage, not even last night. The surge started rising upon a remote shore. It drew nearer, rising up within her, rising up over all her mind, drowning her. She was weeping desperately. 'I am so lonely!' she cried, and strangled the cry. All resistance was broken down. She did not see Rob, did not feel his touch, nor hear his whisperings. 'Oh, I am so lonely!' she cried, and turned and twisted in the bed and choked her mouth. Her cry hit against the utmost bounds of the world, hollow and lonely as a world of the dead. The terror of this loneliness now attacked her, and as Rob bent over she clutched him blindly, not thinking of him, crying out in a terrible hysteric fear. Her hands were strong and one set of fingers dug into his neck, causing a blinding pain. But he kept on whispering her name, pleading with her for God's sake. At last she sank back saying, 'Leave me.' He covered her with the clothes and withdrew; and when the hiccoughing sob had died down and he thought she was asleep, he stretched himself on the floor by the fire.

A quietness came on Rob after that night. He was kind to Elie in unobtrusive ways, but often he sat brooding by himself. Months passed and then Rob one morning looked on Elie's pale face. He kept looking until she said to him sharply, 'Go away to your work.'

'Elie, it's not that?' he whispered in the daylight.

'Away you go!'

She turned from him, but he followed her and presently went away blinded. From that moment he developed an itch to follow her about like a dog and often had deliberately to restrain himself. Often, too, he caught himself laughing huskily in a quiet corner of the mill. Jealously he began to watch now the work she did, and forestalled a heavy task with remarkable intuition or cunning.

One afternoon he said to her in an off-hand way, 'Some of the boys were talking of coming down to see me tonight.'

'Do you mean McHamish from the Heights and that crew?'

'No, no! I mean, there will be no drinking at all! You can be dead sure of that! Do you think I would let these packmen trouble your sleep?' He was incredulous and indignant – the old scoffing Rob in full if cunning feather. She saw the cunning in his eyes. The itch within him to vindicate his manhood before them! In his off-hand pride he would drink them royal! At the moment, however, he behaved more like a girl trying to shoo chickens into a barn. And before he left her he said, 'The dry weather is going to hold, I think. Uh, you might as well bar the door on yourself.'

'And on you too,' she answered, and heard his husky delighted laugh as he disappeared.

That dry weather was holding right into this March morning upon which Mairi went hunting some lichen for a scarlet dye. It was the dead hungry season of the year between the stir of life at the root and the lark singing overhead. As she returned upon the crest by the birch wood she paused, as she always did, to look down upon the Riasgan.

Often of late when she gazed at the Riasgan she saw it like a place awaiting the torch of destruction. Some of this fatalism had entered into her talks with Elie and had in some mysterious way helped them both to that wisdom which apprehends with a healthy calm the transitoriness of life.

Work was going on in the little fields; and all around the houses, and particularly on the slow slopes beyond the houses, the cattle were wandering, lean and restless, searching for the first growths. Mairi knew every house and its every inhabitant. Gilleasbuig the whitebearded, terribly fluent in prayer since his wife had died from a bruise she got in the groin. His strength was failing and he depended now almost entirely on the help of neighbours, who dug his ground and looked after his beasts. On his part he prayed for them and at them and, however some of the young might scoff, he brought to illness and death a certain dignity which responsible parents gravely welcomed. The old soldier had died, and in his place was another army pensioner, a one-armed bachelor named Donald Mackay, with a sister, Elspet, who could keep a ceilidh-house entertained with regimental stories for whole nights. She had followed her husband, who had been killed in action. Morach, mother of Seumas og who had the second sight, had now attained an age in which the extraordinary

clearness of her eyes gave to her frail body almost a trans-
parency. Murdoch's happy household, with Seonaid large
in child for the fourth time. Alie Munro's . . . Dark Mairi's
eyes ran over the households, saw the old, the middle-aged,
the young men and women, the children; and though it
would have taken her many nights to relate all their personal
histories, yet even as her look wandered she had the feeling
of the conjoint story within her, as of something very ancient
and very intimate. And now because of the strength of this
oneness or intimacy, her premonition of disaster became
unnaturally edged. Just as an animal or human being in
the final moment of death may be seen with profound
clarity, so Mairi now saw the Riasgan's brown pelt stretched
against the impending stroke.

She began the descent, forgetting the Riasgan in the vague
mood the sight of it had engendered, until, near the gable
of her house, she looked again and saw what were undoubt-
edly two strangers at widow Gilchrist's door. In the instant
of her glance she knew something was wrong.

The men left that house and went to another. Children
now began running from door to door. Dogs started barking.
Men and women appeared. The strangers were carrying
things in their hands. They were leaving one at each house.
At each house there was a colloquy. Occasionally Mairi
could hear a raised voice, mournful or angry, but always
a woman's.

There was no doubt now in Mairi's mind. They had
been forewarned of this, and though they had not believed
somehow that it would happen to them, yet now lo! it was
happening.

But happening so quietly that clearly others than Mairi
could hardly believe it. Here and there a man stood quite
still, or walked with slow feet as if he had been numbed
or stupidly entranced. The women were more active, but
in a futile restless way, some of them bolting into their
homes as into a burrow.

A few boys followed the strangers at a distance, taking cover when they could, as if these men-gods from the all-powerful outside world might turn and rend them.

Mairi remained by the end of her house quite motionless. In a little while she saw Colin break away from the group of boys and come hurrying at great speed, as if to elude the dangers behind him. Quickly he climbed and, through his breathlessness, gulped, 'They are warning them out!' Back into his face had come the veiled fear that had been natural to it some six years before.

'Yes,' she answered.

He glanced at her and went and stood a little way behind her.

Only one of the men came up. He named Mairi and handed her the notice of ejection, telling her, for he knew the people could not read, that it was a summons upon her to remove herself, her beasts, and all her belongings at the May term coming. Plots of land had been allotted at a certain place by the sea. Everybody was being removed, and if she was wise she would be ready in good time.

He spoke his part gruffly but not unkindly. Perhaps he did not like his duty, though he was getting used to it and was clearly prepared to be abrupt enough.

Mairi, however, never spoke. The man looked at her, then turned away.

Mairi went into her house with the paper in her hand. Colin followed her to the door, then stole on his bare feet to the partition, whence he saw her sitting by the fire, gazing at the paper with the magic called writing upon it.

That by Act of Sederunt of the Lords of Council and Session, dated the fourteenth day of December, one thousand seven hundred and fifty-six, entitled 'Act Anent Removings', it is provided, That it shall be lawful to the Heritor, or other Setter of the Tack, in

his option either to use the order prescribed by the
Act of Parliament, made in the year fifteen hundred
and fifty-five, entitled 'Act Anent the Warning of
Tenants', and thereupon pursue a Removing and
Ejection . . . AND TRUE IT IS, That MAIRI BETHUNE or
SUTHERLAND or DARK MAIRI, Subtenant, Occupier or
Proprietor of the lands of RIASGAN BURN and of
HOUSES . . .

She turned the folded paper in her hands.

. . . and to leave the same void and redd, to the end
the Pursuers or Others in their names, at the afore-
said respective terms, enter thereto and peaceably
bruik and enjoy the same in all times coming thereafter . . .

She turned the folded paper.

. . . one of the Sheriff Officers of Sutherland, in His
Majesty's Name and Authority, and in the Name and
Authority of the said Sheriff-Depute, lawfully
Summon, Warn and Charge you, the before
designed . . .

She laid the paper on the form beside her and pushed it
away to a little distance with her fingers.

While this dumb visitor and herself kept silent company,
Colin retired round the corner of the house. He was now
entered upon his teens, but the hunted 'innocent' expression of his early years was on his face and his eyes, open
and unwavering, were expectant of the blow – not to
himself, not to the Riasgan, but to Mairi, the one person
in the world to whom he talked freely. Pushing away the
paper with her fingers, giving it a place in that fire-lit gloom
that had been the very core of security . . .

Quite suddenly and without any physical warnings he began to cry, standing where he was.

*

A lot of the men had been on the hill when the eviction notices had been served. Davie had expected to find Mairi swaying and mournful and a dark, almost hostile, gloom gripped him as he entered.

She greeted him with quiet welcome, 'Well, Davie, have you got home?' and set about preparing supper. They ate it in silence and then, without saying where he was going, he arose and went out.

This behaviour of Mairi's turned his thought to an excessive bitterness against what was about to happen. Murdoch greeted him with that enigmatic glistening smile that used to sit in his face at moments when he was being desperately baited. Seonaid, however, was without any smile, but not without energy. Her child was due to be born a month after the May term and life for her was an extremely material affair.

She cursed the chief and the factors, called them worse than murderers, for a decent murderer would kill and be done with it. Even a sportsman hunting over the hills never tried to drive his quarry into a place where it would have to eat its own offal and die. Dirty hounds!

Davie was shocked by her violence. The old challenging Seonaid spoke like a virulent middle-aged woman. Yet she had never looked so well nor so comely. Her smooth full cheeks were tinged with red, her dark hair was thick and full of life, a large-bodied threatening woman, her feet on the earth floor.

She rent Davie suddenly. 'You can smile and look away! What are you doing? What are any of you doing? Men you call yourselves! You'll blow the pipes and march away to the wars like strutting cocks! Yes! oh, yes! But when it comes to standing up for your own, you haven't the spunk of one of Angus's linnets!'

'Hmff,' smiled Davie.

'Hmff,' retorted Seonaid. 'I tell you if I wasn't in the condition I am in, I'd lead every woman in the place against them.'

'I think Davie and I—' began Murdoch; but she snapped him up. 'Yes, you're so kind; you're frightened I'll be violent. So you'll go away and talk it over with fools like yourselves. I know you. Many's the long year I've known you both, God knows why.'

'Look here, Seonaid—'

'It's all right,' she interrupted her husband again. 'Do what you like. Only there is one thing of which I warn you. Out of this house I won't go until I'm carried. And I swear that by the bairn there that you have wakened. Out you go!'

Davie looked back at her. She threw him a brilliant smile, in which there was, however, an almost agonised bitterness.

They did not speak as they walked away in the dark, until at last Murdoch laughed, saying, 'She's naturally upset!' and still in the same laughing voice let out a stream of terrible blasphemy that the limp-and-thud of his crippled walk stamped upon the earth.

In old Angus's there was a full house, but at the door, muttering, 'I'll be back in a minute,' Davie walked away towards the barn. Murdoch called after him, knowing in an instant that Davie would not return and guessing at the reason.

'I was shouting to Davie,' he explained to Anna, as the house looked up at his entry, glad of any distraction; 'but something seemed to overcome him.'

The house smiled, welcoming Murdoch. One or two glanced slyly at Kirsteen. They all hated gloom, however decorous it might be to show gloom on occasion.

'How's Seonaid taking it?' asked Anna.

'She's as wild as the Devil,' replied Murdoch.

A few laughed.

'And what do you think of it yourself, Murdoch?' asked old Angus.

'Oh, I suppose it is the end of us here. Though Seonaid was saying that if the men amongst us had the spirit of your linnets, we'd put up a fight. She would take the skin off the Big Woman herself if she had the chance this night!'

'She would, the same Seonaid!' said Angus.

'How are we going to fight?' asked young Art.

'How do men usually fight?' asked Murdoch, smiling his infernal smile. He seemed in gay spirits. The old uncertainty and gloom began to settle back on the company, but now in more troubled fashion.

'Fighting!' said Alie Munro. 'We would stand a chance against the soldiers, wouldn't we? If they send a regiment of Irish, with guns and flags flying, because a sheep-manager took a run to himself, what would they send if Art there hit the great Heller with a sod?'

'They would give the command to Wellington, I know,' nodded Murdoch. 'But we might manage that. The only difficulty would be that when we had defeated Wellington, we would then have to defeat the factors, and after the factors, the sheriff, the police and the jailers. We would have to defeat the world. And then we would have to go to the Bad Place, for it is the Almighty Himself who is bringing this upon us for our sins. Heller is the Almighty's chosen instrument.'

Everyone began to feel uncomfortable.

'The fiddle is my own instrument,' added Murdoch. 'Where is it?'

Discomfort became acute, but the fiddle was passed to him.

'What would you like, Kirsteen?' He eyed her with his dark-smiling malice.

'Whatever suits you,' replied Kirsteen, with her own smile.

Murdoch laughed. 'I wonder!' he pondered, plucking the strings.

'You're talking a lot,' said Alie, 'but what can we do?'

'Not a thing,' said Murdoch. 'It would be wrong to do anything.'

Murdoch began to play. The sharp edge of bitterness cut into them. They hated his playing. Murdoch knew that. 'Come on, Kirsteen. Get your partner,' he prompted, warmed up already and breaking into a swift-footed reel. This was intolerable, and when a young fellow *hooched!* the sound pierced like a lance.

'Forbear, Murdoch. This is not easy,' said old Angus kindly.

'What?' said Murdoch. 'Why, what's wrong?' This question having gone too far, he admitted it with a quick smile. 'All right, then. If you don't like my playing, what about the *Aged Bard*? It's full of memories at least, and most of us will have little else to live on for a long time.' Three men entered, attracted by the amazing sound of the fiddle.

'O place me by the Riasgan stream that flows softly
    with gentle steps,
Under the shade of the birch trees lay my head . . .'

repeated Murdoch. 'Come away with it, Angus!'

There had been for a moment such a true rhythm in his voice that several, feeling drawn to that immemorial land of escape, begged Angus to go on. Why not? Why should they not forget for a little?

But Angus shook his head. Murdoch laughed abruptly, as at a cunning joke. He seemed irrepressible tonight, whereas usually he had to be begged to do anything. And now Murdoch felt that his own mood, which had been falsely induced, was beginning to get a real hold of him, bringing through the malice a true reckless gaiety, and, more maliciously than ever, he decided to impose it upon them all.

The youths who were sensitive became reckless in response. Eyes grew brilliant, hands bold. The girls, from being shy, squealed with laughter and cross-talk. A restless terrible gaiety began to grip them all. A neighbour of old granny Gilchrist's started to weep. 'Och, och the day!' she intoned, swaying her aged body. One of the girls, Seana, dark, vivid and seventeen, got hysterical with laughter at sight of her.

'Ach, leave them, Anna,' said old Angus.

Suddenly Murdoch was perceived to be making his way out. At once he was gripped and hauled back roughly, caught in the act of stripping away the gaiety and exposing the underlying fear and shame.

'I must go,' he said. 'Seonaid is all alone.'

Into the uproar Seumas og came, cold and sunless and staring out of his greenish-blue eyes. 'There's a smell of burning,' he announced quietly.

Everyone grew silent as Angus, his old friend, welcomed him to a seat. Murdoch regarded him with so narrow a concentration that several saw a sudden insane challenge in it.

The silence was pierced by the girl Seana, who cried out, 'I'm coming!' as if answering someone outside.

They all looked at her and saw her slowly realise that no one else had heard the crying of her name beyond the window. She went pale as death.

Anna comforted her, telling her she had got into an hysterical state and had imagined it. But the girl, grown very quiet, hardly listened to her. 'I'm going,' she said. And before anyone could answer, Art remarked, 'I'll go with you.'

Seana looked at Art as though they were alone and she was discovering him out of her wide eyes.

But Art laughed awkwardly. He was a tall handsome youth, dark, with colour in his cheeks. 'Come on!' he said in his lively way. That he should thus disclose his secret passion for Seana came as unexpectedly to himself as to the others, yet the moment gave his act a manliness that went about her like an arm, setting them both apart like two figures in a fatal story. Art cried, 'Goodnight!' briskly, flashing his smile, and they were gone. Inside, the folk listened to their footsteps dying into the night, whence that voice from the other world had come calling the girl away. The girl would go soon; for the voice could not have been far distant, as it cried to Seana with that dreadful intimacy that they all knew even if they had never experienced it. *Seana!* passing with the wind of the night like a peewit's cry, *Seana!*

One of the girls looked sick. Kirsteen was pale and bright-eyed. Upon all was the supernatural fear of the voice beyond the window. No one would go home this night except in company, and then hurrying. Only the fey person would wander, hunting the cry down the wind. Art would be having his own struggle now.

Towards this immortal fear Kirsteen, alone amongst them, was drawn by a dreadful fascination. Against her sanity and pride she knew herself being drawn, felt the craving grow upon her. Fleeing through the dark night, destruction might come upon her, out of the air, carrying her to what shore, leaving her dead without a mark. And together with that, but farther back in her mind, her actual hurrying feet brought her round the corner of the barn – to meet a shadow – that could not be there . . . The night . . . *he's out there.*

She hardly heard the voices of recovery, which were neither forced nor false any more. Only in Murdoch did the Devil linger. He was challenging Seumas og, who was obsessed by his 'fire'.

When Seumas's eyes, however, got fixed fairly on Murdoch's, they never wavered. Murdoch got the impression of long glass rods coming at him; either that or the glass eyes themselves were drawing nearer. But pride would not let him break the look.

Seumas og said, 'I see blood – near you,' and turned his eyes from Murdoch as if he had not been looking at him, but at the blood. Murdoch's ruddy skin became discoloured; his smile grew sickly. The rest were attracted to the point of self-oblivion. Quiet as a shadow Kirsteen slipped away. The night met her, hovering over her on black wings. On swift feet she gave herself up – making for the barn . . . Murdoch arose. Seumas og got up and brushed past Murdoch. They heard his feet following where they had not heard Kirsteen's.

'He's restless tonight,' said old Angus.

The company was now extremely listless. Alie Munro said it was high time they were home. The talk that all had naturally expected had not come off, because of Murdoch and his queer mad mood. Yet they knew that the talk had come off to its final bitter end.

A girl's voice said, 'Where's Kirsteen?'

'What's that?' asked Anna.

Kirsteen was nowhere. Yet she had been there a minute ago. She could hardly have gone out without someone observing her.

Murdoch gave a laugh. Several looked at him.

'She'll be out about,' said Angus, 'for some reason.'

What reason? – *out there*.

'Don't you be frightened, Anna,' said the old weeping woman in haunted tones. Several of the younger folk could have slain her. They began to chatter, and the house to empty.

But on the doorstep Anna was frightened to call 'Kirsteen' into the night.

Hector and Angus went round the house. It was pretty dark. What could have taken the girl? Where in the world could she have gone?

'Let us go in,' said Angus. 'She'll come.' To Anna, he said, 'She won't be long.'

They knew from his quiet manner that he was going to worship.

The Bible stories and the tenets of the Christian religion were very familiar to all the people, many of whom could quote from Scripture at great length though few of them could read, and none in the household of Angus or in any similar household of the Riasgan.

Anna and Hector and Angus og followed the old man to his knees. His prayer was one of quiet humility. It was notable in that place that certain fiery men were, in the onset of their humility, inclined to grovel before the awful omnipotence of the Almighty. Angus was not of that kind. There was so little he understood that he left all in God's hands, knowing that God, in His mercy, would do to them what was beyond their wisdom to understand. But he beseeched God to give them the power of acceptance, to grant them the will and the strength to bear their sorrows and their tribulations in the spirit that would find grace before Him. Sometimes it was difficult to keep evil and rebellious feelings out of their hearts and in the dark of the night they were often troubled and sore afraid, but, O God, what sat at the heart of their heart was not evil, but would be kind and gentle and would give to the stranger – even to the dark stranger, O God . . .

As this new and terrible thought came upon old Angus and for a little left him silent, Angus og's blinking eyes caught a movement by the entrance; his head tilted and he stared at Kirsteen or at this wild apparition of his sister with its glistening eyes and white face and scarlet mouth. The eyes flashing upon him affected him with a cold uncanny sensation. Their triumph over him was unearthly. Her bare feet made no sound as she passed to her stool and kneeled and bowed her head, and hid the fire under the arch of her body.

*

Mr Heller took it upon himself to fulfil Seumas og's prophecy of fire a few days thereafter. Why, he argued, lose

a whole year's new growth for the sake of an overconsci-
entious observance of the law these next two months? The
tenants had to go at the end of May in any case; but he
must burn the heather now, in March, or not burn it that
year. May, with the growth on, would be too late. And
much of this old rank heather was good for nothing. By
sweeping it away he would be giving new tender shoots a
chance. Mr Heller had a theory that he could reclaim great
portions of that land from heath into grassy pasturage. Was
he going to be deterred in the good work merely because
he had no legal right to interfere until after the May term?
Absurd, in view of all the advantages that would accrue
to him and the relatively slight disadvantages to the tenants.
One has got to be reasonable in matters of this sort, and
Mr Heller was given to planning several moves ahead. In
many ways the Riasgan represented ideal wintering for
sheep, and good wintering was the foundation of his whole
scheme. The birch wood for shelter, the present cultivated
ground for fine pasture, and the slopes as excellent hill-
feeding once they had been burned and in due course
surface-drained. Now in the intricate business of dividing
his flocks into hirsels, after the best Northumbrian fashion,
and moving them from place to place, according to age
and the season of the year, Mr Heller had marked the
Riasgan as one of the chequers on his vast board. Moreover
there was a certain part there that with its deer hair sufficiently encouraged would make an excellent ground in mid-
July for his speaned lambs, where the bleat or crying for
their mothers would soon leave them.

At first the people of the Riasgan thought that some of
the boys, under the mysterious if immemorial urge of the
spring, were at their games of making fires along the river
banks and among the pale grass or the grey whin bushes.
The burning smell came to aged nostrils with that odd
disturbing sensation of forgotten rites and new birth. It was
the time of natural scarcity, but the year was on the turn

and warmth and summer days and plenty lay ahead. The illusion of perfect security could be deeply experienced, for lurking dread of the May term gave but a keener 'memory' to the prickling aromatic smell.

But such volumes of smoke, dense and obscuring, were unusual. Folk came to their doors; those working in the fields paused and stared. The lean beasts now started running hither and thither in ghostly fashion through the smoke. Then over the breast of the hill, from the direction of the mill, came a wide wall of fire, throwing torn sheets of flame into the thick convoluting masses of smoke, carrying everything before it, hissing and crackling and terrifying.

From her house on the opposing slope Dark Mairi looked down upon it. Davie, with a cry, pointed out two men with torches – the factor's men! Deliberate and planned! In a mad run he started for the Riasgan crofts, little Colin tumbling after him. At the stream he yelled to Colin to go back and look after his granny.

'I want to come.'

'Go back, or I'll kill you!'

Colin returned slowly up the hillside. When he regained the house his granny had vanished. He had meant to avoid her under the bitter stress of his feelings, but the silence in the house now alarmed him and he called on her loudly.

The Riasgan was almost completely obscured by the billowing smoke. Here and there could be glimpsed men and beasts running. As the red wall of fire advanced against the houses, the whole scene had something infernal about it.

From its awesome fascination Colin awoke to find his granny descending the slope with the home beasts. The ewes were twisting their tether round her legs. The old cow, far gone in calf, was advancing by fits and starts and grunting at the scene below, whence the barking of dogs and bellowing of cattle could now be distinctly heard.

She called him, but instead of running he went moodily towards her.

'We'll herd them here,' she said. 'We don't know what place they'll set fire to next, but they won't likely burn this bit or they'd burn the whole wood.'

There was no trace in her of that anger and madness which he had seen burning in Davie. Her underlying grief and anxiety were being used up in action. She was trying to save all she could. Whatever the treachery or natural calamity she would first and always save what she could.

In a few minutes Colin was released from his moodiness over Davie's anger towards him and went running about doing Mairi's bidding.

No one came near them all day. The fire worked round the houses of the Riasgan, and in the darkness its wall was visible far up Tomich way. It looked beautiful and magical and terrifying in the night. Out of the house Colin was drawn every now and then to gaze upon it, until the darkness frightened him and he drew his granny with him. She went simply and together they regarded in silence that far-glowing red, against which occasional dark figures moved like demons.

*

Davie did not come home that night. Mairi and Colin sat up very late awaiting him, for Mairi was full of foreboding as to the fate of the cattle. After the barren winter they were lean and hungry, and when they were like that they were incalculable and stupid. In addition to the two milch cows they kept about the house, she and Davie had eight beasts in the wandering herd. Although Davie was in many ways careless and impractical, he was secretly proud of his live-stock. And as Mairi talked, Colin understood Davie's murderous look by the stream.

At last Mairi smoored the fire, invoking the Three of Light, and they went to sleep.

Colin awoke to find the fire burning brightly in the darkness, with Davie sitting by it, his face black and hanging, his eyes closed.

This evil dream was so real that terror paralysed him against movement or sound. Into it Mairi came with a steaming bowl. Davie roused himself, and as he opened his mouth the rim of his lips showed pale as the belly of a trout.

'You're tired, poor lad!' murmured Mairi.

'That's good,' he answered, lowering the bowl. He wakened up quite naturally. 'I think I ran a hundred miles,' he said with a friendly, almost an amused, voice. 'I could sleep.'

'You'll just lie down at once as you are.'

'I think I will.' And, getting up, he went towards Colin, who started violently, though not now altogether with fear. 'Awake, Colin?' Davie lay down beside him.

Colin stuttered.

'Hush, go to sleep!' said Mairi.

'It was the cattle,' Davie told him. 'Remember the one you called Elie? She fell and broke her leg and we had to kill her. But I think the others are all right so far. The hot ground – in their feet – lot of them dead – stupid – make you mad.' He was asleep.

The last day or two a new friendliness had come to Davie, which that fierceness by the stream had so violently shattered. But now it was restored. As Colin, arisen, drew in whispers from Mairi the story of the night, they were both aware of the sleeping Davie. In the last hour Mairi had caught a glimpse of the early natural boy, the friend of Angus and the speaker of proverbs. What had wrought this change in him she did not know, but it had been powerful enough to overcome such a dreadful night as he had been through. This had touched her breast with a quick affection for him and, deeper than that, a sense of dependence upon him. She felt now that they had come well out of the evils of the night and the loss of the heifer, Elie, was somehow like a tribute paid for deliverance from disaster.

\*

Many more beasts, however, were lost in the coming days. The land that had been burned was the best early spring feeding, and the cattle would persist in straying back upon that black wilderness. The stores of hay or straw or potatoes were insufficient to hand feed so large a herd. In favourable seasons it was a lean time; now, in the case of one or two unlucky tenants, it was nearly disastrous, for all foresaw the dire need of having as many beasts to dispose of as possible at the summer sales, if they were to get through the coming autumn and winter on the sterile slopes by the sea.

Angus's household carried over a score of cattle and a considerable number of ponies, sheep and goats. The sheep were reared for their wool and were otherwise not of much consequence. From the cattle sales money was got to pay rent, to buy meal or otherwise finance an economy that, in the main, required very little cash. Angus or Hector had lost five cattle and were now, in view of the restricted feeding, faced with the need of selling half-a-dozen. Yet beasts were in such poor condition that very little could be got for them, for who were in a position to buy? Furthermore, Tomas the Drover had sworn that they need not expect any drovers to come into their country this year, because of its widely reported unsettled condition. Tomas had made it out that this was part of the factor's plans for reducing the people to utter submission. For the Highlander, according to Mr Heller, could be assertive enough so long as things were going well with him, but immediately things began to go from bad to worse he caved in and became servile and abject. He had no stamina, no staying power; either up in a burst of vanity or pricked flat.

'The position, briefly, is this,' the Drover had said, for

behind all his bombast and love of rhythm he was, as
Hector knew, not only a shrewd, but a knowledgeable,
man. 'You have the ground and your cattle. What you plant
and sow in your ground now, you'll have the right to come
back and harvest. They can't go against that. At the end
of May it will, of course, be too late to do anything with
the new plots you're getting – assuming you'll ever be able
to do anything with them! However, the plan is to pay no
attention to the removal notices, but to go on working the
ground and laying in all the stores you can, against the
famine of winter. About the cattle, God knows; feed them
somehow. And if it comes to the sea patches in the end,
there will always be limpets and weed on the shore, and
by the time the tangle is finished we may have learned to
eat one another. After all, as the minister was saying last
Sabbath, God tempers the wind to the shorn lamb, and we
are thus being given the chance of proving ourselves lambs
of God. Though our fleeces are now scarlet, they shall be
bleached white as snow . . . For all the time, as has now
been revealed, God was on our side. In his pride the anti-
Christ went marching across the world, but God moved in
the hearts of even the heathen Russians, so that they gave
up all they possessed, destroying their country and burning
with their own hands their great city . . . The French
Revolution was bred in the iniquity and sins of the people,
who denied God and became atheists, who spread their
hellish doctrines until we have at this day amongst us wolves
who are secretly encompassing the destruction of Christ's
sheep. Beware! I know you! . . .'

Tomas had the last Sunday's sermon almost by heart,
and two or three now listening to him felt more than a
trifle uncomfortable, for the real sermon that God had a
controversy with the land for the people's wickedness had
made an impression upon them. Nor was the Drover openly
impious.

Hector returned home, inexplicably depressed, with only

two clear ideas in his head: that he must till all his available ground and feed his stock somehow.

This depression settled upon the Riasgan. Even grumbling or threatening talk became meaningless and tiresome, often a hideous sort of mockery. Each man or woman worked steadily but without zest; a few said openly that it did not greatly matter whether they worked or not.

The women were less depressed than the men. Mairi worked her ground early and late. For some mysterious reason there had come upon their isolated little place a curious access of life, almost an optimism, and Davie helped Mairi with a will, and certainly worked with a persistence he had never previously shown.

Old Angus sat in the centre of his growing coil of heather rope. When they would be cast forth upon the beaches, they would have no shelter until they built and roofed a dwelling with their naked hands. Had he had only himself to think of, he might not have greatly troubled over that dwelling, for he was now come to the stage of that Aged Bard whose desire was to rest by the streams and the primrose banks of the land which he knew and for which he had the deepest feelings of kinship and peace. The time had come for Angus not to wander, but to lie down, and if he might not yet for a time ease him consciously in his lying, then to die.

As Kirsteen entered the barn she saw, for the first time, a frailty in the flesh of her grandfather. His bent neck was scraggy and full of a myriad wrinkles; the light from the door penetrated his thin grey hair and exposed the brittle skull; the loose skin on his hands had a bluish tinge as from perpetual cold and the fingers fumbled now and then in their deft action. Above him a cock linnet was in full song. The song had attracted her, acting upon some mysterious influence of spring in the soft air. She had come in with her heart full of an irrational happiness, and now stood quite still.

He looked up at her, but his expression wore its habitual quiet pleasantness as a weary mask.

'Isn't he fairly singing?' She peered into the wicker cage. 'It's the time for it.'

'Yes,' she answered, suddenly feeling she wanted to cry. As she touched the cage the bird stopped singing. 'He's a beautiful singer.'

'Ay, he's pretty good. Is there anything you're wanting?'

'No. I just came in to see you. I've stopped him singing.'

'He'll start again. His heart is that way.' He looked upward at the cage. 'See how restless he is. There he is setting himself to it.'

The linnet let out a note or two and hopped, trilled and steadied. The twin bills when they opened were like the husks of an oat. How delicate, how frail! But this frailty was irradiated with light, almost transparent, when turned with its song to the sun.

The old man's eyes gathered light and a touch of that cunning pleasure which may sometimes be seen in the glance of a craftsman. His eyes, too, seemed to have dwindled and got rounder with the years; and somehow there was all at once a greater kinship between him and the caged bird than between him and his kind.

Kirsteen could not look at him openly, could not move. She was caught up into a vision of age that is death and singing that is spring, and its sheer poignancy made her tremble as hardly love's hand could.

Though she knew love's hand; the dark vision round the barn. Davie had been there when she had gone out that night, out under the unearthly voice that had called Seana, her body possessed, compelled, until it could have flown through the whole dark world. And he was there, at the spot where they had met before; and all in a moment, though the darkness would not let them see their shame, the shame was there. But now she could not turn back.

Neither spoke; and while the dark tide of time went

between them, neither moved. Her trance caught up a misery that heard the tide break on the hills. She knew he wanted to go away. She wanted to go away herself. Inaction became terrible and humiliating. She felt her face go white and cold. No one had ever been shamed like this. A nervous sickness began to rise into her gorge.

His body wavered out from the wall. His head was turned away.

They had to touch to break the spell, but they could not touch. The spell was upon him, but how could she touch? The shame, the marrow shame, was hers forever.

Impulsively she caught his arm. He was trembling, but remained still and did not turn his face towards her. She let go his arm and felt weak and like to faint. She did not know why she had come here. The madness was spent within her, and the ugliness of her flesh was cold upon her bones. She did not hate him: she did not want him.

'Don't go,' he said, taking her hand. She tried to free her hand. He held her with a grip that was deliberate and cruel.

'All right, you can go if you like,' he said, releasing her.

She staggered a step, then stood like a fool, unable to do one thing or another.

She had never experienced anything like this humiliation. The queer lonely aloofness in him paralysed her. The flame of her spirit was dead. She felt beaten and unclean.

'Don't go,' he said. That roused her. He stepped close, but did not touch her. 'Don't leave me.' His voice was quite cold.

'Never again.' Her voice was calm.

'I know,' he said, and looked away.

'You have shamed me.'

'I know.'

'I'll never forgive you.'

'It's not that. That's nothing.' He looked at her. 'Don't do it.'

All this talk meant nothing. She was going. Voices of folk departing came from the house. Hand in hand they went quickly round the barn and leaned against the wall, listening. The barn divided the folk. As the danger of being discovered increased, they found each other's arms; as the danger seemed to be upon them, they clung and kissed madly. She moaned a little as footsteps were going by them . . .

Kirsteen lowered her eyes from the cage and looked at old Angus. A faint flush gave her rather thin face a delicate smoothness. The quick-spirited crease that came between her eyebrows was gone and her eyes were wide and full of feeling.

'You're looking well these days, Kirsteen.'

She smiled.

'Has sense come to Davie at last?'

Her body twisted away shyly.

But he had not much spirit today. 'Ah well,' he said, 'may the Lord be good to you both.'

'Don't say that.'

'What?'

'Don't say it like that.'

He regarded her. 'You'd like all the world to be singing out of the throat of the linnet! . . . I'm old, lassie; my singing days are over.' He said this bleakly, and somehow she felt that his understanding and his sympathy were dying with his body.

An urge came over her to throw her arms about his neck; but that would now be wrong. For the first time in her life she saw that he was thinking about himself, and it shocked her more than anything she had yet noticed.

'Are you sad today, Grandfather?'

'No,' he answered. 'I wouldn't say that I'm sad. If you asked the ground out there that has been burnt if it was sad, it wouldn't hear you.' He started on his rope-making. 'I'm old, Kirsteen. That's all that's wrong with me. Maybe

I wouldn't have noticed my age and one day I might have slipped away from you; but you see we are now to be driven away and I realise that I'm done. You'll have no love of the things about you yet, because all your life is in front of you. But all my life is behind me. It's here in the barn and out there, coming and going; its living face. And now all I'm wanting is its peace about me. I should like to have died here, Kirsteen. There's nothing sad in that, lassie. You would not grudge me that peace, would you? . . . Ah, there you go. Though it's foolish of me to think you could understand. You are afraid of death and hate death. But I am not afraid and I would talk about it to you, like the Aged Bard.' At that some of the old humour came back into his face and he smiled.

'You're not old – like that – yet.'

'I'm older than that,' he said; 'so that it's not the primrose bank I'd be thinking of, but the bare earth itself.' He looked out of the door and his thought got lost in a stare. She wiped her cheeks.

He had not been moved in any way, however. He would have liked to talk about death, but now in its forewaste he forgot about it and about Kirsteen. With a little sigh he began weaving his rope again. Then suddenly his round eyes were twinkling upon her. 'You'll be thinking I'm mournful?'

'It's a wicked sin,' she said fiercely.

His fingers paused thoughtfully. 'We haven't done much harm. That's true. They might have left us. I think they might have left us. It's a desolate thought – to think of all our hearthstones turning cold and the sheep passing over them. You won't understand that yet,' he said, 'but it makes nothing of all we have done. Colder than the grave itself, that. All that we have done and our forefathers have done, back through time, the very memory of us, is wiped away. In the Word itself there is the saying, the abomination of desolation. It took me to this day to understand it.' His head drooped and he looked fixedly at his hands; while he still looked at them they began weaving the rope which coiled round him on the earth floor, moving and slithering, coil by coil, like the mythical serpent of his race.

But to Kirsteen, subject to unaccountable compulsions and flashes of vision, he was weaving his own shroud.

As she went out he called to her, conscience-stricken a little, but she did not answer.

Against the back wall of the barn she leaned, gazing up the rising ground to the hill-crests. Between the deep clouds the blue of the sky had a light that was all freshness and promise. The notes of the linnet had now the extra magic of distance, and all at once she was aware of larks overhead, interweaving their songs until the upper air was alive and invisibly patterned with them. The haze on the mountains was like the smoke-bloom on ripe blaeberries. The air was quick with the smell of newly turned earth and manure. All was suggestive of the awakening of life, and the coldness in the sunlit depths of the sky was the coldness of a drinking well.

'It's a wicked sin!' she muttered passionately. This keen coldness, bright as the light in the clear blue, ran quickening everywhere. It was in her body quivering keen as if risen from the well. And behind her nostrils there was the memory of a fragrance that went back, back, past the drift of spring fires, to the dim smoke-blue horizons of time.

It was a bitter sin! Bitter! Bitter! 'It's bitter!' she muttered, turning a little to the wall as if Davie were there. This expectancy of life and beauty about the black burnt heath broke her heart.

She would tell Davie in the dark. They met in the dark secretly. They loved the dark with its hidden wildness, and they triumphed over the light in which men's deeds were deliberate and evil.

In the dark, too, she had broken down the spell on Davie. They both knew it had been a spell, and if she had gone away that time when the voices stopped her they would never have come together again. He had not wanted her. And even when he had kissed her, it had been with a perverse cruelty. For a little while they had both been out of their senses, like wild cats.

Kirsteen left the wall of the barn. From its corner she could see Mairi on the plot below her cottage, her blunt body lifting like a dark seal in one of her own sea stories. Davie came with a creel on his back and emptied its contents on the earth beside her, then went back towards the cottage, where he stopped for a moment.

She looked around to see if anyone had observed her wave, but everywhere folk went about their tasks, the children herding or carrying or working with the older people.

A sudden vision of this land, as perhaps old Angus saw it, came upon her, the people close to the earth, the children about them, a slow kind abidingness in it, bare and austere, in the singing March weather.

## FOUR

May came in wet and stormy but the grain was sown and the potatoes planted and the gloom of the weather, though it added to depression, assured even pessimistic minds that no violent hardship could be wantonly and suddenly added to their lot. They would surely be allowed to remain over the May term; and then, as their cattle got into condition and their ground was cleaned, the business of removal might be considered. But in their hearts the hope still lingered that by some providential chance they might not have to go at all.

The May term passed; the first half of June passed. Nothing happened. Men left their homes to attend to their cattle, now coming into condition, and to try to sell what they could where a market offered. Besides, they had little desire to be about their homes in order to argue with ground officers or other emissaries of the factor. They had their work to do.

On a forenoon of lowering skies, spitting cold rain, Colin was sent by his granny with a brew in a little wooden pail to Morach, mother of Seumas og, who was now confined to her bed. Like all the other boys he was mortally frightened of Seumas og, but the beautiful little pail comforted him. It was made of wood in the shape of a barrel, with thin brass bands round it and a swinging brass handle. He far preferred it to Mairi's other treasure, the old silver brooch that was big as the palm of her hand. There was, in truth, nothing like it in the Riasgan, and he knew that his companions would want to look at it again, and one or two would probably come with him right to the door if each were allowed to carry it a little distance.

In this he was not disappointed, though the last fifty yards he had to go alone, the others, however, giving their solemn word that they would wait for him where they were whatever happened.

Seumas og appeared suddenly round the corner of the house and in a quiet word invited Colin to enter. He worked his croft very efficiently, and from one little field had removed a boulder weighing many tons without any conceivable means.

The old woman's face was extraordinarily shrunken; nothing but skin and bone, with the eyes burning out of it in a terrifying kindness, as if all the sweetness of the world melted there.

She made the usual compliments, asking after his grandmother and Davie and for news of Elie, of whom she was clearly very fond. Her emaciated right hand kept clutching the bedclothes. In the dim light of the covered-in bed her gaunt ghostliness was emphasised every other moment by a 'remembering' in her voice, as though she inhabited two worlds.

Colin, aware of Seumas og behind him, answered her questions in a word. At last he was able to say that his grandmother had sent him with this drink, which was to be taken at night and in the morning after being warmed to the same heat as the blood.

She thanked his grandmother. She thanked himself. She called on Seumas og to empty the pail and wash it out clean, and get Colin a piece of bread. While this was being done she engaged the boy again in conversation, asking him his opinion about the present sad position of affairs, and if he had heard what the people were saying. For herself, she thought the worst was going to happen, and that immediately.

Seumas og was never coming back with the pail.

The old woman, deep now in her own thoughts, did not miss her son. She was, indeed, moved at having someone to speak to who could tell her of the world outside. And Colin was so used to speaking at length to his granny that, once the first fear was over and Seumas og outside, he gave the old woman a lot of news in an intelligent way. He was still deeply uncomfortable, however, and at last said, 'Well, I must be going now.'

But she pointed out that he couldn't go without his pail and wondered what on the earth was keeping Seumas og.

Finally Colin had to take leave of her.

The first thing he noticed as he came out was that his companions had disappeared. At the corner of the house, his back to him, Seumas og was standing with the pail in his hand.

But as Colin reached the corner his eyes lifted from the pail to a group of men about the dwelling of Gilleasbuig, and to his recent companions standing warily at a little distance from them. Men and women, too, were coming out from their cottages to see what was going on. All at once there was something ominous in the scene. Colin could hear the shouts of some of the men about the house. They might have been carrying dead or dying beasts or injured human beings from the dwelling. Suddenly he saw old Gilleasbuig, his head bare, staggering about amongst the men, raising his arms and lamenting in a loud voice, his hair and beard white as a flag in the wind.

Terror of the sight put everything else out of Colin's mind. Seumas og had vanished. He started running towards his group of friends, now at a stone's throw from the dwelling, but pulled up short of them, afraid to go nearer. None of the other boys knew what he knew about the agonies and punishments of life. Its nightmare was bedded deep in him.

He could hear Gilleasbuig, who was now not so complacent to the powers that the factor and his crew of sheriff-officers, constables, ground officers and other servants of authority were summarily putting into force. He too had

talked of the Lord having a controversy with the land for
the people's wickedness, and, in His providence, and even
in His mercy, having sent this scourge to bring them to
repentance. But now that he saw the 'controversy' being
exercised against himself, by men made reckless by drink,
abrupt and foul of tongue, his natural feelings were roused
and with Isaiah he cried, 'Woe unto them that join house
to house, that lay field to field, till there be no place, that
they may be placed alone in the midst of the earth.'

A man's elbow knocked him in the belly. As Gilleasbuig
doubled up, he gave a woeful moan. There was an abrupt
laugh; the voice of the leader rose sharply. Several of the
men now began tearing the thatch away. No sooner was
the roof off than the walls were attacked. Dense smoke
began to ascend; a bright tongue of flame leapt up. In a
few minutes the humble dwelling was on fire. The officers
of the law walked away, leaving Gilleasbuig alone with his
chest, his straw-bottomed chair, his iron pot, and one or
two domestic utensils. From their midst he prayed to God
with uplifted arms. The heat of the fire scorched his face;
the rain spat upon him.

At sight of the fire the boys had retreated. Some had
run home crying the tidings. But the old folk were already
gazing from their walls with a dumb and dreadful impotence. Even men in the flush of manhood, like Hector
Sutherland, were stricken in this way and had in their eyes
the staring look of the condemned. They remained by their
gable-ends, waiting. There was nothing they could do. When
the police enter a man's house with a warrant, he permits
them; when they arrest him, he does not rebel. But these
men had not merely the police against them, and all the
power, civil and military, the police stood for, but, more
potent than these, their age-long spiritual attitude to the
authority of their chief and of their God. They were defeated
not merely in their outward but also in their inmost possessions. So much was this the case that one or two of the

younger men who were not on the hill appeared sullen and callous, muttered to themselves, made no effort to approach the destroyers, but, rather, seemed to slink away from them.

Thus each house was attacked in as isolated a way as was Gilleasbuig's.

When Colin saw them approach the house of Seumas og, in upon his trembling fear came the vision of his little pail. They might throw it out from the house before they burned it. He ran to Angus's barn, where the old man, his son Hector, Anna and Kirsteen were standing looking up at Seumas og's.

'Go you up, Hector,' said Anna in a broken voice.

'What's the good in my going up?' muttered her husband.

'Go you,' said Anna. 'They need someone.'

Hector did not want to go. He hated approaching the men. But it was natural to him to obey Anna. She turned away into her own house, crying to Kirsteen to come with her, and Hector set out for Seumas og's. Little Colin ran after him.

'Where are you going?' Hector asked.

Colin looked at him and murmured, 'I left my little pail.'

A sardonic smile touched, for a moment, the weary hawk-nosed face, then Hector went on. At a little distance from the cottage he said, 'You wait here.'

There was no appearance of Seumas og anywhere. The roof was being demolished and a man with a torch was about to set fire to it.

Hector went up to him. 'There's an old bed-ridden woman in there,' he said inoffensively.

'Who told you?' asked the man, with a jeering threat.

'I'm telling you,' said Hector quietly. 'I'll take her out.'

'Who the hell are you?' he shouted, and a man came up whom Hector believed to be Mr Heller, though he had never actually seen him in the flesh before.

'What do you want?' demanded this man in English.

Hector had no English and replied in Gaelic.

'He's saying there's an old bed-ridden hag inside,' explained the man with the torch.

'Oh, is he?' A venomous intensity gathered in the factor's expression. Hector was not an evasive specimen of the native; on the contrary, his large frame and clear-cut features gathered a certain aristocratic antagonism. 'Get out of here,' said Mr Heller; 'you lazy devil, clear out!'

Hector gave a pace or two before this explosive violence.

'What about the old woman?' cried the man with the torch, his eyes gleaming.

'Damn her, the old bitch, she's lived long enough. Let her burn!' cried Mr Heller.

The men, half-mad with drink and the growing lust of destruction, gave a laugh. No half-way measure with their factor! Burn the bitch!

Most of them were decent men normally, with wives and families; kin in blood and tongue, a few of them, to this man and his bed-ridden woman. Having over-stepped the bounds of decency, they must go farther and farther, to keep themselves in countenance; while destruction, once let loose even in temperate kindly men, feeds on its own wild hilarious lust.

Where the thatch was torn from the roof, fire leapt up. A woman, shouting frenziedly, rushed in at the door. Hector with his great stride followed her and together, choked and blinded, they groped their way to the aged invalid, picked her up in the bedclothes, and stumbled back through the falling faggots. When he got outside Hector found that the bedclothes were on fire. He laid Morach on the ground and crushed out the fire with his arms and hands, bestriding her in a way that raised a lewd laugh. Her mouth was open, emitting choking dry sounds as from internal pressure through a pinched wind-pipe. Her eyes rolled. Her whole body heaved, as if the invisible hand were strangling her.

'Get her out of there!'

Hector spoke gently to her and soothed her. She gazed at him now in an insane way and began to gasp and then to moan quiveringly. It had set in for a day of cold rain. She would perish in the open in an hour. His eyes were scorched and stinging, and the smirched skin of his face was an angry red. Wrath was rising slowly in him. He picked her up in his arms and began walking past the burning house.

As Morach saw her home in flames, she started crying in a high dolorous voice. Her neck was not strong enough to keep her head steady and it waggled to Hector's stride. The gaunt witch face behaving in this ludicrous fashion in the arms of that large quiet man set the incendiaries into a roar of laughter, not jeering laughter but hilarious mirth. It was the funniest damned thing they'd ever seen! The niceties of respect for the factor's presence had abated. They were all a jovial crew and in it to the neck. Let Factor Heller order: they'd obey to the last. But who said another drink?

Factor Heller was a wise man. This work had to be done: it would, by God, be done thoroughly! That Gael should curse Gael, that this breed should destroy itself, was necessary for the new order of Progress. Clear them out! Rid the land of such human vermin! For himself and his schemes, he had imported, and would continue to import, thank God, real human beings from the south!

As Hector paused with his burden to glare back at that crowd and challenge it, Mr Heller's vindictive look passed into a grim smile. Not the joke, but the sheer witlessness of the fellow's thinking he could get house shelter here – for himself or his burden!

House by house they took before them, giving the occupants a brief space in which to haul out their belongings, before destroying the dwelling. Pitiful mothers, miserable old men, moaning old women, wailing children, left islanded with their one or two earthly possessions and no home or shelter in the broad world for them. It was a remarkable landscape, acquiring slowly an unearthly demoniac appearance.

Seonaid was ready for them! Hers was perhaps no idle boast that if she had been in fit condition she would have mustered the women of the Riasgan against the burning gang. Her condition, however, was obvious, for she was very heavy with child. As she stood before her doorway, with her three children round her, she looked the vengeful mother of all the tribes of men. Indeed, though it did not so happen in the Riasgan, in certain other parts of the country the women did combine against the officers who came with the notices of removal and put them to rout. But such knowledge of legal procedure was not yet general amongst the people, and the Riasgan, like the rest of the vast territory under his lordship's sway, was caught in this matter in all its primordial innocence. And if the women proved in this respect the shield and guard of their men, it was because they assumed to themselves, in virtue of their motherhood, a position within nature that was outside man's punitive laws. Their men had too often been captured and hanged for offences of trivial significance in the past to risk them now. Their opposition to this attack was based not on man-made legalities but on the inalienable rights of flesh and blood upon the face of the earth which man inherits under God. It struck at them in their homes and in their children. If Murdoch had been there with Seonaid, she would have put him behind her, recognising him in his man's shape as mere meat for factor's jaws. She regarded the approaching gang as brutes and fiends, and when she recognised two of them as being of her own people, her cheeks flamed with anger and shame.

But Mr Heller knew the feminine mind by this time. Sometimes it whined ingratiatingly and then lashed bitter-tongued; sometimes it had quiet dignity and, before force, bowed its head and wept; sometimes it wisely and at once set to its business of saving all it could. But however it acted, Mr Heller proceeded according to his plan.

Seonaid's hostility grew as they approached.

'Get out all your belongings at once,' said a man to her; 'and hurry up!'

'I dare you to touch this house! And you,' she said to the man who had spoken in her own tongue, 'have you no shame that you would go burning the houses of your own people? Turning out old men and women and children to perish as if they were lower than the brute beasts! Have you—?'

'Get on!' shouted Mr Heller to his men.

Seonaid swung round on him. 'You, you dog! I would shut your mouth for you, foul as it is—'

'Damn you, get ahead!'

A couple of the men approached the wall, but Seonaid bore down on them.

'It's my roof, and I defy you to burn one stick of it!'

Her flaming vehemence was not without effect, especially on those who knew Gaelic. They had not encountered anything quite like it. And when she caught one of the two and heaved him against the other, so that both stumbled drunkenly and banged their heads, there was not even a laugh.

Her back to the wall, she defied them. The two men whom she had treated so carelessly glared at her. In her bulging condition she ought to have had more shame, the dirty bitch! The bairns were clinging to her skirts and whimpering like pups, burying their faces every now and then against her ample legs. She had a fierce black beauty, full of bone and strength. A young woman, but already heavy and powerful. It was as difficult to advance against her as against an enraged mother-beast in its cave-mouth.

It was not a moment for delay. The lust of destruction in its hilarious exercise of brute strength must continue to feed upon itself and be fed. Mr Heller's fierce shout was responded to. Seonaid turned, climbed the low wall of her home, and began tearing away the thatch in great sections and throwing it to the ground.

They knew what she was about and paused uncertainly. The houses in the Riasgan, as elsewhere, had been built by the people themselves. The woodwork consisted of couples made from birch trees that, fixed in the ground, arched over from opposite walls and, meeting, were secured to each other by wooden pins. These were left in the rough condition in which they were taken from the woods, but as the woods were deemed the landlord's property, so were the couples in the people's houses. However, from their peat bogs, to which they had an inalienable right, they dug the ancient moss fir or bog pine, dry tough resinous wood, mostly root. A yard or so in length, an inch or two in diameter, the pieces were placed lengthwise from couple to couple and supported the thatch. A great number of them were needed for a home and they were very valuable and accounted one of the few indispensable possessions of any family man. Furthermore, they were his own, actually and legally. With a sufficient stock of them, he could erect a new home almost in a day. Seonaid was now proceeding to make certain that what was hers she would keep, for though it had been rumoured that wood might be found at the new place and that Mr Heller was accordingly against the removal of these battens, Seonaid put little trust in rumour and none at all in Mr Heller.

The battens began to fly from the roof, and though the enraged woman did not look round it chanced that several of the men, including Mr Heller, had to duck smartly. Some began to laugh, for it also chanced that the wind blew about the woman and now and then exposed sections of her naked thighs. A remark was flung at her. She let fly a batten: 'You filthy brute!' Then she tackled the roof with renewed energy, taking a stride upward, and suddenly, and with a wild scream, disappeared from view.

'Break the place down!' cried Mr Heller, who was now in a furious rage. At this rate it would be dark before they were finished. Besides, he wanted everything destroyed. He knew his people! He was not doing this damned work to amuse himself! If roof-trees and battens were left them, their houses might be pulled down today but tomorrow they would be built again. He would not trust them as far as he could spit an oath.

In this he was possibly drawing upon his native shrewdness rather than experience, for large numbers had already been removed quietly enough. But the general temper was growing increasingly sullen, and clearly if these people had meant to go they would have made some preparation. Things had arrived at the stage where the rabbits had to be ferreted out of their warrens and the holes destroyed.

The children, who had bolted inside the house when their mother had gone on the roof, were screaming in a maddening fashion. Suddenly one of the men who had been tearing at the turf wall let out a shout and backed away. 'By God, she's having a bairn!' He looked vastly incredulous, as if someone had hit him in the wind.

'Let me see!' Another looked. 'Jesus!' he said, with a mouth of disgust. They all had a look, for it was something none of them had ever actually seen.

'Get her out of there!' cried Mr Heller.

They looked at each other. Hell, it was a sickening mess! Their faces twisted into a half-shamed grin. What in the blazes could they do? Outside their scope altogether, this!

'Better get hold of some bloody woman or other,' one man muttered. They were all sick a bit at the stomach. The filthy bitch! Damn, they felt awkward! Walk away and leave her. They could come back . . . Something should be done . . .

Two men set off to find a woman and flushed Kirsteen from a ditch. They shouted to her. She waited. 'The woman up there fell through the roof and—' But Kirsteen was already making for the cottage. They yelled to her but she paid no heed. They had meant to tell her to hunt up an old woman. They swore and decided they would have to find an old woman. They spoke in Gaelic and suddenly one of them cried, 'God Almighty, I hate the whole filthy business!' and crushed the ground solidly with his feet. When they reached old Angus's their distaste for what they were doing made them truculent and ruthless and brutal.

\*

From her cottage on the hillside Dark Mairi looked upon this slow-spreading scene of devastation. The rolling smoke was flattened out by the wind and pinned down by the cold deliberate rain. Less and less time was being spent at each house. The screams of children were ringing in Mairi's ears. The groups of the homeless were like condemned beings by pits of fire in a smouldering hell.

Little Colin stuck closely by her, his face very smooth and pale. He was terrified. Now and then he said, 'Maybe they'll not come here, Granny.'

'Yes,' she always answered. 'They'll come here.'

In the end it almost looked as if the boy would be right. But if theirs was the last house, the gang were clearly in the mood to celebrate at it the conclusion of their labours. Mr Heller declined the ascent, and with two of his principal henchmen awaited below. When Mairi saw them coming, she immediately began hauling out of the house all her belongings. She had everything in readiness for this; and by the time the men were upon her, Colin and herself were dragging the last and main treasure, the meal chest, clear of the walls. Two of the men swayed forward to help; they were drunk and collided; they roared with laughter; their faces, streaked with torch grease and soot, gave them an infernal appearance. Two more came to help them. The meal chest was lifted clear of the ground, carried a pace or two to the edge of the watercourse, and with a heave sent hurtling down the steep rocky channel. The lid shot open and the meal burst in a cloud on the air.

That was the best chest yet! As Mairi wailed, one of the men humorously stuck the butt of his burnt-out torch between her legs. She doubled up with an *ouch!* that increased the laughter.

'Spunk in the old witch yet!' shouted the humorist, whose bald head was black and whose lower lip troughed drolly like a pig's.

In her high thin voice she screeched to Colin, 'Go up!' and immediately he scrambled towards the hollow where the beasts were.

'Go up!' mimicked the droll fellow, who had no Gaelic.

When it looked, however, as if they weren't going to have much fun, they began to get what proved the best fun of the day.

Mairi was strongly addicted to keeping fowls and in prosperous times carried a fair stock. She liked them, and without ever consciously studying their ways got to know them with natural intimacy. A week ago she had performed a successful operation on an ailing hen by slitting open its crop, emptying it, and sewing it up again. They did not willingly give themselves into her hands, but when they were feeding about her feet she had no difficulty in picking one up here and there and feeling it for an egg. She knew by the very look of them when they were secretly contemplating laying away and took measures accordingly.

When the men had appeared and got Mairi grunting with fright, the fowls, like Seonaid's children, had bolted indoors. As the roof was being demolished they cackled and scurried. At the first flash of fire they made for the open.

And now started the sport of trying to catch them. They had thrown several snarling dogs and pups to the flames already. Luath (or Swift), Hector's favourite dog, had shared this fate. But these hens would make real pigs laugh. Though they had the whole wide world to escape into, they ran round the house in circles. Men fell and rolled over trying to catch them. The humorous fellow, who was sitting with the cock between his legs, lewdly encouraged the chase and at last rallied the fortunate hunters, for the resinous battens were now in full blast, crackling and belching a whole houseful of flame.

'Get ready!' he called. He had the two legs of the dangling squawking rooster in his right fist. He uttered an infamous sentence, and then crying, 'With these words I commit your soul to hell!' he swung the brute round his head and let go. The cock righted himself in mid-air exactly over the flames, flapped, screeched, and fell plumb into the furnace, his feathers curling in a puff of fire as he disappeared.

Before the sport had right finished, a loud whistle came from below.

'To hell with him, does he think we're dogs?' spluttered the humorous man, his red-veined eyeballs distended.

'Come on!'

'Come on, bedamned!'

They all, however, began immediately to go down.

\*

Seumas og, when he had seen the wreckers coming, had taken to the hills and was the first to convey the tidings to some of the absent men. For a time they were uncertain whether his few words did not represent a 'vision'. They spoke amongst themselves and finally had the cattle rounded up, for they did not know where next the blow might fall. On coming in sight of the smouldering waste that was all that was left of the Riasgan, each man instinctively made for his own home. The crippled Murdoch went at a great pace, falling frequently, gibbering oaths like a tortured lunatic. Angus og had a fixed smile through which his blue eyes shot gleams of cruelty and cunning. Davie accompanied him on the run. Some of the older men called on their

Maker to witness the end of them. Many blasphemed loudly. As they parted, each voice could be heard going its way.

At Angus's, Davie found the old man sitting on his chair among the family possessions. Angus og looked over the possessions and around the burnt buildings, his eyes slotted and calculating. The old man, the cold rain beating upon him, seemed to have sunk into a stupor. He gazed up at Davie blankly, then recognised him and his eyes brightened.

'It's the end, Davie.'

'Where are they?'

'Looking to the wounded.' A groan came from a pile of bedclothes by his hand. 'That's old Morach. We had to make her bed there and cover her from the rain. She'll not be long in it.'

Davie looked about him with the raked restraint that is in the fierce quickness of the hawk. His eyes were brighter than fire on tears.

'They threw my cage with the cock linnet right into the heart of the flames,' said Angus. 'Many a time he sang where he perished.' He was thoughtful and quiet. Davie became aware of his divining eyes. 'It's no use, Davie, my hero. We can do nothing. If you ran after them and did anything foolish, you would only leave the old folk and the little ones to perish. We are like the children of Israel in the hand of Pharaoh. And now we shall have to arise and go to the promised land.'

From the humour of the last words the irony ran like an underground stream upon the deep land of death.

All at once Kirsteen was upon them, breathless, flashing a tragic look at Davie, but not rightly seeing him nor caring. There was blood on her bare hands and arms. She bent over Morach and from among the clothes pulled out a linen sheet, which she rolled tightly, her back to the rain, and without a further look at the men, was gone into the thick evil-smelling gloom of the smoke.

Davie stood for a time quite motionless, staring after her. There had been something about her dreadful as an apparition. Then his head fell forward and he started walking away. Vaguely troubled at not having taken leave of Angus, he half turned and saw the old man, now on his feet and looming large in that infernal gloom, slowly stoop over the covered woman. A drift of black smoke blotted him out.

The crying of the very young was incessant, a thin pitiful wailing, in which the gusty frightened weeping of older children was maddening as torture of the flesh.

From the direction in which Kirsteen had gone, Davie suspected that some terrible injury had befallen Seonaid. Deeper than his thought, so deep that it was sunk in mire, he felt the guilt of himself and of Murdoch and of all the men. He remembered the flash of Seonaid's face and her condemnation. She had been right.

And because they were impotent, utterly and bitterly impotent, they were none the less guilty. This evil should not have happened. It should never have been allowed to happen.

From the stress of these blind futilities, he began to ascend the hill, exhausted, and with a vague misery-haunted mind. Passionate rebellion had passed in a few moments to the mood in which anything could happen to him, even death itself.

All the same, it was bitter to look on that blackened heap, from which, though the fire had died down, smoke continued to roll. It had been his home. Damn, it was hard. Tears stood in his eyes. 'O Christ!' he called, and sat down and began to weep. He could have fought and died gladly; he could have torn the enemy with abounding fierceness, careless of what happened; he could have . . . but they had leaders no more . . . the leaders had betrayed them to the enemy . . . the leaders were the enemy. Then his mind took a terrifying leap and there beat upon his brain the ultimate words: *there is no enemy*. Down upon his mind rolled the dark acrid smoke, shrouding the words and their lucid moment of utter negation.

He could see no one about the ruin, but presently he caught a black head bobbing above the edge of the water-course. He went across and stood looking upon Dark Mairi combing the meal from the water with her fingers and laying it on a flat stone. She had quite a little mound. On another stone were gathered sodden pieces of oatcake. Below in the stream lay the chest, one side of it staved in. When he spoke she started, cowering from a blow. Then she saw it was Davie and she straightened herself, saying through her thin smile, 'You frightened me.' As he turned away he saw Colin up the hillside watching him.

From the ruin Davie brought red embers and with a few peats from the small outside stack, he built a fire in the place by the burn where Mairi boiled water for washing clothes. On this he set the iron pot. Colin brought down the beasts and Mairi milked the cow and fed the calf. Out of the wet meal she made a mess of porridge and the three of them supped it with milk. She also showed Davie four roast fowls, but from their blackened bodies he turned away with disgust. 'They'll do for the journey,' she said, 'when I have cleaned them out. I have a lot to do yet,' she added. There was a drop of cold water at her nose. The bones of her face were clearly defined under the stretched skin. Her whole face and skull had gone expressionless as a death's-head and cold to the centre of the brain. This coldness was tireless and resolute. She had made her moan. The tide of it had washed by. Fate would never do her down until it killed her, and it would not kill her with tragic emotions. It would have to throw her roughly and brutally, and even then she would crawl, and keep on crawling, until it hit her finally. And never would she crawl so resolutely, so blindly, as when she could save and gather for her own people.

Even when Davie had told her about Kirsteen and the sheet, and had suggested she should go and see Seonaid, she answered with preoccupation that she would go in a little while. Then she began running her thread of design upon what remained to be done.

At last she went away with Davie, and Colin was left behind. His clothes were wet against his skin. The evening fell rapidly under the lowering skies, and his teeth began to chitter. In this early gloom of the night he caught, for the first time, the voice of the wind upon the hill behind and in the wood. He listened to it intently and once looked stealthily up as it passed overhead and far out above that place of desolation, whose points of light glowed redder and angrier as the darkness deepened. In the throat of the wind he caught the voices of human beings crying upon the night, in swaying forlorn rhythms, *ooooooo, aaaaaaa*, so sad, so forsaken that despair passed from them to the far hills, leaving . . . but rose again on the wind and passed to the hills once more . . . to rise . . . to fall . . . *aaaaaaa* . . . leaving death behind. Or were the dead risen, their voices on the wind . . . and the voices of the long dead . . . spirits wandering in the night, the disembodied dead? . . .

In the low turf shelter they had prepared for Seonaid, she lay pale as beeswax. Mairi had ministered to her and told Murdoch she would live though she had lost nearly all her blood. 'The child had died, and that had been a good thing,' said Mairi. It had been suffocated by its mother's blood. The pain that Seonaid had would likely be no more than the result of her fall. If Anna had not got the blood stopped, he, Murdoch, would have had no wife this night. Dark Mairi told him all this simply. It seemed to settle him. Mairi said she would come back in a little again. Murdoch drew the wet blanket over the three children that crouched round him as he sat near his wife's feet. Davie could not see his face. What could be said? He was looking away when he felt Murdoch rising darkly behind

him and shouting, 'What the hell do you want? Go away!'
He knew Murdoch had not moved, but all at once, without
a word, Davie walked away. He could not get Kirsteen out
of his head. All the blood-drained tragedy reflected back
on her ghost-face and she flitted through the night, eager,
scared, but resolute. Instead of the rain's lessening with the
rising wind, it was actually getting heavier and colder. It
killed resolution, bogged it in spite when the body jolted
and stumbled. What a night out of hell for the suffering
and bloodless!

'Morach's gone mad,' said Kirsteen at his elbow.

He jumped.

A rain gust blew her almost against him.

'My father made a shelter and a fire in the lee of the
barn wall. They carried her round there. She was sitting
propped up when my brother Angus came out of the gloom.
She screamed: "There's Heller! There's Heller!" It was
horrible. She's raving.'

There was an uncanny something about her, as though
she were telling one horrible thing to hide another, using
her voice to hide herself from her own sight.

At a touch she might scream and fly into bits. Her mind
was haunted by what she had seen. He did not know what
to do and stood dumbly with half-turned head. His lips
began to mutter. 'Don't, Kirsteen – don't—' He wanted to
tell her not to do too much, not to— 'Never! Never!' she
cried shrilly and was gone. He called her name loudly and
started running after her. But he could not find her
anywhere. Dark Mairi he saw crouching by a fire brewing
something in a pot. All night Mairi would move about on
silent errands, sure of her purpose. There would be nothing
bright about her telling folk to cheer up. But those she
spoke to in her practical way would find their feet touching
bottom. 'Take you that.' And with it they would take some
of her persistence and begin to crawl out again. Some of
the ruins were completely deserted and no one seemed to

know where their owners had gone. Round Hector's fire, however, a number of folk were now crouching. But Kirsteen was still not there. While Davie stood debating whether he would go into the circle of light, he saw on its far rim a crowd of phantoms approaching. There was one he knew . . . Eoin. It was the advance-guard of the evicted from Tomich . . .

*

The wind's voice drove little Colin towards the cow. She had her calf, however, and did not want him. The calf began sucking, and though it was part of his duty to prevent such illicit loss of milk, Colin only crept a little nearer. He was now so watchful, so intensely wary, that his body felt light as a leaf. It was, indeed, chilled of feeling to the bone and his bare feet had become quite numb. When he was staring at some dubious thing the driven rain drops would sting his eyeballs and for a moment his body would shiver all over and his teeth click. There were so many dubious things, black things that he was certain had never been there before. Two of them moved where they crouched. But one did not move so long as he stared at it; yet when he looked away and looked back, he was certain it had come nearer. The cow dropped her head and lifted it with a low moo. The calf stood against the off side of her belly, Colin by the near side. The cow stepped two paces away as if it had been hit, and Colin's heart leapt into his mouth. Out of the throat of the night, as it yawed on the hill-crest above, came the devil cries of the past, rising on black wings from the industrial lands, the mills, up to the crest, the nameless horror coming up . . .

Colin had often had nightmare from the mills and the terrors of his early childhood, particularly when he had first begun to realise security in the Riasgan. In the night-mare, things and beings had a horrible distinctness and life, but in his waking hours he knew, rather, their vague threat. More and more had the threat dwindled, but he never lost this consciousness of a past, and when he first learned from his companions that he was a bastard, that past took singular shape and being. He was different from the other boys with whom he played, and they could throw him with a word into that shameful world beyond the mountains, the wandering road of the beggar, the child labour of the mills, the black dwarfed folk of the mines, the lies and cruelties and terrors of that wheel-spinning human-devouring world . . . to the far plains on which fought the soldiers, of whom his father, who had betrayed his mother, was one.

All that was behind him, beating up on the wind, hunting over the hill-crest: to find below him the Riasgan in ruins. Both worlds were in him. Between them he now stood quivering, waiting to be discovered and destroyed.

When he heard the cry, he knew the *invisible thing* was at last approaching. The high piercing wail rose through the wind and against it. When it rose again it was nearer. Then from the black ruin itself, it *cried his name*. As a darkness within the darkness it came towards him.

If terror had held him rigid until he had actually been touched, he would probably have gone out of his mind; but the restriction was removed a moment before and he screamed.

His mother cried his name now in an astonished terrified scream herself; as she got him in her arms her legs gave way, and on the wet ground together they wept and clung.

Colin, my little love, my white love; Colin, my sweetheart. She nursed him against her full breasts and brought such warmth to his frozen body that his teeth would not stop chittering.

Where is granny? Where is Davie? Her questions got mixed with her endearments, with her caresses. And at last he started stammering. This was the refuge in which he had so often taken shelter.

'I was frightened for you,' she said. 'I had a feeling. The mill was torn down. Rob was in a terrible state. He hit one of them, and then – oh, dreadful! Old Gilleasbuig staggered in. He was raving and praying. I wanted to come. Rob would not let me. I stole away. Little Colin, we are by ourselves once more.'

The tender green leaves were on the birch trees and the wind thrashed amongst them with a roar like the sea. The rise and fall of the sea on the far shores of the world. Ruin in the night of the world. Ruin.

She followed the twist of Colin's head and hearkened to the night coming over the crest above them. But so dark was the night she could not see the crest, could not see the wood.

A sharp pain struck her in the side. She thought of Rob and had a moment's vivid fear for the child in her womb. Then she crushed the boy to her and in a low tender voice, rhythm-haunted as if she had gone fey, she began wondering where in this night of ruin they would go.

\*

Daylight found the homeless on their weary, ragged, straggling march to the sea. Several, who had departed during the night to friends at a distance, had had the new and terrible experience of not being received across the threshold. Of all that happened at that time, this denial of hospitality was the most bitter and destroying; for it struck not merely at the body, but at the living root of the spirit. Back into the dawn of time, hospitality had been the spontaneous law; of life's many blessings, surely the rarest, with its welcome and its brightness; for in the giving and the receiving, courtesy found laughing phrases and pleasant manners. Whatever ills beset them, in their hospitality they conquered, and with open hands dispensed bread and kindness and shelter. 'The door of Fionn is always open and the name of his hall is the stranger's home.'

But this ancient law Mr Heller superseded with the new law of the estate, which set the pains and penalties of instant eviction upon any who would show hospitality to the homeless. Never had there been a time in all their history when hospitality would have been more gladly given and more deeply acknowledged. Through the ages it might have been ripening for this moment of perfect necessity. Yet in the stormy darkness, when the woman with her children or the old man with his exhaustion knocked at the ever friendly door, the inhabitant, deep in shame, had to say, 'If I take you in, my house too will be destroyed and we also shall become destitute and homeless.' Indeed whereas those at his door had, if they could reach it, at least the barren seashore before them, he would not have even that.

From the door they turned away into the pitiless night, blaming him not. But the eyes of the man within the house would turn in upon himself and find that the inner house of his spirit had become unclean, and know, moreover, that whatever happened to him of plenty or grace or ill, it would nevermore be cleansed in time. In this uncleanness already evil coiled with beaded degrading eyes.

Four men carried Seonaid on a rough bier. The mad woman, Morach, was propped up on a pony and old Angus was one of the two who walked by her side. Now that the worst had happened, Angus had lost his despondency and won a new access of strength. Ponies, milch cows, calves, barking dogs, sheep, goats, men, women, and children, in a long disconnected line, went winding on the footpath between the hills. Already, as a community, cohesion had gone. They were stragglers after a battle rather than a simple people moving to new lands.

During the night Mairi had come upon Elie and Colin, and had been suddenly angry with Elie and told her she was in no condition to be wandering about. Elie was meek, replying that she wanted to see her own people. Mairi left her abruptly and came back with Davie. Holding Colin's hand, she ordered them away to the mill. Without a word they had gone.

Now in the grey-skied summer morning she was last to leave the Riasgan. Wet and without sleep she still appeared to draw steadily on deep sources of energy. Two fowls she had unexpectedly found sheltering near the ruin had defied her efforts at capture. They had grown wild. Colin chased them and turned them until their wings were trailing and the boy himself could run no more. Seeing how spent he was after the night, Mairi told him to go with the beasts and join Hector.

She caught the fowls by giving them a little of the precious meal, tied their legs, and tidied up her few belongings, burying what she had been unable to remove beneath the small peat stack.

Then she rested for a little. Davie, Art, Angus og, and other young men would be rounding up the cattle behind the hill and driving them away. There was no one left. The Riasgan had shrivelled and grown smaller, like an old person who has died. Smoke was still drifting from the black sores on its skin. Life had been there. Life would be no more.

# PART FOUR

# ONE

As it hit the rocky headland the sea spouted up in a column of water that spread out fanwise, remained for a moment in white languorous suspense, then slowly fell back; fierce impact – lovely suspense and fall – repeated and repeated, not hurriedly, but with all the deliberation of an ocean's power. On shelving rocks by the tide's edge, the same alternation was displayed in myriad form of rush and swirl and choking gurgle, brimming moment of satiety, and white recession. There was something of the wild beast in it, recalling ceilidh-house stories of the lion or leopard that pounces from the jungle and withdraws with the human being in its jaws. The tangled manes of seaweed heaved with the tidal surge, thrust through the roar and froth, grew languid in the moment of attainment, then slowly lay back under the caress of the receding water.

In summer sunshine the action may have a certain fascination; under a dark October sky, the ferocity is apprehended and feared.

Between the cliffs, on a small sweep of rough shore, an old woman stood looking over the swaying waters. There was little wind, and an occasional small snowflake came out of the air and disappeared. Looking into the dark sky she imagined beehive battalions of them on their way.

The woman grew anxious. On the ledge to her right hand a man had been caught on a summer's evening by a swirl of water and drowned before his wife's eyes. 'I wish they'd come,' she muttered to herself. The boat was old and some of the planking so rotten that a knife blade could be thrust into it as easily as into a cheese. If the four men aboard had known anything about the sea, they would never await disaster like this. The sea was rising without wind. When that dark sky broke . . . She wondered if she would climb up on to the cliffs again. They had gone too far out, searching for the hard ground. They did not know how to take land bearings. They had bought the boat from the little fishing creek far along the coast. It was a boat which the fisherman himself had discarded as unsafe. He had told them this and taken very little for it. In good weather it would be all right with strong bottom boards, and they might as well wreck this one as a better one to begin with! The woman wished she herself had gone out with the skilled fisherman; then she could have kept the men right.

All at once she saw the boat coming round the spouting headland, and so close in that her heart stood still. Their very instinct should tell them to keep away from that! she thought. The oars were lifted high off the water and fell into it again uncertainly, giving the boat, lying squat to the surface, the appearance of a drunk crab using its toes as feelers.

Usually, as they drew near the pebbled runway where she stood, Alie Munro would shout, 'Horo Mhairi!' particularly if they had landed a cod. Tonight the men said nothing at all.

'I'm glad you've come,' Dark Mairi welcomed them; 'it's going to be a stormy night.'

'We lost our best line,' said Hector quietly, as he stepped from the boat and held her. 'It got stuck on the bottom. We tried for a long time, but in the end we had to pull. It parted in the middle. We'd better draw her up a bit.'

Many who had been watching from the cliffs now arrived and helped to draw up the boat. Mairi said that when the tide was full in it would wash over her this night. The men were dispirited at the loss of the line and because they had failed again to find the ledge of hard ground – the haddock ground. But they pulled the boat up beyond high-water mark, as Mairi suggested. Soon all the community knew that the best line in Hector's boat had been lost.

Mairi went on to her own place carrying seaweed in her hand-basket. Her holding was all of half an acre and soundly rented. It rose so steeply that the earth, when turned over with the crooked spade, could be kept from rolling away only with the greatest care; and she had had to build her cottage not with but against the slope. Hector had an acre below her where the ground flattened out before taking the plunge over the cliffs. As Mairi stood at her door on this late October afternoon, her eyes could readily sweep over the cabins of her neighbours. Murdoch's was the third on her right and he had had very bad luck with whin and boulders; while Seonaid had been of little use to him that summer. His loom had been destroyed in the burning but they had saved a little money in the Riasgan, and if only they could get through the winter and spring without spending it all, and if Seonaid got her strength back in the meantime, they might win to life yet. Rob and Elie had the finest holding of all, extending to two full acres of steep but not over-rocky soil. Mairi's mind darkened at thought of Elie and she turned to go in, but before entering she sharply lifted her eyes to the hillside above. Colin was coming down it, weeping as he ran. Her heart clutched in pain and she moaned quiveringly, acknowledging tidings that had not yet been spoken.

The hillside up to the crest was all that the folk had for rough grazing. If his lordship's conception of progress, so ably worked out by Mr Elder and Mr Heller, was to be effective, it was manifestly essential that the barren parts of the coast to which the people were evicted should be strictly defined, and any crossing of the boundary by the dumbest of their brutes be duly punished. The brutes, with little moral instinct and moved by memories of their ancient pastures, of green hollows between hills, of rich river banks and sheltering birch woods, had to be continuously watched, for once they crossed the boundary the shepherds were waiting to trap them into a pen some thirty yards square. When inside that pen they could be redeemed only with cash, though on occasion a shepherd would show great leniency by accepting from a person who had no money some valuable article of use or adornment. In the early days of their new, meagre, and overstocked pasture, the beasts had been wild and restless, and the pen was more often than not charged to the gate with horses, cattle, sheep, and goats, trampling or goring one another, and setting up an infernal neighing and lowing and bleating. Occasionally, too, when in the very act of trespassing, the brutes would be so hurriedly turned back by the herds and the shepherds' dogs that, in the excitement, many of them went clear over the cliffs, while not a few got broken legs. Twice little Colin and his friends had come on a broken-legged beast with its eyes picked out by birds and its flesh half-eaten by dogs, though it was still alive.

Mairi had had her losses, but her stock so far had been fortunate enough to escape the pen. Colin had been very vigilant and luck had been with her, and after a time the restlessness in the brutes had calmed down.

Now her turn had come.

'What were you doing?' she asked.

'We were making little houses,' he confessed, gulping and shamed.

On some broken ground near the crest of the hill the young lads turned the weary hours of herding to an adventure by building tiny turf houses, into which they crawled with excited feelings of security and escape. When it was raining, to peer out of the door of such a dwelling upon cloud-swept mountain ridges, upon the marvellous uprising floor of the sea that never spilled back, upon near slopes where beasts and humans were grown small and slow, stirred feelings of delight. 'Boy, look at Seumas og! isn't he getting wet?' And from their half-magic shelter they chortled with glee.

Mairi understood this. She entered and sat by her small fire, her hands falling open, her head drooping. Colin saw virtue drain out of her as he looked. He was frightened that Davie might come home before the two cows were redeemed. Davie had been away for days at the Riasgan trying to harvest some of the crops. It would be awful if he came home with his burdens, dead-tired after these endless miles, to find that Colin had let the cows be captured. It would be awful!

She lifted her head and looked at him in a queer way. He grew afraid.

'You go outside,' she said.

In a little while she appeared, her plaid drawn tight round her head. Without a word he went with her.

When at last they came in sight of the pen, it was half-dark and the fine occasional snowflake was seen only in the instant before it struck the eyeball.

'Wait you here and watch,' she said.

But when he was left alone the lowing of the beasts in the pen was uncanny and heart-rending. They were crying exactly as if they were about to be killed. He had seen the pen before: restless sounds out of their nostrils, the bellow, eyes glancing, heads pushing up over buttocks, pashing and stamping . . . He lost sight of Mairi. Nothing happened. The shepherd must have gone away. All at once there was furious dog-barking. Before he knew what he was doing he was retreating; but quickly he pulled himself up and hesitatingly began to recover ground. There was nothing in the world he feared more than shepherds' dogs. A long time elapsed. Now he was trembling, but valiantly he went nearer. At last he discerned Mairi standing before a tall man. Colin could not see the man's eyes as they rested on

Mairi's old silver brooch, as big as a small plate, full of intricate design and open work, and with the figure of a galley in the middle. By her gesture he saw that it was her all. Pitifully, ingratiatingly, with her thin mindless smile, she held it out. He took it and examined it, and knew it was old and real silver. All right, he would take it; but he would not take anything like that from her a second time. He had had enough of this! She did not understand his words, of course, but she gathered their import from the flash of his eyes. All the same, she could see he was not displeased. He whistled his dogs and for a few minutes there was pandemonium in the pen. Smartly he withdrew the birch bars, but before he could get them in place again two three-year-olds had followed Mairi's two cows. Swearing, he set the dogs at them. All four beasts made away at a great speed, tossing their heads at the dogs and hitting out with their hind legs.

Mairi began waddling after them, crying out to Colin, who was now running like a hare, his fear of the dogs lost in blind action. But he knew how to head them off and where. Shouting the cows' names, he raced madly. His cries brought other lads on the scene. The brutes were turned. The shepherd came over the skyline. At last there was a piercing whistle. The dogs withdrew. One of the three-year-olds had pitched and rolled over. For a time he would not move, but while they were poking his bones he all at once surprised them by getting to his feet. For a little he stood quite still, slavering at the mouth, then trotted off, his eyes glancing, a threat in his nostrils. Granny Gilchrist's widowed daughter had got him back cheap!

As the darkness settled, the snowflakes grew more frequent. Mairi began to wish Davie would appear and several times went to the door. She had an uneasy feeling about him; there was something ominous in the night. She hoped the boat was high enough up.

'It's going to be a nasty night,' she said to Colin.

'Will I go down to Hector's to see if there's any word?' he asked. There was relief in his mind because the cattle had been saved, and now he would do anything gladly. Indeed he seemed eager to do something, so light his heart felt. A step came in at the door. Their faces stared at Elie as she entered; then Mairi welcomed her.

'I heard about the cows,' Elie said, smiling. Her cheeks had fallen in as when she had come back from the south, but there was also about her face a tired haggard expression, and when the smile passed anyone could see she was not well. But now the bright expression remained in her eyes. Elie would never be a mournful visitor if she could help it. In truth, at times, when she snuggled her shoulders to the fire, she seemed to desire to draw out whatever brightness was lost in the gloom of the world.

Mairi told her what had happened. 'It was the change of weather. The beasts felt it coming and wanted to go away to their old shelters. The boys could not know that and I don't blame them. You can go down to Hector's,' she said to Colin. And he went away, secretly elated.

'How are you feeling?'

'Pretty much the same,' answered Elie. 'I don't mind it, though it leaves me so tired. One gets used to anything.' She smiled again and a confiding, almost hungry, look came into her eyes.

Her body had 'gone wrong' ever since Rob's child had been stillborn: legacy of the eviction night. Mairi had held out hope that time would put her right. But the look in Elie's eyes had nothing to do with that at the moment; it was a hungry look for something to grip, some bright core that she could hang on to. Her trouble frequently brought upon her extreme despondency, especially after a period of seeming to drag her body behind her, with its burning centre of pain at the root of the spine.

She lived pretty much alone, for though Rob went away for long periods she could not have Colin with her, because

she was never sure when Rob would come back. He went
away professedly to look after the crops behind the mill,
but she knew that actually he went to the Heights, not yet
cleared, where with some wild spirits he distilled whisky
and lived a riotous life. He had no interest at all in their
new holding. He spurned it, he hated it, he cursed it. And
all that, she felt, had arisen because she had failed him with
the child and then had become unfit for him.

Yet not altogether, for she knew her man now; but it
certainly rounded off the bitter rebellious feelings the eviction had roused in him. Like nearly all the men, Rob was
not naturally an earth worker. He had not the patience for
slow monotonous digging. And as an occupation, he
despised it. It was a woman's job, like spinning wool! They
could get on with it! And she had failed him, damn her!
Nothing but bloody misery!

Elie knew that, at certain moments, Rob hated her mani-
acally. Once in terrible words he had cursed her, and cursed
her son, and cursed Davie, then walked out of the house
for a week. Ever since he had first begun to visit Elie at
Dark Mairi's, he had hated Davie, hated him vindictively,
without reason, blindly. In that cursing, Davie's name had
come out of him before he knew what he was saying, and
when he did realise the horrible thing he was hinting at,
he raised his arm to smash her out of his sight in sheer
madness at having given the lurking thought away, though,
in fact, until that moment it had hardly been a conscious
thought to himself. Her look saved her; the steady expression of her frank eyes; those eyes that had not yet failed
to make him throw up his arms and call on Christ and
stamp dementedly away.

She understood Rob. In months before the eviction, he
had been extraordinarily kind to her and gentle. In conceivable circumstances he would murder people for her sake
and die for her. But the circumstances would have to be
arranged, and life apparently could never be relied on in

this matter, certainly not to arrange them in a way that would flatter Rob.

Anyway, she knew quite definitely or fatally that he would never come back to her now and live as they had lived; in some way, and soon, death would interfere. She saw clearly at last that in life things always moved towards death. 'I'll die.' And all the web of circumstance, of suffering and hopelessness, would be rolled up and put away, leaving the clean peace of blankness where it had been. It was the certainty of this that produced calm.

She did not want Rob to come back.

'That's because you're not well,' said Mairi. 'It's the dampness that's giving you that stabbing pain. But once we get into the new year and the good days come, you'll mend. And if it does not go back itself, I know a woman in Ross-shire who is skilled in putting it right. There's no trouble in all the world for making a person feel down-hearted like yours.' Then Mairi told her a story about a woman she knew who had been similarly afflicted. It was a long matter-of-fact story but it sounded like a legend. Elie was held by it, and in the rhythm of Mairi's voice caught again the half-haunted sensation of sunlight on a remote place.

They spoke then about ailments hitherto unknown among the people, many of them kept secret out of a sense of shame or humiliation.

'I know I'm only one,' said Elie.

'It sometimes helps to know that,' said Mairi.

That was true.

'Davie didn't come home tonight?'

'No. I wish he had.'

The secret fear that haunted Elie was that of Rob and himself meeting at the old mill. 'Rob does not like Davie.'

'And Davie does not like Rob,' replied Mairi. 'But you needn't be frightened of that. There are several of them up there and they would never allow anything desperate to be done.'

Elie saw suddenly that that was true. Rob would never attack Davie in an evil unexpected way. There would first be 'words', face to face. A weight lifted off her back, for she had had a persistent picture of Davie being cut down in a dark and terrible moment at the ruined mill.

Out of this talk a quiet intimacy was born and the rhythm of the words flowed over the mind soothingly. That peat was scarce, that the winter would yet see houses fireless, gave to the yellow tongues of flame a friendliness that was precious. How well off they were to have a fire! Elie's eyes grew tranced by the flap and flicker that ascended like slow thoughts out of the dreaming core.

She awoke to find Mairi still staring mindlessly into that red heart. The small dark eyes, the bone ridges running from cheek-point to ear, the face itself, as if hands had gone over it, making it small and compact, the neat flattened ears beneath the hair drawn tightly back, sleek as some water animal's, now of an indeterminate grey-black but still strong and coarse, and over all a faint darkening or dirtying of the earth: there was no easy response there, rather a hard remoteness, cool and strong like a stone, or like a bit of the earth one had loved . . .

Elie got to her feet, strangely refreshed.

'You're not going, are you?' said Mairi, the thin smile on her face like a breath of air on grey water.

'Yes. I'm sorry you had to give your brooch.'

'It was in my family a long time. That's true. I remember the day my grandmother told me its history. Some of my ancestors, the Bethunes, were famous healers . . . But what is it, after all? And I had to give it or give the money.'

Elie was silent.

'I mean Colin's money,' said Mairi, with a little sigh, getting up. 'And I wouldn't use that unless our need was desperate, and it has never been that yet, thank God.'

Elie moved to the door without saying a word or looking at Mairi. The wind had risen and it was black dark outside.

'They'll never come this night now,' said Mairi, smelling the threat in the wind.

'I'll run,' said Elie, using the old impulsive phrase. 'Goodnight, Mairi.'

Tears stung her eyes as she went through the wind that plucked at her plaid and whisked snowflakes into her face. The brooch *or* Colin's money: Mairi had nothing else. There was something lovely in the bitterness of the world too . . . here she was crying again, crying as if her heart would break . . . lovely and kind.

*

Davie and Angus og and Art and the others did not return until two days thereafter. They had realised, they said, when they smelt the snow coming, that they must get all the potatoes out or leave them in the ground for good. So they had done their best. The shepherds and their dogs had been nasty enough, but didn't realise that the boys were using the old mill ruin as a sort of encampment.

There lay a good joke in that!

Davie related it in Hector's, with old Angus and Anna there, Kirsteen and a handful of girls, old men and young, quite like a ceilidh of the Riasgan days.

The youths were rather proud of themselves for having dared the ruined mill, which was well known to be haunted by old Gilleasbuig's ghost. Gilleasbuig had been one of two greybeards who had never turned up after the eviction. His body had been found by a shepherd within the ruined walls of the mill, where apparently he had crawled round and round, licking the meal dust out of corners and off low ledges, before death stiffened him.

What praying would have been there! All his favourite phrases . . . were heard a month afterwards in his very voice by a couple of men from the main glen carrying at dead of night a bag of malt on their backs.

'But really we had to stay there,' Davie explained; 'the ground had gotten so soft for the ponies' feet. The Riasgan stream is out over its banks – I've never seen anything like it. Your lower field yonder where you had the barley was ankle deep in water. Alan there was wading in and hauling the stuff out by the roots, most of it flattened – and talk about cold! We haven't been dry since we left. And the fences we built – all gone. The shepherd himself had a couple of cows brought up. You know how they tried to chase us off in the summer-time and keep us from watching the crops – well, they've won, for what we have saved, apart from the few potatoes, was hardly worth bothering about. It really has been wicked!'

Davie laughed, and his laughing tickled his throat and brought on a fit of coughing. His face was thin and pale, but his eyes were very bright and full of mirth.

'But what I was going to tell you is about the mill. We had to stay there. There was nowhere else. The old houses are flat to the ground, and it was worth our lives to have built a shelter near them. Not but that we'd have done it, if it hadn't been that that might have given them an excuse to destroy the crops. How they hate us going in yonder! And their dogs, when they go round you with their heads down and their teeth showing – man, I would have liked fine to have knifed one or two of the brutes.'

'We'll do it yet,' said Art. 'I would never lie easy in my grave if we didn't do it.' Several of the boys now got talking at once, their eyes sparkling. Coughing had become a fashion. They were full of an eager gaiety, as if they had come through some marvellous adventure. 'If we hadn't got that drop of whisky we'd have died!' They laughed.

'In the distance we heard a dog bark. The shepherd's, sure! What would we do now? If we were found the whole place would be flattened out, and though it's pretty draughty, there's good shelter in one corner. We had a whole heap of stuff gathered there too. It was a shepherd right enough, coming along with two dogs, and by the cut of him we knew he was the fair fellow who had discovered Gilleasbuig's body. In the mouth of the night there was something very quiet about him, and he was wrapped in his plaid to the chin; it was like a great sheet round him. His dogs were at his heels. They didn't look like dogs that would have been barking. Their dogs rarely bark anyway, the brutes! The ponies were round the back of the wall and Alan had slipped away to make sure they could not be seen. We heard his feet coming back so we felt sure they must be all right. Unless the dogs therefore smelt us, there was a good chance that the fellow would pass by. On he came, not very fast but silently. It was getting uncanny. Then we saw, in that half-dark, the hackle of one of the dogs rising and his head go down and forward. Now he couldn't have smelt us, because the wind was coming from him, and he couldn't have seen us, because we were peering through narrow slots between stones that we had put on the coping. At last we knew that it really was the shepherd in the flesh, because when the dog growled he spoke to him sharply but not too loud. But there was something about it . . . and then *up out of the earth* there came an awful groan.'

Two of the lads turned their faces away. Davie looked like a ghost himself. Alan was serious and awed.

'Our flesh went cold. Art, here, slid to the ground in a faint. The shepherd stood still as death. Then Gilleasbuig's voice started to pray, not as if it was beside us, but again as if it was under us, hollow as a noise in a cavern. And the voice roared and fell – you know the way Gilleasbuig used to cry out when he was "wrestling with the Lord". Show them, Alan.'

'I couldn't,' said Alan quietly. Then all at once they were startled by the loud voice of Gilleasbuig proceeding from his mouth, 'And, O Lord, remember us who walk in the paths of deceitfulness and sin. Look down upon us, O Lord, who in Thy providence and in Thy mercy has sent us this plague of shepherds and factors to bring us to repentance, even as you sent upon the Egyptians the plagues of locusts and frogs and other dirty beasts. And, O Lord . . .' arose Alan's voice till the company swayed and shook in the wild gusts of it.

And then Alie Munro said solemnly, 'God bless me, do you mean to say it was Alan all the time?'

Whereat the laughter increased.

'You should have seen the shepherd take to his heels!' cried Iain. 'And one of the dogs – one of the dogs – let out an awful yelp. Ach!' he choked with mirth.

'Why?' asked Alie.

'Go away!' yelled Iain.

'You see,' said Alan soberly to Alie, 'I had my head in the hollow where the water-wheel was. When I took it out and stood up to see the effect, the shepherd was running as if he was going to finish with a long jump. You know the way you run up to the stand?'

'I do that,' said Alie. 'Wasn't I the longest jumper of my day?'

The house got caught in a more helpless gust.

'I know you were. That's why I said it,' nodded Alan. 'Well, one dog had seen me peering round the corner. I knew that. That's why I had prayed so hard, because I was frightened. And they may laugh if they like, Alie, but you can understand me when I say that I was praying with deep unction.'

'I can that,' nodded Alie. 'It was the time and the place for it.'

'It was,' Alan nodded back. 'Well, this dog, instead of departing with his master, didn't he come a step or two nearer! I picked up a stone the size of your fist. It hit him.'

'No?' Alie slapped his knees. 'Where?'

'In a delicate part,' said Alan.

Alie put his head back and roared.

'When the dog yelped, the shepherd trod on his plaid and went heels over head three times.'

'Capital!' Alie whacked his knees. He was getting a grip of the whole thing!

In the midst of the amusing remarks that followed, Art's face went sickly white and he glared before him, as if he was seeing something or was going to vomit. One or two noticed it. Anna asked him if he was feeling all right.

He looked at her with vacant eyeballs, from which the lids had receded. Then he put his fists up to his eyes and screwed them there. After that he kept his head lowered for a little. Lifting his face, he smiled in a sickly way, wetting his lips with his tongue and making a dry clacking sound in his mouth.

Kirsteen was ready with a bowl of water.

'It's all right,' he muttered. He was trembling so violently, however, that he shook the water out of the bowl. Kirsteen helped him.

'Not enough cold potatoes,' remarked Alan wryly.

'I'll be going,' said Art.

'I'll go with you,' said Alan.

'No,' said Art. 'I'm sorry. I'll go alone.'

'Very well,' said Alan. 'I'll be your shadow on the snow.'

Outside they heard Art being sick and Alan encouraging him. Somehow that relieved them.

'Poor boy,' said Anna. 'I don't know how you all lived up there.'

'He ate a raw potato today,' said Seumas og. 'I saw him.'

They all agreed that was enough to do it.

'Man, I've never known anyone get it so quick as that. I thought at first he was *seeing* something,' said Alie.

The girls' mouths twisted at the old fool, but they smoothed into a quick laugh when Iain said good-naturedly,

'He would have to see it quicker than you, Alie, or he might miss it altogether.'

'My eyes are as good as yours, my boy, but I'll say nothing. You had a hard time of it, but you did well. And wasn't Alan the lad, frightening the shepherd like yon?' His eyes twinkled. He would like to go all over it again.

But they could not quite get back their former ease. Little Colin, thrilled with the night's adventure and fun, felt the constraint. And when, in a little while, there came the far sound of old Roy's pipes, everyone visibly started – and listened.

Before two notes of the theme were played, Colin knew it was Patrick Mór MacCrimmon's *Lament for the Children*. And though he was sitting there in the midst of people, he began to experience all the quivering emotions that would have beset him had he been alone in the night. Sometimes these emotions grew beyond enduring and the body for relief could have stalked on great legs and stretched its arms to the sky, crying, crying, and scattering the stars; but more often – ah, more often – it curled over like a boulder and cried into the earth, while the notes of the music, like the waves of the world, broke over it; while at still other times, the living breath drew the notes in and sent them forth from the breast quivering like an instrument on which the white cold lights of the northern world advanced and withdrew, rayed out and vanished, flickered and died.

Sad seven times – ah, Patrick MacCrimmon of the seven dead sons.

'It's a hard tune that,' said old Angus. Hard on the piper; hard on them all; hard on the world. He had grown smaller in the last year, but the expression of his eyes was still linnet-bright. However old he might grow, he would never lose his faculties. 'He plays it well for his years. But I think it's not himself that's playing now; it's his sorrow.'

At these words the playing and the night came into the house, and visitors got up and prepared to go away.

Outside, the snow was spectral white under the blue-black star-thick sky. A shadow came over the snow towards them. It was Alan. 'Seana is gone,' he said. Seana was dead.

Davie had to turn his head. Kirsteen's face was waiting for him white as marsh light. They stood secretly as in a desert place, then with Colin he walked away, the weeping of the girls in their ears.

When they came near their door, Davie stopped. Colin knew that a feeling had come over him not to go in, never to go in, a mad blind feeling to take to the mountain paths, to the heights, to go away, away, to ease the chest, to break the bonds, to fall, and, falling, die.

'He's mad,' said Davie harshly. It was, in truth, said that old Roy had gone a bit off his head, ever since that night of the eviction, when he had played somewhere or other, not any lament, but a brand new march, improvised for the occasion, and christened, *Into the Sea*. As far as could be made out he had put himself at the head of an imaginary army, and, deceiving them with his wild irony, had led them towards the only place that was left the Gael, the World-under-the-Waves. How he had lived through that night no one knew, though several cottages in the glen vouched for the sprightly devil-playing and some said they heard the army crying on the wind as they went past. All that was certain was that when he did turn up and Seana had dried his clothes, she found his kilt flaked with salt.

As Davie stood swithering, the music ceased, right in the middle of a movement, as if someone had stuck a knife in the bag. Something had gone wrong! Others apparently had thought the same, for they also were running through the crisp snow. There appeared, however, to be nothing wrong with the old man, who refused to speak and walked away with his own thought towards the house.

Davie and Colin this time did not falter, but went right

into their own home. Mairi was not there. They had it to themselves.

'Are you hungry?' asked Davie.

'A little bit,' replied Colin.

'So am I. Ach, let us forget it!' Davie sat down and straightened up the fire. He did not now seem to be in the least sad about Seana. Colin was grateful for this and felt his heart warm. 'Lord, it was cold up yonder,' said Davie pleasantly. 'Wet all the time, and at night—' He shuddered. 'What wouldn't we have given for this?' His smile flashed.

'Were the shepherds bad?'

'There's one fellow I'd like to knife. I may yet,' he said companionably. 'But – they're only – ach, this place is damned, like a place thrown outside hell. I'm leaving it.'

Colin's mouth fell open in intense dismay. 'When?'

'In the spring – when I get you through the winter. You're a big fellow now and with granny you'll manage all right. How's your mother?'

'Fine.'

Davie looked at him. It was known that Colin's father had been wounded and it was later rumoured he was dead. The regiment had left South Africa for home over a year ago.

'Was Rob not at the mill?' Colin asked.

'No,' said Davie quietly. 'Hasn't he come back?'

'No,' replied Colin.

There was silence for a little, then Davie put his hand on the boy's head. 'You're one of us.'

Colin's eyes grew bright.

'All right, Colin, my little hero,' and Davie gave him a squeeze. Then he laughed at him.

Colin had to try his strength to save himself.

'There's granny!' said Davie, cowering away from him.

Colin swung round; but there was no granny.

'That was a lie!' challenged Colin.

'I said granny was there.'

'Where?'

'Over there – where Seana is – helping to dress her body.'

Colin went pale and quite still.

Davie smiled, his eyes glittering darkly, and slowly twisted his mouth, mocking him.

*

Elie returned from Seana's funeral in the mood that made her home feel very empty and silent. Once when she had gone to the door she had thought she had seen a man move among some boulders and whins away along the hillside, as if he were hiding there. Probably it was no more than a black calf. Anyway, one could not readily think of Rob, however shame-faced, waiting for the darkness before entering his own door.

An hour before she died, Seana had been talking brightly about what she would do when she got up. Her cheeks were wild roses, her eyes remarkably clear and shining. Then the inner fire flared up and burned her out. Such a trouble had never been in her family before; nor had any of the other families experienced it. She had not been meant for this world, they knew . . .

Toasted oatcakes and cheese, and Roy, with his pipes, had set them to the dance, for he would have the funeral conducted decently and bravely according to the customs of his fathers. So wiping their tears they had turned from the dead Seana and danced. Salt and earth, for the spirit and the body, on a plate on her breast below the white rose and the ghostly red of her delicate face.

Elie by her peat fire got into one of those long trances that more and more drew her away from the world, from the pains and the penalties that were sometimes less real than the noise of distant waters falling in the night.

As the darkness touched her with its hand, she got up obediently and went to the door. A big man was approaching from the boulder clumps with a burden on his back. It was the black-whiskered McHamish from the Heights, who had piped at her wedding.

He had to drop the bag of meal at her feet, for she seemed unable to move. From the bag she looked up into his face.

'Isn't Rob in?' he asked.

'No.' And then she said, 'I thought you had him on your back.'

He could see she had thought that. He was a quiet man and did not know what more to say. Rob had left him with the first flakes of snow four nights before to return home. It was he himself who had prevailed on Rob to go and had indeed accompanied him for several miles. It had turned out a dirty night.

'I said I would come down with this. He used to be very good to us when he had it.'

'Won't you come in?'

McHamish half faced round and looked at the death-white hills. 'I'll take in the bag, but I'm not waiting.'

He lifted the bag in his arms and emptied the precious meal into the chest.

She thanked him in her timid way. He protested that he would have nothing to eat, but she poured boiling water into a bowl of meal and stirred it to a thick mess, added some milk, and handed him a horn spoon. The new meal was fragrant.

He asked her how they were getting on, but his dark uneasiness shamed his fierce if innocent nature and when he had finished eating he got up and went away. She watched him at a little distance stand and gaze at the hills, as if wondering what place, of all the places, should be searched first.

She had seen that death would interfere, but somehow she had never in the most tranced moment thought that it was she who would be left.

\*

Cold driving rain dissolved the early snow and turned their world into the darkness of the dead heather. Throughout the winter the resources of the people dwindled away and the stormy weather was against sea or rock fishing. Mairi's knowledge of edible seaweed and shellfish was useful, and as she used to be seen in the birch wood and on the rocky uplands gathering roots and lichen for colour, now, back bent, she could be seen like some sea-animal haunting the edge of the tide.

As in all times of war or famine or other natural calamity a people grows superstitious, turning to strange fetish-worship, so Mairi's people lost the brightness or magic of their old beliefs and, through fear, degraded them into dark ways of snatching a personal benefit or staving off some threatening evil.

This was seen particularly in the manner in which the folk began to look upon Mairi herself. In exchange for cattle, nets of a sort had been procured for catching herring, and after much cogitation it was decided that if Mairi could be got to put one of her charms on the nets, not only would loss be avoided, but luck ensured. Her old stories about people of the West who would wade into the tide and pour out ale to the seagod came back to them.

Moreover, this was a new and dangerous venture, for herring-boats must be out all night on the sea and who knew what gods or demons moved on that heaving darkness?

They met on the beach in the first of the night and Mairi made the men walk sunwise round their craft. Then she blessed the craft and she blessed the men, but she did it in the name of the Three-One, ever-living, ever-mighty, ever-lasting, who brought the Children of Israel through the Red Sea. 'Sain and shield and sanctify; be seated, O King of the elements, at their helm, and lead them in peace to the end of their venture.

*God of the elements,*
*King of the elements,*
*Spirit of the elements,*
*Close over us,*
*Ever eternally.'*

She had smiled then her thin smile as the boat moved off, but those who had been watching slipped away so that Mairi's eye might not fall upon them.

The night remained without storm; the net was filled; and in the morning a string of herring was left at Mairi's door.

After that the people avoided her more and more, and only when illness or other evil attacked them did they ask her aid; and the usual way was to go to Elie and say ingratiatingly, 'I wonder if you could get Dark Mairi . . .'

Little Colin lived with his mother, since Rob's body had been found on the hills, and often he would be sent on such an errand; but he did not like it, because it was bad enough to be a bastard without being taunted with having a witch for granny, a thing that befell him readily enough when he quarrelled with any of his companions.

The New Year festival was celebrated amidst poverty, sickness, and illicit drink. There were whisperings of immoral happenings at a certain house where boisterous nights were held – visited by men who wandered the countryside on heaven knew what midnight business. Death and disease were in the air.

'Not on the primrose bank any more,' said old Angus, 'but on the midden.'

'Where would you expect,' asked Davie, 'when the primrose banks were taken from us? What does it matter where we die?'

'It matters how we die,' said Angus.

'Perhaps.' Davie gnawed at the grin on his lips.

'I agree with Davie,' said Kirsteen, her eyes flashing. 'I

think Heller's new society of sheep-farmers has put the last and the blackest lie of all upon us. Fifteen hundred sheep stolen last year! What a terrible, terrible lie!' she said passionately.

'Their own shepherds stole them,' said Angus og. The quiet tone drew their glances. He was thin, with a perceptible stoop at the shoulders, but the smile on his face had a disillusion that was evil.

'Anyway,' said Davie, 'it was a good enough excuse for putting up pens and hunting us out of our crops with their dogs! You can imagine what a cry-out there would have been if one of us – one of us – had been found taking one sheep! How the shepherds must have watched – and hoped – for that!' He laughed.

'Hsh, Davie,' said Anna.

'Hsh yourself,' said Davie, with a sudden flash of good humour. 'We have hshed long enough. I'm not going to let this eat me away into gloom and death. In fact,' he said, getting up, 'I'm clearing out in the spring and Kirsteen says she'll come with me.'

There had been three phases in Davie's growth: the boy who loved the neatness and the excitement of the proverb game; the youth who became rather reserved and secretive, if occasionally fierce enough; and now the young man breaking defiantly through, crushing sensitiveness with a laugh. As Anna looked fixedly at him, she saw the three struggling excitedly in his face, and making his body hitch from leg to leg swaggeringly but awkwardly. Indeed deep in his dark eyes there was still the old weak sensitiveness begging her not to misunderstand, not to think he was being rudely assertive . . . yet if it came to that, his mouth did not care.

Anna dropped her eyes and did not look at Kirsteen. Old Angus was watching Davie, his mouth slightly open. Angus og, the only other in the room, glanced at his sister with a sarcastic smile. But Kirsteen was not looking at anyone, for this was the first time that Davie had asked her to go away with him.

'Where were you thinking of going, Davie?' asked old Angus.

'Oh, I don't know. The world is big. When Captain Grant and his wife Muiril went away, you remember they said that in the spring they might get a ship to take any of us who wanted to go with them to America and found a colony of our own.'

'Ah, Davie,' said Angus, in a tone of such unconscious appeal that clearly when Kirsteen and Davie went the light of his life would go with them and the light of that land.

Anna looked at her daughter. 'Would you go with him?'

Kirsteen lifted her face and looked fairly at her mother. 'Yes,' she answered.

Anna breathed deeply and bowed her head again.

Davie, his face extraordinarily quickened, was now standing dead still. His eyes were alive and triumphant. The flush of heat that went burning over him started him coughing.

'You'll have to watch that cough,' said Anna.

'It's nothing,' said Davie, his body now quivering like an athlete's. 'But I must be going.' He hesitated, vaguely moved to comfort them with the words that it might be a long time yet, but in the end all he said was good-night.

Kirsteen went after him quite openly, and when she paused at the door he caught her by the arm and led her away. The sea wind was cold and spitting rain. They went on up the face of the hill until the rough ground stopped them.

'It's a cold barren place this,' said Davie. They stood looking back against the darkness and the rain.

'You said you would go.' His voice was quiet.

'Yes,' she answered. 'I'll go with you anywhere you like.'

There was no emotion now. It was the old terrible feeling

of the exposed bone and marrow. All in a moment there was something bitter about it like ashes.

'I would be sorry to go – and leave them,' she said.

He was silent. She needn't go unless she liked. The black night was full of hideous spite.

Now they found they could not speak to each other and they began to descend the hillside. As they went they instinctively hunted for a sheltered place into which to take this misery of their world and of themselves. Soon they were alone at the heart of it, so far in, so lost that they sat looking out. The loneliness slowly bred a secretive friendly feeling, not unlike what Colin and his companion, little Alie, experienced when they peered out from the door of their tiny house upon the diverse world.

'You would be sorry to go?'

'Yes,' she answered.

Yes again, and only that! Obstinate, because she knew her true heart! He chuckled drily.

'You do not understand,' she said, 'how cruel you can be at times.' There was a quiet but almost bitter resentment in her voice, though its tone was also reflective, nearly smiling.

'Would you go to America?'

'I would go to the end of the world.'

'It sounds like a challenge,' he laughed. 'Would you take me with you?'

'I'm not sure,' she answered. 'I doubt it.'

'Kirsteen,' he murmured, with mock seriousness. But his voice trembled. He wanted to touch her, but found he could not. 'You blow me on your breath like thistledown.'

'You make me do what you like, but I'll never give in to you,' she answered.

'How much can I make you do?'

'Everything,' she said sadly. 'Weak I am, to my shame; but I'll never give in to you.'

'Light and fire, they say, can never change their nature, which is to pierce the darkness where cruelty is and evil.'

Their hands, becoming entangled, began to tremble. Their smiles trembled on their faces. The light and the fire sent up their flickering tongues into the darkness until the travail of their identity was lost in the one flame.

## TWO

But the spring brought a new and fierce interest that acted on the people as sunlight acts on things that crawl in holes. Though destitute and indeed desperate, they were stirred to hope, even to exultation; and old women who shed tears proclaimed God's goodness. God would never desert the faithful. The wicked would be punished. As young Alan, after listening to the women, said, 'God's the boy!'

Petitions or memorials to his lordship on behalf of the evicted had been common enough. But these had always been sent back to the factors for their attention and any action they thought fit. But suddenly, like the old fiery cross, the amazing news went round the country that one of the king's sheriffs was among the people taking particulars of the fire-raisings, house-destroyings, and other illegal actions of Mr Heller, with a view, should the evidence be sufficient, to raise a criminal charge against that gentleman.

Evidence sufficient! There was enough evidence to smother him in fire and brimstone in the bottomless loch of hell!

And it was no wild mad rumour. The sheriff-substitute of the county arrived, empowered to take a precognition of the case and, if necessary, to apprehend Mr Heller. Amongst the Riasgan colony, Hector and other responsible men were questioned with precision, their answers having to be such as they would swear to in a court of law.

Both his lordship and her ladyship were behind the forces of the law, as could be gathered from what they had written. Ah, if only they had listened to their own people and not to the infamous factors, none of this evil would have happened! But things might yet be put right and the old order restored. To think of going back to the Riasgan! *O place me by the little streams that flow softly with gentle steps* . . . Stranger, if not more lovely, things had maybe happened in the history of the world!

The people came out of their holes and filled their lean bellies with talk. 'Horo Mairi!' they would now shout to Dark Mairi, and when they heard her muttering to herself as she dug the steep ground, they were sure it was going to go hard with Heller.

And for Mr Heller the affair was really beginning to look serious. The 'change of tenancy' had proceeded at an ever-accelerating pace, and comfortably-housed educated persons, observing from a distance this sustained effort at Progress, had applauded it. As one contemporary historian and humanist wrote of it, 'Of late years the landlords have very properly done all they could to substitute a population of sheep for the innumerable hordes of useless human beings who formerly vegetated upon a soil that seemed barren of everything else.'

That was the critical and humane note that had sustained Mr Heller, under Mr Elder, in his endless and arduous endeavours. Not only had he seen the interior of his vast territory being gradually swept clean of the useless human hordes, but could congratulate himself upon the construction of a road which would link up the handful of sheep-farmers' residences. The hordes had not required roads, for their cattle droves preferred the soft turf of the ancient passes; and now on the sea-beaches they required them less than ever, for even the wild drovers would not risk coming into a country inhabited by people of such unsettled ways and evil repute. Though here again, bent on educating the uncivilised, Mr Heller rigorously exacted the road-tax of four shillings on every male of eighteen or over, going the length, where payment could not be made, of seizing goods to a value that would also cover the expenses of collection, even if no legal process had been entered into. Nor was there any injustice in this, inasmuch as the sheep-farmer with his fifty thousand acres also paid his four shillings – though, of course, his shepherds were exempt.

Moreover, in addition to vast sheep-farms and roads to link them up, efforts were being made to erect lime-kilns, salt-pans, and tile-works, whose products, cheaply produced by imported labour, would help forward the beneficent work of construction. Even the sea-fishing, which the hordes would have to pursue or perish, could be made a source of pride, of profit (on the customary $6^{1}/_{2}\%$ basis), and of justification. Nor was historic worth forgotten, for an ancient castle, suitably adapted, was made to fulfil the requirements of a real jail.

But because these schemes were beneficent and just and full of that larger vision that looks towards the future by paying a dividend on the present, the simplest plant that grew could be 'fitted in' in a way that was truly marvellous only because it was obviously providential. Birch woods, for example, not only wintered sheep, but Providence (foreseeing Mr James's apologia of a slightly later date) designed the young trees to shoot up vigorously during the summer months, so that by the time the sheep are turned into them the tender parts have got beyond their bite or the bark has become objectionably strong and bitter. But that was only one aspect. The thinnings of the birch trees were designed for smoking red herrings; the tree itself for barrel staves; and its crooked bits as knees for boats. 'A system which a few interested and malignant persons have attempted, for selfish or pecuniary or still worse motives, to revile,' concluded Mr James, moved by the very spirit which animated his lordship and her ladyship in their active support and furtherance (the need being great) of the Scottish Society for the Propagation of Christian Knowledge.

'Which is all very true,' said Mr Heller, 'but where the hell do I get out?'

'Well – you see – his lordship now desires—'

'*Now*,' said Mr Heller. 'Quite so. The hounds are out – so one hunts with them.'

'Something—'

'Something had to be done. And again I'm the one to do it. His lordship is righteously indignant that any servant of his should act in a wrong or illegal manner. As if his lordship and her ladyship didn't know every move we made! Hm! Put not your trust in princes! All the same, by God, I'm a lawyer, and a charge of culpable homicide and fire-raising in an open court, where the prosecution is actively against me with a crowd of witnesses – that's another story. I don't like it.'

'There's a risk, you think? I can understand you. But let us look at it practically. Assuming our case is proved to the hilt, as it will be, then at one blow we not only clear ourselves from all these ugly rumours that are going about the country – and about Parliament – and you yourself admit that that must be done – well, we not only do that, but we get the express sanction, as it were, of His Majesty's court to clear out the whole country, root and branch, into the Pentland Firth. We're either going to throw in our hands – or go on. And clearly we cannot throw in our hands now that this is upon us. This is the one moment when we have got to justify ourselves up to the hilt.'

Mr Heller, staring grimly at nothing, reserved comment.

'Now let us examine the risk,' proceeded Mr Elder. 'In the first place Scotland is ruled by a certain few, who are supported by the landed aristocracy. London, so to speak, has farmed Scotland out to them. The Lord Advocate is supreme. Even in Edinburgh, the judge specifies the fifteen out of the forty-five who are to form his jury. In the country circuits he names the whole forty-five. That is, the jury of fifteen in your case would contain, beyond question, a majority of landlords, with a minority composed mostly of factors like ourselves. You know how sheep-farmers, ministers of the gospel, and justices on this estate are with you – and on every other estate, *necessarily*. And as for the landlords, all their own clearance schemes hang on this decision.

'Now let us examine it from the point of view of the Government. In the first place, the Government have the means of getting what they want. The Lord Advocate rules. But why should the Government, in your case, be absolutely against an adverse decision? Obviously because such a decision would not only implicate his lordship but also all the leading Highland proprietors throughout the country, who have already evicted on a wholesale scale. The Government would damn themselves. Look at it calmly. His lordship and her ladyship have sanctioned proceedings. Why? In order that their acts and their instructions to us may be reprobated and damned? No, no. A decision in your favour is as certain as that the sun will rise tomorrow.'

'That's well enough,' said Mr Heller; 'but it's not what's worrying me. It's not the evictions themselves that are to be called in question: it's *how* they were carried out in stated cases.'

'Sheriff-officers and constables and you yourself were there: is your conjoint evidence of no value against illiterate witnesses, whose incoherences will have to be translated? Again, what were the circumstances? If they had not been compulsorily removed, you know, and everyone knows, they would never have removed. They simply would not have gone. Well, we must have the power, the force, to remove them – or else his lordship can throw his charters in the fire. That's the crux of the whole thing. You served proper legal notice. When the term had passed, the land was your tenancy. You had to act, and you took the only steps that would have been effective. However,' said Mr Elder, 'we are anticipating. I do not think that your learned friend will go the length of requesting your company officially.'

'All the same—'

'Quite. But – there are more powers behind you in this than you quite realise.'

'Oh?'

'If it goes the whole length, the result is certain. That's my view. And there's been so much talk these last few months that something definite had to be done. We have had the Church and the military. Quite as spectacularly we shall have the law.'

'God, if this goes through all right, I tell you I'll make it pretty hot—'

Mr Elder nodded sympathetically. 'That,' he said, 'is, I think, the proper attitude.'

*

Then the news came of Mr Heller's arrest. The trial was on before a High Court with judge and jury. Along the sea-coasts and up into the uncleared glens, the tidings sped on the feet of the wind. Truthful witnesses were ready for the journey to the northern capital. As the investigating sheriff wrote to his lordship, 'After much patient perseverance, I examined about forty evidences . . . and it is with the deepest regret that I have to inform your lordship that a more numerous catalogue of crimes, perpetrated by an individual, has seldom disgraced any country, or sullied the pages of a precognition in Scotland.' The crimes would include wilful fire-raising 'with most aggravated circumstances of cruelty, if not of murder', the demolishing of houses whereby the lives of the aged were endangered if not actually lost; the demolishing of barns, kilns, &c., to the great hurt and prej-udice of the owners; the burning of heath pasture before the legal term of removal; and 'innumerable other charges'.

Oh, Heller was done for! *Into the Sea* with him, Roy, my hero! Little Colin led grey Angus to a linnet's nest in that spring of poverty with its thin lovely sunlight of hope. 'It's good,' said the old man, 'to be out of the cage.'

*

Then the news came of Mr Heller's acquittal; honourably acquitted amid the compliments of the presiding judge.

'To this measure,' reported Mr Heller's counsel, 'his lordship seems to have been induced, chiefly for the purpose of satisfying the public mind and putting an end to the clamours of the country.'

His lordship's purpose, thus precisely defined, had been achieved.

Tomas the Drover, as the last living witness to Galgacus and Ossian, also summed up the affair, though with little respect, it is to be feared, for the august manner in which the High Court had with such notable impartiality arrived at the fine essence of legal justice whereby Mr Heller was acquitted with compliments and the sheriff-substitute dismissed in disgrace.

'What came you out for to see?' cried Tomas, now a veritable doubled-up rag of a man, with burning eyes and pointed skeleton-arms. 'Fools!' (Though he had previously taken much credit to himself for Mr Heller's incarceration.) 'Fools! That great court was not dealing with history, with truth, with justice – it was dealing with law. And as the law of the land – the law *of the land* – is against us, how could it decide but in its own favour? Heller and her ladyship own this land. Who gave it to them? The law. Who made the law? Landlords like her ladyship in times past. At one time the land belonged to us all. There were no "sheep-skins" then. But now it belongs to her ladyship and is administered by the lily-white hands of her parasites. They have the law's right to clear us off the land, which our fathers fought and died for, to clear us into the sea, into nothingness, into hell. It is out of their great mercy, their deep concern for their "subjects", that they allow us to rot on their sea-beaches. Let us give them thanks for that. We have not gone far enough in our appreciation. We have not gone low enough. We have not yet begged to be permitted the four-legged honour of kissing their backsides. But that will come – though I doubt if even then we shall be considered worthy of so signal and chaste an honour.'

The schoolmaster was enjoying this effort in bardic satire by his pupil (by far the oldest of the handful who attended his little turf dwelling in the main glen). He was a big man with a dark brown beard and eyes of such irreverent penetration that they had at an earlier age effectively prevented preferment from school desk to pulpit.

'But do not let us show our ignorance by blaming her ladyship, as if she were the first to throw honour aside and foul her heritage in a manner that would revolt the stomach of an African slave-dealer. For the slaver at least traffics honestly in human bodies and enlists the aid neither of Progress nor of Jesus Christ. She is not the first to turn from the ancient ways of our people, ways that, wherever they wandered, never forgot fidelity unto death, courage, and the fine laughing virtue of hospitality. She is not the first to betray them and make for herself a name that must to every Gael while the world lasts stink of the unforgivable sin of treachery. For I am cursing her now not for dispossessing the people of their own land, not for having made the law that gave her the power to dispossess her own people, not for having burned them out of their ancient homes, not for having made them wanderers and beggars and eaters of filth, not for the angels of insanity and disease and death she sent amongst them, not even for having tried to justify herself in the eyes of the world by employing an army, by using Christ's Church, by weighting the balances of justice: not for any of these things in themselves, not for any bodily hurt these may have done us; but because in using all these things, in doing all these things, she has broken the spirit of her people, she has destroyed the soul

of her people; as surely as if she were Judas, she has cruci-
fied the Gael.'

The Drover had shown unusual restraint and was now
leaning towards his audience, as if the suppressed demonic
fire were about to issue from his outstretched hands. The
schoolmaster's face was creased in a smile of disintegrating
satire. 'Not exactly a legal summing up, but it has its points!'
he remarked to the man at his elbow.

'I said she was not the first,' resumed Tomas. 'I saw
what happened in Glen Tilt. It's a beautiful glen, fertile and
full of the finest grazing, where the people from all time
had enjoyed salmon-fishing and hunting on the hills. A
strong and hospitable people, who had defeated the enemies
of Scotland on many a bloody field – until Atholl, their
chief, for his own wanton pleasure, drove them out; not
only drove them out but violently pressganged the young
men for service in the American war, and when that war
was over tried to sell them to the East India Company –
and was prevented only by a mutiny in the regiment. And
today Glen Tilt is like – what all our glens will be like
tomorrow. Six hundred men followed Glengarry to
Culloden; but *Marsali Bhinneach*, widow of a Glengarry
chief, evicted over five hundred from their homes in
Glencuaich to make room for one south country shepherd
– and that was the year after our lads enlisted to fight for
their country against the anti-Christ, Bonaparte. For years
now ships have been carrying their human cargoes from
the land of the Chisholm. Not only evicting, but selling
them into slavery – as the Macleod of Dunvegan and the
Macdonald of Sleat tried to do long ago in that black and
infamous story of the *Soitheach-na-Daoine*. Whatever the
chief, whatever his name, from Argyle to Caithness, from
the wilds of Inverness to the Western Isles, he is carrying
out this work of ruin and death. There have been horrors
and barbarities that would in their treachery shame the
cannibals of the southern seas. And the worst of these the

world will never know, because, driven like dumb brutes, like dumb brutes we are voiceless.

'That is the doom that has come upon us, we, the clan of Cuchulain and Ossian, of Ninian and Columba, we who stood with Galgacus and while we were yet heathen hurled back the Roman conquerors of the world. "See," cried Galgacus, "these plunderers of the world, stimulated by greed, by ambition, by a hunger that is never satisfied. To ravage, to slaughter, to usurp under false titles – *false titles!* – and where they make a desert they call it peace." Then we were "the noblest sons of Britain, undebased by slavery and far from the view of servile shores". *Then* – not now. *Then* as heathen, not *now* as the children of Christ, taught by our minister to accept our debasement and slavery as ordained by Christ, as commanded by the loving and ever-merciful Christ, whose doctrines of humility and brother-hood her ladyship interests herself in propagating throughout this her barbarous and heathen realm.

'In Galilee, on Calvary, the Roman was an invader and a conqueror. There may be that excuse for him. But what excuse can there be for the chiefs of our own clans, acting not in a strange land, but at home upon the hearthstones of their people? No treachery like this has been known in the whole history of the earth, and Time itself will be so shamed that it will tear the Gaelic tongue out of the mouth of the world lest the memory of it be spoken amongst men.'

The schoolmaster eyed his pupil keenly and a wild cold-quickening surmise touched his features. Could it be possible that Tomas was himself caught in this doom, was himself experiencing something of the agony of the Crucifixion? Was this why his frenzy would not come upon him, why the final curse could not be spoken?

'I said we did not blame them for murdering the body: we blamed them for murdering the soul; we blamed them for taking an order of mankind, faithful and loyal, who in the course of the ages had given light to the world and courage and a tale of deeds dressed in great music and story; for having taken that order to which they themselves belonged, and for thirty fleeces of wool to have betrayed it in its own garden and destroyed it.

'But finally it is not even that. Even that I could have forgiven them. For if our end has come upon us, let us go. But O God, O God, how my soul cries out that we had gone cleanly, that the history of our people had been rounded off in a way fitting its brave and loyal past! But the chiefs are blood of our blood and bone of our bone, and by their meanness, their vileness, they have dragged us in bitter degradation to their own level and shamed us forever before the peoples of the world.'

This strange bundle of rag and bone stood with outstretched hands, the curse that would not come choked at last by a sob in the throat. Then it fell to the ground and began writhing, while a light spume bubbled at the mouth.

## THREE

On a day in July of that year, Elie came to the corner of her house and looked up the slope towards Mairi's cottage. There was no smoke from the chimney but that did not disturb her, for the day was warm with a soft wind blowing over the hills from the west. The floor of the sea glittered under the noonday sun, and there was everywhere a peace that stilled action. Actually Elie saw no one anywhere, and for a moment she got a vivid impression of all living things having withdrawn into that quiet rest that is like the trance of death. Touched by a misgiving, not altogether on Mairi's account, she started for the cottage and, at its door, called the old woman by name. There was no response, and inside in the gloom the fire was all but out. Even as she looked at its ruined face, the last ember, red as an open mouth, fell and was buried in a puff of ash. For Mairi to let her fire go cold, day or night, was so unthinkable that Elie listened to the silence in the room with fear. If Mairi had been going away for any length of time she would have smoored her fire. Elie went out and looked around the cottage and about the hillside, then walked over to Murdoch's place and found Seonaid and her two youngest children at home.

'You're merely restless, Elie!' Seonaid's dark eyes smiled at her in a peculiar way.

Elie returned the smile frankly, and the joke passed between them like a drift of smoke. A week before Hector had learned from a returned disabled soldier the story of how his son Colin had been struck in the head by a ball, and had had great difficulty in getting his memory back.

Hector had faced up to the story but the man had sworn an oath that there never had been any question of an insane mind, and that he was hiding nothing. If Colin had not yet come home, he would come home, as he must be discharged for good. He certainly would not be embarking with the others for America. The man was so positive about this that when Hector had had time to think over the matter with Anna, he hardly dared know what to believe or hope.

Seonaid and Elie had discussed the news but Elie had shown nothing beyond a natural and deep concern for Colin; even in talking, her look had been fixed as if dispassionately regarding something at a great distance. Seonaid, grown to dislike that look, had tried to rally Elie, and though Elie smiled, Seonaid saw that in her there was no belief. Elie's health had improved and in many ways there was about her a quiet happiness, often a deep tenderness, but it seemed to have no centre, no core. Her face, thinner than ever, had lost its dreadful gauntness, without gaining purpose. She was more untidy in her person and her house than she had ever been, yet out of untidiness and disorder she seemed to gather a certain warmth or comfort. She often gave Seonaid the uneasy impression of nestling to that still centre where life is forgotten.

For Seonaid herself had grown strong again and worked the earth better than any man; a powerful full-bodied woman, with living eyes ever wary of easy sentiment or doleful expression and a tongue caustic enough to frighten any but the free-minded. Murdoch and her three children she ruled with decision and wisdom – and on occasion with a dark-eyed relaxation that gave to their conjoint being the depth and ripple of a pool. She showed the first trace of uncertainty when Elie mentioned Mairi's abandoned fire.

'Since Davie went away with Kirsteen she has grown a bit queer. She lives entirely within herself. And you know what they say?'

'I know,' said Seonaid. 'The fools! When you think in

the old days how good she was to them! And all this last
winter, how many has she saved from death! You say she
lives within herself. She doesn't. She lives outside herself.
I see her here, there, down on the strand among the boulders, wherever I look, and I know that nobody has ever
forgotten herself as Dark Mairi has.'

'That's true,' said Elie. 'I have the queer feeling that at
last she has forgotten herself entirely.'

Seonaid became thoughtful and murmured, 'Last night
Murdoch was talking to her about dyes.'

In the end they decided that she had probably gone
hunting lichens and plants and roots. But where? Could she
conceivably have set out for her old haunts in the Riasgan?

'Don't laugh at me, Seonaid, but I knew this morning –
I had the feeling – I—' She stopped.

Seonaid looked closely at her. There was a faint flush
now on Elie's cheeks and her eyes were bright. She had
grown awkward too, as if conscious of Seonaid's mistrust.
She was hiding something – probably a dream!

All the same, it was odd about Mairi. And Seonaid agreed
that if she didn't come back in an hour or two, it might
be as well to send Colin on the hunt.

Elie suddenly became relieved and grew amusing over
Mairi's recent absent-mindedness. 'She was talking away
to the earth she was turning over. "Now you lie there,"
she would say, patting down the clod. "That's you, my
dark one." You would think the earth was a family she
was keeping from rolling down the hill!'

Talking of Mairi, the two women grew friendly and
companionable. A reflection of the old golden glow of the
Riasgan – the ceilidhs, the music, the summer shielings, the
lonely lovely care-free days of youth – touched their mood,
and for a time they forgot the horrors of the last year, the
nightmare of the winter, the hunger of their present lot, the
meanness in it beyond hunger that was killing brightness
and trust and giving suspicion two faces.

When Elie at last went home, she could not sit still, and finally departed to the peat-bank for her son, who was carrying the dried peats to a loose stack, whence they could be sledged home by the ponies. She saw him stagger under the light creel, for lack of varied and nourishing food had sapped his young strength. She told him of her fears, and at once and with a serious man's air he said he would go.

She fed him extravagantly, moving about with a restless excitement. Twice she asked him if he didn't think it was too far. Should she go with him or what? She did not know what to do. When his face had gone serious in the peat-bank and the eyebrows had flattened, she had seen his father.

When he started off, the very sight of his thin young body overcame her, and she turned into the house and broke down. She shouldn't be sending him! She shouldn't! she cried to the apparition on the crest of the wood.

\*

The apparition on the crest of the wood did not hear her but yet was disturbed by a vision of her face moving down the grassy hollow and looking back. That look, withdrawing and pale, the loneliness of denied life in it, going away . . . So deep an impression had it made on the old familiar hollow that its unbearable ecstasy was readily evoked. And then, swift as the flash and twist of eyes and supple body, hands thrust upward, cupping the face: *Colin, my dark love.*

But he hardly heard the words through the bleating of the lambs, whose mothers had been taken from them two days before. All the Riasgan was full of this bleating. Whenever his thought paused, the myriad crying rushed into its silence like waters from the desolate hills.

There was nothing that could have been so desperate or so torturing as this. He could have been prepared for silence, for desolation; with a certain irony he could have remembered the promise of land to the soldier who would fight for his chief and his king; he could have looked upon the scene as evidence of faithlessness so black that bitterness before it goes numb; the end having come upon this world, let it be rolled up in the silence that is death's due – and forgotten. Let it be forgotten, let it pass! The little pathways with their memories, their ghostly, their golden faces; the green arable land with the slow rhythm of the labour songs; the stooping, the walking, the running bodies; firelight in the houses and bright eyes, mouths quick in words and laughter; and quick hands; the darkness, the darkness under the stars, and voices dying into the night; and music: let them be rolled up and crushed between the hands of death and put away; out of the faithlessness and cruelty – are they not due the final decency of peace?

The crying of the lambs was like the crying of dead or unborn children. All the earth had little lambs' mouths. The sentimentality of it was monstrous.

Maddening; throwing its wavering shadows over the vanished faces, so that as ghosts they withdraw, the pale look stricken, and fade.

Bleating around the black ruins, by the hearthstones, in the fields, crying upon the mothers, the lost mothers, treading upon the dead mother . . .

The small dark figure of the woman came within his vision that had fallen upon the trance wherein even the action of crushing pain at last ceases.

She might have come out of the hillside; and presently she seemed to enter it again, leaving a dark boulder to mark the spot. The boulder moved and there she was coming on, small and tidy, not going anywhere so much as having business where she was at each moment, alive and wandering, like a hen or a dog.

This air of preoccupation with practical affairs was perceptible even from a long distance. The human mother carrying on her ancient solitary business with the earth, talking good and familiar sense with boulder and flower and rock, and now and then following a root below the surface; in easy accord, the communion sensible and so full of natural understanding that silence might extend into eternal silence, for wind and sun to play upon.

At last the woman too seemed to hear the lambs, for she stood still on a green patch of ground for a long time. The Riasgan was like a wave rising over her. She dwindled before his eyes, and when next he was aware of her she was walking from one dark ruin to another. Now the lambs had come running about her, their heads uplifted, clamorous.

She must have offered some words of explanation, for they came close against her legs, and some got in her way.

When she sat on a blackened heap, she became invisible, but the lambs gathered all around the ruin. Then he could discern the oval of her face, like a hand.

After a long time, he observed a man with two dogs come over the rise from Tomich and stand and stare at the curious way the lambs were behaving.

Presently the woman was moving towards the stream, beyond which uprose the birch wood, the lambs still following her, their bleating for all the world like an earnest and anxious pleading.

A shrill whistle pierced the air.

The woman proceeded quietly, not even turning her head.

The two dogs started. The raucous voice of the man directed them fiercely. The lambs swirled and swayed in a white wave against the woman. The dogs were foiled and became furious; for they were not shepherding the lambs, they were hunting the woman.

They were hunting the human quarry out of this place. It was their only sport. They leapt among the lambs, and one, madly eager to be in before his fellow, sprang at the woman. She screeched as she went down and the brute ripped and tore. The white wave swirled away from her.

The second dog pounced, and the two snarled and slashed, but not the woman now so much as each other, for they were mad with excitement and the sharp whistle with calling them maddened them still more. The first dog got his teeth in the second dog's throat. They rolled over. The shepherd now was running. He arrived on the scene at the same time as the man from the crest of the wood.

This man from the crest of the wood had eyes only for the shepherd, and their concentration was so inhuman that the shepherd gave ground, calling his dogs. The man was dressed in kilt and jacket of no local cut, and from his right fist protruded a knob of ebony. As the wrist flexed and lifted, the steel blade flashed.

'Get out!' yelled the shepherd. 'Prince!'

The dog leapt, overthrowing the man in his stride; then yelped sharply as the black knife slashed and went home. From the ground-swirl, the man slowly reared himself. The shepherd, who had called off his second dog, was retreating. The man followed him, blood trickling from his throat; staggered and stopped; then turned back to the woman.

'Mairi!' he said, lifting her head. The sightless eyes stared at him.

Feeling the wave coming, he threw himself on his back; for a little he fought against it, then let its waters flow over and obliterate him.

His eyes opened on a blue sky, ribbed here and there with white cloud, firm high cloud and a blue full of early evening light. Odd sounds pierced the incorporeal ease of his body, and turning his eyes he beheld a boy clawing at Mairi's shoulders and crying in a wild whisper, 'Granny! Granny!' Terror had turned his face greyer than hunger.

'She's dead,' said the man, slowly turning over on his side.

The breath went from the boy in a small grunt.

'The dogs got her.' The man sat up and felt his neck where the blood had congealed. The thought of hydrophobia turned his dark eyes bleak in a pitiless humour. 'I'll have to wash this.' He looked closely at the boy; then slowly looked around. There was no other human soul in that place.

He would wash his neck in the stream and then he would go and cut two small trees. The boy could pluck heather for a rope. Muttering these words, he went down into a pool and scrubbed his neck until the wounds flowed freely. With moss he padded his neckcloth and bandaged the wounds.

By the time he had cut and dressed two young trees and brought them back to where the dead woman lay, the boy had yards of a heather rope coiled in a ball. Criss-crossed with the rope, the slim birches made a bier upon which they stretched the old woman, the man switching round the straw-pocket from her side to her stomach. Pale roots and grey lichen stuck out from it: the crimsons and yellows and purples of her own and the earth's business.

'Do you think you can manage an end?'

'Yes,' answered the boy.

'We'll take it in easy stages,' said the man; 'time matters no more.'

And thus the father and son set out with the body of Dark Mairi for the distant shore.